# *Simon Says Die*

## Also by Lena Diaz

*He Kills Me, He Kills Me Not*

# *Simon Says Die*

**LENA DIAZ**

AVONIMPULSE

Excerpt from *He Kills Me, He Kills Me Not* copyright © 2011 by Lena Diaz.

EPub Edition APRIL 2012 ISBN: 9780062136329

Print Edition ISBN: 9780062136367

10 9 8 7 6 5 4 3

*This one is for my readers. Your e-mails and letters are deeply appreciated. You are why I do this. Thank you.*

*With deep appreciation to Todd P. Huhn, DO, MPH, for brainstorming clever, maniacal ways to kill people—fictionally speaking of course. Any mistakes are entirely mine.*

*And always, a heartfelt thank you to my agent, Nalini Akolekar, and my editor, Esi Sogah, for your constant faith and support.*

*Simon Says Die*

*Prologue*

FEAR HAS A smell—sharp, tangy, with a biting edge—like sweat, but more intimate, more powerful and addictive than any drug.

Simon was an addict, and it had been too long, far too long, since he'd had his last fix.

*That was about to change.*

He stood by the computer desk and picked up the pile of paper from the printer. He ran his finger down the profile of the woman in the photograph on the first page, across the pale skin of her arms, the upper swells of her breasts. Her dark hair was silky, shiny, barely brushing her shoulders. Laughter filled her deep blue eyes, crinkling them at the corners. Who was she thinking about when she smiled that way? Someone she cared about? Someone who cared about her?

"Simon, was there anything else you wanted me to print?"

His gaze slid reluctantly from the photograph to the blonde, slightly overweight woman sitting at the computer. Her muddy brown eyes were framed with makeup she probably hadn't worn in years. Her dress was bright yellow, new. She must have looked forward to tonight all week, thinking he'd invited himself to her house to finally take the next step, to become her lover.

*He was definitely ready to take the next step.*

Her hands hovered over the keyboard as she looked at him expectantly.

"No, I have what I want." He set the pictures back down. "You're sure no one will be able to tell you hacked into those Web sites?"

She grinned. "I didn't have to hack in after all. I just created a fake profile and got some of them to friend me. From there it was easy to get access to the others, and all their information."

*Stupid woman.* "Erase the profile."

Her grin faded. "What's wrong?"

At her wary look, he forced himself to relax and give her a smile meant to charm and reassure. "I don't want them to know. Not yet. What's the fun of a practical joke if they find out too soon, right?"

Her smile returned, but it wasn't as bright as before. "Um, right."

He closely watched her this time, as she undid everything she'd done, deleting her profile from the site.

When she was finished, she pushed back her chair and stood to face him. "You've made me curious. What kind of joke are you going to play?"

"Curiosity can get you in trouble, my dear."

She gave a little laugh. "What, like curiosity killed the cat?"

He cocked his head to the side. "Actually, I was thinking more of something a bit . . . different. Have you ever played the game *Simon says*?"

"Simon says?" She gave another laugh—a nervous laugh. "A child's game. Isn't that a bit silly for adults?"

"Not the way I play." His voice was deep, seductive.

He edged behind her and she half-turned, looking up at him. Her body tensed as her subconscious began to sense the danger that her conscious mind wasn't ready to accept.

He settled his hands on her shoulders.

She jumped and tried to pull away. "Stop that. You're making me nervous."

"Hush, now," he whispered. "That's not how you play the game. You can't do anything unless Simon says you can."

Her swallow was so loud he could hear it. She jerked her head, looking around the room, as if she'd only just realized how alone they were, how vulnerable she was. "Wh—what does Simon say to do?" she croaked, her voice shaky.

He leaned to the side so he could see her face. Like a frightened rabbit, staring into the eyes of the snake that is about to strike, she stood unmoving, paralyzed. He inhaled deeply, briefly closing his eyes, reveling in the scent of fear oozing out of her pores.

Oh, he was going to enjoy this one.

*Very much.*

He squeezed her shoulder with one hand as he slid his other hand down her spine, delighting in her shiver. He reached behind his back, lifting up the edge of his jacket to pull out his knife.

The poor little rabbit didn't even try to get away. She stood frozen, her breaths coming out in short little bursts. He tightened his hand on her shoulder.

She shivered again, tensing . . . as if to run.

*Too late.*

He caressed the cold steel of the knife's blade behind her, closing his hand around the hilt. Leaning down, closer, he softly pressed his lips against her taut cheek. Some of the fear left her eyes, replaced with a pathetic spark of hope.

"Simon?" Her mouth curved in a tentative smile.

He moved his lips next to her ear. "Simon says . . . die." He plunged the knife into her back.

## *Chapter One*

FBI SPECIAL AGENT Pierce Buchanan could think of only a few of his experiences more pathetic than standing on his former lover's front porch, waiting for her to answer the door. Like having the woman he loved dump him, as he was reaching into his pocket for an engagement ring—the same woman whose porch he was currently standing on.

*Yep. Pathetic.*

If his best friend hadn't begged him to check on his kid sister, Pierce sure as hell wouldn't be here right now.

As he raised his hand to knock on Madison's door again, a man darted around the corner of the house from the backyard and ran to the road out front. A woman with shoulder-length dark hair ran after him.

Pierce clenched his jaw. No point in knocking again. Madison wasn't home.

She was chasing a man down the street.

He narrowed his eyes. Was that the bulge of a gun beneath the edge of the man's jacket? A sinking feeling settled in his stomach. What was she thinking? Was she *trying* to get herself killed?

He vaulted over the porch railing, landing in a painful crouch on the brick walkway, three feet below. His knees throbbed in protest, an insulting reminder that a thirty-five-year-old agent shouldn't pull stunts as if he were still a twenty-year-old kid fresh out of the academy.

Madison didn't react when he shouted a warning about the gun. Either she didn't hear him, or she was too stubborn to listen.

He'd put his money on stubborn.

His GTO was parked down the street. His 9mm was in the glove box. But the car was in the opposite direction from where Madison was running.

*Too far away. Not enough time.*

He blew out a frustrated breath and took off across Madison's front lawn. Fifty yards ahead, she raced up one of the manicured paths of Savannah's Forsyth Park after the man with the gun.

A bright blue trolley was unloading tourists. They scrambled out of Madison's way like a gaggle of geese, honking their displeasure as she and her prey disappeared behind some trees.

Pierce shouted an apology as he vaulted over an elderly couple sitting on a bench. The sky erupted in a haze of gray and white as a flock of pigeons flew up in front of him. He waved his arms to ward them off, and he barreled through the same tourists Madison had scattered only moments before. He threw back another apology and sprinted down the path where Madison had disappeared.

Panic shot through him when he rounded a clump of oak trees, only to see an empty, winter-brown field spread out before him. Unbidden, an image flashed through his mind—Madison's tiny body, broken and bleeding, riddled with bullets. The thought of a world without the sexy little smart-ass sent a sharp jolt of pain knifing straight to his heart.

*Much to his disgust.*

He slowed to a jog, steeling himself against the curious stares of the people walking down the paths. It was a safe bet they hadn't expected to see someone in a business suit sprinting through the park. It certainly wasn't what *he* had planned when he'd gotten up this morning.

A faint shout sounded from behind a row of two-stories on the opposite side of the field. He took off toward the sound, emerging onto the street behind the houses in time to see Madison and the man she was chasing disappear down another side street.

Pierce veered down a parallel road, hoping the shortcut would help him catch up to Madison before she caught up to the gunman. Near the end of the block, he raced down a cross street and tore in between two houses, emerging onto a narrow road several yards ahead of Madison.

His relief was short-lived when Madison stumbled to a halt, her face draining of color. But she wasn't staring at him. She was staring off to his right, over his shoulder.

He whirled around. The man Madison had been chasing wasn't running anymore. He was standing in the middle of the street, his face hidden in the shadows beneath his hooded denim jacket.

*Pointing a gun at Madison.*

That sinking feeling twisted Pierce's gut again. Today of all days, why couldn't he have worn his Kevlar vest?

*Pathetic.*

He lunged in front of Madison just as the gun went off.

MADISON STOOD OUTSIDE the ambulance, watching Pierce lying inside on a gurney, while an EMT pressed a white piece of gauze against his chest. The gauze came away bright red, and Madison's breath caught at the sight. She clutched her hand to her own chest, and swallowed past the tightness in her throat. Thank God the bullet had gone clean through his side without hitting anything vital.

What was he thinking to risk his life like that—*for her?* And what was he doing in Georgia in the first place? He should have been safe at home in Jacksonville instead of playing hero.

Her stomach rebelled when the EMT pressed a fresh piece of gauze against the jagged flesh. She held her hand against her mouth, willing the nausea away. Blood had never bothered her before, but this was *Pierce.* The thought of him hurt—especially because of her—made her stomach churn.

Like a horror movie, the shooting played through her mind in slow motion—the deep-throated boom of the gun, the high-pitched whistle of the bullet, the sickening thud as Pierce fell to the ground.

His brow furrowed. "You okay?"

"How can you possibly be worried about me? *You're* the one who got shot."

An amused smile flashed across his face.

"This isn't the least bit funny," Madison said. "Why weren't you wearing a vest? You're an FBI agent, for goodness' sake. You should always wear your vest. You shouldn't ... you shouldn't ... you just ..." she sputtered into silence.

"I never thought I'd see you speechless. And I didn't realize seeing you again would be so dangerous. Next time, I'll wear body armor."

"Stop treating this like a joke. You could have been killed."

His smile faded and he gave her a puzzled look. "I'm okay. Stop beating yourself up."

She clenched her hands and looked past him to the red and blue lights flashing on the police cars behind the ambulance. Lieutenant Hamilton stood with three uniformed officers, talking in low tones next to one of the cars. Even though he'd already taken Madison's statement, the lieutenant's suspicious gaze never wavered from her as he spoke to his men.

When she'd answered his questions a few minutes ago, he hadn't believed her any more than when he'd questioned her earlier in the week. She'd been telling him the truth before.

*But not now.*

He wouldn't believe her if she told him the truth. She wasn't sure she believed it herself. The gunman couldn't be who she thought he was. It wasn't possible.

Was it?

She turned back toward Pierce, just as the EMT pressed a piece of tape over the bandage across his right side. Pierce's lips whitened.

"That must really hurt," Madison said.

"It's just a scratch."

"It's a bit worse than that, Special Agent Buchanan." The EMT helped Pierce into a sitting position then began to bind his chest with white gauze. "You've got a couple of busted ribs."

Madison's stomach clenched again. This wouldn't be the first time Pierce had broken a rib, or even the first time he'd been shot. His body was covered with battle scars from his years in law enforcement tracking down the worst kinds of violent offenders.

She'd tried to coax him to tell her how he'd gotten all his injuries, however, getting him to talk about himself was about as easy as getting her mother to ignore a sale at Macy's.

When her gaze traveled past his short dark hair, her pulse began to race for an entirely new reason. She mentally glided down the path her fingertips had traced so many times—over his hard bare chest, across the ripples of his stomach muscles, to the top of his waistband. Unwelcome heat flashed through her.

She raised her gaze and saw the same heat reflected

back in his whisky-colored eyes. She sucked in a breath and looked away, only then noticing that the EMT had stopped his work and was glancing curiously between them. Madison returned his stare until his neck turned red, his fingers fumbling with the gauze.

Pierce grinned and shook his head.

That familiar, sexy smile sent a sharp jolt of longing through Madison. Her belly tightened as a memory teased her senses—that same sexy smile curving his lips as he bent over her in bed, the last time they'd made love.

"Aren't you cold?" Frustration added a sharp edge to her voice. She was tempted to grab the blanket lying beside him and toss it over all those hard planes and muscles. "You should cover up."

"That would make it hard for the EMT to bandage my ribs, don't you think?"

The teasing note in his voice told her he realized the effect his near-nakedness was having on her, the same effect it had always had on her.

And he was enjoying it.

She forced herself to look at his face. "What are you doing in Savannah? Why did you run after me?"

"So, you *did* know I was following you. Did you hear me shout a warning about the gun too?"

Her face flushed with heat. "I heard someone yell something behind me, but I wasn't sure what they'd said."

His brows rose in obvious disbelief.

"I'm not reckless." She hated that she felt the need to explain her actions. "If I'd known he was armed, I wouldn't have chased him."

*Not until she'd gone back inside her house and grabbed a gun.*

"You're not reckless? Did it occur to you that the man you were chasing could be the killer who's been in the papers? The one who's killed two women so far, leaving 'Simon says die' notes on their bodies?"

Her faced flushed even hotter. "Honestly, no, it didn't." Admitting that, out loud, wasn't doing much for her pride or her sour mood. "Stop changing the subject. Why are you here?"

"Why were you chasing that man?" he countered.

She waved her hand toward the patrol cars. "I already told Lieutenant Hamilton. That man was trespassing on my property. I went outside to confront him, and he took off. I didn't think—I just reacted—and took off after him."

"Why didn't you call nine-one-one?"

"I did," she snapped. "The *first* time I saw someone watching me. And the second time. And the third. But that man is always gone by the time the police bother to arrive."

His eyes widened. "This is the *fourth* time you've seen him watching you? And you thought it was a good idea to chase him?" He swore and shook his head. "Why didn't you tell Logan you had a stalker when you called him this morning?"

She went very still. "How did you know I spoke to him this morning?"

He glanced uneasily at the EMT before answering. "He called me, said you sounded upset, distracted. He asked me to check on you."

"Ha. Check *up* on me you mean," she said, crossing her arms. Honeymoon or not, her brother was going to get an earful about this. She should have known better than to call him. But when she'd seen that same man in her backyard again, she'd wanted her police chief brother's advice. After hearing his voice, how happy he sounded, she couldn't bring herself to tell him anything that might make him worry. He and Amanda had been through so much. They deserved this happy time together.

A terrible suspicion flashed through her as she thought about what Pierce had just said. "Wait a minute. I talked to Logan less than an hour ago. Jacksonville is at least three hours away. Are you in town on a case?"

He didn't look like he wanted to answer. The tiny lines at the edges of his eyes crinkled and his mouth hardened into a flat line. "I don't live in Florida anymore. I live here now."

Her breath left her in a rush.

*Pierce lived in the same city she did.*

That thought pounded at her like a drumbeat, as though a hand were squeezing her heart and pressing against her lungs.

It shouldn't matter.

It shouldn't matter that he lived so close. It shouldn't matter that she could run into him at the grocery store, or pass him on the street. It shouldn't matter that she could reach out right now and run her fingers across his golden skin.

It shouldn't matter, none of it.

But, damn it, it did.

She cleared her throat, twice, before she trusted her voice again. "How long have you been here?"

The EMT flicked a glance at her and set the gauze down. "You can lower your arms now, Agent Buchanan."

Pierce eased his arms down, watching her with a wary expression on his face. "A couple of months."

*Two months?* He hadn't bothered to mention that he'd moved when he'd seen her at her brother's wedding. She hadn't told him she'd moved either, but then she'd had no desire to talk to him since he was so busy with the ridiculously young, beautiful redhead he'd brought as his date.

*She'd probably missed her curfew to hang out with him at the wedding reception.*

But *Logan* must have known that Pierce had moved to Savannah. Pierce was like the brother Logan had never had, especially after everything they'd been through last year saving Amanda from a serial killer. And he wouldn't have asked Pierce to check on her if Pierce was hours away in Jacksonville.

"Logan knows you live here, doesn't he?" She didn't bother to wait for his reply. She already knew the answer. "He should have told me, *before* he talked me into buying a house here. *You* should have told me."

"What difference would it have made if you'd known?" he asked. His brows drew down in a dark slash. "Would you have run away again?"

She blinked at his well-aimed barb and took a step back. She wished she could step back from the truth just as easily. He was right. She *had* run away from him.

But not for the reason she'd told him.

"Mrs. McKinley?" a voice called out from behind her.

Startled, she whirled around, and stumbled against the curb.

"Whoa, there." The policeman who'd spoken to her grabbed her elbow, steadying her. "Are you okay, ma'am?"

She grimaced when she put some weight on her ankle.

"Let's have the EMT check that."

"No, no, I'm fine."

The policeman gave her a skeptical look. "If you're sure, I'm supposed to escort you to the station. Lieutenant Hamilton wants to question you some more. And you'll have more privacy away from this crowd." He nodded toward the curious onlookers behind the police line. "Is there someone you want me to call to meet you there? Your husband?"

"There's no one to call. My family doesn't live around here. And my husband is . . . dead."

Madison tried to put weight on her bad ankle again, but as soon as she did, a sharp pain shot up her leg and she had to grab the policeman's arm for support.

"Get into the ambulance, Madison." Pierce scooted over on the gurney to make room. "The police can question you later."

She hesitated. She didn't want to be secluded in the back of the ambulance with Pierce, especially a *curious* Pierce who might barrage her with questions all the way to the hospital.

Then again, she could use the opportunity to try to convince him not to tell Logan what had happened. If the gunman was who she thought he was, the life she'd tried to build for the past year and a half was about to come crashing down. She needed some time to figure out what to do and how to protect her family.

She took a wobbly step forward and grabbed one of the metal handles by the ambulance door.

The EMT opened his mouth as if to protest, but promptly closed it when Madison stared at him in challenge. She hauled herself inside and plopped down on the bench across from Pierce. The EMT spoke through the glass window to the other EMT driving the ambulance, then pulled one of the doors shut.

"Just a minute," the policemen called out, stopping him before he could close the other door. "Agent Buchanan, the lieutenant wanted me to let you know that he called your boss, like you asked. Agent Matthews said he'll meet you at the hospital with your fiancée."

## Chapter Two

PIERCE GRIPPED THE edge of the emergency room examining table he was sitting on. Seeing Madison again, seeing her at the wrong end of a gun, had been a punch in the gut that still had him reeling. When she'd bent over him as he lay on the street after getting shot, the concern and fear in her deep blue eyes had him wanting to reach up and hold her, to pull her close. He'd wanted to bury his hands in her thick hair and breathe in the scent of jasmine that always clung to her soft skin.

But then his brain had kicked in, and he remembered the way things had ended between them. And he knew that look of concern was the same look she'd give anyone if they were hurt. It certainly wasn't because she cared about *him*.

He looked over at the green curtain where a nurse had taken Madison over half an hour ago. Why had her face turned so pale when she heard he had a fiancée? Madison was the one who'd broken up with him. Why would she care if he'd moved on?

"Agent Buchanan."

He reluctantly turned back toward the young doctor who'd just stitched him up. *Too* young. Probably some boy genius who'd graduated from high school when he was thirteen. A boy genius who'd already taken far too much of his time. He needed to wrap up the case he was working on, and he still had a dozen questions to ask Madison about the shooting this morning.

Like why she'd begged him not to tell Logan what had happened.

"If you won't allow us to take X-rays, you'll have to sign a form acknowledging you're refusing treatment against medical advice."

"My ribs aren't broken. X-rays are a waste of time."

"You have a medical degree and forgot to mention it?" The doctor grinned at his own joke.

Pierce narrowed his eyes. "I don't have a medical degree, but I'm pretty damned good with a gun."

Boy genius made a choking sound in his throat.

"I'm sure Special Agent Buchanan will be happy to undergo any tests you think are necessary." Pierce's new boss, and longtime friend, stood in the curtained doorway.

Pierce shook his head in defeat. So much for questioning Madison without any more delays.

"Supervisory Special Agent Casey Matthews." His boss stepped forward to shake the doctor's hand. Then he held the curtain back. "And this lovely lady is his fiancée, Tessa James. I assure you, Doctor, Special Agent Buchanan *will* cooperate."

The doctor enthusiastically pumped Casey's hand. "I appreciate your help. He's been fighting to leave from the moment he got here." He gave Pierce a smug grin.

Pierce stared at him until his smile disappeared. The kid was so easy to intimidate; he almost felt guilty.

Boy genius's wide-eyed gaze darted around the room. "Someone will be back in a few minutes to take you to radiology." He turned and fled.

"Did you enjoy flustering that boy?" Tessa stepped to the examining table and clicked her red nails on the shiny stainless steel surface.

"He was wasting my time." Pierce flattened his palms against the table to hop down, but Casey blocked his way.

"You haven't been X-rayed yet," Casey reminded him.

"I need to talk to Madison."

"The woman involved in the shooting?" Tessa asked.

He nodded.

"Lieutenant Hamilton was leaving with her when we walked into the ER."

A feeling of dread curled inside Pierce. He hadn't missed the suspicious glances Hamilton had aimed at Madison earlier. The lieutenant thought she was hiding something.

So did Pierce.

But he didn't like the idea of her in the high-pressure atmosphere of an interrogation room. Not because she'd be scared—just the opposite. Her brother called her "trouble" for good reason. Madison's temper could get her into a tight spot if the police got her riled up. She was a firecracker with a short fuse, and when she went off, she was usually the one who got burned.

"She twisted her ankle earlier," Pierce said. "Did she seem okay?"

"She was favoring her right leg a bit," Casey said. "But she seemed fine. No cast or crutches." He rapped his knuckles on the table. "You should have called me. When one of my agents is involved in a shooting, I shouldn't have to hear about it from Savannah-Chatham Metro PD."

"It was a flesh wound, no big deal."

Tessa placed her hand on top of his. "Possible broken ribs is definitely a big deal."

He eased his hand away. "What are you doing here?"

"Where else would your doting fiancée be?" She grinned.

"She was with me when Hamilton called." Casey's voice held a note of impatience. "I want answers. Who is this Madison woman? Why were you at her house this morning?"

"Her brother, Logan Richards, is a friend of mine. He's out of the country on his honeymoon and asked me to check on her. That's all there is to it. There's nothing federal about this."

"This became *federal* the moment a federal agent got shot." Casey frowned. "Wait, Madison—that name sounds familiar." His eyes widened. "Is she the same Madison who—"

"Tessa," Pierce interrupted, giving Casey a hard look, "would you mind going to the house to get me a fresh shirt? I'd rather not wear a hospital gown when I leave."

She rolled her eyes. "You don't have to invent an excuse to get rid of me, *darling.* Don't forget our appointment tonight. I've got everything set. If we pull this off, the case is over. If not, you'll be stuck with a fake fiancée a lot longer than you'd hoped." She stepped out of the room, her high heels clicking down the hallway.

Casey yanked the curtain shut and turned around to face Pierce. "Are we talking about *the* Madison? The widow you dated a few months back?"

Pierce started to cross his arms, but the tug on his stitches stopped him.

He'd only spoken once to Casey about Madison, the weekend she'd broken up with him. He'd gotten roaring drunk, and didn't even remember making the phone call. Casey had reminded him about their conversation in embarrassing detail the next day when he'd called to make sure Pierce was okay.

"It's not what you think," Pierce said.

"I sure hope not. Please tell me you didn't transfer to Savannah just so you could be near the same woman who dumped you."

"I didn't even know she lived here until her brother called me this morning. The last I knew, she was living in New York."

"How did you two hook up in the first place if you didn't even live in the same state?"

"Her brother is the police chief I helped with that last serial killer case I worked on. She visited Logan during the investigation, and she and I hit it off."

Casey raised a brow. "Hit it off? From what I recall, it was a bit more serious than that. You two were—"

"Drop it."

Casey laughed. "I'm just saying that—"

"Drop. It."

Casey raised his hands in surrender. "Okay, okay." His look turned thoughtful. "How did she end up in Savannah?"

"She mentioned something about her brother encouraging her to buy a house here. As to why, I have no idea."

"Is this the same brother who encouraged *you* to transfer here?"

Pierce tensed as he realized what Casey was implying—and damned if he didn't agree. Logan was trying to get him and Madison back together. The next time he spoke to Logan he'd let him know what he thought of his interference. And he'd let him know, in no uncertain terms, that the odds of him and Madison getting back together were exactly zero. She'd made her feelings, or lack of them, perfectly clear when she'd left him. And he had too much pride to put himself in that position again.

No matter how sexy and appealing she was.

A wry grin tilted up the corner of Casey's mouth. "You've been set up."

"Yeah, got that. I'll deal with Logan later. Right now, I need to keep his reckless sister from getting herself killed. And you're going to help me."

IN THE SHORT time since she'd moved to Savannah, Madison had never once been tempted to go on one of the infamous ghost tours. But as she sat on a bench in Colonial Park Cemetery and watched another ghost tour walk by, she had to admit their entertainment value was far better than she'd expected.

They were certainly entertaining *her*.

"Where have you been all day?"

The sound of a deep, male voice beside her had Madison grabbing her Colt .380 pistol out of her jacket pocket. An iron grip clamped around her wrist. Madison looked up, then collapsed back against the bench in relief.

*Pierce.*

He swore under his breath and slid onto the bench beside her, forcing her to move over to make room for his broad shoulders. He took the gun, pointing it toward the ground as he checked the safety. His mouth drew into a tight line, and he handed the tiny pocket-pistol back to her. "I'm going to assume you have a license for that."

*Nope, but she wasn't going to admit it.*

She shoved the tiny gun back in her jacket pocket, grateful none of the departing tourists seemed to have noticed anything.

"How did you find me?" She knew she'd have to face him sometime, but she'd hidden out in the library most of the day, hoping to put off the confrontation a bit longer. She still wasn't sure how she'd explain her actions this morning. And she also wasn't sure what she'd say if he brought up the subject of his fiancée. Part of her was actually happy for him that he'd found a woman he loved who loved him in return.

The other part of her wanted to use his fiancée for target practice.

"I put the word out I was looking for you," he said. "A friend at Metro PD called when he saw your car parked in front of the cemetery. I put the word out hours ago."

His earlier question—*Where have you been all day?*—hung in the air between them.

She wasn't about to tell him she'd basically hidden from him all day. "Since you're out of the hospital, I guess you were right about the ribs not being broken."

"Scratched and bruised. How's the ankle?"

She lifted her jean-clad leg, revealing the pink-colored bandage she'd chosen at the hospital, wrapped around her ankle. "A light sprain, barely hurts anymore, especially with the painkillers they gave me." She lowered her leg as the image of Pierce being shot flashed through her mind again, as it had so many times today. "I never thanked you for risking your life for me this morning. You could have been killed."

"Thank me by telling me who you were chasing, and why you were chasing him."

Her pulse started pounding in her ears. If he suspected what she suspected, he'd do one of two things. He'd either insist on telling Logan so her brother could help her, or he'd insist on helping her himself.

The first option didn't appeal to her at all.

The second option appealed to her far too much.

"Who was he?" he repeated.

"I have no idea." She shoved her hair back behind her ears. "Some vagrant, I suppose." She'd tried to sound flippant, but the way his mouth tightened told her she'd failed.

"Describe him."

"You saw him too," she hedged. "*You* describe him."

"I only caught a quick glimpse."

"You're a trained FBI agent."

He shrugged.

She crossed her arms and sat back. "Apparently, neither of us got a good look at him."

His expression hardened. "You didn't get a good look at the shooter, huh?"

"Nope." She shoved her hair back behind her ear again.

"All right. I'll play that game. The man you were chasing was a few inches shorter than me, about six feet tall. Thin, maybe a buck seventy. Caucasian, between thirty-five and forty. Faded jeans. New, white sneakers. Denim jacket, waist-length, unzipped halfway. The hood was pulled up, so I couldn't see his face. He was wearing a black T-shirt under the jacket. How am I doing so far?"

He'd gotten every detail right. She forced a nervous laugh. "You should have been the one the police interrogated if you saw him that well."

"They did interrogate me. After I left the hospital, I went to the station to give a statement, and to talk to you. But you were already gone."

"I had nothing else to say so I left."

"Hamilton told me his men investigated each of your

nine-one-one calls, and they never found any evidence to support your claims about a stalker. Is that why you took the law into your own hands today?"

She bristled and crossed her arms. "My *claims*?"

"You should have called the police this morning. Vigilantes get themselves—*or other people*—killed."

She drew in a sharp breath. "That's not fair. I never asked for your help. And the people I did ask for help— the police—threatened to arrest me. Did Hamilton tell you that part, that he threatened to arrest me for abusing the nine-one-one system and for filing false police reports if I called again?" She jabbed her finger against his thigh to make her point. "When the law lets you down, you have no one to depend on but yourself."

He grabbed her hand, flattening it against his leg. "I'm sure they were bluffing. They wouldn't have arrested you. And if you felt the police had failed you," he continued, "then why didn't you tell Logan what was going on? Hamilton would listen to a police chief, regardless of his jurisdiction. Logan would have made sure someone helped you."

Madison couldn't concentrate with his warm hand holding hers. It felt far too good, and seeing him again made her realize how much she'd missed him. She reluctantly tugged her hand out of his grasp. "I couldn't ask Logan for help. He's on his honeymoon, or had you forgotten?"

"Even Italy is only a phone call away. He would have helped, and you know it."

"You're right. He would have helped. But Logan's version of help would have been to cut his honeymoon short and come here. I couldn't let him do that."

"Give your brother some credit. He thought you were in some kind of trouble this morning, and he didn't cut his honeymoon short. He called *me*. And he made me swear to help you. You're not getting off the hook by denying what we both know. You're in the middle of some kind of trouble. And until you tell me what that is, I'm sticking around so I can keep you from getting hurt."

She jumped to her feet. "Logan shouldn't have called you. I can take care of myself."

He eased off the bench and stood, towering over her. "Right," he snapped, "that's why you almost got shot this morning, because you can take such good care of yourself. You need help, but as usual, you're too stubborn to admit it. Tell me who the shooter was."

She shoved her hair back behind her ears. "I don't know."

His face tightened. "Yes, you do."

"You think I'm lying?"

"I *know* you are."

*Why couldn't he just let this go?*

She took a step back and darted a glance toward the front gates. Her convertible was parked just outside the entrance. Could she reach it before he caught up to her? He was wounded, which should slow him down. If she surprised him, he might not react fast enough. She felt in her pocket for the clicker to unlock her car.

"Who's the shooter?" he demanded again.

"I told you, I don't know."

"The hell you don't."

She took another step back.

He closed the distance between them and gripped her

shoulders. "You don't have a head start this time. You wouldn't even make it to the gate. Who's the shooter? I'm not going to ask again."

She tried to wiggle out of his grasp, but gave up when his hands tightened on her shoulders. She stomped her foot in frustration. "Why would I lie about knowing who the shooter was?"

"Good question. Why would you? You're an intelligent woman, *Mads*. If you saw a stranger watching your house, you'd call the police, no matter what B.S. they'd said about arresting you."

*Mads*. What a ridiculous nickname. At least when her brother called her "trouble," that made sense. Pierce was the only one who'd ever called her Mads. It was silly. It wasn't even cute.

*And every time he called her that, it made her go all melty inside.*

She took a deep breath and tried again. "*You* might not think the police would have really arrested me if I'd called them, but I do. That's why I didn't call." The excuse sounded weak, but it was all she could think of with over six feet of angry male glaring down at her.

"You chased after that man instead of calling the police," he continued, as if she hadn't spoken, "because you knew who he was and didn't want the police to know. But you underestimated him, thinking you could catch up to him and confront him, not realizing he was armed."

Good grief. The man was like a hound after a fox, which didn't bode well for the fox.

"What does the gunman have on you?"

"Nothing," she squeaked, her voice rising with panic.

The disbelief on his face was far more damning than any accusation he could have spoken. For several minutes the tension stretched out between them. Then he shook his head and released her arms. He scrubbed a hand across the stubble on his jaw.

Madison slumped with relief, only to stiffen again when Pierce pulled his cell phone out of his jacket pocket. Unease crept up her spine.

"What are you doing?" she asked.

He pressed one of his saved contacts and showed her the face that appeared on the screen.

*Logan.*

She gasped and tried to grab the phone.

He held it up, out of her reach.

"Don't do this," she said. "He's probably asleep. It's like"—she waved her hands in the air—"three or four in the morning in Italy right now."

He held the phone to his ear. "One ring."

"He's your best friend. How can you ruin his honeymoon?" She dug her nails into her palms. If Logan knew what was really going on, he'd feel it was his duty to help her, to fix things. It was too late to fix things. If he even suspected what she thought was going on, and that she was determined to take care of this on her own, he'd try to stop her. She couldn't let that happen.

"Two rings."

"That man was just some crazy vagrant, a homeless guy." She shoved her hair behind her ears. "I'm sure he won't be back."

"A homeless guy, with brand-new sneakers, and an expensive Sig Sauer 9mm pistol." Pierce shook his head. "Nope. Not buying it. Three rings."

What was she supposed to do? She couldn't tell him the truth. But she couldn't let him involve her brother either. "Hang up the phone."

"Four rings."

Panic flooded through her. She'd have to tell him who the shooter was. She'd just have to figure out later how to keep him from figuring out the rest. "Fine, you win. I'll tell you who he is. Hang up."

"Not without a name."

She heard the sound of a voice coming from the phone—Logan's voice.

"Hey, man," Pierce said into the phone. "Sorry to wake you, but I knew you were worried about your sister. I checked on her like you asked."

Madison shoved Pierce's arm, pushing the phone away from his mouth. She reached her arms up behind his neck and tugged him down so she could put her mouth next to his ear. She whispered a vile name she'd hoped never to pass her lips again.

His eyes widened. He stared down at her and slowly put the phone back to his ear. "No. Everything is fine. I just wanted to let you know she's okay. Kiss Amanda for me. Gotta go." He ended the call and lowered his phone. "Tell me again."

"You heard me. The man who shot you is Damon . . . Damon McKinley. My dead husband."

# Chapter Three

MADISON SAT IN the passenger seat of Pierce's vintage, dark blue muscle car, methodically considering different ways to torture him. She shoved at the handcuffs he'd snapped on her wrists at the cemetery, before carting her off like a prisoner. The man was determined to keep her with him—with, or without, her consent.

By the time Pierce pulled into his garage, in a cookie-cutter subdivision Madison would never have pictured him in, Madison had gone from furious to seething.

Pierce opened the passenger door and squatted in the opening to unlock the cuffs.

"Behave," he warned, as he took them off. He twisted away just in time to avoid her fist.

She rubbed her wrists and climbed out of the car, ready to give him hell. But her anger drained away when she saw the bloodstains on his white shirt.

"You're bleeding." She stepped toward him, her hands outstretched.

He jerked away. "Uh-uh. After hearing your plans for vengeance the whole ride here, I'm not letting you get that close."

"I didn't think you were listening."

"You were hard to ignore."

"You want to bleed to death, fine. Your choice." She turned around and leaned into the back seat to grab her purse. She let out a surprised yelp when he grabbed her by the waist and pulled her out of the car.

"Leave it. You can get it later." He unlocked the door between the garage and the house, flipped on a light, then stepped back to allow her to precede him. "After you."

"You're just afraid I'll shoot you." He'd taken her Colt .380 out of her jacket pocket at the cemetery and had tossed it into the back seat, along with her purse.

"You're right. Getting shot twice in one day is not something I want to add to my list of pathetic experiences."

She paused. "Pathetic?"

"Never mind."

She moved past him through the kitchen, which was open to the family room beyond. She stopped beside a white leather couch, wrinkling her nose in distaste at the less-than-inspired neutral color palate.

"Either come with me into the bedroom while I change my shirt, or keep talking so I know you aren't running off." Pierce disappeared through a set of double doors beside the fireplace.

Heat spiked through Madison at the idea of following him into the bedroom. He'd always been able to set her blood on fire with the slightest touch, the brush of his lips against the curve of her neck, the stroke of his warm hand across her hip. She moved away from the doors, away from temptation.

Even if her past didn't stand between them, there was a far bigger barrier to overcome.

His fiancée.

The idea of him with another woman was like a bucket of ice water, washing over her heated skin.

"Why shouldn't I run?" she taunted, still angry about being handcuffed, and angry that he was trying to force her to let him help her.

"Because I'd have to catch you again, and that would really piss me off. I'm already late for a meeting." His voice was muffled, as if he were in a closet.

She ran her fingers across the cold glass top of the brass coffee table, with its vulgar display of flea-market-quality statues. The man she remembered had favored antiques, like the car he drove. Simple lines, nothing fancy, or gaudy.

The paintings on the walls displayed a nauseating lack of talent. She could have painted something better back in her high school art class. Pierce was strong, solid, reliable, and sexy as hell. This house didn't reflect any of that.

His fiancée must be the one with the tacky decorating taste.

She turned away from the offensive paintings and started in surprise.

The same young woman he'd brought to her brother's wedding stood in the entryway just inside the front door. Her long, red hair hung down in luxurious waves across her pale shoulders. She raised a perfectly plucked brow and started toward Madison, her high heels clicking on the marble floor.

"Pierce." Madison raised her voice to make sure he would hear her. "You've got company."

The woman stopped in front of her and crossed her arms over her ample chest.

The sinking feeling in Madison's stomach told her who the woman was even before Pierce stepped out of the bedroom.

The lousy decorator.

*His fiancée.*

"I'm not *company*, darling. I live here," she purred, her green eyes riveted on Madison before they flashed to Pierce. "What's she doing here?"

Madison stiffened and gritted her teeth in the closest semblance of a smile that she could manage. "I'm here to take you to the shooting range, *darling.*"

Pierce gave Madison a warning look before turning his attention to the redhead. "Tessa, why are you here? You're supposed to be . . ." He glanced at Madison before looking back at the other woman. "You had an appointment."

"We *both* had an appointment. I called, but you didn't answer your cell." Her long-lashed eyes zeroed in on Madison. "I guess I know why."

"We need to talk." He grabbed her hand and anchored her beside him.

Madison stepped away, not wanting to get any more involved in this dispute than she already was.

Pierce pointed at her. "Wait right there. Do *not* make me chase you again."

"Again?" Tessa exclaimed. "What is going on?"

Miserable, and more uncomfortable than she could ever remember being, Madison inched farther away from the unhappy couple. Pierce pulled Tessa into the bedroom and closed the double doors.

Determined not to dwell on the image of Pierce shut in the bedroom with that *cover model*, Madison turned away. She froze when she noticed what she'd missed when she'd first entered the room.

Photographs, dozens of them, tucked into the bookshelf, sitting on an end table. Pictures of Pierce with his long-legged fiancée. Pictures of them at dinner in a fancy restaurant. Pictures of them laughing with another couple, cooking steaks on a grill.

*Kissing.*

Pain knifed through Madison, stealing her breath. Her pulse hammered in her ears. She'd given him up, afraid to trust feelings that had happened too fast and burned too hot, desperately afraid she was making the same mistake she'd made with her former husband.

But instead of fading in time, those feelings were stronger today than they'd ever been. And right now it was killing her seeing him with someone else. She had to get out of this torture chamber. But she didn't want to run out the door and make him think she was running away again.

Retreating to the hallway on the opposite side of the family room, she occupied herself exploring the two bedrooms. Other than the subpar decorating, they looked like any other guest rooms—except that one of the rooms had a closet full of men's clothes.

She ran her fingers over the smooth, cool fabric of a light blue shirt. The faint smell of soap and cologne teased her senses. She couldn't resist pulling the shirt close, and breathing deeply. There was no mistaking whose clothes these were. They belonged to Pierce.

Was Tessa such a clotheshorse that she couldn't give him enough space in the master closet? Madison moved to the chest of drawers on the other side of the room and reached for the handle on the top drawer.

"Looking for something?"

She straightened at the sound of a woman's voice, Tessa's voice. She was standing in the doorway, one of her pale, slender arms angled behind her, while her other hand tapped impatiently on her tight emerald-green skirt.

Madison glanced past her.

"He's not here," Tessa said. "He had an important meeting."

"He left me here? With you?" She didn't bother to hide her surprise, or her relief. Leaving her with "pretty face" meant she was no longer Pierce's prisoner. Madison didn't care that the woman was several inches taller than her. *Most* people were taller than her, and she'd rarely met anyone she couldn't outfight—if it came to that. "Well, in that case, I'll go home now."

"I don't think so." Tessa pulled her other hand from behind her back, revealing the pistol she was holding. She aimed it toward the floor, gripping it with the confidence and poise of someone who knew how to handle a gun.

Madison's respect for her went up a notch.

"Pierce wants you to stay here until he gets back," Tessa said. "He explained that you were . . . unhappy about being here. He also told me how sneaky you can be. If you give me any problems . . ." she shrugged, letting her unspoken threat hang in the air between them as she tapped her thigh with her gun.

Well, well, well. Pretty face had some backbone to go along with that gun. Madison nodded to let her know she wasn't going to try anything—yet.

Tessa stepped back to let her out of the bedroom.

When they reached the family room, Madison turned around, warily watching the other woman. "Now what?"

Tessa patted the couch. "Sit, watch TV, make yourself something to eat. I don't care what you do, as long as you don't try to leave. When you're ready to sleep, there are extra sheets and pillows in the hall closet."

"Sleep? How long will Pierce be gone?"

Tessa sat on the far end of the couch, her actions so smooth and graceful it made Madison feel far older than her twenty-eight years.

"He should be back by morning," Tessa said. "Until then, you and I get to enjoy each other's company."

Madison nearly choked on the bile rising in her throat. Enjoyable was not a word she'd use to describe being forced to spend time with Pierce's fiancée. If she and "red" made it through the night without killing each other, it would be a miracle.

MADISON DECIDED TO show Tessa some mercy. After all, where was the fun in yanking out all that salon-perfect hair when the woman was sprawled across the couch, in a dead sleep?

She didn't even move when Madison took her gun away and set it on the kitchen counter. And the gun wasn't even loaded.

Madison rolled her eyes in disgust and settled into the recliner across from sleeping beauty. *She* would certainly never threaten someone with an empty gun.

Neither would Pierce. Madison had always admired how competent he was, his quick reflexes, his skills as an investigator. He could handle himself in any situation. And he sure wouldn't fall asleep while guarding someone.

Tessa let out a loud snort.

Madison shook her head and closed her eyes. When would Pierce be back? Was he working a case? He was good at what he did for a living, one of the best, but she couldn't help but worry. After all, he was injured. His reflexes had to be off.

When the sun's first rays peeked through the window blinds, Madison was still wide awake. A few minutes later, a metallic screech sounded from the garage as the door began to raise, followed by the reassuring rumble of Pierce's GTO as he pulled inside.

Tessa jerked awake, blinking to focus. She lifted her empty gun hand and her eyes widened. She frantically patted down the couch.

Madison hid her smile and peeked out through her lashes, enjoying the other woman's frenzied panic. When she spotted the gun on the counter, she let out a string of curses and hurried into the kitchen, tucking the gun away just as Pierce stepped into the kitchen from the garage.

The sound of his deep voice as he spoke in muted tones to Tessa soothed Madison's worry. Her relief turned to annoyance as they continued to whisper to each other. She wished she could hear what they were saying. Then again, maybe it was a good thing she couldn't.

She tried to tune them out so she could catch a few minutes of sleep. She'd give Pierce hell later for leaving her with his snoring fiancée all night. And then, somehow, she'd convince him that she didn't really need his help.

## Chapter Four

MADISON COVERED HER yawn and looked out Pierce's car window at the FBI office building on East Bryan Street.

After nodding off in the recliner this morning, she'd been shaken awake an obscenely short time later. Pierce, looking impossibly refreshed, as if he hadn't been awake most of the night himself, had driven her to the cemetery to retrieve her car. Then he'd followed her home and had waited while she showered and changed.

In spite of her brilliant arguments about not needing his help, he'd bullied her into going with him to give his boss a statement about the shooting.

He opened her car door and offered her his hand.

She swatted his hand away and covered another yawn as she climbed out of the car. She'd wipe that grin off his face later, once she got enough caffeine into her system.

One cup of coffee was not enough to wake up her "nice" gene.

The lettering on the glass door of the building declared that it was a technology center, rather than a field office like the sprawling complex in Jacksonville, where Pierce used to work. Its stark, plain facade had none of the Southern charm Madison associated with the rest of Savannah's historic district, which was probably why the FBI had tucked it away, a block off Reynolds Square—so no one would notice it and complain.

"After you, Sleepy, or should I call you Grumpy?" He held open the front door.

"How about I call you Dopey and we call it even?"

He laughed as she trudged past him into the tiny entryway that didn't even boast a receptionist.

She couldn't help it if she wasn't cheerful Snow White today. Being handcuffed, kidnapped, held prisoner by a cover model, and then hauled to the FBI building on just a few hours sleep did not make her want to burst into song and play with bluebirds.

"You can't ignore me forever." He slid an ID card into an electronic reader on a metal gate. It beeped and clicked open.

"I'm not ignoring you." She stepped through the gate. "I just don't have anything to say."

He looked suspiciously close to grinning again as he led her down the hallway to an elevator. She crossed her arms after they stepped inside, daring him to smile at her.

"Are you never going to forgive me?" He punched the button for the second floor.

"You left me with your fiancée and told her to shoot me if I tried anything."

His lips twitched. "She told you I said that?"

"That's the way I took it."

He laughed. "I'm sure she was only teasing." His grin faded and his face turned serious. "As for her being my fiancée, I've been trying to tell you—"

She held up her hand to stop him. "And I already told you this morning that I don't want to discuss her. Your personal life is no longer my business. You don't owe me any explanations."

He gave her an odd look, but before she could figure out what that look meant, the elevator door slid open. A man in a dark gray business suit was leaning against the far wall, apparently waiting for them. He straightened and held out his hand. "Mrs. McKinley, I'm Special Agent Casey Matthews. Thank you for coming."

She shook his hand without enthusiasm. "I'm only here because Pierce would have ruined my brother's honeymoon if I didn't agree to talk to you. This is a total waste of time."

His eyes widened, and he glanced at Pierce.

"She's actually a marshmallow inside once you get past the prickly spikes."

Casey let out a bark of laughter, but sobered when Madison glared at him.

"I apologize for the inconvenience," he said. "I'll try to make this as painless as possible."

He led them down an interior hallway lit by harsh overhead lights, into an expansive room full of low-walled cubicles. The two dozen or so men and women sitting in front of computer monitors watched them with open curiosity. Madison got the impression they didn't get civilian visitors very often.

Casey took them to his office in the back corner, one of the few offices in the open room with real walls and a door. The computer on the wood laminate desk looked expensive and new, but the two cheap vinyl chairs in front of it were the typical, low-budget government variety. The tiny table that separated the chairs was only big enough to hold a couple of file folders.

Or maybe a cup of coffee.

"I don't suppose there's some coffee around here somewhere?" Madison asked. "The FBI guys on TV always have coffee."

Pierce sat down in one of the vinyl chairs. "I'll get you some after we leave."

Casey smiled. "No need to wait. I'll be right back."

As the door closed, Madison edged over to the window and pretended interest in the street below, even though the only things she could see were the cars parked up and down the curb, and a couple of squirrels scurrying toward the corner.

"If it makes you feel better, I don't want to be here with you any more than you want to be with me," Pierce said.

Madison stiffened and turned around.

"You're surprised," he said. "Did you think after you left I was sitting around, miserable, hoping you would come back?"

*Why not? She'd been miserable, missing him.*

"Of course not." She took the seat across from him. "I'm glad you've moved on. Theresa seems like a great girl."

"Tessa."

"Whatever. I really don't care." She crossed her arms over her chest.

Pierce stared at her, his dark eyes searching, as if he were looking for the answer to an important question. "No, I guess you really don't."

Before she could figure out what *that* meant, the door opened. Casey stepped into the office, closing the door behind him.

"Here you go." He handed Madison a Styrofoam cup of coffee, and set some cream and sugar packets down on the table.

"Thank you." She ignored the cream and sugar and clutched the coffee between her hands, breathing in the comforting aroma. She took a deep sip. The coffee was bitter, and only lukewarm, but she didn't care. The smell alone was starting to wake her up, and the caffeine rush would finish the job in a couple of minutes. She took another sip as Casey sat down behind his desk.

His lightly graying hair was military short, like Pierce's, but he was far less imposing than the intent man sitting across from her. She imagined any criminal facing Pierce Buchanan had to be a shaking ball of nerves by the time he finished questioning them. She'd never thought of him as intimidating back when they were dating, but as he sat there watching her now, the little hairs stood up on her arms.

"Mrs. McKinley," Casey said, "I don't know how much Special Agent Buchanan told you about why he brought you here, but basically, since one of my agents was involved in a shooting, I have to perform an investigation into the incident."

She set her cup down on the table. "What is it that you want to know?"

"Let's start with your version of what happened yesterday morning."

"There isn't much to tell. I looked out my kitchen window and saw a man in my backyard, the same man I've seen several times in the past few weeks, watching me. I called my brother to get his advice—"

"Why didn't you call the police?"

"Technically, my brother is the police." She waved her hand in the air. "Regardless, I'd already called them several other times to report the same man watching my house. They never arrived in time to catch him, so they chose not to believe he'd even been there. They weren't exactly receptive to more calls from me."

"Fair enough. Then what happened?"

"After I ended the call with my brother, I watched the man in my backyard for a while. And, well, there was just something . . . familiar about him." She glanced at Pierce, wondering how much he'd told his boss. "I decided to confront him. He ran as soon as I stepped outside."

"How many times have you seen him before? Where did you see him?"

"I didn't come here to talk about those other times. I'm here to talk about yesterday's shooting."

"Standard background questions," Pierce said. "It helps frame the overall investigation."

She grudgingly continued. "The first time I saw him was three weeks ago, right after I moved in. He had the hood of his denim jacket pulled up, just like yesterday, so I couldn't see his face. He was standing on the sidewalk leaning against an oak tree. Technically, he wasn't on my property. When I passed by my window half an hour later, he was still there. Watching my house."

She remembered the alarm that had shot through her. The way the man held himself, the way he stood, had reminded her of Damon. That, more than anything else, was why she'd called the police that first time. She'd hoped they would catch him and prove her irrational fears were groundless. "He never . . . did anything . . . other than stand there. But something about him made me uncomfortable."

"And the other times you saw him?" Pierce asked.

"The second time, he was closer, standing in my back-yard by a storage shed. The next time, he was actually on my front porch when I turned into my driveway." She rubbed her hands up and down her arms, remembering how shocked she'd been to see him standing there, peeking in her front window.

Pierce leaned forward, his forearms resting on his knees. "What did he do when he saw you? What did *you* do?"

"He ran. I called the police. I'd hoped they'd find a fingerprint or something, figure out who he was and why he was so interested in my house."

"Or you," Casey said.

She nodded, swallowing hard. "Or me."

"Yesterday morning," Casey said, "you stepped outside to confront him."

"Yes."

"And he ran?"

"Yes."

"And you chased him?"

She felt her face heating up, just like when Pierce had asked her the same thing. "With hindsight, I know that was foolish. But at the time, honestly, I was just angry. This man kept watching my house, openly, like he didn't care if I saw him. I mean, it's like he . . ."—she shook her head, struggling to put her impressions into words— "it's like he wanted me to see him, like he was trying to scare me. I wanted to talk to him, to ask him why he was watching me, and make him stop."

*And prove to herself that the man who haunted her nightmares was really dead.*

She clutched the arms of the chair. "You know the rest. Pierce jumped in front of me when the man pulled a gun. I heard the gunshot, saw Pierce fall to the ground . . ." her voice trailed off. She tried not to let the horrible images from yesterday crowd into her mind again.

Casey folded his hands on his desk. "Mrs. McKinley, Pierce told me you think the man you saw is your husband, that you think he faked his death."

She straightened in her chair. "I thought the purpose of this meeting was to clarify *Pierce's* involvement in a shooting, not mine. I've already spoken to the police about this."

"Why didn't you tell them about Damon?" Pierce asked.

"How do you know I didn't?"

"I read your statement."

Madison clamped her lips shut and crossed her arms.

Pierce sighed heavily. "We're trying to help you."

She looked at Agent Casey. "The idea that my dead husband is running around Savannah trying to scare me is ridiculous. I was overwrought yesterday. The shooter bore a resemblance to my husband, but he's not my husband." She looked back at Pierce. "My husband is dead." She rose from her seat, but Pierce quickly stood and moved to block her way.

"You're not the kind of woman to have hysterics, or imagine things. I don't buy for a second that you've changed your mind. You believe the shooter was Damon." His face softened as he reached out to gently sweep her bangs out of her eyes. "Mads, talk to me. Let me help you."

His use of her nickname in that low, intimate tone nearly made her knees buckle. But instead of stepping into his arms as her traitorous body wanted, she pushed past him, bracing herself against the tingle of awareness that shot through her when his chest brushed against hers.

This time he didn't try to stop her. She yanked the door open and stepped outside the office, only to stop short when she saw who was standing a few feet in front of her.

If it weren't for the long, red hair, Madison might not

have recognized Pierce's fiancée. In contrast to her sex-kitten look last night, Tessa was all business today in a charcoal gray suit, with a conservative skirt that hung past her knees, and sensible flat shoes. An FBI badge clipped to her jacket proclaimed her as Special Agent Tessa James. She and Pierce worked together.

How cozy.

Tessa grinned sheepishly and stepped forward with her hand out. "Mrs. McKinley, I'm sorry I couldn't tell you the truth last night. We had to wait until the case we've been working on was resolved. I couldn't risk blowing our cover."

Madison made no move to shake the other woman's hand. "Cover?"

Tessa lowered her hand and her brow wrinkled in confusion. "We've been working a case. The engagement was fake." She glanced past Madison. "You didn't tell her?"

Madison slowly turned around. Pierce was leaning against the office doorway, his hands shoved in his pants pockets.

Heat crept up Madison's neck. She felt like a fool, the only one *not* in on an inside joke. Now all of those men's clothes in the guest bedroom made sense. And she couldn't even be mad at Pierce. He'd tried to talk to her about his fiancée several times this morning. Each time he brought the subject up, she'd shut him down, refusing to listen. He must have been trying to tell her the truth.

Part of her was thrilled that he wasn't really engaged. But that part was overshadowed by the part of her that felt like a total, complete idiot.

"I'm sure I can find my own way out." She shoved past "pretty face" and hurried through the long row of cubicles.

By the time she made her way out of the building onto the sidewalk, her embarrassment had settled into a cold, hard knot of resentment in her stomach.

She closed her eyes and leaned back against the brick wall, taking deep breaths as she struggled for control. *Control.* That's what she needed to do, control this crazy situation instead of allowing others to control her.

All her life she'd been the baby, sheltered, protected. Her mother, father, and even Logan had smothered her with good intentions. They'd made decisions for her until she wanted to scream. When she'd met Damon, her family didn't approve of him, which made him more appealing to her. She'd decided it was time to take a stand, to make her own choices.

So she'd chosen Damon.

*You've been a very bad girl.*

She held her hands over her ears to block out the memory of Damon's voice. A whimper escaped between her clenched teeth.

"Miss, are you okay?"

Her eyes flew open. She forced her hands down and drew in deep, gulping breaths. A businessman holding a briefcase stood on the sidewalk in front of her, a look of concern on his face. His gray suit made her think of the agents inside the FBI building, which had her anger surging all over again.

"I'm fine. Thank you." At his doubtful look, she said,

"Headache. I just need to . . . get some water, and take something for it." She hurried down to the corner onto the next street, leaving the stranger behind.

*You shouldn't have snooped. Curiosity can get you in trouble. Remember that.*

No!

She clutched her hands to her chest and forced her feet to keep moving. All these months she'd convinced herself Damon was dead. She'd been in denial, assuming the autopsy report was wrong, that sloppy police work had missed the bullet in his burned-out corpse.

*The bullet she'd put in him.*

But now she knew better. Someone else had died in that car crash. Damon had killed another man and faked his own death. Now he was in Savannah, watching her. Why? What did he want? Money? Revenge?

Tears stung her eyes. She'd finally seen the evil inside him, but it had been too late. Far too late.

An image of her father's beloved face the last time she'd seen him suddenly swam through her mind.

*Forgive me, Daddy.*

## Chapter Five

"DON'T WORRY," CASEY reassured Pierce. "Agent Williams followed Mrs. McKinley out of the building. And he'll keep an eye on her until you catch up."

Pierce nodded and sat down in front of Casey's desk. He wasn't happy about letting Madison out of his sight, but with another agent shadowing her, she couldn't get into too much trouble. At least, until she figured out she was being followed and shook her pursuer, which he wouldn't put past her.

"Williams had better stay alert," Pierce said. "If Madison realizes she's being followed, she'll give him the slip just to be ornery."

Casey laughed and reached for his keyboard. "What was her husband's name?"

"Damon McKinley. He died in a car accident about eighteen months ago." Pierce stood and circled around behind the desk.

"Location?"

"Madison and Damon lived in Manhattan, but the accident was outside of the city." The idea of Madison being married to another man didn't sit any better with Pierce today than it had when he'd first met her. Not that it should matter. Any future he might have planned with her was destroyed when she left him. That part of his life was over, and he needed to focus on what was important, keeping her safe until her brother could take over that job.

Casey's fingers flew across the keyboard. A moment later the screen displayed a newspaper article with a picture of a mangled, burned-out car.

"Single-car accident," Casey said. "Rain-slicked road, high-speed turn. He lost control going around a corner, wrapped the car around a tree."

"It's unusual for a car to catch on fire like that. The body was burned beyond recognition."

"Rare, but it does happen—if there are enough fumes in the gas tank and it ruptures. What kind of finances are we talking about?"

"Damon had money before he married Madison. He wasn't outrageously wealthy, but they were comfortable. Madison's father had several life insurance polices that paid out millions to his wife and kids when he died. Her brother, Logan, invested their money and grew it into a fortune in a fairly short amount of time, mainly in real estate and dot-coms. He has a knack for buying low and selling high, and getting out of markets before they crash."

"Remind me to ask him for investment advice. Did Damon die before, or after, Mrs. McKinley's father?"

"A week or two after."

Casey frowned. "Why would a man fake his death, when his wife just inherited millions of dollars?" He clicked an icon on his desktop and performed another search.

"I agree it doesn't make sense."

A few searches later, another document filled Casey's screen. "We can rule out insurance fraud. He didn't have insurance, none that I can find anyway, unless it was an amount too small to show up on federal radar. Kind of unusual not to have life insurance. Self-employed?"

"From what little Madison would tell me on the way here, I gather he was an entrepreneur. He invested in small businesses up and down the East Coast. But he was very private about his work, and Madison wasn't all that interested in it. She focused on her own work as an assistant curator in one of the museums in New York."

Casey relaxed in his chair. Pierce leaned back against the desk.

"Did she tell you anything about the marriage? Why she thinks her husband would want to kill her?"

"She isn't exactly confiding in me right now. The only reason she agreed to come here is because she feels guilty about me getting shot, and she's worried I'll tell her brother about it. She says she doesn't want to ruin his honeymoon, but I don't buy that. She's hiding something. Damned if I know what it is."

Casey tapped his fingers on the desktop. "When you

went to the station to talk to Hamilton, did you discuss whether this could be related to the 'Simon says' case? I haven't heard anything about that killer stalking his victims before he kills them, but it's possible."

"He didn't think the two were related. He still hasn't invited the FBI in on that case?"

Casey shook his head. "Hamilton's stubborn. He wants to handle it himself. Honestly, he's got some crack detectives over there. They might solve it without our help anyway. Hopefully soon, before more bodies pile up. There've been three murders now."

Pierce shook his head. "What about Madison? Can you think of an angle that would give us jurisdiction to look into her husband's death? If Damon's alive, someone else died in his place. We might be able to convince NYPD to invite us in to investigate."

"Maybe, but exhumation is expensive. Without credible evidence, I don't see NYPD paying for it. I sure can't justify it in my budget. I suppose we could ask Mrs. McKinley if she'd be willing to cover the cost, sounds like she could afford it. But what would be the point? It'd be nearly impossible to confirm the vic's identity. The fire most likely destroyed any viable DNA. Does Damon have any blood relatives, so we would have a DNA profile to compare against?"

Pierce shook his head. "Damon was adopted."

"Dental records?"

"Madison said her husband refused to go to the dentist because he'd had some kind of bad experience as a kid."

"This is all beginning to sound rather convenient."

"My thoughts exactly. Body burned beyond recognition, no DNA, no dental records. I'm inclined to understand why Madison believes he could still be alive."

Casey steepled his hands over his chest. "How long were they married?"

"A little over a year."

"They should have still been in their honeymoon phase, and yet she thinks he's trying to kill her. What kind of marriage did they have?"

Good question, one that had gnawed at Pierce since yesterday morning. "I haven't had much of a chance to ask her all those details yet. It was a struggle getting her to answer just a few questions on the drive over."

"Why is she so reluctant to involve law enforcement?"

"I'm not sure if she's reluctant to involve law enforcement, or if she's just frustrated over the police's handling of her nine-one-one calls, and reluctant to involve *me*."

Casey pursed his lips. "What did Damon have to gain by faking his death?"

"I think the only person who might be able to answer that is Madison."

Casey punched the clear key, erasing the contents of his screen. "The police didn't find any evidence to back up her reports that someone was stalking her. The only verifiable facts are that she chased a man and he shot at her. Playing devil's advocate, I can think of several explanations, and none of them involve her former husband faking his death and coming after her."

Pierce let out a long breath. "I agree. The most obvious

explanation is that the man she chased was casing the house to rob her. When he couldn't shake her, he shot at her so he could get away. I can ask Hamilton if there have been any burglaries in the area, but I think he would have mentioned that when I spoke to him earlier."

"Fledgling burglar? Casing his first house? It could explain why she saw him watching her house so many times. He was nervous, not sure what to do. Where does she live?"

"East Gaston Street. One of those historic mansions, worth a cool million, easy. Might be closer to two."

"A burglar's dream."

"I don't want to dismiss this without a thorough investigation," Pierce said. "I want to make sure she's not in danger. If your theory is right, then no one is after her. The burglar will move on to an easier target. He won't want someone to spot him in the same neighborhood after all the attention caused by the shooting. But if your theory is wrong, anything is possible."

Casey nodded and glanced past Pierce, as if making sure the door was closed, before looking up at him.

"Any chance you'll let this go, leave it to the locals?"

"None. Metro PD doesn't have the resources to put someone on guard duty over Madison, or to dig into this and figure out what's really going on."

"What do *you* think is going on?"

He thought for a moment. The facts pointed to this as a one-time event, most likely the burglary scenario. But Madison was too nervous. She was hiding something. She was convinced her husband was after her. He didn't see how she could be that sure without having a really good reason.

Like being *certain* her husband wasn't the one who'd died in the car crash.

He shook his head. "You're probably right about all of this. But I have to follow up and make sure she's safe. I'd never forgive myself if something happened to her when I could have prevented it."

Casey's brows rose. "Because you're still hung up on her?"

He clenched his hands beside him. "Because I promised her brother I'd keep her safe."

Casey didn't look like he believed his excuse.

Pierce wasn't sure he believed it either.

"Well," Casey said, "unless new evidence comes to light, I can't classify this as federal. And unless Savannah-Chatham Metro PD invites us to participate in the investigation, there's nothing we can do. If you work this case, it will have to be as a civilian, on your own time. Now that your undercover work is wrapped up, you've earned some time off."

"Shouldn't take more than a few days."

Casey gave him an arch look. "I'm not thrilled about this. I think you're still emotionally involved with Madison McKinley."

Pierce stiffened. "My past relationship, emphasis on *past*, is not relevant."

"I'll spare you the standard lecture. But if you do something stupid because you're distracted, and get yourself killed, don't expect me to cry at your funeral."

Pierce gave him a bland look. "I'll keep that in mind."

"You do understand there's no way I can officially help."

"Understood. But, if you *were* to look into this, hypothetically speaking, what do you think you could do?"

"Well, hypothetically speaking, of course, I could operate on the assumption the shooter really is Damon McKinley. I could build a dossier on him, see what's lurking in his background, follow the paper trail, starting in New York."

"When will you have something for me?"

Casey grinned. "Give me twenty-four hours."

MADISON STEPPED OUT of the taxi onto East Bay Street, clutching her heavy purse to her side. Since Pierce had refused to give her back her Colt .380 unless she produced a concealed weapons permit, she'd had to go home after leaving the FBI building to retrieve her much bulkier, heavier, .357 Magnum. And just to be sure his police buddies couldn't track her down again, she'd taken a cab instead of her flashy red convertible.

She'd also printed out a list from her computer, a list that detailed some of Damon's investments that she'd found while snooping on *his* computer. That was the first time she'd seen his irrational temper.

And the first time she'd realized something was very, very wrong.

Some of the legal documents she'd copied from the folders in his desk drawer all those months ago were also in her purse. He'd supposedly sunk money into small businesses in most of the major East Coast cities, including a handful here in Savannah.

The few investments Madison had looked into after her husband's estate went through probate had turned out to be bogus. She didn't expect the ones in Savannah would be any different, but it was a starting point. If he knew the businesses well enough to write fake contracts about them, Madison figured he knew the area. As her brother had often told her, people tend to follow patterns, whether they realize it or not. They return to the familiar.

Hopefully that meant someone at one of those businesses knew him, and might have seen him recently. It was the only way Madison could think of to try to track him down. The alternative was to sit in her house and wait, and worry when he might show up again.

And what he might do.

Sitting around, being on the defense, had never been her style.

She sidestepped a group of slow-moving tourists, maneuvering her way down one of the bumpy, stone access ramps to East River Street, taking special care with her weak ankle. The brisk air coming off the Savannah River had her wishing she'd brought a scarf to cover her neck. She flipped her jacket collar up and hurried past the outdoor market to a brick building with a black and orange sign out front boasting its name, MacGuffin's Bar & Grill.

The restaurant hadn't opened for the lunch crowd yet, and no one answered the door when she knocked. She'd been a waitress in more than her share of restaurants to earn her way through college. If this place was typical, there were probably at least a couple of staff members inside getting the restaurant ready to open. Which meant the service entrance was probably unlocked so the staff could easily come and go.

She headed around the side and found the service door. As she'd expected, it was unlocked. She stepped inside, blinking as her eyes adjusted to the dimly lit interior. The smell of roasted peanuts and stale beer hit her nostrils.

"We're closed," a tall man said, standing in the narrow hallway, blocking her way. He wore faded jeans and a black T-shirt with the restaurant's name on it. "We're not open for another hour. And it's customary to use the front door." He pointed toward the front of the restaurant.

Madison gave him her best smile. "Sorry to bother you. I'm Madison McKinley. I have urgent business with the owner. Is Mr. MacGuffin around?"

"Is he expecting you?"

"I didn't get a chance to call ahead, but it's very important."

"If you're a salesman, he's not buying."

"I'm part owner of this restaurant, and I need to talk to Mr. MacGuffin."

His eyes widened. "Part owner? Well, that's a new one. Come on. I'd like to see his face when you tell him that."

Madison frowned at his retreating back, and followed him as he weaved his way through the tables to another door at the end of the hallway. He entered a large, cluttered office and ushered her inside. An older man was sitting behind the desk that took up a good portion of the room. Papers littered nearly every inch of the wooden surface. More papers were piled in stacks on the floor.

"Boss, this lady wants to talk to you, says she's part owner."

MacGuffin looked just as surprised as the other man had. But his look of surprise smoothed into a smile as he held out his hand. "Joshua MacGuffin."

She shook his hand. "Madison McKinley."

The look on his face didn't change when he heard her last name. Madison took that as a bad sign.

"Have a seat." He motioned to the chair in front of his desk. "Close the door, please, Todd." He smiled at the man in the doorway.

Todd didn't look happy to be left out of the discussion, but he didn't argue. He closed the door with a solid click.

Mr. MacGuffin leaned forward. "Well, now. Since I'm the sole owner of this establishment, I'd be very interested in knowing why you believe you have a stake in the place. I do hope someone hasn't rooked you out of some money, young lady."

Madison was fairly certain how this would end, even before it began. But after being such a bad judge of character with Damon, she no longer trusted her instincts. So even though this man's kind face and gentle way of speaking reminded her of her father, and she sensed he was telling the truth, she plunged ahead with her questions.

"My husband, Damon, bought half of this restaurant for two hundred thousand dollars. I've got the paperwork right here." She took a sheaf of papers out of her purse and placed it on the desk.

MacGuffin studied the contract, pushing his thick glasses up on his nose before turning the top page. He scratched his balding head, his lips moving as he read. When he looked up at her again, he was no longer smiling. He grabbed a piece of paper from one of the piles on his desk and set it down in front of her. "This is my signature here." He pointed to the bottom of the paper, then flipped to the signature page on the contract she'd brought. "And this is supposedly my signature on your paper." He looked at her over the top of his glasses. "I'm no handwriting expert, but—"

"They aren't the same."

He smoothed his fingers across one of the pages. "What did you say your husband's name was?"

"Damon McKinley."

"Can't say I've ever met him. Name doesn't sound familiar. But I'm sure my lawyer will be interested in meeting him."

Madison pulled the sheaf of papers toward her. "Damon died in a car accident."

Sympathy immediately flooded Mr. MacGuffin's eyes. "My sympathies, Mrs. McKinley. I hope you have some other means of income besides that alleged investment."

She shoved the papers into her purse. "I didn't have any plans to liquidate his holdings in this restaurant in any case. But I can't understand why he'd go to such lengths to pretend that he'd invested in your restaurant, why he'd create a fake contract."

"Two hundred thousand dollars is a lot of money. Perhaps he needed a way to explain away some kind of loss. A gambling debt, something like that."

"He never showed me this contract. I found it on my own. So it's not like he tried to use it to explain any losses to *me*." She didn't tell him she'd found it by snooping through her husband's things. Instead, she let her statement hang in the air so that Mr. MacGuffin would assume she'd found it after her husband died.

"Forgive me, but did your husband engage in . . . illegal activities?"

She clutched her purse in her lap. "Not that I can prove. Although, I do admit that I suspected as much."

He nodded. "Then it's entirely possible he planned to use that fake contract to try to take my restaurant from me. Perhaps he was going to approach my heirs someday, to place a lien against my estate. There are all kinds of schemes con artists use. Unfortunately, I've seen quite a few of them. This one, however, is new to me."

He stared at her curiously. "You said you didn't plan to liquidate. If that's the case, may I ask why you're here?"

She considered lying, but she'd done far too much of that lately, and it was leaving a bitter taste in her mouth. "I have reason to believe my husband may have faked his death, and that he's in Savannah. I'm trying to track him down."

"Oh dear."

"I forgot to bring a picture of him with me." She'd been in too much of a hurry to leave the house before Pierce caught up to her. "But if you've seen him, or if you see him in the future, I'd appreciate it if you'd let me know." She described him as she scribbled her name and cell phone number on a piece of scrap paper from her purse. She slid the paper across the desk. "He has distinctive, extremely light blue eyes, hard to forget."

MacGuffin took the paper and slid it into his top drawer. "I don't interact with the customers much these days. I spend most of my time in the office doing the ridiculous amount of paperwork the government requires from small businesses." He smiled ruefully. "I can't say that I've seen him, but I'll have Todd put the word out with the staff."

"Thank you. I appreciate it."

"Of course. I hope I can help, as long as you don't plan to try to take half my business with those fake documents of course."

The hint of steel underlying his tone surprised her. He was obviously more suspicious of her motives than she'd realized. She pulled the contract back out of her purse. She held the pages in the air and tore them in half before setting them on the desk.

"Does that satisfy you, Mr. MacGuffin?"

"Almost." He picked up the torn pages, swiveled in his seat, and Madison heard the unmistakable sound of a paper shredder in action. Mr. MacGuffin turned back around. "Now I'm satisfied."

## Chapter Six

THREE HOURS LATER Madison was suffering from a chronic case of déjà vu. She hopped off the trolley, giving the driver the bribe she'd promised him so that he'd let her on board without a ticket and drop her off in front of a bed-and-breakfast that wasn't on his tour route.

Damon had supposedly sunk fifty thousand into this particular investment, but Madison expected that was as much a lie as the five other places she'd visited today. Everyone she'd spoken to told her the same story. They didn't know who Damon was and the papers she had were fake.

Some of them, like Mr. MacGuffin, had been polite, even concerned about her. Others had been outright hostile. She had business cards from two lawyers in her purse, and the verbal threats to go along with them.

She went inside the bed-and-breakfast. Twenty minutes later, with the bed-and-breakfast just as much a bust as she'd expected, she stepped outside and marked it off her list. She shoved the list in her purse, then looked up, directly into Pierce Buchanan's dark eyes.

His Pontiac GTO was parked on the curb. He was leaning back against the door, his arms crossed and his long legs stretched out in front of him. For a moment it was as if the past few months had never happened. She remembered their first couple of dates in the Panhandle, when he was still helping her brother wrap up the loose ends of the case they'd solved together. After the third or fourth date, she'd decided not to see him anymore. Everything was too good, too perfect, which scared her. She'd gone her own way, but that had only lasted a few weeks.

She'd missed him, was desperate to see him again. She'd gone to Jacksonville, and he'd welcomed her with open arms. They'd spent evenings going to the beach, or floating down the St. Johns River on a boat they rented for the day, watching barges go by on their way to the port.

Everything had been so wonderful, until a jewelry store called while he was at work and left a message on the answering machine. The engagement ring he'd ordered was ready to be picked up. The walls had begun to close in on her. The thought of getting married again made her sick with fear, and she could barely catch her breath.

When he came home, she'd told him a cruel lie, because she didn't want him wasting his life hoping she'd change her mind and come back. She'd told him the one thing that she knew would make him let her go: "I don't love you. I'm ready to move on."

Madison ruthlessly pushed the past out of her mind. "What are you doing here?" she asked.

He straightened and opened the passenger door. "That was the last place on your list, right? Let's grab a late lunch, my treat."

She put her hands on her hips. "What do you mean, that's the last place on my list?"

"You mark a name off that piece of paper every time you come out of a building. It looked like this bed-and-breakfast was at the bottom of the piece of paper, so I thought you were done for the day."

"What list?" she repeated. Had he actually followed her today, and she hadn't known? That thought had her both irritated and alarmed. If *he* could follow her so easily, who else could? She glanced around, rubbing the arms of her coat as she searched for a familiar silhouette in the shadows.

*Damon.*

"The list you shoved into your purse," Pierce answered.

She looked back at him and crossed her arms. "You've been following me all day?"

"Technically, no. Another agent followed you until I could wrap up a few loose ends. *Then* I followed you."

Her face flushed, and she whirled around. She strode past his open car door and headed down the sidewalk.

"Coward." His insult echoed up the block.

She stiffened but kept walking.

The sound of a powerful engine revving up spurred her to walk faster. Pierce's GTO whipped into a parking spot on the curb ahead. As he got out of his car, she hurried around the corner onto Congress Street.

She heard his footsteps right before his arm clamped around her shoulders. He pulled her to a halt, facing the building in front of them.

"Molly MacPherson's Scottish Pub and Grill." He read the sign over the door. "Not exactly what I had in mind, but it'll work. Let's get a beer, Mads." He anchored her against his side, in spite of her attempts to pull away.

She raised her elbow, bluffing, because she would never really hit him in his bruised ribs.

He grabbed her arm. "Do it, and I'll have you locked up for assaulting a federal officer. Don't think I won't."

She tried to twist away, irritated that he'd believed her bluff so easily. This time he let her go.

"This is twice you've kidnapped me. Isn't that a felony or something?"

His face tightened into angry lines. "You and I are going to talk. We can do it here, or at the police station. I'm sure I can convince Lieutenant Hamilton to arrest you for something." He cocked a brow. "Like carrying a concealed weapon without a permit."

Madison sucked in a breath and moved her purse to her other side, away from him.

The hostess approached them and asked about their seating preference.

Madison tamped down her irritation and smiled. "A booth please."

"Away from everyone else," Pierce added.

The hostess nodded, grabbed napkin-wrapped silverware and some menus, and led the way toward the back corner of the restaurant.

Molly MacPherson's wasn't the kind of place Madison would normally pay more than a passing glance. She preferred smaller places with local flavor, without all the tourists. Judging by the Savannah T-shirts most of the diners were wearing, and the shopping bags cluttering the floor beneath their tables, just about everyone in this place was a tourist. The folk music piping out of the speakers was also a bit loud, but the beat gave the place a happy atmosphere, and she could feel her mood lifting already.

When she passed a kilt-wearing waiter, she couldn't help but be intrigued. Wasn't there a rumor about what men wore beneath their kilts—or rather—what they *didn't* wear? The waiter, noticing her interest, gave her a playful leer and a wink. Madison grinned, winked back, and stopped to ask about his kilt.

As if guessing her intent, Pierce shook his head and grabbed her around the waist, steering her to their booth.

Madison frowned at him, her mood sinking again as she slid into the seat with the wall at her back. She glanced toward the entrance, reassuring herself that Damon wasn't standing there. She had no reason to believe he'd followed her today, but if an FBI agent had followed without her knowing, anything was possible.

Instead of sitting on the other side of the table, Pierce slid in next to her. Since he didn't seem to be watching the door like her, she assumed he just wanted to be able to discuss Damon without anyone overhearing them. She also noticed he sat with his injured ribs facing away from her as if he still didn't trust her. She blew out a frustrated breath.

Her mood soured even further, until she began to notice how warm and cozy it was sitting close to him. This wasn't the first time they'd sat beside each other in a booth. When they'd gone out to restaurants together in the past, they'd often sit next to each other instead of across from each other, so they could hold hands beneath the table, or exchange a more intimate touch—a kiss on the nape of her neck, the brush of his breath against her ear, her hand on his thigh.

She shivered at the memory. Pierce glanced at her in question, and she looked away.

The waitress arrived and took their drink orders. They sat in silence until their drinks arrived, along with an order of potato scones the waitress had recommended.

Madison took a bite of one of the scones, but she barely tasted the almonds and raspberry preserves. She kept trying to close her mind to the memories that swirled around her, so she could focus on whatever questions he might ask her, but sitting this close to him was playing havoc with her concentration.

It was all she could do not to bury her nose in his shoulder and breathe in that intoxicating blend of soap and cologne that she always associated with him. She didn't realize how much she'd missed him, or how much she cared about him until she'd seen him jump in front of a bullet for her.

She drew a shaky breath.

In spite of his earlier quip about getting a beer, Pierce had ordered water. He took a sip and turned slightly toward her as if he were about to ask her something.

Madison took another bite.

"You can stall all you want," he said. "I'm not going anywhere until we talk."

The scone sat like sand in her throat. She chased it down with a generous sip of Diet Coke and shoved the plate away. "There's really no need for another inquisition. As you can see, no one took any shots at me today. No one followed me."

He raised an eyebrow.

"Okay, except for the FBI. Other than that, no one followed me." She couldn't help glancing at the door again. But she realized that was a mistake when he looked toward the door too. The frown on his face when he looked back at her told her he knew exactly why she'd looked toward the entrance.

"I'm still a little jittery from yesterday," she said in explanation. "And tired. But other than that, I'm fine. You have no further obligations to my brother. You can go back to Tammy and forget all about me."

He sighed heavily. "*Tessa*. Her name is Tessa. And we shared that house for undercover work."

Jealousy slammed into her so hard her eyesight blurred. "How much *undercover* work did you two do?"

He rolled his eyes and ignored her question. "Speaking of houses, it's too dangerous for you to stay in yours. Until we know whether the gunman is coming back or not, you need to stay somewhere else."

She clutched the edge of the table so hard she was surprised the wood didn't crack. She wasn't about to let another man order her around. She rested her hand on Pierce's thigh beneath the table and batted her lashes as she leaned against him. "You don't think Terry will mind if I stay with you two, do you?"

He glanced down where her breast was pressed against his arm, before he met her gaze. "Careful, Mads. I'm more than capable of finishing anything you start."

The waitress stopped to see if they were ready to order.

Madison flashed her teeth in a false smile and rubbed her hand up the front of Pierce's shirt. "I'm not hungry anymore, *darling*," she said, mimicking the tone and endearment she'd heard Tessa use.

Pierce captured her hand in his and gifted the waitress with one of his sexy smiles. He put his other arm around Madison's shoulders and hauled her up against his side. "Please ignore my bride's poor manners. She's just ticked that I dragged her out of bed. I told her we have to keep up our strength." He winked and the waitress blushed fire red.

Madison kept her smile in place while she ground the heel of her sneaker into the top of his shoe. His pained grimace was extremely satisfying.

"We had to leave the room anyway," she said, in the same sexy, flirty tone he'd just used. "We had to get some more of those little blue pills." She cupped her hand conspiratorially. "You know, for his little . . . problem."

The waitress blinked like an owl and her mouth fell open.

Pierce slid his hand down the side of Madison's arm.

And pinched her.

She let out a yelp and jerked away from his hand, throwing herself against his side.

"Whoa, honey," he said. "Let's save that for the motel. And don't you worry. I brought plenty of batteries to power those toys you love so much." He winked at her gasp of outrage.

Madison ducked under his arm and sprang from the booth, leaving him to settle the bill. She stalked outside and marched down the sidewalk, her face so hot she barely noticed the cold air. When he fell into step beside her a few moments later, she stopped and faced him with her hands on her hips. "Batteries? Toys?"

"Blue pills? My little problem? Did you think I would let something like that go?"

"You deserved it after that comment about dragging me out of bed."

He let out a short laugh, without a trace of humor. "You started this, hanging all over me back there. If I didn't know better, I'd say you were jealous."

"Ha, jealous? Of who?"

"Oh, let me see. Theresa, Terry, or was it Tammy?"

She turned around, but he stepped right back in front of her. She tried to take a step back, but he grasped her shoulders and held her in a firm grip.

"Let me go," she demanded.

"Not until you answer me."

"I don't remember you asking a question."

"Are you jealous?"

"Why would I be jealous of . . ." her voice trailed off. She was about to make up another "T" name but she didn't want to give him more ammunition. "Why would I be jealous of Tessa?"

He frowned. "Good question. Why would you? May I remind you, you were the dump*er*. I was the dump*ee*."

She poked him in the stomach, careful to avoid his ribs. "I did *not* dump you. It was just . . . over. We were finished with each other."

He grabbed her hand in his, his blazing eyes inches from hers. "*You* might have been finished, baby, but *I* was only getting started."

She didn't know who moved first, but suddenly they were in each other's arms. She tugged him against the wall of the building beside them, and kissed him back as fiercely as he was kissing her.

It had been so long, too long, since she'd felt this way. Heat coiled deep inside her, and she wiggled her hips, cuddling against him. She slid her fingers into the waistband of his pants, trying to free his shirt so she could feel his skin against hers.

He made a choking sound and broke the kiss, grabbing her roving hands. He took a deep, shaky breath as he forced her back. "Stop," he rasped.

She frowned and stepped closer, tugging her hands out of his grasp. "Why?"

He drew another deep breath. "For one thing, we're on a public sidewalk."

Her eyes widened as she looked around at the small audience they'd gained—an elderly couple shaking their heads as they walked by, two teenaged boys grinning and whispering a few feet away, making no attempt to hide their interest.

She shrugged. The delicious heat he'd awakened still curled through her. She'd missed this. She'd missed *him*. She ran her fingers down the front of his shirt. "Then let's go to my house where we can be alone."

He grabbed her hands and firmly removed them from his chest. "What about your *husband*? If your stalker is who you think he is, you're still married."

She twisted her fingers beneath his until she was holding his hands. "We're not married. I divorced Damon."

He stilled. "What did you say?"

She pulled a hand free and reached up to play with the hair at the nape of his neck. "There's no reason we can't enjoy each other for a couple of hours, like old times."

He grabbed her hand again, "That's not going to happen. Play your games with someone else. I'm not getting back on that merry-go-round." He pulled her toward his car and yanked the passenger door open. "Get in."

She plopped down on the seat, blinking against the unexpected moisture in her eyes at his merry-go-round comment. She'd definitely met her goal of making sure he didn't try to stop her when she broke up with him. Maybe she shouldn't have tried quite so hard.

He slammed her door shut and crossed around the front of the car to the driver's side. He got in, but instead of starting the engine, he grabbed her purse.

"Hey, what are you doing?" She tried to grab her purse back, but he held it out of her reach.

"I'm trying to keep you out of jail, but you're making it extremely difficult." He took out her .357 Magnum and shook his head as he shoved the gun under his seat. "Are you hiding any more weapons I should know about?"

She glared at him. "Why don't you search me and find out?"

His jaw tightened as he tossed the purse in her lap. He turned the key, making the engine roar.

"Where are we going?" she demanded.

He slammed the gas pedal, throwing her back in her seat. "Neutral territory."

MADISON STOPPED IN front of the sign, "October 9, 1779. In Memory of Those Who Fought Here." Beside her, Pierce stared across the expanse of brownish-green grass that spanned Battlefield Park.

"How is this neutral territory?" Madison asked.

"No cops." Pierce glanced down at her. "No guns. Just you and me, on a battlefield. Seems appropriate. We're about to do battle. And we're not leaving until one of us wins."

With that ominous statement, he grabbed her hand and hauled her to a bench that looked out over the grassy fort. She reluctantly sat beside him and tugged her hand out of his grasp. The man was far too bossy.

And far too appealing.

How could she want to hit him and kiss him at the same time?

He leaned back and propped his arm behind her. "We need to talk."

When she didn't say anything, he sighed heavily and pulled his arm back, then twisted to face her. "Please."

That one little word, spoken so softly, was her undoing. The man had taken a bullet for her. The least she could do was try to answer his questions, or at least, she'd answer what she could without revealing too much. That bitter taste was already coming back in her mouth because of the lies she knew she would have to tell.

"WHY DID YOU go to MacGuffin's?" Pierce asked. "The place wasn't even open."

Madison's eyes widened, and Pierce saw a flash of panic cross her face. He could practically see the gears spinning in her mind, searching and sifting for that elusive answer, the lie she would tell to get him to leave her alone.

Tough. She could lie to him all day, and it wouldn't matter. He wasn't going to leave her alone until he got the truth.

"MacGuffin's," he repeated.

She stared out over the battlefield. "Damon . . . mentioned the place a few times. I thought someone there might remember him, that maybe they'd spoken to him and might know where he's staying."

"You thought the man that you think is trying to kill you might hang around that place, so it was a good idea to go there?"

She winced. "When you put it that way, it doesn't

sound like a very good idea. But I always keep a gun with me." She frowned at him. "Or at least, I did."

He wanted to shake some sense into her. Thank goodness Casey had sent an agent to keep an eye on her. The agent had later told Pierce he spoke to her right outside the FBI building, that she had claimed to have a headache and seemed upset. Right now, Pierce was the one with a headache.

And its name was Madison.

He had to concentrate to keep his voice even, and his exasperation from showing on his face. He needed information, and getting Madison's hackles up wouldn't get him anywhere.

"And did they?" he asked. "Did anyone at MacGuffin's remember Damon?"

"No. And before you ask, no one remembered him anywhere else I went either. I got nowhere today." She waved her hand in the air. "Honestly, I don't see how you detective-types figure out who the bad guys are, or where the bad guys are, with so little to go on." She chewed her bottom lip. "Maybe tomorrow I'll check out the museums. Damon was always big on art. If he's in Savannah, he couldn't resist going to the museums. Someone has to remember him."

She wasn't going anywhere without him, but he'd straighten her out about that later. He watched her closely as he asked his next question. "I need you to answer me truthfully, Mads. Did Damon ever hit you?"

## Chapter Seven

MADISON'S FACE TURNED bright red, and she looked genuinely outraged. "Do you really think I would have stuck around if Damon had ever hit me?"

"It happens. Even strong women can feel trapped in those situations, unsure what to do. Leaving isn't always as easy as you'd think it should be."

She wrapped her arms around her waist. "Well, regardless, he never hit me."

He waited for her to shove her hair back behind her ears. That was her "tell," like a neon sign letting him know she probably wasn't telling the truth. It wasn't an infallible test, but judging by the look on her face, he was confident she wasn't lying now. Damon hadn't abused her. Relief swept through him.

"Then what was so horrible about your marriage?"

"What makes you think it was horrible?"

"You think he's trying to kill you. Is that your idea of a *good* marriage?"

She wrapped her arms around her middle. "It wasn't always that way," she said, her voice quiet and small. "When I met him, he was charming. He doted on me, and I was crazy about him. My brother tried to warn me things were going too fast, that I didn't know enough about Damon. Actually, no one in my family liked him very much. But I didn't want to listen. We were married two months after we met."

Two months, about the same amount of time *he'd* known her when she'd ended their relationship. He hoped that thought hadn't figured into her reasons for leaving him. Being compared to Damon didn't sit well with him one bit.

"Go on," he said. "What happened to make it all go wrong?"

She smoothed her jacket and drew little circles on her jeans with her fingernail. "The first five or six months were wonderful. After that, I guess the strain of lying all the time was too much for him. That's when I saw the real Damon."

"What do you mean?"

"It started when I saw him with another woman in a restaurant. He didn't know I was driving by, never saw me."

"He was having an affair?" Pierce asked.

"I thought so, but I couldn't see how that was possible. We were happy, or so I'd thought. I didn't want to confront him and feel stupid if she was just a business associate. But after that, I started watching for signs, hoping I was wrong."

She sighed. "I couldn't let it go. It kept eating at me. We argued. I accused him of cheating. He was so surprised he started laughing. He was genuinely amused that I thought he was having an affair. And relieved."

"Relieved?"

She nodded. "It was . . . odd. I knew he was hiding something, but he'd rather me think he was having an affair than tell me what he was really up to. That's when I started following him."

"You followed him?"

"Oh, come on. Don't look at me like that. I didn't think he was dangerous. I just knew my marriage was falling apart, and I wanted to know why. We didn't get along. We argued all the time. Then I discovered some hidden files on his computer."

Pierce put his finger beneath her chin, tilting her head up so that he could look her in the eyes. "What was in the files?"

She stared at him a moment, then pushed his hand away and stared out across the field. "He lied about his finances. I found spreadsheets detailing private accounts I knew nothing about, and purchases. He was spending tens of thousands of dollars a month."

Pierce grimaced. "You were broke."

"No, not at all. That's the weird thing. We had too much money, way more than we should have had, the way he was spending money. I confronted him, demanded to know where all the money was coming from. When he found out I'd logged onto his computer and looked at his files . . ."

She shivered and Pierce took her hand in his. She looked down at their joined hands, her brow wrinkling. But she didn't pull away.

"That's the first time I was ever afraid of him." Her jaw tightened. "But not the last."

The bleak sound of her voice told him far more than her words. He had a feeling he wasn't going to like the answer to his next question. "What did he do?"

She vigorously shook her head, her dark hair brushing back and forth across her shoulders. "It doesn't matter. Our marriage was over. He grabbed his laptop and left. He disappeared for two weeks. No phone calls, no e-mails, nothing. That's when I filed for divorce."

Her eyes had a slightly wild look to them, as if she would bolt if he pushed her any further. So he decided not to press her on that topic. For now.

"Did Logan or your mom know about the divorce?"

"No, no one did."

"Why didn't you tell anyone?"

She swallowed and briefly closed her eyes. "At first, I was too embarrassed. I hated that my family was right about him. Later, when my dad's health got so bad . . ."

"Go on."

She drew a deep breath. "Damon showed up again when my father was admitted to the hospital. He acted supportive and sweet in front of my family, as if nothing bad had happened between us. I played along, but I wouldn't let him back into the house. I'd changed the locks. And I was never alone with him, even though he asked me, several times, to speak in private."

Her grip on his hand tightened.

"A few days later, my father was dead." She was silent for a long time. Finally, she shrugged. "A week after that, Damon died in the car accident. I never thought about canceling the divorce proceedings. I'd totally forgotten that I'd even filed, until my lawyer contacted me. He said since Damon had been declared dead, obviously there was no point in finalizing the divorce. But . . ."

She tugged her hands away from his and shoved her hair back behind her ears.

Pierce steeled himself for whatever lie she was about to tell him.

"I guess I just wanted those papers to make it feel official, that it was really over. So I had the lawyer push it through." She shrugged. "There wasn't any point in telling anyone after that."

He didn't believe for one second that a judge would waste his time processing a divorce when one of the parties in the divorce had been declared dead. He made a mental note to press her about the divorce later. He frowned as a new thought struck him. "Damon didn't know about the divorce?"

"No one does. Except you."

"Then, if he's alive, he would assume if something happens to you, he'd inherit your money."

She blinked at him in surprise.

"You never thought about that?" he asked.

"Well, sure, but I thought if he'd been declared dead,

he'd have no claim to my estate." She wrinkled her brow. "Even if that's not the case, I still don't see how he'd think he could get my money, not after faking his death. He obviously . . ." She swallowed. "He obviously killed someone, put his wallet, jewelry, clothes, on some other man and staged the accident. He'd be arrested for murder if he turned up to claim my estate, wouldn't he?"

In a perfect world, yes. But Pierce had seen far stranger things happen. Justice didn't always work the way it should.

"Faking your death isn't strictly illegal. There'd be questions, lots of questions. He'd have to come up with an incredibly plausible explanation for how another man died in his car, and why he didn't come forward at that time. But if there's no physical evidence, and he can explain his actions away somehow—he could still inherit. Can you think of any reason he'd want to pretend he was dead? Was there some reason he needed to disappear?"

Her eyes widened as she looked down at her feet.

Pierce sighed. Once again, she knew something, or at least suspected something, and wasn't telling him. "You can afford to live wherever you want. Why not just move back to New York until all of this blows over?"

Her head jerked up. "I just moved here. I'm in the middle of renovations. And I love this city. I don't want to leave."

"Even if it means you could be killed?"

She waved her hand in the air. "I'd be just as much a target if I went back to New York. He found me here. He'd just find me again there." She shook her head violently, her dark hair flying around her shoulders. "I will not let Damon control me or dictate where I live. And I'm not going to spend my life running away. This ends now, here, whatever it takes."

The stubborn set of her shoulders told him arguing that point wasn't going to make a difference. Truth be told, he'd rather she stayed here anyway—because that way he could help her.

If she'd stop being stubborn long enough to realize she needed his help.

"How certain are you that the shooter was really Damon?"

Her shoulders visibly relaxed, as if she were relieved that he wasn't going to press her further about moving away. "As sure as I can be without getting a closer look at him, or seeing his face." Her brow scrunched together as if she were concentrating, trying to remember the face of the man she'd seen. "I guess I could be mistaken. But I was so sure it was him."

"Let's assume the shooter wasn't Damon. Is there anyone else who might have a reason to hate you?"

She shook her head, looking completely miserable. "Only you."

His stomach lurched at the vulnerability on her face. He had to curl his hands around the bench to keep from reaching for her and pulling her into his arms.

"I don't hate you," he said.

Her gaze searched his as if she were trying to see if he were telling the truth. He knew she wanted more . . .

a touch, a look, some kind of reassurance. But that was more than he was willing to give.

She dropped her gaze to her lap.

He suddenly felt like a jerk for not giving in to the urge to hold her. Too late now. The moment was gone. "Someone tried to shoot you yesterday," he reminded her. "Whether he's Damon or not remains to be seen. I think it's entirely likely the shooter won't strike again, that he's moved on to find another victim. But until we know for sure that you're safe, you need someone to watch your back. I propose a truce."

"A truce?"

"An agreement. You stop trying to investigate on your own, and I promise I'll do everything in my power to figure out who the shooter is. I'll keep you safe."

She seemed to consider that, and cocked her head to the side. "Why do you want to help me? After the way I ended things between us, I wouldn't expect you to care."

"I didn't say I cared." He immediately regretted his harsh words when her eyes widened and she turned away. What was it about her that brought out the worst in him? He let out a long sigh. "I made a promise to Logan to keep you safe. I always keep my promises. So, how about it? Truce?"

She chewed her bottom lip and stared off in the distance, over his shoulder. "Did you really mean what you said? That even if Damon is alive, he could get away with faking his death? He wouldn't go to prison? He'd get away with . . . murder?"

The way she'd said "murder" had him wondering if they were talking about the man who'd died in the car accident . . . or someone else. He watched her closely as he answered. "It's certainly a possibility. It all depends on the evidence. Is there something else you know about Damon that you aren't telling me? Something he did?"

She blinked and refocused on him. "Nothing I can prove."

Before he could ask her what that meant, she waved her hand in the air. "Back to the truce. I'll accept your help, on one condition."

Leave it to Madison to make it sound like she was doing him the favor when he'd already gotten shot protecting her, and was burning vacation days to help her. The woman was completely exasperating.

And even though he hated to admit it, completely adorable. That sass and fire was one of the main things he'd always liked about her. "What condition?"

"You can't tell Logan about this, any of it. I don't want him to suspect I'm in danger. And I especially don't want him to think Damon might be alive."

"Why are you so worried about Logan knowing about Damon?"

"Because Logan would want to fix everything. And there are some things he just can't fix. I'll accept *your* help, but with that one condition. Take it or leave it."

What "things" was she talking about? He wanted to shake her in frustration, but he knew that would get him nowhere. Sooner or later she was going to have to be honest with him. He just hoped it wasn't too late, that someone didn't get hurt—or worse—before she decided to tell him what she suspected Damon had done.

"All right, deal," he said. "But I have a condition of my own. You're moving in with me. It's too dangerous to stay at your house while the stalker is still out there."

Her eyes widened in surprise. "Where do you live?"

"Does it matter?"

A mischievous grin curved her lips. "Not as long as Tessa doesn't come with us."

He didn't bother to respond to that ridiculous statement.

She stared at her shoes, deep in thought, as if carefully considering whether she could stand to live in the same house with him for the duration of their truce.

If it weren't for his promise to Logan, he might very well have gotten up right then and told her to forget it. He and Madison had shared themselves in every way two people could, and she was worried about him sleeping under the same roof?

"Okay, deal." She suddenly held out her hand.

He hesitated, belatedly wondering what he might have just gotten himself into. But when a look of uncertainty crossed her face, he blew out a breath and shook her hand.

"First things first, give me that list you had earlier today when you went to MacGuffin's," he said. "And tell me what you were really doing there."

She rolled her eyes. "I didn't figure you believed me about that." She grabbed her purse and dug inside. She pulled out a small packet of papers and plopped them in his hand.

"What's all this?" he asked. He flipped through the pages and glanced up at her. "Contracts?"

"Alleged contracts. I found those in Damon's things when I was . . . suspicious of him. That list"—she pointed to the paper on the bottom of the stack—"contains the names and addresses I got from the contracts. I visited all of those places to see if the owners really knew Damon, and if maybe he'd contacted them recently."

"You said alleged. They're all fake?"

"Yes, as confirmed by each person I spoke with today."

He flipped through all of them again, looking more closely at each page. "I don't see anything with MacGuffin's listed on it."

"That's because Mr. MacGuffin shredded the contract. He was suspicious of me, thought I might be trying to pull some kind of scam. I let him have the contract so he'd know I wasn't trying to cheat him."

He folded the papers and held them in his left hand. "I'll give these to Casey, see if he can find anything useful." He pulled her to her feet and tugged her toward the car. "Come on, let's go."

"Are we going to scout out the museums for Damon?" Her voice came out in choppy pants. Pierce realized she was jogging to keep up with him.

He slowed his longer stride to match hers. "It's getting too late in the day to go museum hopping. I have somewhere else in mind." He stopped beside his car and opened the door for her.

She slid inside. "Where are we going then?"

He couldn't resist baiting her. "To see Tessa."

She let out a string of curses as he shut the door. He struggled to contain his answering grin as he headed toward the driver's side of the car, all the while marveling at how such ugly words could pour out of such a pretty little mouth.

"THAT SHOULD BE everything." Pierce stuffed the last of his shirts into the suitcase and snapped it closed.

Madison watched without enthusiasm. She hated being in the house he'd shared with Tessa, regardless of whether his personal relationship with the other agent was real or not. Jealousy was a useless emotion, and Madison hated being in its grips. But she couldn't seem to do anything about it.

Pierce set the suitcase on the guestroom floor and rolled it into the kitchen. He set it by the door that led out to the garage.

Madison followed, pausing beside the white couch in the family room. According to Pierce, Tessa was coming over to return his keys now that their case was over. They had to wait until she arrived.

She glanced at the double doors at the end of the family room. "If you were living out of the guest room, how did you get a fresh shirt the other day out of the master bedroom?"

"I kept a few changes of clothes in there for appearances, for when we had people over."

Her face flushed at the knowledge that he'd treated her like any common stranger, continuing the charade of being undercover, even when it had only been the two of them in the house when he'd gone in that room for a shirt.

He headed out of the kitchen toward the double doors. "That reminds me, I need to grab the clothes out of the master closet too."

Madison stopped in front of one of the bookcases and picked up a picture of Pierce and Tessa, the one where they were kissing. "This sure looks real."

He paused beside her, took the picture, and laid it facedown on the shelf.

"Would it matter if it was?"

*Yes, damn it.* She looked up at him, suddenly wanting to tell him the truth about why she'd left. She searched for the right words to let him know how sorry she was for how she'd ended things, the lies she'd told him, and the real reason she'd broken up with him. "Pierce, I—"

"Am I interrupting?"

Madison stiffened and turned toward the kitchen. Tessa had perfect timing, along with her perfect complexion. Madison gritted her teeth and batted her lashes at Pierce. "Where did you put my three-fifty-seven, *darling*?"

His eyes narrowed as he gave her a warning look. "Thanks for meeting me here, Tessa."

"No problem." She gave Madison a wary glance and stepped into the family room. "It will be a relief to get out of this tacky place and back to my own apartment."

"You didn't have a say in decorating this house for your assignment?" Madison asked, surprised.

"Are you kidding? Have you noticed the pitiful art-work on the walls? And could you possibly imagine a more colorless existence? Next time I go undercover, I'm going to insist that I have some input on the decor." She wrinkled her nose.

Madison clamped her mouth shut to keep from laughing. Damn. She'd have to strike through "tacky decorator" in her *why-I-don't-like-the-redhead* column. Of course, there were still plenty of other reasons left in the column.

Like the kissing picture, for one.

"Do you need help with your things?" Pierce asked.

Tessa shook her head. "No, but I have that information you wanted." She looked at Madison. "That is, if you don't mind giving us a minute?"

"Actually, I—"

"Madison can stay inside while we talk in the backyard," Pierce said.

*Not even close to what Madison had planned on saying.*

Pierce gave her another warning look before heading outside with Tessa. The man really should have been a high school guidance counselor. He was a master at the *behave-or-else-guidance-counselor-death stare.*

Too bad it was wasted on her.

She sat down on the couch and tried to be good, to give him privacy. But after a couple of minutes she gave up. She'd never been good at being good. She crept over to one of the back windows and peeked through the blinds.

TESSA LEANED AGAINST one of the oak trees in the backyard, a concerned look on her face. "How are the ribs?"

"A little stiff. I'll be good as new in a couple of days. You said Casey has some news already?"

"An initial report, yes. He said to tell you he's still digging." She reached into her purse, pulled out a manila envelope and handed it to him.

He slid the report out and scanned the first page.

"I admit I was surprised when I walked inside and saw Mrs. McKinley," Tessa said. "I didn't expect her to be with you."

He glanced up from the page. Something in her tone put him on alert. "I'd hoped to have her settled somewhere safe by now, but she's being stubborn. Things seldom go as planned when Madison is involved."

"Yeah, I can see that. She's something else. Has quite a temper."

Apparently, the dislike between Madison and Tessa wasn't all one-sided. After Madison's target-practice comment yesterday, and her asking for her gun a few minutes ago, he could understand Tessa being wary. But she didn't know Madison well enough to judge her.

Madison's bravado was her way of dealing with a world that assumed she was weak because of how petite and fragile she looked. And her outlook was jaded from being brought up by an older brother who constantly warned her how dangerous the world was. She'd protected herself by building that tough, sarcastic shield to hide her true emotions. Pierce felt privileged to have been one of the few people she'd ever let in past that shield.

"She has a good heart. She's been through some rough times." He skimmed a few more paragraphs of the report.

"How did Casey get into the NYC medical examiner's database?"

Tessa was frowning when he glanced at her, but her face quickly smoothed out. "He did mention he called in a favor he'd been saving, and that you owe him. Big time." She stepped toward him and peered at the report. "I think what you're interested in is on page five."

He flipped to the indicated page, which gave the medical examiner's conclusions. "Not much here."

"Depends on what you're looking for. Everything seems straightforward. Damon McKinley died in a car crash. Freak accident, nothing suspicious. I'm not sure what you thought you'd find."

*Something to explain why Madison felt Damon could still be alive.*

He lowered the report. "I was hoping for something more."

"Casey said you'd say that."

He slid the pages back into the envelope, then slid it into the large inside pocket of his jacket, exchanging it for the packet of papers Madison had given him earlier. He handed them to Tessa.

"What are these?" she asked, flipping through them. "Contracts?"

"They're contracts Madison said her husband created, allegedly fake. Can you get those to Casey for me?"

She shoved them into her purse. "No problem." She glanced back at the house, and tapped her fingernails against her thigh.

"Something bothering you?" Pierce asked.

She smiled a sad smile and leaned against the tree again. "I may be a relatively new investigator, but even I know you didn't meet me here just to get that report, or to turn over your keys—or those contracts."

"You're right. I wanted to tell you that I'm taking Madison to my house until I get to the bottom of this stalker business. I'm not sure how long I'll need to watch over her. A few days, a week, maybe more."

"Your house huh?" She pursed her lips. "Well, I guess that means our first date you'd promised after the case was over is on hold." She glanced at him. "Or canceled entirely." Her voice sounded brittle, and she was no longer smiling.

He wasn't sure what to say. He couldn't seem to gather any enthusiasm for setting up a future date with her, even though he'd been looking forward to getting to know her better—before he'd seen Madison again. He nearly groaned out loud when that realization struck him. "Things are . . . complicated right now."

"No more complicated than they were before." She held up her hand to stop his next words. "It's okay. I'm the one who pursued you, even though it was obvious you were still hung up on someone else. I don't have to look too far to figure out who that is. She's watching us out the back window."

The urge to grin at Madison's outrageous behavior didn't seem appropriate, so he was careful to keep his face blank. "She's my best friend's sister. I owe it to him to keep her safe. Later, maybe you and I can try again."

"I think we both know that's not going to happen." She tapped her fingernails against the tree. "It's probably for the best. Office romances have a way of turning out badly. This way neither of us has to transfer to Alaska when it all falls apart." She held out her hand. "I guess this is our official good-bye, at least, on a personal level."

Knowing Madison was watching, and that she was already acting like a jealous shrew when it came to Tessa, he hesitated. But when Tessa started to lower her hand, he realized it wasn't fair to her to end things this way—even though nothing had really quite begun between the two of them.

He reached for her hand, and instead of shaking it, he pulled her close to give her a kiss on the cheek. She turned her head at the last second, and her lips met his. Pierce was too surprised by her bold action to immediately pull back.

The only time they had ever kissed was for that picture inside the house, and that had been the day they'd met. The kiss had been awkward and uncomfortable for both of them since they were strangers.

He'd always expected that if he and Tessa ever *really* kissed, once they got to know each other better, he'd feel something, anything. But instead, all he could think about was the kiss he'd shared with Madison on the sidewalk, how his heart had slammed in his chest, and how he'd ached to make slow, sweet love to her again.

With Tessa, he felt . . . nothing.

He reluctantly pulled away, cursing the fact that the woman who set his blood on fire was a little hellion who was just as likely to shoot him as to kiss him.

## Chapter Eight

MADISON LET OUT a pent-up breath when Pierce stopped his car in the driveway of her brightly colored colonial so that she could pack a suitcase. Her stomach was still churning, after witnessing that tender kiss Pierce had given Tessa. Thank goodness he didn't realize she'd seen it.

She jumped out of the car and hurried up the brick path. He caught up to her in the foyer as she was disabling the alarm. He wrinkled his brow and gave her one of those *what-are-you-thinking* looks as he locked the door behind her.

"Wait here." He drew his gun and headed into the family room.

She crossed her arms and leaned against the wall, impatiently waiting while he methodically searched every possible hiding place on the ground floor, including the kitchen and the hallway that led to the mother-in-law suite. When he came back into the family room, he headed up the stairs with his gun still drawn.

Madison shoved away from the wall and plopped down on one of the couches. A few minutes later, when Pierce came back down, his gun was tucked away.

"Didn't find any bad guys up there, huh?" she asked, not bothering to hide her sarcasm.

"Just one. I tossed him out the window."

She reluctantly laughed and was rewarded by one of his sexy grins. Regardless of all the hurts and secrets between them, he could always make her laugh. "I'm surprised you didn't search the basement too." She chuckled and stood to go upstairs.

"Basement? Where's the entrance?"

She groaned. "I was being sarcastic."

"I know. I'm still going to search the basement."

She shook her head and pointed toward the back hallway. "There's an inside entrance in the hall closet. I'm guessing the former owner put it there so he didn't have to go outside to do the laundry. I'm going to have the staircase moved one of these days."

"Stay here," he ordered again, as he headed toward the basement stairs.

When he came back, she hopped off the couch. "Give me fifteen minutes to pack." She headed up the stairs, but stopped and turned around when she realized he was following her up. "I don't need your help packing my bras and panties."

His mouth quirked up. "You sure about that? I wouldn't mind."

Even though she knew he was teasing, the idea of his hands running through her underwear drawer had her feeling flushed. If it weren't for the fact that she needed to pack without him seeing *what* she packed, she'd see if he were bluffing.

"Fifteen minutes," she repeated. "You already searched for bad guys. I'm perfectly safe."

He didn't look happy letting her go upstairs by herself, but he nodded and turned around.

She hurried up the stairs, down the long hallway to her bedroom. She grabbed one of her larger suitcases, and tossed it onto the four-poster bed. She shoved far more clothes into it than she needed, trying to ensure the suitcase was full enough to explain the weight.

Then she stood back to judge her handiwork. She grabbed several more pairs of panties, the silkiest, sexiest ones she had, and sprinkled them on top. That should deter Pierce if he searched her suitcase, which she assumed he would do.

The man probably thought he'd taken all of her guns when he took her Colt .380 and .357 Magnum. But he hadn't even made a dent. She'd heard too many horror stories from her brother and his law-enforcement friends through the years not to be hyperaware about all the kinds of evil that existed in the world around her.

And having been married to Damon, she knew all about evil.

She clenched her jaw and headed into her closet. She took two pocketknives and shoved one into her bra, and one into her front jeans pocket. Then she crossed to her suitcase and stored two 9mm pistols with loaded magazine clips in the bottom of the suitcase, under a stack of silky thong underwear and some lacy bras. She wasn't sure that was enough to deter a thorough search. What else could she do?

She tapped her finger against her jaw. Ah, yes! She hurried into the bathroom, reached under the cabinet and pulled out the perfect thing to keep him from searching her suitcase well enough to discover her cache of weapons. The one thing that made even the toughest of men stutter and blush.

*Tampons.*

She grinned as she tore the box open and headed back into the bedroom. She dumped every last one of them into the suitcase.

MADISON SMOOTHED HER hand over the bumps on the rustic wooden front porch railing as Pierce stood next to her. A log cabin was the last place she would ever expect him to choose to live. She'd always thought of him as a city slicker, like her, not the type to surround himself with acres of trees, or to live miles outside of town.

He'd surprised her several times since forcing himself back into her life again. She'd never realized how tenacious he could be, how stubborn, how loyal. He had every right to turn his back on her and not help her, especially when she'd fought him every step of the way. That's what most men in his situation would have done. But he'd made a promise to a friend, and because of that promise he was doing everything he could to help her.

She couldn't help wishing that he wanted to help her because he cared about her, not because of some stupid promise to her brother.

"Not what you expected?" he asked, watching her closely, as if it were important to him whether she liked his house.

*He* wasn't what she'd expected. She was beginning to think she'd never really known him at all, that she'd missed something important by not spending the time to peel back all his layers. "No, I can't say that it is."

He must have seen something in her eyes, because his smile faded.

"Something wrong?" he asked.

What was wrong was that she'd made a terrible mistake by breaking up with him. And it was too late.

She sighed. "Just tired. I didn't sleep well last night with Tessa the Terrible holding a gun on me."

He laughed and unlocked the door. He entered a code into the beeping alarm keypad and rolled both of their suitcases inside. "I never would have thought I'd like anything but a condo or an apartment like I had in Jacksonville. But your brother teased me about my city ways one too many times, so I thought I'd give it a try." He shrugged. "I'm still getting used to it, but so far, it's not half-bad."

Madison stepped inside. Pierce shut and locked the door behind her. There was no point in him giving her a tour of the house. The entire floor plan was visible from the entryway. The kitchen was a tiny collection of cabinets and appliances in the back, left corner of the main room. Two doors opened off the short hall to the right. Both were open, revealing a small bathroom and a bedroom.

*One* bedroom.

Pierce left his suitcase, the one he'd brought from the "undercover" house, sitting by the entertainment unit to the right. He rolled Madison's suitcase down the short hall into the bedroom.

Following behind him, she glanced at the bed before looking back toward the hall to see if she'd missed a second bedroom somewhere.

"The couch folds out into a bed," he said, in answer to her unspoken question. "You get the luxurious master suite."

"Ah, heaven." She took a few steps past the bed and peeked into the bathroom, which was the same one visible from the hall, accessible by two different doors. At the end of the bedroom was a small deck. She tugged open the sliding glass door and stepped outside to breathe in the crisp, cool air that smelled heavily of pine.

There was no yard to speak of, just the woods, creeping up toward the house. The sun was beginning to set, so she couldn't see a lot of detail, but what she did see was so beautiful she was beginning to wonder if she'd made a mistake moving into town.

Out of the corner of her eye, she saw Pierce lift her suitcase up on the bed. And just as she'd expected, he unzipped it and opened the top in his never-ending quest to rid her of her arsenal. Then he froze.

The shocked look on his face was priceless as he stared down into the suitcase. A few seconds later, without touching anything inside, he flipped the top closed, zipped it, and left the room.

Madison was still grinning a few minutes later when she unpacked the bare minimum of clothes and toiletries she'd need for the next few days. Everything else remained in her suitcase, to cover her guns. She took her knife out of her jeans pocket, and the one from her bra, and shoved them under the layer of thongs and tampons before heading into the main living area to check on Pierce.

He was tucking in the sheets on the pullout sofa bed. She was about to offer to help when her cell phone rang.

She pulled it out of her pocket and frowned at the unfamiliar number. "Hello?"

"Mrs. McKinley, this is Joshua MacGuffin. I believe I may have seen your husband."

MADISON TOOK A bite of her blueberry bagel, but only because Pierce kept frowning at her untouched food. Normally, breakfast was her favorite meal of the day. And on a typical day, she would have loved dining at this beautiful café on East River Street, looking out at the Savannah River. Today, however, was anything but typical, especially with Lieutenant Hamilton sitting across from her.

The lieutenant took a loud slurp of his coffee and wiped his mouth on his napkin. "I hope the meeting with

MacGuffin will be quick. I've got my own meeting to go to, with the 'Simon says' taskforce."

"Making any progress?" Pierce asked.

"Not really." He grimaced. "Don't tell that to the media."

"You know the FBI would be happy to help if you invite us."

Hamilton raised a brow. "Does that include you?"

"No, I'm out of the serial-killer business, at least for now. Had my fill."

"Can't say that I blame you. I don't have much of a stomach for it myself. Nasty business. So, what time did you say this MacGuffin meeting is?"

"Nine o'clock," Pierce said.

Madison shoved her bagel back, tired of small talk. "Shouldn't we get going? We don't want to be late."

Pierce reached for her hand beneath the table and squeezed. Apparently, that was his signal to be quiet. If his hand didn't feel so good on hers, she'd let him know what she thought of his penchant for bossing her around. Instead, she wrapped her fingers around his. He glanced at her in surprise, but didn't pull his hand back.

"We'll make it in plenty of time," he said. "It's a two-minute walk from here."

"As for time," Hamilton said, "It would have been nice to have a little more notice myself. Like maybe when I'd questioned someone at the police station, they could have clued me in that they thought the shooter was their late husband miraculously come back to life."

Madison opened her mouth to object, but promptly

closed it when Pierce squeezed her hand again. He was probably right. Anything she had to say to Hamilton was only bound to get her in trouble.

"Madison knew her story was difficult to believe," Pierce said. "She didn't want to burden the police with it until she had some kind of proof. When Mr. MacGuffin called last night to say he might have seen her late husband, I decided it was time to fill you in on her suspicions."

Looking somewhat mollified by Pierce's diplomatic explanation, Hamilton nodded. "What exactly did MacGuffin tell you?"

"He said he was walking through the restaurant last night when he saw a man who fit Madison's description of her late husband, right down to the unusual light blue eyes. The man was signing a credit card receipt and looked up just as Mr. MacGuffin was walking by. That's when he noticed the eyes."

"Did he talk to the guy, ask his name?"

"No," Madison said, unable to keep quiet any longer. "Mr. MacGuffin said he was so surprised that he rushed back to his office to call me. He wrote down the date and table number so that he could pull the man's credit card information from the cash register, but he got interrupted with some kind of problem at the restaurant before he could make the call. He forgot about it until he got home and pulled my number out of his pocket, and by then it was getting dark. He said he has problems seeing at night, so he wanted to wait until this morning to go back to the restaurant. He called me to make the appointment."

She'd offered to go pick him up last night and drive

him to the restaurant, rather than wait. But Mr. MacGuffin had politely refused, telling her he'd had a long day and was already settled in for the evening.

Hamilton took another long sip of his coffee. "Okay, let's assume he can figure out which credit card receipt is for the guy he saw. You don't actually think if your husband faked his death that he'd get credit in his real name, do you?"

"Of course not. But Pierce thinks we could get a judge to make the credit card company give us more information on the cardholder. It might be enough to figure out where Damon is."

Pierce released her hand and Madison immediately missed the warmth of his touch.

"I doubt it would be that simple," he said, "but at a minimum we could track his movements, see if there's a pattern. We might find out where he's living, if he isn't paying his rent in cash. Finding him should be fairly easy, if he sticks to any patterns. Most people do."

Hamilton was already shaking his head before Pierce finished his last sentence. "No judge is going to issue a warrant based on a widow's belief that a man looks like her dead husband." He wiped his mouth and cleared his throat. "Mrs. McKinley, believe me when I tell you that I completely understand how you could see someone and think he was your dead husband. I lost my wife to cancer a couple of years ago, and to this day I can still see a face in the crowd and swear she was my Amy." His mouth quirked up in a wry smile. "But you and I both know that's not possible. It's just the mind playing tricks on us."

Some of Madison's irritation with him faded after hearing how his voice had softened when he said his late wife's name. Still, it didn't really change her situation. "Lieutenant, I can tell you loved your wife very much. And maybe that explains why you think you see her. But my case is different. I thought I loved my husband when we got married, but it quickly changed. I made a terrible mistake. And there is no part of me, none, that wants to see him again. I'm not imagining things. The man who's stalking me, the man who shot Agent Buchanan, is my former husband. He murdered some other man and staged his death. I'm convinced of it."

"Why?" Pierce asked. "Why are you convinced? Did something happen to make you think Damon wasn't really dead back when the car accident happened?"

She cleared her throat and shoved her hair back behind her ears. "No, of course not. It's just that, the man I've seen, reminds me so strongly of Damon."

Pierce narrowed his eyes at her. She had the distinct impression he knew she'd just lied. She hated lying to him, but she couldn't exactly tell an FBI agent that she'd shot her husband the night he'd died, and that since the autopsy didn't find the bullet, she was worried the man in the car wasn't him.

Oh, for a long time, she'd convinced herself he was dead, that the bullet must have remained inside the burned-out car, or the medical examiner missed it. But now she realized the real reason the medical examiner and police hadn't found that bullet. The man who died in that car wasn't Damon.

"Regardless." Pierce turned back to Hamilton. "A judge wouldn't need to know about Madison's suspicions to sign a warrant to get the credit card information. All the judge would need to know is that we're trying to find a man who shot a federal officer, and that two people—Madison and me—described the same man that Mr. MacGuffin described. That might be enough for a warrant."

"Maybe," Hamilton conceded. "Of course it all depends on whether Mr. MacGuffin was able to find that credit card receipt." He took another sip of his coffee, and held it between his hands as if to warm them. "Let's assume the stalker really is your husband, Mrs. McKinley. You said you're from New York? That's where you and your husband lived?"

"Yes, Manhattan."

He nodded. "Did you have the house here when you were married?"

"No, my brother recently advised me to buy my house as an investment."

"If it was an investment, why did you move in rather than rent it out?"

"I didn't right away. I hired Mrs. Whitmire as a property manager to oversee the property. But then, you know all about that."

Pierce leaned his forearms on the table. "Who is Mrs. Whitmire?"

"She's a property manager. She hired a cleaning crew for me to clean the house once a week, and a landscaper to keep up the yard. Several weeks later, she called to ask me why I'd sent her a note canceling the company's service. But I didn't send a note. I flew to Savannah to see what was going on, and I filled out a police report. Someone forged that note."

"You knew about this?" Pierce asked Hamilton.

"I found out after Mrs. McKinley made that first nine-one-one call. I personally questioned the property manager, to see if there was a connection. I couldn't find any evidence to corroborate whether the note was real or a forgery. It was printed out, not handwritten. There wasn't anything else I could do. And since no one had been hurt, I didn't pursue it further."

"I'll talk to Mrs. Whitmire myself and make my own determination."

"It was a forgery," Madison insisted. "Why would I lie about something that insignificant?"

Pierce put his hand on hers beneath the table again. She drew a deep breath and decided to let him have the lead in the conversation.

For now.

Hamilton crossed his arms and sat back. "The point I was making was that if Mrs. McKinley lived in New York, how would her husband know to go to Savannah if he was after her?"

"Good question, one I intend to answer." Pierce pitched some money onto the table and stood. "But first, it's time to go meet Mr. MacGuffin."

"ARE YOU SURE Mr. MacGuffin meant nine a.m. and not p.m.?" Hamilton hugged his jacket against the wind and peeked into the front window of MacGuffin's. His nose was bright red from their brief walk from the café. He kept stomping his feet to keep warm.

Madison couldn't imagine what the man would do if he had to endure a *real* winter, like in New York.

"I'm sure." Pierce knocked on the door again. "Someone's inside. They're coming to the door."

Madison recognized the man she'd met earlier, Todd. He had a heavy ring of keys that jangled against the door as he unlocked the deadbolt. He pushed the door open and motioned them inside.

Lieutenant Hamilton was the first to enter. He moved away from the door opening and gave a dramatic shiver before plopping down in a chair at one of the round tables.

Madison shook her head and sat down in the chair farthest away from him.

Todd closed the door and introduced himself. "I'm sorry you wasted a trip out here. I didn't have your number, Mrs. McKinley, so I couldn't call to cancel."

"Cancel? Is Mr. MacGuffin running late?" Pierce hadn't bothered to sit like Hamilton and Madison. Instead, he'd moved to stand directly behind Madison's chair.

"Mr. MacGuffin called me late last night," Todd said. "He told me he'd made an appointment to speak to Mrs. McKinley this morning, but that he couldn't make it. A family emergency came up and he won't be back for about a week. He said to offer his apologies."

"Did he say why he didn't just call me back to tell me?" Madison asked.

"It was after midnight when he called me. He didn't want to wake you. He had no such worries about waking me." He covered his mouth and let out a huge yawn. "I was too tired last night to think straight and get your number to save you the trip this morning. Sorry."

Lieutenant Hamilton rested his forearms on the table. "Did Mr. MacGuffin explain to you why he was meeting Mrs. McKinley in the first place?"

Todd rubbed his jaw, which was covered with whiskers. He obviously hadn't shaved yet this morning. His T-shirt and jeans were wrinkled, as if he'd grabbed them off the floor in his hurry to make it to the restaurant to meet them.

"He did mention something about some man she was looking for, and that he'd thought he'd seen him, but that he wasn't sure. I think he might have changed his mind after calling you."

Hamilton let out a loud breath and pushed himself up from his chair. He gave Madison a long look before crossing over by her chair to face Pierce. "Next time, I'd appreciate it if you could wait until you're sure you have something before calling. I'm happy to help, I really am, but I'm slammed right now. Without some hard evidence about who the shooter is, I'm pretty much done with this investigation."

Madison started to rise, but Pierce's hands were suddenly on the tops of her shoulders, keeping her in her seat.

"Sorry to have wasted your time, Lieutenant. Thanks for coming out," Pierce said.

Hamilton nodded and headed out the door.

Pierce released Madison's shoulders.

"What was that all about?" She shoved up out of her chair.

"Just keeping you safe."

"Safe? From Lieutenant Hamilton?"

He gave her a droll look. "From yourself."

She narrowed her eyes at him, but he'd already turned to speak to Todd.

"Are you certain it was your boss on the phone?" Pierce asked.

Todd looked surprised at the question. "I've been working for him for five years. Yeah, I'm sure."

"Did he sound like he was under duress?"

"If you're asking if he sounded upset, yeah, sure. His granddaughter is in the hospital. That's why he had to leave. So, yeah, he was upset, with good reason." He lifted his ring of keys, making them jingle. "Sorry you wasted your time, but if there's nothing else . . ."

Pierce pulled a business card out of the pocket of his suit and handed it to the other man. "When you hear from Mr. MacGuffin again, have him give me a call."

Madison and Pierce walked down the sidewalk back toward the café. There were so many tourists out already that Pierce and Madison had to step off the sidewalk onto East River Street to get past them. The brick pavers were bumpy and uneven, which was aggravating Madison's still healing sprained ankle.

"Ouch." She grabbed for Pierce's arm as her ankle twisted beneath her on a particularly uneven paver.

"I've got you." He grabbed her around the waist.

"Hey lady, watch it." A young man on a bicycle swerved to avoid Madison. He threw back a nasty insult and punctuated it with a hand gesture. He was still laughing when he turned down a side street.

"That kid's mom must be so proud," Madison said.

"I wouldn't call him a kid. And his mother probably gave up trying to tell him what to do several years ago, about the time she kicked him out of the house." He steadied her on her feet. "Are you okay?"

She gingerly tested her hurt ankle, and to her relief she was able to stand pain-free. "Yeah, thanks." She laughed. "Aren't we a pair? You with your bruised ribs, and me falling all over the place like a drunk."

A slow smile curved his mouth. "At least we—"

A scream filled the air. Pierce grabbed Madison and hauled her against his side.

"Where did it come from?" she asked.

"Up ahead, around the corner."

Another scream, shouts. A wave of tourists began running down the block in the same direction where the biker had gone. Shouts of "call nine-one-one" sounded from up ahead.

Pierce tensed beside Madison. He put his hand on the small of her back. "How's that ankle?"

"It's fine. I just lost my balance. I know you want to help. Let's go." She took off at a jog, and he grabbed her hand, keeping her close as they both hurried to the end of the block.

They were forced to stop because of the wall of people crammed into the street. Sirens sounded in the distance.

Pierce, taller than most of those around them, craned his neck as he tried to see what everyone was looking at. When he turned back toward Madison, his entire body radiated tension. He urged her over to the wall of the building beside them. "Stay here. I'll be right back."

"Wait, what did you see?"

But he was already pushing his way through the crowd. Red and blue lights flashed as a police car turned onto the other end of the street.

Madison gave up trying to see anything. But soon the crowd began to part and move back as one of the police officers who'd arrived worked to move people out of the way. "Unless you're a witness, move along. Make room," he barked.

People grumbled and complained but moved back.

The man directly in front of Madison stepped to the side, and she finally saw what everyone else was looking at.

Lying in the middle of the road, his neck twisted at an impossible angle, was the young man who'd cursed at Madison just moments before. His bike was discarded beside him and his sightless eyes stared up at the bright, sunny sky that he would never see again.

Madison gasped and clutched her throat.

Pierce was crouching next to the body, beside a police officer. From the gestures the officer was making, the two of them appeared to be discussing a white sheet of paper lying on the dead man's stomach.

Madison clutched her throat and turned away. On the other side of the street, directly across from her, a familiar figure stood in the crowd. She couldn't see his face. The hood of his denim jacket was pulled up over his head. But she knew who he was.

*Damon.*

Madison screamed Pierce's name, and Damon disappeared back into the crowd. The people around her moved back, and suddenly Pierce was beside her, gripping her shoulders.

"Mads, what's wrong? Are you hurt?" He ran his hands up and down the sleeves of her jacket, as if searching for injuries.

She shook her head and leaned to the side to try to see around him. She whipped her head back and forth, searching the crowd.

Pierce gave her a little shake. "What is it? Why did you scream?"

She swallowed past her thickness in her throat. "Damon, I saw Damon."

PIERCE ENDED THE call and shoved his phone in the pocket of his suit jacket. The café he and Madison had been in an hour ago had been completely transformed into an impromptu police headquarters. Police officers stood around talking, or sitting at tables interviewing witnesses.

Not that there were any real witnesses. So far no one had stepped up to say they'd seen whoever killed the bicyclist.

Pierce rubbed Madison's back in the chair next to him. "You sure you're okay?"

"I'm sure. Quit worrying about me. What did Hamilton say?"

"Pretty much what you'd expect."

"He thinks I imagined seeing Damon."

"That sums it up. However, he does believe you saw the shooter. So he's taking the statement you gave very seriously."

"I know Damon is the shooter. Do you . . . think he killed that boy?"

"You saw a man fitting the description of the shooter, wearing the same denim jacket. But you didn't see his face. You don't know that it was Damon. Was there blood on his jacket?"

She crossed her arms. "Not that I saw, no."

"That boy was stabbed, just like all the other 'Simon says' victims. The killer would have had blood on him."

She blinked up at him. "What makes you think it was the 'Simon says' killer?"

He blew out a harsh breath. "Because he left the same kind of note he leaves on all his victims. Hamilton confirmed the wording and the writing are the same."

"Then . . . maybe Damon . . . is the killer. Maybe he stabbed that boy, and zipped up his jacket to cover the blood."

"I already mentioned that possibility to Hamilton. He thinks it's highly unlikely. The killer wouldn't have stuck around in the crowd and risk being discovered."

She rested her face in her hands, looking worried, defeated.

Pierce wished he could make her feel better, but short

of catching her stalker and proving he wasn't Damon, he didn't know what else he could do to give her peace of mind again.

"We're through here," he said. "The police are looking for the man you described. If he's still in the area, they'll find him. We might as well go."

She looked relieved to be leaving. "Do you want to go see Mrs. Whitmire now?"

He opened the door for her, and they headed outside. "I didn't think you'd be up to talking to her today, after . . ." He nodded toward the yellow tape down the street.

Madison followed his gaze, then quickly looked away. "I want to talk to Mrs. Whitmire now. No sense in wasting time."

Keeping a close watch on the people around them, Pierce walked her toward his car. The killer who was stalking Savannah had just struck within a few hundred yards of where Madison had been. Could it really be a coincidence that she was being stalked, and the "Simon says" killer murdered someone a few hundred yards from her?

If the killer was the same person stalking her, that blew a big hole in Madison's belief that her dead husband was her stalker. Pierce couldn't imagine that a killer narcissistic enough to leave those notes would use a fake name.

So what did that mean? Were two people after her now? How the hell was he supposed to protect her from a stalker *and* a sadistic killer?

## Chapter Nine

"YOU'RE CERTAIN THIS is *not* the man who dropped the note off, Mrs. Whitmire?" Pierce asked.

Madison sat impatiently while Pierce continued to question her former property manager. So far, he wasn't doing any better than she had when she'd questioned the woman.

Mrs. Whitmire squinted down at the black-and-white printout of Damon's driver's license that Tessa had faxed over.

"I'm sorry," she said. "I thought I was sure, but I guess it could be him."

"What about his eyes?" Madison asked. "Did he have pale blue eyes?"

"He caught me outside, and he was wearing sunglasses, dear. I didn't see his eyes." She shoved the paper back across her desk. "Perhaps if you had a better quality photograph?"

Pierce glanced at Madison sitting beside him. "I assumed Mrs. McKinley had a picture of her beloved husband in her purse."

Madison smirked at him, but smoothed her face into a smile when Mrs. Whitemire turned to her. She twisted her hands in her lap, trying to portray the grieving widow. "I'm so sorry. With Damon gone, I just couldn't bear to keep his pictures with me. It's only been eighteen months. The memories are still so fresh."

The manager's eyes moistened with sympathy. "Understandable, dear. I'm so sorry for your loss."

Madison wiped a fake tear from under her eye. "Thank you."

Pierce rolled his eyes.

Madison kicked him.

He coughed to cover his reaction. The property manager looked at him, her eyes wide.

"I wasn't involved in the original investigation," Pierce continued. "Bear with me if I ask some questions you've already answered. But can you tell me whether the housekeeping service you hired to clean the house ever reported anything odd at Mrs. McKinley's house?"

She shook her head. "They cleaned once a week. Never mentioned anything."

"What about the yard service? Did they ever see anyone hanging around?"

Mrs. Whitmire huffed. "I have to assume not. The man I hired never bothered to call me each week like the cleaning service did. All he did was cash my checks. I didn't even have to fire him. He just stopped showing up on his own. I didn't even know he wasn't taking care of the yard until the cleaning service told me the weeds were getting overgrown. He'd better not ask for a recommendation. He certainly won't like what I tell anyone about his lack of professionalism."

Pierce exchanged a glance with Madison. "He just stopped showing up? When was that?"

She tapped her fingernails on the desk. "Hmm. Probably around the same time Mrs. McKinley fired our service." She looked down her nose at Madison as if she'd committed some kind of unforgiveable faux pas.

"I didn't fire your service," Madison insisted. "Someone else created that note."

"If you say so." Mrs. Whitmire looked across her desk at Pierce. "Was there anything else you needed?"

Madison crossed her arms and sat back, tapping her foot.

"Actually," Pierce said, "if you could give me the contact information for the yard service, I'd like to ask them a few questions."

She turned around in her chair and opened a filing cabinet. A moment later she handed Pierce a business card. "It's just one man, Kevin Newsome. He was starting up his own service, and I thought I was being nice by helping him out. I'll never do that again."

It sounded like Mrs. Whitmire had done her one good deed and intended to never help *anyone* else again. Madison eyed her with distaste.

"Thank you," Pierce said, taking her hand. "You've been very helpful."

The older woman blushed, actually blushed.

Madison thought she just might be sick.

Pierce ushered Madison out of the office to his car.

"Where are we going now?" she asked, as she buckled her seat belt.

He pulled out his cell phone and punched a button. "I want to talk to your yardman. I'll see if we can make an appointment." A minute later he shook his head and ended the call. "No answer. I'll call Hamilton, see if he can send an officer over to do a wellness check."

"A wellness check?"

"Go by his place of business, or his home if he's not there, make sure he's okay." He made the call to Hamilton, nodding his head to let Madison know Hamilton had agreed to his request, then he pocketed his phone. "I assume you have some photographs of your husband back at your house."

"I'm sure he's in some of the pictures of my family, and my wedding album of course."

"Let's get a better picture than that driver's license photo. If Hamilton locates Mr. Newsome, we can take the picture by and ask him why he stopped taking care of the yard."

She put her hand on his forearm. "*If* he locates Newsome? You think something happened to him don't you?"

His jaw tightened. "From what Mrs. Whitmire said, Newsome was just starting out and couldn't even afford to hire helpers. A man in that position isn't going to just not show up at work one day, unless something is wrong."

MADISON AND PIERCE headed through the family room into the front room of Madison's house. It was originally supposed to be a dining room. It connected through an archway to both the kitchen and the family room. But Madison had set it up as her home office. She paused in front of one of the bookshelves, frowning when she didn't see the picture she'd wanted to give to him.

After her husband died, knowing what he'd done, she certainly hadn't kept pictures of him sitting around. But this particular picture had been one of her favorites of Logan, so she'd kept it, even though her husband could clearly be seen in the background.

"Something wrong?" Pierce asked, studying the collection of picture frames on the shelves of the other bookcase.

Madison edged a picture of her and Pierce behind a picture of her mom so that he wouldn't see it and ask her why she still had it.

She moved another picture of Logan and her mother to the side to more clearly see the frames sitting behind it. "I could have sworn there was a picture here that had Damon in it."

"Are you saying some pictures are missing?"

"I don't see how they could be." She glanced around uneasily. Her security alarm hadn't been tripped, and Damon certainly didn't have any keys to her house. "I'm probably wrong about what I unpacked. I still have tons of boxes in the attic. I must not have brought down all the photos I thought I'd brought down." Or at least, she hoped that was what had happened. It made sense. And it was preferable to the alternative—that someone had been in her house and taken the picture. She didn't have to think very long about who that someone would be.

She led the way up the stairs and down the long hallway. Stopping outside her bedroom door, she pressed one of the boards in the wall and it slid back to reveal the hidden staircase.

Pierce's face lit with interest as he stepped inside the little alcove. "Do these stairs lead anywhere besides the attic?" He ran his hands along the pocket in the wall where the door had slid.

"Just the attic. You can only get to the basement from the stairs in the back hallway on the first floor. She led the way up the stairs with Pierce following behind. He kept running his hands along the wall.

"Are there any other hidden passageways in this house?"

"Nope, sorry. Just the one." She paused at the top to open the door. "No one could sneak in here without setting off the security alarm, if that's your worry."

He stilled. "Did you change the alarm code after you moved in?"

"Of course." The way his brow tightened with concern had her feeling uneasy again.

She slid the pocket door into the wall and flipped on the overhead lights. The two small dormers let in almost no natural light because of the centuries old oak trees that hung over this side of the house.

He gently moved her to the side and made a circuit of the room, looking behind each stack of boxes, in every possible hiding place. "All right, come on in."

For once, she didn't feel aggravated at his over-protectiveness. After everything that had happened today, his vigilance was reassuring.

While she read the labels on the boxes stacked against one wall, he felt along the far wall—the only wall not blocked by boxes.

"What are you doing?" She opened the box in front of her.

"Looking for a hidden door."

"There aren't any others. And all the exterior doors, and the windows, are wired into the security system."

"What about the dormers?" He finished his examination of the wall and crossed to the small windows.

"It's a three-story drop from the attic to the yard below." She pulled an album out of the box and sat on the floor. "There aren't any balconies, no access from the outside."

"What about gutters, downspouts? If they're solidly attached to the house, someone could climb up those. Or they could climb the oak trees."

"I hadn't thought about that," she admitted, as she flipped the pages. "I suppose if someone was really, really determined . . ." She rubbed her arms and glanced around the room. The stacks of boxes suddenly took on more sinister shapes. She vowed to get better lighting up here once this was all over.

Pierce crossed the room and sat on the floor beside her. "Did you find any pictures of Damon?" He peered over her shoulder at the album she was holding.

She looked back down and turned another page. "Maybe I have the wrong album." She quickly flipped through the rest of the pages, then set it aside and pulled another one out of the box in front of her.

"What about framed pictures?"

"I haven't come across any yet." She flipped through the album and sat back. "I must have mislabeled one of the boxes."

They searched together, opening up box after box.

"Here," she said, relieved to find another album in a box filled with winter clothes. "I don't know how this ended up over here, but there should be plenty of pictures of Damon in this one. This is the album I made the first month after we got married."

She knelt on the floor with the album sitting on a box in front of her. Pierce knelt down beside her.

She flipped a page and pointed to a photo. "This is Damon, but it's not a very good picture. He's looking away. You can't see his face very well."

She frowned. "Here's another one, but it's not very good either, blurry. There have to be some better pictures in here."

"Don't you have some professional pictures from your wedding? Maybe one of those is a close-up."

"We eloped to Vegas. The only picture I got there was fuzzy and out of focus."

"Vegas? You?" His voice was laced with surprise.

"Is that so hard to believe?"

He stared at her intently, as if he could divine her thoughts if he stared hard enough. "I can't see you wanting a Vegas wedding."

"Exactly what kind of wedding do you think I'd want?"

"Nothing flashy, like Vegas. Nothing traditional either. Something flirty, fun. Outdoors—a beach or a garden, maybe under an oak tree. You wouldn't want a lot of guests, mainly family, a few friends. The dress would be easy to move in. You'd want to be comfortable and free, not restricted by a long, tight gown."

She stared at him, too surprised to say anything. She'd hated her Vegas wedding. She'd only agreed to it because Damon had been so excited about the idea of going to the casinos. Going to Vegas was his dream, not hers. If she could have gotten married the way she wanted, she'd have had an outdoor wedding, much like what he'd just described.

How could he know her so well when they'd known each other for such a short amount of time? She frowned and dropped her gaze. She flipped a few more pages in the album, then froze.

"What's the matter?" He looked over her shoulder, instantly in tune with her and realizing something was wrong.

"They're gone. They should have been right here." She pointed at a blank page. "There were four pictures on this page that my daddy took when we got back from Vegas. I remember, because my mom insisted I put on my wedding dress and let them take some pictures, even though Damon was fussing the entire time."

His eyes narrowed. "You're sure they were in this album?"

She pointed to the rectangular outlines on the page where the pictures used to be. "I'm positive."

"You wouldn't have taken them out? Maybe destroyed them after he died?"

"No."

"Do you have *any* good pictures of your husband?"

"I already looked through the other albums. This is the last one." She quickly flipped through the rest of it. "Every picture of Damon is either blurry or . . . missing."

"When was the last time you looked at the albums?"

"When I packed up my Manhattan apartment and moved here."

He gently but firmly pulled her hands back from the cover and set the album onto a box.

"What are you doing?" she asked.

He grabbed her hand and pulled her up, then tugged her behind him as he headed toward the door. "I'm getting you out of this house. Now."

## Chapter Ten

FIFTEEN MINUTES LATER, Pierce stood behind a patrol car next to a policeman. Madison was sitting inside the back of the car, glaring at both of them through the rear window. She wasn't happy one bit about being locked up in the car. And Pierce didn't have to hear her to know what she was saying.

Her hand gestures were perfectly clear.

Hiding his grin behind a fake cough, he turned his back on her and leaned against the rear bumper. "Thanks, Officer Crowley. I appreciate you keeping Mrs. McKinley safe while Hamilton oversees the investigation inside the house."

"No problem." The officer cast a wary look toward Madison. "I don't think I've seen a woman that angry in a long time. You're going to have your hands full later."

"I don't mind," Pierce said, and he meant it. He'd take whatever abuse she wanted to dish out if it meant keeping her safe. "I'll check on the techs and see how it's going. I'll let you know when Hamilton gives the all-clear to let Mrs. McKinley back in the house."

"Yes, sir. I think I'll just wait outside the car. Feels pretty good today. The weather's been fairly mild for January so far."

Pierce laughed and the young officer smiled in return. They both knew why he wasn't getting into his car.

Pierce headed up the front walk and went inside the house. Another uniformed officer was standing in the family room with Lieutenant Hamilton. They both turned around when Pierce approached. The uniformed policeman nodded in response to something the lieutenant said and hurried out the front door.

"Agent Buchanan." Hamilton held out his hand. "No offense, but I'd hoped it would be a bit longer before we saw each other again."

Pierce shook Hamilton's hand. "Got any leads on that murder off East River Street this morning?"

"No, but it's early yet. We're still looking for witnesses and canvassing the area. We did talk to a few people who saw someone in the crowd that matched the description Mrs. McKinley gave, but no luck getting a lead on where that guy went, or even if he's the shooter in the park."

"What about Mr. Newsome, the yardman? Did your men conduct that wellness check?"

"Not yet, but we will. It might be a day or two. We've had a few other higher priorities, as you know." He cocked his head. "I don't recall inviting the FBI to help me with any of my current investigations, but you sure are popping up a lot. Are you sure your involvement isn't official?"

"I'm on my own time, a friend of the family."

"I see." He didn't sound convinced.

"Have your techs found anything upstairs?" Pierce asked, not wanting him to pursue that line of questions. Casey and Tessa were both looking into the case now after Pierce had called them this morning to tell them his worries about the murdered bicyclist. But without an official invitation to join the investigation, they could both get in trouble if Hamilton found out.

"Hard to say. Lots of prints, but we don't know yet if they belong to Mrs. McKinley or the burglar. No signs of forced entry. Is she certain she always locks up and sets the alarm when she leaves?"

"She says she does, but I've sent a request to her alarm company for a report on when the alarm was set or disarmed. Should be ready later today," Pierce said.

"You'll share the report with me, of course?"

"Of course."

"And you'll let me know if Mrs. McKinley realizes anything else is missing—besides some old family photographs. It seems odd someone would break in for pictures, in an attic no less, without taking something else of value." He glanced around the room, his gaze settling on the desk visible in the home office that adjoined the family room. "Like the laptop sitting on that desk, for instance."

Pierce conceded the point. "If the shooter is Mrs. McKinley's husband, the break-in makes sense. He doesn't want anyone to have any pictures of him so he can continue in whatever new identity he's assumed."

"I suppose that makes sense, if you buy the whole undead scenario, which I don't. Not without some kind of hard evidence."

"Lieutenant?" One of the police officers leaned inside the front door. "There's something out back you need to see."

"WHY WOULD SOMEBODY trash everything in the back-yard?" Hamilton asked.

Pierce wondered the same thing. Ruined shovels, hammers, rakes . . . they all littered the backyard with their handles sawed in half. Nothing else was disturbed, not that there was much else in her yard to destroy even if someone wanted to.

For a home with a price tag well over a million dollars, there was virtually no landscaping. The only structure was a small shed that had presumably housed the tools. In contrast, the front of the house was thick with orna-mental trees and shrubs, and carefully manicured brick paths going up to the front door and out to each side yard. Pierce figured the lack of landscaping in the back must be because of the renovations Madison had mentioned ear-lier. Although it wasn't clear what types of renovations were being done. The house itself was untouched.

"Could be a teenage prank, unrelated to the burglary," one of the policemen said.

"Doubtful," Lieutenant Hamilton said.

"I wouldn't count on it," Pierce said at the same time. He exchanged a rueful glance with Hamilton. Apparently neither of them were strong believers in coincidences.

Officer Crowley, the police officer who had Madison in the back of his patrol car, stepped around the corner of the house and approached the small group. He had a pained expression on his face. "Agent Buchanan?"

"Yes?"

"Mrs. McKinley is demanding, quite forcefully, to be let out of the car so she can see what's going on back here. She said something about making a list of everyone she's going to sue if she isn't let out in the next minute. She sounds serious."

"Oh, I have no doubt she is." Pierce laughed at the worried look on the policeman's face. "Lieutenant Hamilton, do you mind if Mrs. McKinley comes back here?"

"Not as long as she doesn't touch anything and stays out of the way." Hamilton waved toward the officer. "Go ahead, let her out."

Pierce strode to the side of the house so that he could watch Madison. When the car door opened, she burst from the vehicle. To say she was furious didn't even come close.

As she stalked across the lawn toward him, he struggled not to laugh. She looked liked an adorable little pixie, all stirred up, her face red, her eyes flashing. He couldn't wait to find out what kind of outrageous thing she would say when she reached him.

Everyone else watching her seemed to be holding their breath with worry.

When she caught sight of the ruined tools scattered around the yard, her eyes widened and her anger seemed to leave her in a surprised rush. Pierce's amusement faded when he saw the flash of fear in her eyes. Just as quickly, the fear was gone and she was back in control—or at least that's the face she showed Lieutenant Hamilton and the others.

Pierce knew better.

"What happened?" she asked.

"We're not sure." Pierce said. "I assume your tools weren't in this condition the last time you were back here."

She shook her head. "They're not my tools. They belong to the contractor who's adding the sun porch to the back of the house. They've been tearing out the landscaping and the old brick patio to make room for the addition. Are all of the tools ruined?"

"Looks that way." Lieutenant Hamilton stepped forward. "Do you have a number for the company performing the renovations? I'll need them to sign a complaint and write up an inventory of exactly what was destroyed."

"I've got their number programmed into my cell phone inside. I'll go get it."

"No rush. Just text me once you have it. You already have my contact information."

She nodded. "Do you think this is related to the break-in?"

"Hard to say. We haven't found any evidence to explain how someone could have gotten into your house. No scratch marks on any locks. No broken windows or unlocked entry points. Are you positive no one else has a key?"

"I had the locks changed when I moved in."

"What about other valuables that could be missing? Maybe something you don't use very often."

"I'll have to look around and see."

He glanced over at his men. "I think we've done about all we can here for now. I wouldn't normally expend this much manpower on a break-in, but with everything going on . . ." He shrugged. "We'll get in touch with your contractor and let you know if we have more questions later. And I'll have an officer canvas the neighborhood, see if anyone saw anything." He gave Pierce a nod, then moved away to talk to one of the officers.

"Go ahead and get your phone," Pierce said.

"Why?"

"You heard the lieutenant. No rush. This isn't his top priority. I don't want to wait around. I want to talk to your contractor."

MADISON CALLED THE contractor and found they were at another construction site, a Victorian a few streets away. When she and Pierce pulled up to the curb, the first thing she saw was the enormous, dark green dumpster snugged up against the house. Workers with bright yellow hardhats tossed debris out the windows on the second floor into the metal dumpster below, stirring up small clouds of dust.

"Which one is the contractor?" Pierce asked her, talking loudly to be heard over the banging as some pieces of scrap wood fell into the metal dumpster. He stepping around another, smaller dumpster at the end of the driveway.

Madison shaded her eyes from the sun and surveyed the busy site. "I don't see her. Maybe she's inside, or around back."

The sound of a powerful engine had them both turning around. A white, long-bed pickup pulled to the curb behind Pierce's car. There were two men in the cab. The driver started grinning when he saw Madison and Pierce.

"I thought you said your contractor was a woman."

The irritation in Pierce's voice had Madison looking at him in surprise. "She is. I don't know who these men are, but I assume they work for her. The name of her company is written on their truck—B-and-B Construction."

"They don't work for her." He sounded disgusted. "She works for them."

She wanted to ask him what was wrong, but the men from the truck had just reached them.

The first one, a dark-haired man just as tall and muscular as Pierce, and about the same age, grinned widely and pounded him on the back. "I didn't expect you to be here."

The second man was quite a bit younger and looked like he should have been sitting in a college class somewhere. He was just as tall as the first one, but lankier, as if he hadn't quite grown into his frame yet. He nodded at Madison but didn't say anything.

"Who's this beautiful woman standing next to you?" The first man aimed his sunny grin at Madison.

His grin was contagious. And when he added a wink, Madison laughed out loud. She stepped forward to introduce herself, but Pierce grabbed her around the waist and anchored her against him.

She was about to tell him what she thought of his Neanderthal ways, but the sullen expression on his face made her pause.

"Madison McKinley," he said, "This grinning fool is Braedon. And the serious one is Matt. My brothers."

MADISON SAT IN one of the chairs on the back patio, just behind the Victorian's finished sunroom. Pierce had taken the chair next to her, and his brothers sat across from both of them. B&B Construction—Buchanan and Buchanan. She should have realized what the B&B stood for as soon as Pierce's brothers got close enough for her to see them clearly.

The older one, Braedon, looked the most like Pierce. Same build and coloring, but Braedon smiled a lot more than Pierce did. In fact, the more Braedon smiled, the less Pierce smiled.

If she didn't know better, she'd think he was jealous. And wasn't that ridiculous? He'd made it clear after that shattering kiss the other day that he wasn't interested in her. So why would he care if his brother flirted with her?

She glanced at the younger brother, Matt. He looked

to be around twenty, maybe twenty-one. At first, she'd thought he was shy. But after watching him with his brothers for the past few minutes, she realized he was just quiet, intent. He studied everything and everyone around him, as if he were absorbing every piece of information and weighing it for its worth. When he spoke, he chose his words carefully, making each one count.

He caught her looking at him, but instead of winking and grinning like Braedon tended to do, he simply nodded and looked back at his brothers.

"This isn't the first time there have been problems at Mrs. McKinley's house," Braedon said. "Colleen had two slashed tires there last week."

"Did she report any other problems? Did she see anyone watching the house while she and her crew were there?"

Matt sat forward, crossing his arms on the tabletop. "Someone put sugar in one of the guy's gas tanks the day they started pulling out the landscaping."

Braedon raised a brow. "You didn't tell me about that."

Matt shrugged. "Didn't need to. I took care of it."

"And how exactly did you take care of it?"

"He's putting two kids through college. He can't afford repairs like that. I leased him a loaner and put his truck in the shop. I told him the company will pay for it."

"That's a heck of an expense to approve for a kid who's home on a break. Especially when it's not you who'll have to pay for it."

Matt stared at him, not looking impressed with his brother's speech. He also didn't rush to apologize.

Madison tensed, wondering what Braedon would do.

He suddenly grinned and slapped Matt on the back. "Good job, kid." He turned back to Pierce. "I haven't heard of any other problems. The footers for the sun-room's foundation are scheduled to be dug next week. Should we cancel?"

"Yes," Pierce said.

"No," Madison said at the same time. "I'll reimburse you for the losses your company has suffered while work-ing on my project, including the repairs to that man's truck, but I don't want you to stop or delay the schedule."

"Why not?" Pierce demanded.

"Because I'm not going to let some . . . teenage pranks change my plans."

He looked incredulous. "Teenage pranks?"

"Am I missing something?" Braedon asked.

"No," Pierce and Madison said at the same time.

Braedon exchanged a surprised look with Matt.

Matt pushed his chair back and stood. He stepped in front of Pierce. "I'm not sure what's going on between you two. But I do know that Mrs. McKinley paid us to do a job." He directed his next remark to Madison. "We'll have a team at your house next week, as planned, to dig the footers." With that, he walked across the patio and around the side of the house toward the street.

The corner of Pierce's lip twitched.

Braedon grinned and reached across the table to shove him.

He shoved him back, and they both laughed. The ten-sion that had existed between them seemed to evaporate.

Madison frowned, not at all sure why they seemed so amused. "What's so funny?"

"My little brother has grown a backbone," Pierce said. "Braedon, I'd like you and Matt to take over the work at Madison's house. Do you have the time?"

"We'll juggle things around. We'll make it work."

"Tell your men to stay on their toes, and let me know right away if anything goes wrong, no matter how ordinary."

"You got it."

Pierce tugged Madison's hand until she rose to stand beside him. As they turned to go, Braedon put a hand on Pierce's shoulder.

"You're obviously worried there's more to this than some neighborhood kids having fun. If you don't want to tell me what's going on, I'm fine with that. But just because I'm not some hotshot FBI agent doesn't mean I can't help. You get in a tight spot, call me. I'll be there."

MADISON REREAD THE card Mrs. Whitmire had given Pierce. She shook her head and looked back at the padlocked door to the storage unit. "This can't be right. Did Hamilton confirm this was Mr. Newsome's business address?"

Pierce leaned back against the hood of his car. "He hasn't sent anyone to see Newsome yet, so he wouldn't know. Mrs. Whitmire did say Newsome was just starting out. It's not uncommon for people to use a storage unit or even a post office box as their company's address. He probably keeps his mowers and tools here."

Madison shoved the useless card back into her purse. "Do you think the people in the storage company office can give us his *home* address?"

"Not if they understand privacy laws, they won't."

"Can we at least try?"

He shook his head. "Going to a place of business is one thing. Taking you with me to Newsome's house isn't going to happen, not unless Hamilton's men did their wellness check and can assure me there's no danger."

Patience was never one of her virtues, and waiting like this was torture. She ran her fingers across the shiny hood of his car. "Maybe his men already checked on him and forgot to tell you."

He let out a long, slow sigh and pulled out his phone. A few minutes later, he shoved it back into his pocket. "All right, you win. Hamilton said his men spoke to Newsome about an hour ago. He gave me Newsome's address. It's not far from here. Let's go."

NEWSOME'S HOUSE WAS a modest one-story a few miles from the historic district, a block off Skidaway Road, partially hidden beneath towering oak trees with Spanish moss dripping down.

"For a yardman, his yard sure is overgrown," Madison said, picking her way through the knee-high weeds crowding onto the walkway.

Pierce's gaze scanned the yard, the front porch, as if he were taking everything in.

A rolled newspaper was lying on the porch steps. Madison picked it up to take a look. "Today's paper. That's a good sign, right?"

"Possibly. You should have stayed in the car like I told you." He pulled her to a stop when she reached the top porch stair.

"There's nothing to worry about," she said. "Hamilton said his men spoke to Newsome."

"Humor me. Don't move from this spot until I tell you it's all clear." He gave her what she thought of as his *FBI-agent stare* and continued across the porch to the front door. When no one answered his repeated knocking, he crossed to the end of the porch to peer around the corner of the house to the side yard.

She hurried forward and peeked in through the front window, cupping her hands against the glass to see past the glare. "It's fairly clean inside. Doesn't look abandoned."

"For the love of . . . get away from the window." He strode forward and grabbed her arm.

"Wait, I think I see Mr. Newsome."

A shadow, darker than the rest, appeared in the hallway.

Madison waved a hand to get the man's attention, then sucked in a sharp breath.

Pierce yanked her away from the glass and pulled out his gun, every muscle in his body tense. "What?" He edged to the corner of the window. "What did you see?"

She swallowed against the lump in her throat. "Damon. I think I just saw Damon."

"I'M TELLING YOU, Damon was in there." Madison leaned back against Pierce's car in front of Newsome's house, facing off against Lieutenant Hamilton. She didn't understand why he was so inclined *not* to believe everything she told him.

For once, Pierce wasn't giving her one of his warning looks or telling her to be quiet. He was facing Hamilton next to her and looked just as puzzled as she was.

Behind the lieutenant, two police cars sat in Newsome's front yard, lights flashing.

"Did *you* see anyone?" Hamilton asked Pierce.

"No, but I saw Madison's reaction . . . her *genuine* reaction. She saw someone inside, and believes it was her husband. He wasn't wearing a hood this time. She saw his face. That's good enough for me."

She sidled closer to him and put her hand on his waist, lightly squeezing to let him know she appreciated his support.

"It was dark inside. No lights on," Hamilton said, still sounding skeptical.

"It was him," Madison insisted.

"There's no one inside. I should know. My men just broke in Mr. Newsome's front door, a door you, Mrs. McKinley, are going to have to pay for when Mr. Newsome comes home."

"No problem," she said. "I'll take it out of my police benevolent donation this year."

That earned her one of Pierce's warning looks, but it was worth it.

"When your men spoke to Newsome, how did he look?" Pierce asked. "Was he anxious, worried about anything?"

A light flush of red crept up the lieutenant's neck. "Actually, they didn't visit him in person. They spoke to him on the phone. I didn't think it was worth their time driving over here, and it turns out it wasn't. There's no one here."

Now Madison understood why Hamilton was acting so defensive. He was embarrassed that his men had lied to him, but he wasn't willing to admit they'd lied, not in front of another law-enforcement officer.

Pierce swore beneath his breath. "I wouldn't have brought Madison here if I'd known your men hadn't seen Newsome for themselves, and verified his identity. For all you know, the man your officer spoke to on the phone could be Damon McKinley."

"Highly unlikely. I was doing you a favor, a courtesy to a fellow officer, by even having my men make the phone call. There was no evidence of foul play, no evidence of a crime to even warrant the wellness check. And in case you've somehow forgotten, we're a bit busy with some real crimes right now, namely the 'Simon says' killer."

Madison pushed off Pierce's car and stepped closer to the lieutenant. "I'm not likely to forget since I saw that poor young man after he was killed this morning. As for a crime to warrant that wellness check, how about that fake note to the property manager? The note I gave you weeks ago? That's your evidence."

"A printed-out note, not a hand-written one. And no signature. For all I know, you typed that note."

She threw her hands in the air. "Why would I do that?"

He waved his hand back toward the house. "Why would you do any of this? Mrs. McKinley, in the past few weeks we've responded to your calls on half-a-dozen occasions." He held up a hand and began counting off his fingers. "Once to report that allegedly fake note to the property manager—a note that was typed, with no fingerprints besides the property manager's . . . and yours."

She shook her head in frustration. She was so tired of not being believed. "Mrs. Whitmire showed me the note, so of course my prints were on it."

"Three times to say someone was watching you," he continued. "But we never found anyone."

"It would help if it didn't take you thirty minutes to get there when someone called."

Pierce stepped behind her and rested his hands lightly on her shoulders, like he had at MacGuffin's. He was trying to remind her, without words, of the discussion they'd had in his car when they called the police earlier. He'd asked her to be careful, not to do anything to antagonize the police. And she'd promised she would try to keep a rein on her temper.

She drew in a deep breath and clamped her mouth shut.

"Another time," Hamilton continued, "you called to

report a threatening note, and a threatening phone call. Again, the note was typed, not handwritten, and only had your fingerprints on it. And the number the call came from couldn't be traced to anyone."

"Again," she said, using a calm, conversational tone, "my fingerprints were on the note because I'm the one who found it. And even I know, as a civilian, that bad guys can use those throw-away cell phones. No cell phone contract, no way to trace the number. Everyone knows that."

"Hold on," Pierce said. "What threatening note? What phone call?" He leaned down next to her. "You never told me about those."

She felt her face flush. With so much happening, so fast, she'd honestly forgotten about those two incidents. They'd paled next to him getting shot. "It wasn't on purpose. I forgot."

His hands stiffened on her shoulders. Her heart sank as she realized he thought she was lying again.

Hamilton ticked off another finger. "You called another time because a man you chased apparently feared for his life and shot at you in self-defense. Your actions caused a federal agent to get shot."

"Now hold on, Hamilton—" Pierce began.

"Let me finish," he told Pierce, before looking back at Madison. "You reported that someone had stolen photographs from your attic. Once again, we found no evidence of a break-in or that anyone else had been there."

"You're out of line, Lieutenant," Pierce said.

Hamilton held out a hand as if to appease him. "I'm just pointing out the way this looks from my side. Based on Mrs. McKinley's statement a few minutes ago, that she believes her *dead* husband was in this very house, we entered the home to search for an intruder. Surprise, surprise, we didn't find anyone. And, lo and behold, no one has reported Mr. Newsome missing either."

In spite of her good intentions, Madison couldn't stand by and listen to Hamilton's sarcasm anymore. She took a step forward, but Pierce tightened his grip on her shoulders, pulling her back.

"Calm down," he whispered in her ear. His voice was harsh, radiating anger. Was he beginning to side with Hamilton against her?

"From where I stand," Hamilton said, "the only person causing trouble here is you."

Pierce gently shoved her behind his back. "That's enough."

Hamilton held his hands out in a placating gesture. "I'm not trying to be difficult, Agent Buchanan. I'm just pointing out the facts as I see them. I can't waste any more resources on one woman with a fixation on her dead husband. She needs help, not the kind of help my department can provide. If she calls again, someone had better be dead or dying."

## *Chapter Eleven*

MADISON WAS STILL ticked over Hamilton's not-so-subtle insult, basically calling her crazy, and threatening to put her in jail. "I *told* you the police would have arrested me if I'd called them the day of the shooting."

She immediately regretted saying anything. Pierce's jaw tightened and his knuckles whitened on the steering wheel as his car bumped along the dirt road leading to his house. He hadn't said anything at all to her since the lieutenant's tirade.

Was he having the same doubts Hamilton had about her? Was he regretting that he'd ever offered to help her?

"When we get inside, I want you to level with me," he said, his voice tight, harsh. "I want to hear all about that note, and the phone call, and anything else you *forgot* to mention."

She tensed in the seat beside him.

When the house came into view, he had to quickly

turn the wheel to avoid another car parked in front of the cabin. He killed the engine, but instead of getting out of the car, he stared through the windshield at the man standing on the cabin's porch. "What's he doing here?"

The man's arms were crossed and Madison had to squint to make out his face in the shadows from the overhanging roof. "Isn't that Braedon?"

"Unfortunately." He sat back in his seat, seemingly in no hurry to get out of the car. "Maybe if we sit here long enough, he'll leave."

"Why don't you like your own brother?"

His face mirrored his surprise. "What makes you think I don't like him?"

"Oh, I don't know—maybe because you frown and complain every time you see him."

He rolled his eyes. "It's not my brother I have a problem with. It's the notches in his bedpost."

"What's that supposed to mean?"

"Never mind."

She huffed out a breath and opened her car door. "Well, I'm not going to sit here all night. I happen to like your brother. He seems very nice. And he's a lot more cheerful than you."

Pierce jerked his car door open. "Might as well see what he wants."

When Madison and Pierce were close enough to see Braedon's face, Madison saw that his brows were a dark slash across his forehead. He didn't even look at her. Instead, he directed his ferocious glare at his brother.

"Why didn't you tell us you got shot?"

Pierce groaned. "Who told you?"

"Hamilton called Alex, all up in arms, saying you and . . ." He glanced at Madison then, as if noticing her for the first time. His face flushed a light red. "Sorry, Mrs. McKinley. I shouldn't air family problems in front of you."

She waved her hand in the air. "Don't apologize. If you're upset about something Hamilton said, then you can lay that at my feet. Your brother has been trying to help me with . . . a little problem I have. It's because of me that he got shot." She crossed her arms and stepped in front of Pierce. "If you want to yell at someone, yell at me. Leave him alone."

She squeaked in surprise when Pierce's hands wrapped around her waist, and he lifted her out of his way.

"You don't owe Braedon an explanation. None of this is any of his business. And it's not Alex's business either."

"It's none of my business that my little brother almost got himself killed and didn't bother to tell his family?"

"Who is Alex?" Madison asked.

"Bruised ribs and a few stitches aren't something to call home about. I don't need any of my brothers looking out for me."

"Who's Alex?" Madison repeated. "Wait. *Any* of your brothers? Exactly how many brothers do you have?" She glanced back and forth, but neither of the men seemed to even remember she was there.

"You supposedly moved back to Savannah to be close to family again," Braedon said. "Being part of a family means letting each other know when something bad happens. You've worked those serial-killer cases way too long. You've forgotten what 'normal' is."

Pierce aimed a pointed look at Madison. "Let me get her inside. We can discuss this in private."

"We can discuss it at the house. It's Friday night, or had you forgotten?"

Madison frowned. "The house? Whose house? What's so special about Friday night?"

"I can't make it this week." Pierce shoved past Braedon to unlock the front door.

"Austin's home."

Pierce slowly turned around.

Madison watched the staring match between the two brothers for a full minute. "Um, guys, what's going on? Who's Austin?"

Braedon sighed and shoved a hand through his hair. "Alex is . . . was . . . married to Pierce's mom. Austin is our youngest brother. We don't get to see him too often these days. He's been . . . ill. Which is why I'm not going to let Pierce blow off Friday night." He crossed to the top step. "Dinner is in two hours. If I have to come back to get you, I'm bringing the whole family with me."

"THE HOUSE" BRAEDON had mentioned turned out to be a rambling ranch-style home half an hour south of Savannah. Situated on several acres of land, it was surrounded by a white-washed wooden fence on all sides of the property. A fishing pond stretched out to the right side, from behind the house, all the way to the tree line. And just like with Madison's house, there wasn't a garage. Instead, there was a massive, gravel, circular drive out front.

Pierce pulled his car to a stop next to the white pickup, with its bold B&B lettering, Braedon had driven earlier. Two more pickups, all domestic brands, were lined up beside Braedon's truck. A massive SUV—a black Cadillac Escalade—was parked at the end. But front and center, right by the ramp that led to the front door, was one vehicle that didn't seem to match the rest.

It was a custom, blue van with a wheelchair lift on the back.

She glanced over at him, but he'd made no attempt to move once they'd both gotten out of the car. Instead, he stood sullenly beside her, staring at the van.

"This is your father's house?" she asked.

"Technically he's my stepfather, but he's only ten years older than me, eight years older than Braedon. We just call him Alex."

"So—do you like him or not?"

He tore his gaze away from the van. "Why would you ask that?"

She threw her hands up in the air. "No reason. You and your family get along so well. And you seem so excited to visit. Why on earth would I think you had any negative feelings about any of them?"

His mouth quirked, but the threatening grin didn't materialize. Instead, he grabbed her hand, and headed toward the trees on the left side of the property, away from the pond.

She had to jog to keep up with his long-legged strides. "Where are we going?"

"Into the woods."

"Yeah, I can see that. *Why* are we going into the woods?"

"I need to explain a few things before you meet my family."

"Okay. Maybe you could have explained those things during the drive over here?"

He didn't answer. He kept moving with those ground-eating strides while she was forced to run behind him. When they reached the trees, out of sight of the house, he finally let her go.

She immediately plopped down on a fallen tree and took several deep breaths to slow her racing heart.

He frowned. "Why are you breathing hard?"

"Maybe . . . because I just ran . . . a quarter mile?" She drew a couple more quick breaths. "My legs . . . aren't nearly as long as yours . . . in case you hadn't noticed."

His face flushed. "Sorry. I wasn't thinking." He joined her on the fallen tree. "When I saw that van, it brought back some . . . painful memories."

When he didn't say anything else, she crossed her arms, hugging her jacket against her body. The sun was going down, and here in the shade of the pine and oak trees, the sun's warmth couldn't penetrate.

He scooted closer to her, wrapping his arm around her shoulders and pulling her into his side.

She snuggled gratefully against him, already feeling warmer. "Thanks."

"My pleasure." His voice sounded oddly thick.

"So, you wanted to talk." She was desperate to keep from thinking about how good it felt, how right it felt, to be held by him.

He let out a harsh breath. "The house is kind of like my family's home base, where we all gather once a week and on holidays."

"Whose house is it?"

"It was my mom's, passed down through generations. Now it belongs to Alex."

"Then your mom, she's . . . gone?" She hated to think of him losing his mom, the way she'd lost her dad. She put her hand on his.

He twisted his hand beneath hers, interlacing their fingers. "In a manner of speaking, yes. She left when I was in high school. She said she was bored. She ran off with a younger man. Sent the divorce papers back to Alex through a lawyer. She didn't want anything but her freedom. Didn't even want custody of any of us kids. She was more than happy to foist us off on Alex, even Austin and Matt, who were just babies at the time. They're Alex's only biological children, but he took care of all of us like we were his own."

Madison froze. Oh God. His mother had abandoned her children, had abandoned Pierce, giving a similar excuse that Madison had given when she'd left—that she was bored and wanted to move on. She suddenly felt lower than the lowest pond scum. "I'm so sorry," she whispered.

His arm tightened around her shoulders. "It's okay. We all pulled together. When my mother left, Alex became the glue that kept the rest of us together, has been ever since."

She opened her mouth to correct him, to let him know she was apologizing for her own behavior, not his mother's. But she decided now was not the time. This wasn't about her. It was about him, and whatever he'd brought her out here for. "Go on," she encouraged. "What else did you want to tell me?"

He rubbed his hand up and down her coat sleeve. She couldn't help but wish his hand was tracing across her bare skin instead.

"We don't all share the same mom or the same dad. It's a bit . . . complicated. But we're brothers, regardless of whose blood flows through our veins." He watched her carefully, as if waiting for her approval.

She nodded, wondering why he felt he owed her this explanation about his family. Was that why he'd brought her out here? To tell her about his family tree?

"Alex lives here alone most of the time. When Austin isn't in treatment somewhere, he lives here too."

"Treatment?"

"Austin has a neurological disorder, similar to muscular dystrophy, but not quite the same. It's more . . . unpredictable, one of those 'orphan' diseases that's so rare there hasn't been a lot of research on it." His jaw tightened. "Every time Alex hears about some new kind of experimental drug, or a study, he signs Austin up for it. One of these days, probably sooner than later, Austin is going to refuse to enroll in more studies. Alex is way too protective."

He scrubbed a hand over his face. "I didn't mean to get into all that. But I didn't want you surprised when you walked in. I wanted to prepare you."

"I'm so sorry. I can tell you love him, and all of your family, very much. I shouldn't have teased you earlier."

He gave her a pained look as he pulled his arm back from around her shoulders.

She scrambled up from the log. "Is it your ribs? Did I hurt you?" She reached out to open his jacket to see if he was bleeding again.

He grabbed her hands and stood. "My ribs are fine."

"Then, what—"

"In spite of how I've been behaving, my family and I are actually quite close."

She sensed she wasn't going to like what he was about to tell her. "So is mine. Or, at least, my brother and I are close. Mom's another story," she teased, trying to coax a smile out of him. But he wouldn't even look at her.

Not a good sign.

She hugged her arms around her middle, feeling the chill much more now that she wasn't snuggled against his warm body. "Go on," she urged, "before I become a Popsicle out here."

"Stop joking," he said. "I need to tell you something."

She wasn't joking. She really was freezing. But judging from the harsh frown on his face, she didn't think he'd be interested in hearing that declaration. She stared up at him, waiting.

"Braedon was angry about the shooting earlier, because we have no secrets from each other," he said, tensing up, as if expecting her to be upset.

Was she missing something here? "No secrets. Okay, got it. Is that supposed to mean something to me?"

SIMON SAYS DIE   157

He sighed heavily. "If you'll remember, we were going to meet my family once, back when you and I were dating. We were going to go to Savannah, but something came up at work and we had to cancel."

The weekend before she'd left him. She remembered it vividly, because that's when she'd realized how serious he was getting. She knew he wasn't the type to casually invite someone to see his family, and neither was she.

"I remember," she said quietly.

"That was the weekend before—"

"I know." She glanced back toward the break in the trees, growing more miserable the longer this conversation dragged on. Not just because of the cold.

"A few weeks later, I made that trip to Savannah, by myself."

Her stomach jumped with dread as everything clicked. "They know about us? About . . . how it ended?"

He nodded. "No secrets." His expression turned wary, as if he expected her to explode.

She wished, for once, that her infamous temper would come to her rescue. But instead of exploding, she felt like imploding, crumpling in on herself and curling into a tight ball. "They must all hate me," she whispered.

He gently squeezed her fingers. "They don't hate you. I won't let them." His brows drew down in a harsh line. "Then again, it might be better if they did. Then they'd leave you alone."

"What do you mean?" she asked, alarmed by his tone.

"You're too beautiful by far. Once they're certain you and I aren't involved anymore, they'll see you as fair game. Well, Braedon and Devlin will. You're exactly their type, and they're outrageous flirts. I should have told you before we came out here. You don't have to face my family. I can take you home, have Casey or another agent watch over you for a few hours while I get the required family visit out of the way."

She was still trying not to choke up over his matter-of-fact statement about them not being involved anymore, and she was having trouble focusing on what else he'd said. Something about a required family visit? She didn't buy that. He wanted this, to see his brothers, Austin. And he was already here. She didn't want him to have to miss dinner with them or postpone his visit because of her.

Especially since they weren't involved anymore.

She blinked against the burn of unshed tears. She deserved this, feeling miserable, after how she'd treated him. Taking the easy way out, leaving without facing his family, was incredibly tempting. But that wasn't fair to Pierce. She sensed he wanted her with him to face his family, so she wasn't going to abandon him now, not if he needed her. She could consider it her penance.

"Come on," she said. "Let's go up to the house. I want to see this family of yours. If they're anything like Braedon and Matt, I'll consider myself honored to meet them. And if they're mean to me, I'll just be mean right back. I can take care of myself."

She could see some of the tension go out of his shoulders, the relief in his eyes.

"All right, tough girl. Let's go."

This time, as they walked back toward the house, he

slowed his stride to match hers, so she wouldn't have to run to keep up. When they stood outside the front door, he leaned down beside her. "Come on, beautiful," he whispered. "Let's get this family reunion over with. I have a feeling I'm going to have to bash a few heads in to teach my brothers some manners."

She blinked at his compliment, and looked up at him, wondering if he'd even realized how his voice had softened when he'd said it. Was it possible he still cared about her, even after the "no relationship" comment?

He pushed the door open, and she dragged her gaze away from him to face the gauntlet she was about to run. The low hum of conversation went silent as five pairs of eyes centered on them from the couches in the middle of the family room. She instinctively stepped closer to Pierce. He put his arm around her shoulders and pulled her into his side.

"Don't worry," he spoke in a low voice, only for her. "They'll love you." He grabbed her hand and tugged her forward into the enormous room that resembled a hunting lodge. A massive fireplace took up the far wall and had a roaring fire inside. All the walls were painted dark brown and displayed paintings of wildlife, except for one wall that was filled with what looked to be family pictures.

He pulled her to one of three large brown leather couches in the center of the room. Three men were sitting on the first couch, a fourth sat on the couch across from the first one, and a young man sat in a wheelchair between both couches.

"Madison, meet Alex, one of the best defense attor-

neys to ever practice law in the state of Georgia." He
waved his hand toward the man closest to them.

He had coal black hair with tiny threads of silver running through it, and brilliant blue eyes that looked far
too sad, even though he was smiling. "I'm sure Madison
doesn't care about my status as a *semi-retired* attorney,"
he corrected. "Besides, I can't imagine her ever needing a
defense lawyer." He gave her a firm handshake. "Nice to
meet you, Madison."

"You too." Her stomach jumped at his reference to
needing a defense attorney. Her last night with Damon,
their argument, and what she'd done, loomed in her
mind. It was all she could do not to yank her hand away
and run.

"You already met Braedon," Pierce continued. Thank-
fully he didn't seem to notice her discomfort. "And his
constant shadow, Matt."

She nodded and shook both their hands as they stood
and reached out to her.

Pierce turned to the lone man on the far couch. "This
is Devlin, better known as Devil, with good reason. Stay
away from him." Pierce gave his brother a warning scowl.

Devlin grinned and took both of Madison's hands in
his as he towered over her. He was the tallest of all the
men so far, including Pierce, and Madison had to tilt her
head way back to meet his dark-eyed gaze.

"Why don't you sit over here with me, gorgeous?" He
tugged her toward the couch.

Pierce plucked Devlin's hands off her and shoved his
brother onto the couch.

Madison let out a shocked gasp, but Devlin only laughed.

The low hum of the wheelchair's motor had all eyes turning to the last occupant in the room as he pushed a lever and brought the chair to a stop in front of Madison. When she looked down at him and held out her hand to shake his, her mouth dropped open in surprise as she glanced back at Matt.

Matt sighed as if the weight of the world was on his shoulders. "Twins," he said, confirming what she'd just realized. "I'm the older, responsible one. Austin's the baby."

"Five minutes doesn't make me the baby. It makes you the jackass."

"Austin, watch your language." Alex's deep voice filled the room, even though he'd barely spoken above a whisper.

Austin rolled his eyes. "I'm twenty-one, and he still treats me like a two-year-old."

"Trust me, I know the feeling," Madison said. "My brother calls me 'trouble' and still thinks I need a babysitter." She glanced pointedly at Pierce.

Austin's youthful face broke out in a smile as he shook her hand. "Sorry if I offended you with my language." He didn't look apologetic in the least, in spite of his words. He was slow to let go of her hand and gave her a warm squeeze before he did.

Braedon clapped his hands together and rubbed them back and forth. "It's about time you two got here. I'm starving." Devlin and Matt got up too, and the three of them headed out one of the sliding glass doors on the back of the house.

"Pierce, why don't you ice down the drinks," Alex said. "Austin, you can help. I'll escort this young lady outside."

Pierce didn't look at all happy with Alex's suggestion, but he nodded curtly and headed toward the front of the house with Austin following behind.

"Madison?" Alex offered his arm. His mouth curved in a smile that didn't quite reach his eyes.

A feeling of foreboding went through her, but she took his arm and walked with him through the glass doors to a wide deck that extended off the back of the house. The brothers were on the right side, taking steaks out of a cooler and loading them onto two grills that were already smoking. Devlin caught sight of her and gave her a broad grin, before Matt elbowed him in the ribs and got his attention.

"Don't mind them." Alex led her to the railing several feet away from the others.

"I don't mind them at all." She sat beside him. "They all seem very nice."

He nodded. "They're good kids."

"Kids?" She looked toward the grill where the three brothers were arguing about the best placement of the steaks. "Braedon's what, thirty-eight, forty?"

"Thirty-nine. Matt's twenty-one like Austin, of course. Devlin's a precocious thirty. But it's not age that defines how old you are. It's attitude. Trust me, they all have the attitude of a randy college kid. Well, except for Matt maybe. He's always serious." His smile dimmed. "And Pierce. He's serious too, even more now than he

used to be. Something changed him a few months ago."
He turned the full intensity of his ice-blue stare on her.

This was what he'd wanted to talk to her about. The
family patriarch looking out for his son. And he obviously saw her as a threat.

She swallowed and dug her fingernails into her palms.
She looked away, out over the acres of winter-brown grass
and oak trees that dotted the landscape behind the house.
"It's beautiful here. Pierce told me this is *your* house."

She heard his sigh, and from the corner of her eye she
saw him turn to look out over the yard as well.

"It's the family house. It belongs to all of us. I've lived
here for . . . oh, twenty-five years now, give or take. Most
of the time it doesn't seem that long. Other times, it seems
a whole lot longer. Pierce said you were from New York?"

"Originally, I'm from the Florida Panhandle. But
when my family moved to New York, I fell in love with
the city."

"And yet, you moved to Savannah. Any particular
reason?"

She glanced around, wondering what was taking
Pierce so long. "My brother thought I'd like it here. He's
the reason I bought my house."

"What kind of house?"

"An old colonial, on East Gaston Street."

"Nice part of town. What square are you near?"

She could well imagine this man facing a witness in
court. He was quite good at interrogating. "The closest
square is Calhoun. I'm less than a block from Forsyth
Park, between Drayton and Abercorn."

"You aren't far from that amazing center fountain at the end of the park then. I used to roam the historic district whenever I had a chance to get away from work. That's how I know Lieutenant Hamilton, by the way, from the courthouse. We were often on opposite sides of the law, but we've always been friends outside the courtroom."

She clutched the railing and waited for his next question.

"I know about the shooting. We all do. I also know a few more details the rest don't know."

She stiffened and turned to face him. "What details?"

"Everything."

She glanced back at the house and crossed her arms. "Hamilton told you he thinks I'm some hysterical female who's faking threatening notes and believing her stalker is her dead husband. Let me guess. You agree."

"I didn't say that."

"You didn't have to."

"What I think is that you have a ghost in your past that is coming back to haunt you. Whether that ghost is your dead husband, or something *you* did, remains to be seen."

There was no mistaking the threat in his deep tone. "Why don't you just speak plainly? Are you trying to warn me about something, sir?"

"That depends."

"On?"

"On whether you hurt Pierce again."

## Chapter Twelve

THE DOOR BEHIND Alex slid open and Pierce stepped outside. Madison saw his jaw tighten when he looked at her, as if he realized what Alex was doing.

Interrogating her.

She tried to gather her composure, and offered a small smile.

"You're supposed to be grilling steaks, Alex, not Madison." Pierce eyed the other man with suspicion and set a bucket of iced-down beer by the railing. Austin wheeled up beside him with a second bucket in his lap. Pierce grabbed the bucket and set it down beside the first one.

When Pierce stepped toward Alex looking like he was ready to do battle, Madison grabbed his arm.

"Alex was just telling me about your family."

Pierce narrowed his eyes at her. He didn't look convinced.

Alex smiled, his eyes mirroring his approval. "Austin, you need to take your meds before we eat."

Austin's smile dimmed, and he said a few choice words beneath his breath as he wheeled around and headed back inside.

"You shouldn't treat him like a kid," Pierce said.

"You're right, but he hero-worships you, and I didn't want him upset. It's not good for him."

"Why would he be upset?"

"You got shot. I want the details. *All* of them."

Pierce leaned back against the railing and crossed his arms. "Madison, would you mind going inside to check on Austin?"

"Now who's treating him like a kid?" Alex said.

Madison rushed to the door, more than happy to avoid this particular discussion, and to put some distance between herself and Alex. "I don't mind," she said, heading inside.

The sound of cursing led her toward the front of the house into the kitchen. Austin's wheelchair was rolled up to a table and a pile of pill bottles was spread out before him. A bottle of water sat to his right.

He glanced up when she entered the room. His face turned a light shade of red. "Did Alex send you in here to help me? I swear he thinks I can't open these damn things by myself."

She pulled out a chair next to him and took the bottle out of his hand. "Judging by the cursing when I came in here, he's right. But, actually, it was Pierce who sent me in here. He wanted to speak privately to Alex without me overhearing." She twisted the cap off and set it on the table. "How many?"

His mouth twitched and his frown melted into a grin. "You've got some sass in you. I like that." He nodded toward the bottle. "I'm supposed to cut that one in half."

She glanced around, then got up and went to the kitchen counter. She pointed at a knife and cutting board. "Is this what you use?"

"Yeah."

She washed her hands at the sink, then carried the knife and cutting board to the table. After sitting down, she shook out one of the pills.

"I wouldn't have thought to wash my hands first."

"That's because you're a guy."

He shrugged. "I suppose."

"Why do you call him Alex?" she asked.

"Because that's his name."

"Now who's being sassy? He's your father, right? So why do you call him by his first name?"

He shrugged. "I grew up hearing everyone else call him Alex. The 'Daddy' label never took."

They sat quietly for a few minutes, shaking out pills, putting them on a napkin. Madison cut three of them in half, per Austin's instructions. When they were done, she capped all the bottles. "Where do you keep these?"

"On the counter." He waved toward where the cutting board and knife had been. "But I can put them up myself."

"I'm sure you can. But I've got nothing better to do at the moment." She carried them to the counter, rinsed and dried the board and knife, then rejoined Austin at the table.

He started taking the pills, two at a time, chasing them with a swallow of water.

"That's an awful lot of pills. Do you take them every day?"

"On this most recent study, yeah. Some of the studies are worse than others." He shrugged. "None of them seem to do any good for very long. I keep getting worse."

"Worse? In what way?"

He waved his hand toward the wheelchair. "This is new. Before this last study, I could walk . . . sometimes. The paralysis is a side effect of the medication. Temporary, supposedly. I'm starting to wonder if the potential benefits are worth it. But the doctors swear the medication will result in long-term gains like it has for other diseases. If all goes well, in a few months, I should be out of the chair again."

She glanced at his legs. "The pills paralyze you?"

"Yep. Can't feel a thing. Alex is terrified I'll burn myself or something and not know it. That's another reason he sent me in here, I'm sure. To keep me away from the grill." He grinned. "Heck, maybe I *should* burn myself just to see him freak out."

"Very mature."

His grin widened.

"Sounds like the cure is worse than the disease."

He sobered. "Sometimes it is."

"What's the prognosis?" When he raised his brows,

she rushed to apologize. "I'm sorry. I shouldn't be so nosey."

He shook his head. "I don't mind. You just surprised me. Most people avoid looking at my wheelchair, or asking questions. They pretend there's nothing wrong." He took a sip of water. "The prognosis is that the doctors don't know. There haven't been enough people in the world with my disease for them to make any predictions. I could keep losing muscle function and become completely dependent on others for my care. Or I could stabilize and live a long, relatively healthy life. They just don't know."

"That must be incredibly frustrating."

He cocked his head, studying her. "You're not at all what I expected."

"What you . . . expected?"

"You know, for a party girl who dumped my brother to scope out the dating scene in New York."

Her face flushed with heat, and she jumped up from her chair.

"Hold on a second," he said. "Okay, okay, I admit that was out of line. I shouldn't have said that. Don't go."

She crossed her arms over her chest. "Why shouldn't I?"

He waved his hand toward his wheelchair. "Because I'm a cripple, and I'm lonely?"

The puppy-dog look on his face was so ridiculous she couldn't help but laugh.

"Oh, fine. But no more insults."

She plopped down in her chair.

"Those were my words, by the way, not Pierce's," he said. "Pierce was much more diplomatic when he explained about the breakup."

"I'm not talking about that anymore."

"What were their names?"

"Excuse me?"

"The guys you dated. You did tell Pierce you were"—he raised his hands and did air quotes—" 'moving on.' " He lowered his hands. "What's wrong? Can't make up any names fast enough to answer the question?"

"Of course I can." She flushed, realizing how that sounded. "I've met several . . . ah, really nice guys." She waved her hand in the air, desperately trying to think of a name, any name. "There was, um . . . John, and uh, Mike, of course."

"Do John and Mike have last names?"

"I came in here to help you, not play games." She shoved her chair back again.

He grabbed her arm when she started to get up, holding on with surprising strength. "You know what I think? I think you lied to my brother. I think you're still hung up on him. I saw the way you were looking at him when he opened the door. That's not the look of a woman who has moved on."

She shook off his hand and shoved back from the table. "My feelings for Pierce are none of your business. What is it with this family? First, Alex, now you. You sure know how to make a stranger feel welcome." She gripped her chair to stand, but he moved forward, using his wheelchair to block her way.

He grinned. "Did Alex lecture you? He's good at that."

She glared at him and wondered why she'd liked him earlier. She didn't like him at all right now.

He cocked his head again. "If you really wanted to date other guys, you wouldn't act so defensive. So I have to conclude you lied to my brother."

She clutched the chair in frustration. "What do you want from me?"

"Tit for tat. I shared personal details with you." He waved his hand toward his wheelchair. "How about you do the same? Just between you and me. Answer one question, honestly, and we're even."

She crossed her arms. "What's the question?"

"Don't insult me by pretending you didn't lie to Pierce when you broke up. The real question is . . . *Why* did you lie?"

She forced a swallow past her tightening throat. "I never wanted to hurt him. I hated leaving the way I did," she whispered.

"You still care about him."

"Yes. Always"

"Then why did you lie?"

"Because I couldn't tell him the truth. I needed him to let me go. I had to tell him something awful, to make sure he wouldn't try to stop me." She drew in a ragged breath.

He backed away, his expression smug. "My work here is done. I'm starving. I think I'll go outside and grab a thick, juicy steak." He looked past her shoulder. "Oh, hey, Pierce. I didn't notice you there." Austin winked at Madison and wheeled out of the kitchen.

*Damn.* Madison's pulse thudded in her ears. She took a deep breath and slowly turned around.

Pierce was standing in the kitchen doorway. His jaw was tight, his eyes narrowed. She braced herself for his accusations, his barrage of questions.

Without a single word, he turned and walked away.

THE RIDE BACK to Pierce's house was taut with silence. Madison kept waiting for him to demand that she tell him why she'd lied. But just like their earlier car ride from Mr. Newsome's house, he was completely silent.

As soon as he opened the front door of the cabin, she tried to rush past him, fully intending to spend the rest of the evening in the bedroom, hiding like the coward she'd just discovered she was.

But his hand shot out and grabbed her wrist, preventing her escape. She glanced up at him uncertainly, but he wasn't looking at her. He disabled the alarm, locked the door, then reset the alarm, before turning and giving her his full attention.

His jaw muscles were tight, and he looked more serious than she'd ever seen him. Calm, too calm, like a dormant volcano ready to explode. "We need to discuss a few things." His words were short, clipped.

Her stomach sank. He towed her the few steps to the couch. She plopped down, but instead of sitting next to her, he stepped to the small desk against the wall and powered up the laptop sitting there.

He typed for a moment, then he swiveled the laptop around so she could see the screen. "This is your home security alarm company report for the past month, the report I requested after you realized some pictures were missing from your albums."

She frowned, puzzled. *This* was what he wanted to talk about? Not why she'd lied when she broke up with him? She got up and crossed to the desk to view the report. It had yesterday's date. "Why didn't you tell me you had this?"

"I guess I forgot. Kind of like you forgot to tell me about the note and phone call Lieutenant Hamilton mentioned at Newsome's house."

She winced, but she didn't respond to his goading, which she thought was admirable. Instead, she scrolled through the report. "The alarm hasn't been tripped. I already knew that."

"What about the dates and times the alarm was set or disabled? Do they look right?"

She pressed the keys, paging through the report more slowly. "I couldn't swear to every time, of course. I didn't exactly keep a log. But overall, it looks right."

"No one else knows the alarm code?"

"I already told you and Hamilton that I changed it after I moved in. I haven't shared it with anyone—not even you."

He swiveled the laptop back toward him. "Did you use your birthday for the alarm code? Or some other date your husband might be able to guess?"

Her pulse sped up, and she moved back to the couch. "Ah, no, Damon wouldn't know the code. It's not significant." To *him*. It was, however, significant to *her*.

"You're sure?"

The code was the month and day of her first date with Pierce. She swallowed, her throat tight. "I'm sure."

"What's the code?"

"Why?" She tried to think of a reasonable excuse for not telling him the code, but just like when she was talking to Austin, her mind was coming up blank.

"I want to judge for myself if the numbers are a pattern Damon might be able to guess."

"How would you know if it was?"

He waved toward the computer. "Casey e-mailed a file with some information on Damon. I read some of it on my phone earlier. Before I go through the rest, I'd like that code. There might be something in his past, your shared past, that would make him able to guess the code. I've got to figure out how he got in your house to take those photographs from your albums—or even if he did get inside your house. Sometimes moving companies store everything for a short period in a warehouse before making the final delivery. He might have searched through the boxes at the warehouse."

The thought of Damon going through her things had the hairs standing up on her arms. "I suppose that's possible. After the movers packed my apartment, I stayed in New York a few days wrapping up loose ends before I flew down here. They delivered my furniture the day after I arrived. They would have had to store my belongings."

"The code?"

Guys didn't remember things like when they had their first date, did they? Especially when the relationship ended so badly. She drew a deep breath and told him the code.

His dark gaze flew to hers, and for a moment she thought maybe he'd realized the significance of those four numbers. But then he simply nodded, and looked back at the screen.

She let out a relieved breath, feeling as if she'd just been given a reprieve. "If there's nothing else, I'm going to bed. It's been a long day."

"Not yet. I want to know about the note and the phone call."

## Chapter Thirteen

MADISON SHOULD HAVE known Pierce wouldn't let her escape without another inquisition. She sighed and scooted back on the couch. "The note was taped to my front door when I got home, a couple of days after the first time I saw . . . someone . . . watching my house."

"Typed out, not handwritten."

"Yes."

"Do I really have to ask you to tell me what it said?" He stared at her, waiting.

"It said, 'You've been a very bad girl.' "

His brow furrowed. "What the hell is that supposed to mean?"

She felt her face heating with embarrassment. "Damon said that to me, once, after an argument. He was upset that I'd been on his computer."

He sat silently for a moment. "Does anyone else know he said that to you?"

"Probably. I was pretty ticked the first time he said that. I called my mom and vented with her. She's not the best at keeping secrets. For all I know, she blasted it all over the Internet on those social media sites she's so fond of."

"The first time?"

She wrapped her arms around her middle. "He said it one other time. His voice was . . . cold, angry. I'll never forget the tone of his voice that day."

He stared at her intently. "What did Hamilton say about the note?"

"That it was probably some neighborhood kid, playing a joke on the new lady who'd just moved in. In all fairness, he wasn't sarcastic and didn't dismiss it, not at first anyway. He looked into it. He sent his officers to ask my neighbors if they saw anything."

She laughed harshly. "Not that anyone on my street *would* see anything. Most of the homes around me are vacant for the better part of the year, vacation homes. Right now, with it getting cold, most of the owners are in South Florida."

"So, no one saw who left the note."

"No."

"Tell me about the phone call."

She kicked her shoes off and tucked her legs beneath her on the couch. "It was after I saw the man in my backyard, by the storage shed. I was eating breakfast. The phone rang. When I answered, a voice on the line said the same thing the note said. And before you ask, no, I didn't recognize the voice. It sounded . . . odd . . . distorted, like the person speaking was purposely changing his voice."

"But you could tell the caller was male?"

"Definitely. That much I was sure of."

"You think it was Damon."

"Wouldn't you? Knowing what he'd said in the past?"

He didn't answer. He typed a few notes on his laptop. "You mentioned you had files from Damon's computer. You still have those files?"

"Yes, on my laptop, back at my house."

"We can go get your computer in the morning. What about the pictures you think are missing? Are you certain you saw them before you moved, that you didn't throw them away when you were packing?"

She blew out a breath. "We're back to that? Seriously?"

He studied her for a moment. Then he closed the laptop and turned toward her, resting his forearms on his knees. "I'm re-looking at all the evidence, trying to figure this out. Casey texted me earlier, saying he wants a sample of Damon's handwriting to compare to those bogus contracts you gave me. Do you have a sample?"

She pinched the bridge of her nose and shook her head. "Of course not. That would be too easy, wouldn't it?" She rested her head against the back of the couch. "I had no reason to keep anything personal of his after he died. The only reason I kept those contracts was because they had to do with finances. At the time, I thought they were valid investments. But other than those, I don't have anything with his signature."

"You're not giving me much to go on here."

She rolled her head back and forth against the couch,

so frustrated she wanted to scream. It was either that, or shoot someone. And since the only other person in the room was Pierce, she didn't exactly have any options along those lines.

Drawing a deep breath, she tried to focus on answering his questions without totally losing her composure. "I've given you *plenty* to go on. You saw him yourself. He shot you. He's real, flesh and blood, and he's after me. Why? I don't know. You know everything that's been happening—the notes, the shooting. He killed that boy this morning, and Mr. Newsome's missing."

"Maybe."

"Maybe? Maybe he killed the boy, or maybe he did something to Mr. Newsome?"

"Both."

That was it. She'd had enough. She uncurled her legs and stood. "We're done here." She'd just reached the hall-way when he was suddenly in her way, blocking her. She shoved at his chest. He winced, and she jerked her hands back.

"I'm so sorry. I forgot about your ribs. Are you okay?"

"I'm fine." He blew out a breath. "Don't run away from this. I'm trying to help you, and I can't do that without the facts."

"I've given you the facts."

His brows drew down. "I don't think so. How did you push a divorce through for a man who'd been declared dead?"

She froze. "Push it through?"

"No court is going to continue proceedings on a divorce when one of the parties has been declared dead. What did you do? Bribe a judge?"

Her fingers curled into fists. "This is ridiculous. Why would I do that?" Her heart was hammering so loudly she could feel the blood rushing to her ears. She couldn't tell him she'd wanted that divorce in case her worst nightmares were true, in case the man who'd died in that car *wasn't* Damon.

"There's only one reason I can think of," he continued, relentless now that he was grilling her.

"I don't want to hear this." She turned, but he grabbed her arm.

His eyes flashed as he leaned down, inches from her face. "Eighteen months ago, a man died in a fiery car crash. You buried him in a grave with your husband's name on the tombstone. But you never cashed in the life insurance policy."

Panic twisted inside her. She tried to pull away, but his grip was like iron.

"You didn't think I knew about the insurance did you? It took some digging, but Casey found it. There's only one reason I can think of for someone not to cash in a life insurance policy. You knew Damon was alive. All this time, you've known."

She pulled her arm, desperately trying to free herself.

"You pushed that divorce through so you wouldn't feel guilty sleeping around with other men. Did that make you feel less guilty when you slept with me?"

She jerked as if he'd struck her, pain twisting inside

her chest. He was treating her like a tramp, as if she'd slept with tons of guys since Damon's death, and after she'd left Pierce. Was that really what he thought of her? She blinked, determined not to let the threatening tears flow. She wasn't going to let him know how much he'd hurt her. After Damon, Pierce had been that one bright spot in her life, the light that had made the darkness of her past fade away, if only for a brief time. Pierce was her *only* lover, besides her husband. Ever. "Let me go," she demanded.

Instead of releasing her, his grip tightened, and he yanked her closer.

His face twisted with anger. "Did you lie about Damon? Was he really the terrible husband you portrayed him to be? Or did you make all that up?"

She gasped. "What? No. No, I didn't lie. He was . . ." She glared up at him. "I didn't lie. He was an evil man."

"But he never hit you."

She clenched her fists. "No. Not once. No bruises. He was far too clever for that. Just like now. He's being far more clever than you, or anyone else realizes. He's turning everyone against me, making me look like a hysterical female, a fool. He destroyed my family, and they don't even know it. I alone bear that burden. I alone live with that pain every day."

"What did he do?" He enunciated each word, slowly, clearly, as if she were a child, and he was forced to speak that way so she'd understand him. "How did he destroy your family?"

She twisted her arm, trying to get him to let go. When

he wouldn't, she jerked her knee up toward his groin, but he anticipated her action, twisting sideways.

"Let. Me. Go." She gritted out each word.

They stared at each other for a full minute, their eyes clashing like swords on a battlefield. Finally, Pierce released her.

She fled into the bedroom, slamming the door behind her.

## *Chapter Fourteen*

THE SOUND OF the bedroom door slamming echoed through the hallway. Pierce closed his eyes, and leaned back against the wall. He hated that he'd hurt her, but from the moment he heard her security code, his frustration and anger had started a slow boil. How could she use their first date as her alarm code, as if she cared about him, and then continue to lie to him?

His shoulders slumped, and he shook his head in defeat. He didn't know how long he stood there, in the dark, thinking. It was the sound of Madison's soft snores that finally broke through his haze, and had him trudging back to his computer desk.

He plopped down in the chair and powered up the laptop again, to read the files Casey had sent him. Nothing earth shattering, nothing about Damon's life in New York that seemed any different than any other businessman. Either Casey had been a boss too long and had forgotten how to investigate, or Damon really didn't have anything lurking in his background worth finding.

If it weren't for the shooting that had started all of this, Pierce would probably be sitting in Hamilton's camp right now, thinking Madison was a crazy woman, desperate for attention, inventing shadows, faking notes.

He didn't doubt that she *believed* what she was telling everyone. She genuinely believed her husband had come back from the dead to stalk her. But what if her bitter relationship with Damon was clouding her judgment? What if the shooter was just a simple burglar, casing her house, as Casey had suggested? That scenario was just as plausible, hell, more so, than the scenario she believed.

He scrubbed his hands over his face. Logan was due back home from his honeymoon in a few more days. As soon as Logan was back in the States, Pierce was going to call him and tell him to get his butt to Savannah to take over guard duty for his sister. Her baby-blue eyes had sucked him in once, and he was hearing that sucking sound again. He needed to get out while he still could.

Tomorrow he'd get her laptop, and look through Damon's files. But the way things were going, he didn't hold out hope that the files would reveal much. Other than Madison's statements about her husband, there was nothing else backing up anything that she'd said about him, or that she even had a stalker to begin with.

Not. One. Damn. Thing.

MADISON WAS MUCH calmer the next morning as she got out of Pierce's car at her house to get her laptop. He was trying to help her. She had to keep reminding herself of that. He couldn't help it if he had a suspicious, detective's brain. When she thought about everything from his perspective, she could understand his skepticism.

Especially since she *hadn't* told him everything.

"I can open my own door." She stepped in front of him to unlock and open her front door.

His hand closed around hers. He, too, was calmer today. There was nothing of his anger from last night in his eyes, in the gentle touch of his hand on hers. "We have a truce. Remember? Part of our deal is that I'm supposed to protect you. Stop fighting me."

She relaxed her grip beneath his. "You're right. I'm sorry. I don't mean to make this even more difficult for you." She pulled her hand back.

"Even more difficult?"

She waved her hand in the air. "You know, being around me. I know you wouldn't be here if you didn't feel you had to, because of your promise to my brother. I'm not trying to be difficult. Really, I'm not." She waved her hand again. "I think it just comes naturally."

His lips twitched as if he were trying not to smile, but then he gave in to the urge and grinned. "Being with you isn't that much of a hardship. I happen to enjoy your waspish ways."

"My waspish ways?" She put her hands on her hips. "What's that supposed to—"

"Uh-uh." Laughter was heavy in his voice. "You can't apologize and ruin it by doing the same thing you just apologized for."

She blew out a long breath. "Fine. Let's get my computer. I'll try to be nice."

"Don't try too hard. Then you wouldn't be your sweet, stubborn self."

"Now who's being 'waspish'?"

He laughed. "I guess you're rubbing off on me." His smile faded. "Stay behind me until I check everything out."

She raised her hand and saluted him. "Yes, sir."

He rolled his eyes and opened the door. He immediately held his hand out to stop her. "Hold it."

"The alarm is beeping. I have to key in the code before it goes off."

"I'll get it. Wait here." He stepped farther into the foyer to the keypad.

She looked down and saw what he'd seen, a white sheet of paper on the floor. Someone must have slipped it under the door. She leaned down to pick it up.

"Don't touch it." He grabbed her hand and tugged her with him back onto the porch. He squatted down to look at the note. As soon as he read it, he reached into his pocket and grabbed his phone.

A sick feeling flashed through Madison. "What are you doing?"

"Calling Hamilton."

"No, don't. *Please* don't call him. Can't we just ignore this? It's not like he'll figure out who left the note anyway, or how they left it. He'll just assume I'm a nutcase, or worse, arrest me like he threatened."

"He won't arrest you. Even he can't ignore this."

His worry began to filter into her. She leaned over his shoulder to read the words printed on the sheet of paper.

*I'M COMING FOR YOU.*

MADISON JUMPED UP from the wing chair across from Lieutenant Hamilton.

"We're nowhere near to being finished here," he said.

She waved her hand toward Pierce, who was sitting beside Hamilton on the couch, and the three uniformed policemen milling around her family room.

"I don't think I have to worry about my safety inside the house with all of these guns sitting around. I'm just going to the kitchen to make us some coffee."

"It's not your safety I'm concerned about. I don't want you finding another note for me to look into."

"Knock it off," Pierce said. "Madison didn't have an opportunity to leave that note. She's not the one who wrote it."

"Typed it you mean."

"So, your theory is she printed it while I wasn't looking and shoved it under the door? *Again, while I wasn't looking?*"

"You said you brought her here to pack her things yesterday. Were you with her every moment? I assume you carried her luggage to the car. Did she wait inside, maybe make that last-minute check women like to do, to see if she'd gotten everything while you were outside at the car? And was she the last one out the door?"

Pierce didn't answer.

"That's what I thought."

While Pierce and Hamilton were busy arguing, Madison headed into the kitchen. She pulled the pocket door closed behind her. But it only slightly dampened the sound of angry voices coming from the other room.

No surprise, Lieutenant Hamilton was playing the same old tune. He was convinced she was some nutcase who wanted attention. At least he hadn't arrested her, yet.

She grabbed the coffee can and filters out of the pantry, then slumped against the counter. Maybe he was right. Maybe she *was* losing her mind. Nothing in her life seemed to make sense anymore. And she was getting so tired of arguing, of trying to make everyone believe her, to listen to her.

She was starting not to even believe herself.

For the first time since calling Logan the day of the shooting, she seriously considered calling him and telling him everything that was going on. He was one of the smartest men she'd ever met. He'd be able to help her, wouldn't he?

She rested her elbows on the countertop and dropped her head in her hands. Logan was smart, yes. He'd be able to help, but then . . . his curiosity would drive him to keep digging, and digging, and then, when he dug far enough, he'd know her secrets.

What would happen then? No matter how hard she tried to think of a good outcome, she couldn't. No, she couldn't tell him. Not now, not ever. And somehow, she had to keep Pierce from finding out.

Before he destroyed her.

"If you're not going to have forensics look at that note, then give it to me," Pierce said. "I'll look into it. I want whoever is stalking Madison to stop."

Lieutenant Hamilton flipped the plastic baggie over on the coffee table to see the back of the note that was inside. "I want all of this to stop too. We just have different views about how to make it stop."

Pierce was suffering many of the same doubts as the lieutenant. But until he knew for sure what was going on, he had to play devil's advocate, and make sure Hamilton saw all the possibilities. "What does she have to gain by faking any of this?"

Hamilton handed the sealed baggie with the note to one of the policemen to record into evidence. "That's a good question. Since you two seem so cozy, maybe you can help me figure that out. Tell me about her. Should I trust what she says? Has she ever lied to you?"

Pierce started to say "no," but he couldn't very well do that without lying himself.

"Uh-huh," Hamilton said.

"She wouldn't lie about that note, or about seeing Damon at the yardman's house, or about *thinking* it was her supposedly dead husband who shot at her in the park. There wouldn't be any reason to lie."

"Look, you know the long hours involved with law enforcement. We're overworked, and we never have enough time in a day to take care of what needs to be done. In spite of that, my team has responded every time Mrs. McKinley called. We've looked into every single complaint. But so far, other than you getting nicked in the park the other day, none of the calls have amounted to any real, verifiable threats. I can't keep investing my department's resources on wild-goose chases, not when I have some 'Simon says' nut killing people and the press hounding me every day."

"Has there been another murder, since that kid on East River Street?"

"Not yet, but you and I both know there will be if I don't stop whoever is behind this. I tapped your boss for help just this morning. He's analyzing the 'Simon says' notes, and helping us profile the killer. I've got every business in the historic district after me to arrest someone. The tourism business has plummeted. That's my focus right now."

"Meaning you're dismissing Madison's stalker. You aren't going to take this latest note seriously."

Hamilton shook his head. "Exactly the opposite. I'm going to this note *very* seriously. I can't afford to keep splitting my resources like this, so I'm going to throw some manpower at her supposed stalker to get this wrapped up. I'm going to figure out where the paper the note was printed on came from, where the ink came from, the type of printer that printed it, who bought the printer that printed the note, and finally, the computer that was used to compose the note. And then, I'll arrest whoever typed it. It just so happens that I believe I'm going to find out that Mrs. McKinley typed it on her computer, printed it on her printer, and she planted it under her front door as she was leaving with you yesterday so you could find it today."

"Why? Why would she do that?"

"I don't know. Has it occurred to you the woman needs help? Mental help?"

Pierce shoved off the couch and paced in front of Hamilton. "You've totally lost perspective on this case."

The lieutenant shrugged. "Some might say it's you who has lost their perspective. Alex told me that you and Mrs. McKinley used to date, that you were quite serious at one point."

Pierce stopped in front of him. "You have no business talking to Alex about my past."

"He's worried about you, and he has the same doubts about Mrs. McKinley that I do. As soon as it's a decent hour, I'm calling a judge for a search warrant. Until then, I'll have Officer Drayton"—he nodded at the policeman to his immediate right—"ensure Mrs. McKinley doesn't destroy any evidence."

Pierce swore and headed through the archway into Madison's home office. He stood at the window, looking out onto the street. He took a bracing breath, grimacing when his ribs protested. How had it come to this? How had everything gotten so totally screwed up? He stood looking out the window for several minutes, trying to make sense of everything, to clear his thoughts.

When Pierce finally returned to the family room for round two, Hamilton was sitting on the couch, but there was no one else in the room. A feeling of dread shot through him. "Where are the police officers who were in here earlier?"

"Drayton is standing guard out front, to ensure no one leaves with any of the evidence—namely Mrs. McKinley's computer and printer."

Pierce shook his head at that nonsense. "And the other officer?"

"I told him to keep an eye on Mrs. McKinley."

"What are you doing? Are you *trying* to bait her?" He whirled around and headed toward the kitchen. He wouldn't put it past Hamilton to purposely try to goad Madison, to see what she might reveal if she lost her temper.

MADISON GLANCED UP from the automatic coffee-maker when the pocket door between the family room and kitchen opened. A police officer stepped inside and closed the door behind him.

"Ma'am," he said. "The lieutenant wanted me to check on you, see if you needed any help in here."

*Right. Suddenly Hamilton was concerned about her. She didn't believe that for a second.*

She pressed the coffeemaker's ON button. "I think I can handle the incredibly difficult task of making coffee all by myself. Thanks anyway."

When he made no move to leave, she leaned back against the counter. "Was there something else?"

He leaned back against the counter across from her, on the opposite side of the galley-style kitchen. "Just following orders, ma'am. I'm supposed to stay with you, until the lieutenant says otherwise."

She straightened and tapped her fingernails on the countertop. "Is that so?"

"Yes, ma'am."

"How old are you?"

"Pardon?"

"You seem a bit young to be hard of hearing. I asked . . . How old are you?"

His brows drew down. "Thirty-two."

"Then I suggest you stop calling me ma'am. I'm several years younger than you, *sir*."

She turned and yanked open a cabinet to get some coffee cups.

"Let me help you with that, *ma'am*." The police officer stepped forward.

Madison stepped in his way. "What did you just call me?"

"Do we have a problem, here?" He took another step closer, crowding her.

She poked him in the chest. "The only *problem* I have is some policeman standing in my kitchen, watching my every move as if I were a criminal. Back. Off."

"I don't think you want to do that, ma'am," the officer said, grabbing her hand.

"Let me go," she gritted out between clenched teeth, "or I promise you'll regret it."

"Is that a threat?" he reached behind his back.

She tugged her hand out of his grasp, ready to give him hell.

The pocket door slid open and Pierce stepped inside. His eyes widened, then narrowed when he saw the two of them. "Get your hands off your weapon, officer." He stepped between the policeman and Madison, using his bigger bulk and height as a shield. "Now." His voice was low and deadly.

"Mrs. McKinley just threatened an officer of the law, sir."

"Oh, *now* he calls me Mrs. McKinley," Madison grumbled.

"Madison?"

"Yes, Pierce?"

"Shut up."

Her anger left her in a rush. She couldn't help but grin. Prim and proper Pierce Buchanan had probably never told anyone to shut up in his entire life.

Hamilton stepped into the room, his brows climbing as he took in the stand-off between Pierce and the police officer. "What's going on here?" He jerked his thumb over his shoulder and glared at his officer. "Go stay with Williams."

"Yes, sir." The officer left the room, looking relieved.

"You'd better keep a tighter rein on your men," Pierce warned. Without waiting for Hamilton's response, he grabbed Madison's hand. "Come, on. Let's wait in the family room."

She half-ran behind him to keep up. "Wait for what? I've already answered Hamilton's questions. He has the note. He should leave now."

Pierce glanced at his watch. "In about another hour, he's going to make a call, to a judge."

She plopped down on one of the couches, starting to feel nervous at the expression on his face. "And what happens after he makes this call?"

"All hell breaks loose."

MADISON SAT ON the end of the couch, as far away from Lieutenant Hamilton as she could. The uniformed police officers were sitting in her home office now, instead of the family room, at Pierce's insistence. He, Hamilton, and Madison were sitting in the family room. Madison was pretty sure he'd done that to keep her from slugging one of them and being hauled off to jail.

One of these days she was going to have to get her temper under control.

The doorbell rang. Both Hamilton and Pierce jumped up and headed out of the family room into the foyer. Madison clenched her fists, determined not to let her emotions get the best of her. She knew what that doorbell meant.

Hamilton's warrant had come through.

He was going to take her computer and her printer. And there wasn't anything she could do about it. It was ludicrous that someone would think she'd had anything to do with those threatening notes. Why would she do that? It made no sense.

Hamilton gave her a smug look as he headed back through the family room with a white piece of paper in his hand. He slapped it into Pierce's palm before going into Madison's home office.

Pierce sat down next to her. "I guess I don't have to tell you the search warrant came through. Want to see it?" He held up the piece of paper.

"No thanks."

He slid the paper into the inside pocket of his jacket just as the doorbell rang again.

Madison jumped up, but Pierce placed his hand firmly on her shoulder. "I'll get it. Stay here."

She plopped back down on the couch.

Pierce disappeared back into the foyer. The sound of several voices, familiar voices, had Madison jumping off the couch and heading into the foyer as well.

Pierce gave her an exasperated look when she joined him, but he didn't try to stop her.

Braedon and Matt stood in the open doorway, and Madison could see several work trucks behind them, and a group of men unloading equipment off the trucks.

"Are you here to dig the footers? I thought you weren't coming until next week," she said.

"We had a cancellation," Braedon said. "Figured we could fit your project into the schedule today, if you don't mind."

"We do mind," Pierce said.

"No, we don't," Madison said. "I appreciate you fitting me in. Come on. I'll get you some coffee. I could use some friendly company around here. And then you can start right in on the footers. There's no reason not to."

"What's going on here?" Hamilton stepped out of the front room.

Madison took Braedon's arm and tugged him toward

the kitchen. "None of your business." She offered him a smirk. "Come on Matt. I just made a fresh pot."

Braedon glanced back at Pierce and grinned. "Sorry, little brother. Can't disappoint the lady. Matt, you heard her. Come on."

Pierce shook his head at her, but he stepped in front of the lieutenant to provide interference.

Madison headed into the kitchen and grabbed two fresh cups.

Braedon and Matt leaned against the far counter.

"What's with all the police cars out front?" Braedon asked.

"Part of the continuing saga of my stalker problem. How do you take your coffee?" She reached for the cream and sugar.

"Black," Matt said.

"Me too. What do you mean your stalker problem? In addition to the vandalism, someone's after you?"

She handed each of them a cup of coffee and leaned back against the sink. "Someone left a threatening note. It's not the first one. Pierce thinks I should leave town."

"Maybe you should," Matt offered. "At least until they catch whoever is doing this."

"It's not that simple."

"Why not?"

"Good question." Pierce's deep voice sounded from the doorway. "I think it's time to cancel your renovations and leave until everything settles down." From the angry look on his face and his sharp tone, Madison figured his latest encounter with Hamilton hadn't gone well.

She frowned. "If I run away, it's not going to fix any-thing."

"When's the last time you ever stayed in one place more than a few months? You were living out of motels, traveling all over the country when I met you. And from what Logan told me, that was the norm."

The anger in his tone had her clenching her fists. "Well, it's not the norm now. I'm tired of not having a real home, not having any roots. Maybe I've finally found the place where I belong."

He cocked a brow. "Belong? Here? In case you haven't noticed, there's no Ritz-Carlton around here, no Metro-politan Opera house."

She sucked in a sharp breath. "That's not fair."

"Isn't it? Where's the excitement for someone like you in a small, lazy town on the river?"

Was that what he thought of her? That she was a big city snob and couldn't be happy in a small town? Or was it more personal? Maybe he just didn't want her in *his* town. Well, tough. She wasn't letting him, or anyone else, force her to do anything she didn't want to do. She crossed her arms over her chest. "I'm. Not. Leaving."

His brows drew down in a deep slash. "When you should stay, you don't. When you should leave, like now, you dig in and fight tooth and nail. Why do you always have to make everything harder than it has to be?"

Braedon glanced back and forth between them. "Um, guys, shouldn't we be discussing the stalker?"

Pierce scrubbed his hands over his face, as if he were trying to calm down. "You need to leave town, Madison.

Let me handle the investigation. When it's all clear, you can come back then."

"No. I want to face . . . this person, whoever he is, and end it—now, rather than spend the rest of my life wondering and worrying."

"You're not going anywhere." Hamilton stepped up behind Pierce. "Not until I get the forensics on that note and your computer. I want you to stay in town."

Pierce frowned at him, but before he could say anything, the doorbell rang again.

"Who the hell is it now?" He shoved past Hamilton back into the family room. A few seconds later, he came back, his expression grim. "The B-and-B team found more vandalism in the backyard."

The house quickly emptied, with everyone heading around to the back of the house. Madison would have gone with them, but Pierce's harshly whispered command to stay inside had her sitting in the front room. And even if she did want to disobey his Neanderthal order, Hamilton had posted Officer Williams on the porch to make sure she couldn't leave the house.

## Chapter Fifteen

PIERCE STEPPED OVER the ruined valves that controlled the sprinkler system, and stood on one of the few portions of dry lawn in Madison's backyard.

Braedon shook his head, his hands on his hips, as he surveyed the muddy mess. "Someone deliberately cut every wire and broke the valves, causing the sprinklers back here to go nuts and flood the yard. Why would anyone do that?"

"My guess is whoever did this doesn't want you digging," Pierce said. "The question is, are they trying to stop you from digging—specifically—or just from being here at all."

"That doesn't make sense," Matt said. "We weren't even supposed to be here until next week. No one could have known we'd be here today to dig the footers."

"Good point." Pierce glanced around. "This is recent, within the last few minutes. The water has just started to pool around the side. If you hadn't shut it off, the water would be running into the street by now. Whoever did this wasn't trying to hide their work."

"The ground is soaked," Braedon said. "We definitely can't do any digging today. We've turned the water off to the house. We'll have to put a shut-off valve on the main sprinkler line like it should have been done in the first place before we can turn the water back on." He shook his head. "Sloppy work not to have a proper shut-off valve. Just sloppy."

Pierce glanced over at Hamilton. "You're not going to try to blame this on her too, are you?"

He shook his head, looking just as perplexed as Pierce felt. "No, I don't see how she could have done this. She didn't have the opportunity."

"I'll have to go to a supply store to get what we need to fix this." Matt motioned to the rest of the B&B workers. "You all might as well go back to the office, see what other projects you can work on. Braedon and I can handle this mess."

"What are you going to do, Lieutenant?" Pierce asked.

"We'll do what we always do—investigate. I'm not assuming anything. We'll go around the neighborhood, see if the neighbors saw or heard anything. Does that satisfy you?"

Pierce nodded. "That's what I would do."

As Hamilton got on his cell phone, Pierce headed around the side of the house to the front. He nodded to Officer Williams who was standing outside the front door, and headed inside. He was surprised when Madison didn't meet him right away with a barrage of questions about the vandalism. Maybe she was in the kitchen.

He slid the pocket door open between the family room and kitchen, but the kitchen was empty. He checked out the mother-in-law suite, the mudroom, and made a complete circuit of the downstairs.

"Madison, where are you?" he called out, but no one answered. The first stirrings of unease flashed through him.

"Madison," he said, louder this time, as he hurried through the rest of the rooms on the ground floor.

The front door opened just as he was starting up the stairs. He turned around, disappointed to see that it was only Officer Williams.

"Where's Mrs. McKinley?" Pierce asked.

Williams's face showed his surprise. "She should be inside, sir. No one has gone past me except you."

"Search the basement while I look upstairs. The entrance is in the closet in the back hall." He pointed toward the hallway, then jogged up the stairs to the second floor.

A minute later, full-blown panic had him running back down the stairs. Williams was waiting, along with Hamilton.

"No sign of her in the basement," Williams said, before Pierce could ask.

"What's going on?" Hamilton asked.

"She's gone." Pierce headed toward the front door.

"Wait a minute. What do you mean she's gone?"

Pierce yanked the door open and paused. "Missing, vanished, gone."

He slammed the door on Hamilton's next question, then jogged down the front steps. He walked around the house's foundation, looking for footprints, something to explain how Madison had left the house without anyone seeing her. On the right side of the house, away from the driveway where all the trucks were parked, he stopped at the entrance to the basement.

He punched the speed dial for Casey as he bent down to study the ground outside the basement steps. The grass, even though it had turned brown in the cold weather, was still too thick to show any useful impressions. But it was bent back, showing someone had recently passed this way. Or, possibly, one person carrying another?

"Pierce," Casey's voice sounded through the phone, obviously recognizing his cell number. "What's up?"

"Madison McKinley is missing." He straightened. "It looks like someone left the house through the basement, but I can't pick up any distinct footprints."

He tightened his hand around the phone and followed the faint impressions in the grass out to the street where they abruptly ended. "The trail ends at the street. No tire tracks."

"What are you thinking? She left, without telling you?"

"No, she wouldn't do that." His heart slammed in his chest. "He's got her, Casey. Damn it. I shouldn't have left her in the house alone. The alarm was off because the cops were here, going in and out. I shouldn't have left her. Her stalker, Damon, whoever . . . he's got her."

"I'll help in any way that I can. Hamilton won't be

pleased about my involvement since I'm focusing on the 'Simon says' murders. I'll send Tessa over, *unofficially*—as your friend. That should placate Hamilton. But I'll do what I can behind the scenes. Give me the address."

Pierce rattled off Madison's Gaston Street address. "She was taken within the last half hour."

"Get me a vehicle description."

"Working on it." He hung up and headed around to the other side of the house. He expected to see Madison's little red convertible parked in the driveway on the other side of Braedon's massive B&B work truck.

The car wasn't there.

He frowned down at the tire tracks. Again the grass was too thick here to offer any viable footprints to tell him who had moved the car. It could have been anyone.

Even Madison.

What the hell? Had she been abducted or had she snuck out and left on her own? Why would she do that?

He turned back toward the house and stood in indecision. Hamilton was waiting for him on the front porch. The two officers he had brought with him were heading down the sidewalk in opposite directions, canvassing the neighborhood.

Just like they should.

Hamilton was following procedures.

Just like he should.

Was Pierce the one who wasn't keeping an open mind? Was he allowing his past with Madison to cloud his judgment? Was the flooded backyard a diversion? To get everyone in the backyard? His brothers may have turned off the water earlier than the perpetrator would have expected, but eventually the water would have run to the front street. Someone would have noticed, and knocked on the front door to get whoever was inside the house to go around back.

Wait, that didn't make any sense. It couldn't have been a diversion. Madison wasn't staying in the house. No one could have known she'd be there this morning. If Pierce hadn't brought her to get her laptop, she'd never have been here in the first place.

*Unless she'd called someone, to tell him she was there, to tell them to help her get out of the house, away from Hamilton.*

She could have called from the kitchen. She'd been in there with the door closed.

Again, that didn't make sense. Madison would have been outside if Pierce had let her.

Or would she? Maybe she assumed he would stop her?

He shook his head, but even as he told himself that thought was crazy, he couldn't help but think that it made a bizarre kind of sense. Madison had been hiding something from him, all along. He'd known that, and had hoped she'd eventually trust him enough to confide in him.

Was it possible that whatever she'd been hiding from him all this time was something that could put her in jail? That would certainly explain why she didn't want Logan involved. She didn't want her police chief brother to have to choose between his career and helping his sister.

*Especially if she were guilty.*

Of what? What could she have done?

He raked his hand through his hair. *Had* she been abducted? By her *alleged* stalker? Or was she on the run, afraid of what Hamilton might find on her computer? The note had said: I'M COMING FOR YOU. That could be a threat, sure.

Or it could be a promise . . . from someone she knew, someone who was helping her get away, perhaps a lover.

He closed his eyes, surprised at the pain that flashed through him at that thought.

"Buchanan? You coming?"

He opened his eyes. Hamilton was staring at him, waiting. Pierce headed back across the yard and up the steps, sparing Hamilton only a quick glance before opening the front door. There on the wall to the left of the entrance was the hook where Madison always hung her car keys.

Her keys weren't there.

The only way to get the keys was to go into the house. The only way in the house was past the police officer who'd been stationed out front.

Or through the basement.

The question was whether someone entered the basement and took Madison, or whether she'd left the house, of her own free will.

"I assume you called your boss. Did you find anything out?" Hamilton asked.

Pierce studied the other man. No censure, no anger that Casey might be giving him advice, or even helping. Hamilton looked genuinely curious, concerned—an officer helping a fellow officer. Had Pierce only imagined Hamilton was biased against Madison this whole time?

Hamilton was patiently waiting for an answer.

"Casey's still working the 'Simon says' case, but another agent—Tessa James—is coming over, unofficially." His hands tightened into fists. "I found a path through the grass leading out of the basement to the street. I couldn't tell if it was one person, or two. Madison's car is missing, along with her keys."

Hamilton seemed to digest that for a moment. "What do you think happened?"

"I wish to God I knew."

MADISON STRUGGLED AGAINST the cloth that bound her wrists, but her awkward position, with her hands behind her back and her knees drawn up and her ankles tied together didn't give her any leverage.

She was in a car trunk. She knew that even without any light. The fluorescent emergency trunk release glowed in the dark, tantalizingly close but out of reach.

She remembered going into the kitchen for more coffee. Someone had grabbed her from behind. He'd put a sweet-smelling cloth over her nose and mouth. After that, everything went black. He must have somehow taken her out of her house, and put her in this car.

But who? Damon? Or someone else?

From the aches and pains in her back and hips, she knew she'd been in the trunk for quite some time. She shivered, the cold seeming to seep into her bones without the benefit of a coat. But she was thankful it was cold outside. If she'd been left in a car trunk in the heat of summer, she would have baked to death.

She strained against her bonds again, twisting and pulling, trying to get her hands up under her bottom and over her legs to get her hands in front of her. If she could do that, she could pull the trunk release and try to get away before her captor came back.

Several minutes later, she collapsed back against the carpeted trunk bottom, gasping in deep breaths of chilly air. No luck. She was still trussed up just as soundly as she'd been when she woke up.

How long could she survive in this trunk? If she didn't die of hypothermia, she'd run out of air soon, wouldn't she? Or were trunks not airtight these days? How many more minutes, or hours, of good air, did she have left?

*God, please don't let me die. Not like this.*

If someone were near the car, would they hear her in the trunk? What if the man who'd taken her was standing outside? She couldn't lie here and just do nothing. She had to take the chance that someone might hear her, and would help her.

She drew a deep breath and screamed.

TWO HOURS.

Madison had been gone for more than two hours, and Pierce still had no leads about what had happened to her.

He and Matt were the only ones in Madison's home office right now. The police had executed their search warrant, and Hamilton and the others were in the family room discussing next steps.

Matt had surprised Pierce by wanting to help. He'd organized the B&B crew and his brothers, and they were out driving the roads. But in spite of all that manpower, and the BOLO the police had issued to be on the lookout for Madison's bright red convertible, no one had spotted her car.

"It's a lot of area to cover." Matt traced his fingers across the map spread out on Madison's desk.

"I appreciate your help."

"That's what family's for."

Pierce gripped Matt's shoulder and gave him a nod of thanks. He was only just now beginning to realize how much he'd distanced himself from his family over the years as he worked on the serial-killer task forces he used to be on. But his brothers had forgiven him and were doing everything they could to help, pulling together like families were supposed to.

A commotion at the front door had Pierce and Matt looking up. A moment later, Tessa stepped into the room. From the look on her face, Pierce knew he wasn't going to like what she had to say.

"Thanks for coming. This is Matt, one of my brothers."

She shook his hand. "Nice to meet you." She glanced over at the detectives and police officers in the next room. "We need to talk, in private."

"There's a mother-in-law suite off the kitchen. We can go there." Pierce led the way through the family room, avoiding Hamilton's curious glance when he, Matt, and Tessa stepped through the archway into the kitchen.

"Is he coming with us?" Tessa looked pointedly at Matt.

"*He* can hear you just fine, and yes, *he* is coming too." Matt stared at her, as if daring her to try to stop him.

Pierce opened the door to the sitting room that was part of the mother-in-law suite, and ushered the others inside before closing the door behind them. "Matt's helping with the search, and he's smarter than you and me combined. He wants to help."

Tessa shrugged and turned her back on Matt to face Pierce.

Matt, having none of that, sidled around to join the three of them.

She ignored him. "I've got a confirmed sighting of Madison's car at a motel outside of town, just off the interstate."

Relief poured through him. "Let's go."

She grabbed his arm. "Wait, you need to hear all of this."

His stomach clenched. He was already dreading what she was going to say. "Go ahead."

"The car isn't there anymore, but the motel manager saw it, and he verified the tag number when the woman driving rented a room."

"Woman?" Pierce asked.

"A petite woman with shoulder length, dark hair." Tessa pulled a photograph out of her purse. "I personally checked the motel manager's story, and got this picture from the still camera at the check-out desk." She handed it to him.

He stared at the grainy black and white photo, then held it closer for a better look. "It looks like Madison. I'll admit that. But the woman in the picture is wearing sunglasses, inside. Seems suspicious."

"Agreed. Which is why I triple-checked the credit card information. The woman in that photo was driving Madison's car, and paid with Madison's credit card. What was Madison wearing when you last saw her?"

He was holding the picture so hard that it started to crinkle in his hands. He forced himself to relax his grip. "Jeans and a white blouse, with little pink flowers on it. Just like the outfit this woman is wearing."

"This is looking less and less like an abduction," Tessa said.

Matt crossed his arms. "That's just stupid."

She gave him the kind of look someone would give a fly buzzing around their head. "It's a reasonable deduction, based on evidence."

"None of this makes sense," Pierce said. "Why would Madison sneak out of the house and run off to a motel? She's an adult. If she wanted to meet some man . . ." he swallowed and cleared his throat. "If she wanted to do that, she'd do it. She wouldn't sneak around."

"I agree," Tessa said. "Which is why I'm going back to the motel. I'll dig deeper, see if I can find other witnesses. I need a picture of Madison for when I question people. I saw some photographs in her home office. I'll go grab one of those." She started toward the door, but Pierce stopped her.

"That won't be necessary." He pulled his wallet out of his pants pocket. He took out a picture of Madison he'd taken when they were dating, a picture he'd been unable to throw away. Without a word, he handed it to Tessa.

She gave him a sympathetic look, making him grit his teeth.

"I'll make sure you get this back." She headed out the door.

Matt frowned after her. "I'm going to call Braedon and update my map to show where he's searched already." He paused with his hand on the doorknob. "You coming?"

Pierce pulled his phone out of his pocket. "I have to make a call first, something I've been putting off. Be there in a minute."

Matt nodded and headed into the kitchen.

Pierce moved to the window overlooking the backyard, and punched up a number on his phone. The same number he'd been threatening to call since the morning of the shooting.

"Hey, Pierce," the voice on the phone said. "This had better be good. I'm a bit . . . busy at the moment."

Pierce leaned his forehead against the cool glass and closed his eyes. "Logan, Madison's in trouble."

MADISON DREW IN another breath to scream just as the trunk popped open.

SIMON SAYS DIE   213

A patch of bright blue sky had her blinking as her eyes adjusted to the light. A dark figure moved into her range of vision, and suddenly a rough cloth was held over her nose and mouth.

She thrashed and tried to turn her head away from the sweet-smelling cloth, the same smell she remembered from back in her kitchen. She tried to hold her breath as she struggled against his hold. Her lungs started burning. Spots flashed before her eyes, and she finally had to draw a breath.

Her world went dark.

PIERCE REFUSED TO leave Madison's house in case someone called demanding ransom.

Hamilton refused to leave in case Madison magically appeared on her own. He still wasn't convinced she'd been abducted. Neither was Tessa.

But Pierce no longer had any doubts.

Madison had been gone for over six hours now. She wouldn't be gone that long without contacting him. She'd know he would worry, and she wasn't the kind of person who would want him to worry, no matter what kind of problems they had with each other. Something bad had happened. He knew it. He just prayed he could find her soon.

He refused to even consider that he *wouldn't* find her.

Tessa sat down on one of the two couches in the family room to give her latest report to Lieutenant Hamilton and Pierce. Matt was out searching with the B&B

crew. And Pierce had already updated Hamilton about the picture Tessa had from the motel.

The lieutenant was eager for help closing the case, so he wasn't upset at all that Tessa had been digging around. He was a little too happy, in Pierce's opinion, because the evidence wasn't backing up the abduction theory.

"Okay," Tessa said. "Here's where things stand right now. I've spoken to several eyewitnesses who said a woman matching Mrs. McKinley's description, driving Mrs. McKinley's car—as confirmed by still images of the license plate—was seen at the Super 8 motel out on I-95, just south of town approximately thirty minutes after her disappearance. The subject used Mrs. McKinley's credit card to rent a room."

She glanced at Pierce, an apologetic look on her face. "Subject was seen entering the motel room with a man closely matching the description of the man Mrs. McKinley recently chased through Forsyth Park, the same incident in which Special Agent Buchanan was shot. The subject and the unidentified man were seen leaving the motel room half an hour later, and they drove off in Mrs. McKinley's vehicle."

Pierce tightened his hand around the arm of the couch. "If that woman was Madison, she was under duress. The man with her must have had a gun pointed at her."

She shook her head. "Not according to the eyewitnesses."

"He could have had the gun hidden beneath his jacket. Just because they didn't see a gun, doesn't mean there wasn't one."

She put her hand on Pierce's shoulder. "They were seen kissing, passionately, in the parking lot. I saw the still photo from the security camera."

He shook off her hand. "I know everyone thinks my judgment's clouded because of my past relationship with Madison. Maybe you're right. But there are too many things that don't add up here to ignore."

"Like what?" Hamilton asked. He held his hands up when Pierce frowned at him. "I'm serious. If there's something I've overlooked, I want to know about it. You accused me of jumping to conclusions too quickly. I'm just as willing as you to admit I could be wrong. Give me something to go on. There's been no ransom demand, no note, no phone call, nothing to suggest that Mrs. McKinley was taken against her will. And everything we've seen points to just the opposite. So, go ahead, please. Give me something to help me see your side."

Pierce blew out a frustrated breath. "Aside from the glaring fact that Madison has no motive to lie to the police—"

"That you know of," Tessa said.

"All right. That we know of. Aside from no motive, everything else is too . . . perfect."

"Like what?" Tessa asked.

"The motel, for one. How did you find out about it in the first place?"

"I traced her credit cards, found she'd made a charge and went to the motel to investigate. Standard operating procedure."

"Exactly. Madison's brother is a police chief. Before

that, he was a detective in New York City. Madison and Logan are close. I know for a fact that he's discussed police procedures with her on numerous occasions. She knows standard operating procedures. If she wanted to disappear, she wouldn't use her credit cards. And she sure as hell wouldn't drive a flashy, red sports car."

Hamilton looked thoughtful. "When you put it that way, it does sound far-fetched. Considering how carefully everything else was done, I wouldn't expect these kinds of mistakes."

Pierce nodded, relieved to see that Hamilton was at least listening. "The sprinkler system was also overkill. If Madison wanted to create a diversion so she could get out of the house without anyone noticing, wouldn't she have chosen something more reliable or predictable? She didn't have any way of knowing the B-and-B contractors were coming out this morning, or how long it would take the water to go out to the street if they hadn't come along. It could have been a long time before someone actually noticed. As a diversion, the sprinkler system wasn't a good plan."

Hamilton tapped his hands on the table. "Maybe," he admitted. "It could also be that Mrs. McKinley panicked when she realized I was going to get a search warrant. Busting the sprinkler was the only thing she could think of to create a diversion. It wasn't perfect, but it did work. She could have gone outside through that back bedroom, the in-law suite. No one would have seen her."

Pierce crossed his arms over his chest. It was difficult to argue when what Hamilton said made sense.

Tessa pulled a manila folder out of her purse. She placed it on the table, and took out a small stack of black-and-white photos. "These are the still pictures from the motel security camera. They're not the best quality, but I felt they were pretty definitive. You can clearly see the license plate on the car." She handed the photos to Pierce.

He looked at them for a full minute before tossing them back on the table. "That's Madison's car, but that isn't Madison."

She picked up the photos and studied one of them. "What makes you say that?"

"Something is off, but I can't put my finger on it. It will come to me. But one thing I can tell you, whoever the woman in that picture is, she's doing her best not to let the camera get a clear shot of her face."

Tessa slowly flipped through the photos. "You're right. Not one of them shows her full-on. She's wearing sunglasses in half of them, and has her head turned to the side in the rest. All I can say for sure is she has dark hair, the same general build as Mrs. McKinley, and she's wearing the same clothes." She glanced up. "You're not disputing the clothes are you?"

"No, those are Madison's clothes." He didn't allow himself to think what it could mean if someone had stripped her clothes from her body. It hurt too damn much to go down that road.

"Let's say you're right, that she's the victim in this. What's your theory?" Hamilton asked.

"Madison came to Savannah in the first place because someone had impersonated her and fired her property management company. And the person who used to take care of the yard each week has disappeared. Or at least, that's my opinion. Have you actually seen Newsome since we were at his house the other day?"

Hamilton shook his head. "No. But no one's filed a missing person's report."

"Maybe he doesn't have any family to file a report," Tessa offered.

"Possibly. I can get someone to dig a bit more."

"That's a start," Pierce agreed. "Now, why would someone fire the property management company and possibly be responsible for the yardman's disappearance?"

"Because he, or she, didn't want anyone checking on this house," Tessa said.

"Right. If we assume Madison really was abducted this morning, the person who abducted her knew this house intimately. He knew another way inside so he could take her without anyone seeing him. And if we add in all the notes, the phone calls, the vandalism—"

"It's all about the house," Tessa said.

Pierce nodded. "Seems that way. I think someone was living in this house and wanted to get rid of the property manager and yardman so no one would report that he was here. Half the neighbors aren't around this time of year, so no one would even know there wasn't supposed to be anyone in the house. They wouldn't report anything if they saw lights on at night, or a car outside. When Madison came down to check on the house, and ended up staying, the man who'd been living here decided to try to inconvenience her enough, or spook her, so she'd leave."

"If that's the case, why abduct her?" Hamilton asked.

"To make sure she got the message," Tessa said.

"And what message is that?" the lieutenant asked.

"He wants her out of the house."

Pierce shook his head. "I don't think so, Tessa. I think he started out trying to scare her away, but now he's having too much fun. He's changed his plans. He's not worried about the attention he's attracting, or that cops are involved. Think about it—if he was still trying to get her to leave, so he could live in the house, he's ensured that's not feasible by involving the police. He could never live here now, with everything that has happened."

"Then what's his new plan?" Tessa asked.

His fingers tightened so hard on the chair they started to ache. "I have no idea."

## *Chapter Sixteen*

MADISON TURNED HER head into her pillow. She slowly opened her eyes, blinking at the bright, overhead light.

She jerked upright, and had to put her hand down to keep from falling on the soft surface she was sitting on. A mattress, no sheet, on a concrete floor in a small room. Her hair was damp and smelled like shampoo, as if it had just been washed. She was wearing a pair of jeans and a shirt.

And they weren't hers.

Bile rose in her throat at the thought of a stranger being that familiar with her body. Bathing her, dressing her. She had to swallow hard to keep from throwing up.

She shoved her damp hair back from her face, and realized she wasn't bound anymore. She jumped up, then staggered at the first rush of blood back into her limbs. Spots swam in front of her eyes, and she caught herself against the wall.

When she could see clearly again and the dizziness subsided, she looked around, trying to get her bearings. She was in a room the size of a small bedroom, empty except for the mattress. Bars covered the one window, a black square reflecting the overhead light back at her.

A door was set into the far wall. She hurried toward it and grabbed the doorknob. Locked. She tried again, twisting hard, then rattling the knob. She pounded on the door. "Help! Is anyone there?"

She beat on the door, screaming until her throat was raw. Gasping for breath, she collapsed against the wall.

*Focus. She needed to concentrate, think. There had to be a way out of here.*

*The window.*

She ran to the dark piece of glass and cupped her hands around the bars as she tried to see outside. Someone had painted over the glass. She couldn't see anything. The bars were wide enough apart that she could fit her hand between them to touch the glass. She pounded, trying to break it. She took off her shoe and used it like a hammer, but nothing happened. The glass wasn't any ordinary glass or it would have shattered by now.

Trapped. She was utterly and completely trapped.

She turned away from the window and plopped onto the mattress. Her chest was heaving from exertion, and she sprawled backward. Her eyes flew open wide as she saw what she hadn't noticed earlier.

Pictures on the ceiling above her, dozens of them. She scrambled to her feet and squinted up at them, shading her hands from the light.

*Oh God. They were pictures of her family.*

Her mother, smiling at her new husband, standing outside a house. The villa in France, where her mom and her husband lived when they weren't in Manhattan, the villa where her mother was right now.

Above that was a picture of Logan and Amanda, on a cruise ship.

On their honeymoon.

Fear slashed straight to Madison's heart. She'd seen these pictures before, on her mother's social media Web site. Someone had printed them out and taped them to the ceiling. They'd built this prison just for her.

Who, Damon? Why would he do this?

She stilled when she saw a picture that hadn't been on any Web site. A picture of Pierce, in Jacksonville, standing on the balcony at his apartment, flipping steaks on a grill. He was grinning and looking through the open sliding glass door at someone inside. Madison squinted up at the picture. She gasped when she recognized the faint image of the other person, barely visible in the photograph

*She* was the person inside.

She let out a low moan when she saw the next picture of Pierce, lying on the street after he'd been shot while trying to protect her, blood seeping through his shirt.

The message was clear. Whoever had taken her was threatening her family, and everyone she cared about.

Her body flushed hot and a buzzing sounded in her ears. She ran to the door. She rattled the doorknob and pounded on the wood.

"What do you want from me? Who are you? Damon? Are you the coward doing this? If you hurt my family again, I'll kill you. Do you hear me, Damon? You got away once, but you won't get away again. I'll track you down. I'll kill you." Tears streamed down her face as she sank to the floor, curling her fingers against the door.

A sound had her sitting up straight. A footstep, another. Closer, closer, stopping right outside the door.

Her heart was beating so hard she couldn't catch her breath. She waited, watching the doorknob. Praying the door would open, but dreading it at the same time.

A full minute passed. Nothing. No sound. The door remained firmly shut.

She quietly leaned down and laid her head on the cold concrete to peek underneath the door.

Something flew at her, brushing against her face.

She screamed and jerked back.

The sound of laughter echoed in the hallway, floating back to her as the footsteps sounded outside again, getting farther away, fainter, fainter, until she couldn't hear them anymore.

A white piece of paper lay on the concrete. That's what had flown at her from under the door.

Her hand shook as she slowly reached out and picked up the piece of paper. Letters were pasted onto the page, in different sizes and colors, as if they'd been cut from a magazine. When she read what it said, she began to shake so hard her teeth chattered together.

YOUR PUNISHMENT IS ABOUT TO BEGIN.

Twenty-four hours.

Madison had been missing for more than twenty-four hours. Pierce had worked violent crimes long enough to know the exact odds of her being found alive.

They weren't good.

The sun coming in through Madison's bedroom window had him blinking against the harsh light. He'd gone upstairs late last night, so tired he couldn't focus anymore. He'd intended to take a quick nap, but the sun coming through the window told him he'd slept far longer than he'd meant to.

He cursed and jumped out of bed. He rushed through his morning routine, taking a mostly cold shower to try to wake up. Braedon had brought him a travel bag with fresh clothes from his house. Pierce didn't bother with the shaver. He threw on some slacks and a dress shirt and padded in his bare feet down the stairs.

He nodded at Lieutenant Hamilton sitting on one of the couches as he headed into the kitchen for some caffeine. Hamilton looked as bad as Pierce felt. In spite of his doubts about Madison, Hamilton was doing everything in his power to help find her, making Pierce regret the bad thoughts he'd had about the man.

Most of them.

He poured a cup of coffee and took a quick sip, grimacing at the bitter taste, but welcoming the caffeine. He called out to Hamilton from the kitchen. "Heard anything?"

The lieutenant let out a loud yawn. "No, too early."

Pierce took another deep sip. Tessa was still following up on the one lead they had—the sighting at the Super 8 motel yesterday. She was a bulldog when it came to leads, and he had every faith that if there was something to find, she'd find it. She was young, inexperienced but tenacious and clever. If anyone could figure out what really happened at that motel, Tessa could.

Or Logan.

He was the best investigator Pierce had ever met. He could look at a series of seemingly unrelated facts and see the pattern that revealed the truth.

Pierce glanced at his watch. Logan had said he'd try to get a flight out of Italy last night, but he had to take his bride, Amanda, to leave her with his mother and the mother's new husband. Logan refused to bring his wife to Savannah. He said she'd been through far too much to be plopped back in the middle of turmoil again.

Pierce understood Logan's stance, but he hated that he had to wait that much longer for Logan to get here and pitch in with the investigation.

He drained his cup, refilled it, then filled one for Hamilton.

The lieutenant nodded gratefully when Pierce set the cup down in front of him.

"Don't thank me yet," Pierce said. "You haven't tasted how bad it is."

Hamilton laughed, a hollow, tired sound. "As long as it keeps me awake, I don't care what it tastes like. Heard anything from Mrs. McKinley's brother?"

Pierce sat down across from Hamilton. "Last I heard,

he'd just booked a flight to France to drop off his wife. Should've gotten there sometime during the night. Hopefully he's on his way here by now."

"I hope he's as good as you say he is. I'm about out of ideas."

"He is." The sound of the front door opening had him turning around. His brothers, all of them, came through the door, with Alex following close behind.

"None of you should be here." Pierce pulled a chair back from the grouping in the family room so Austin could scoot his wheelchair up. "You did more than enough yesterday, helping with the search. You can't have had more than a couple of hours sleep."

"As ugly as you look this morning," Braedon said, "I'm sure we got more sleep than you did."

Alex shook his head at Braedon. "Matt guilted us into coming. He wants us to work on Madison's renovations. He thinks all the problems B-and-B has had over here are because someone was trying to stop us from digging up the yard, that if we work on the footers, we might find something important that will help with the investigation."

"I should have thought of that," Pierce said.

"We've got a team outside right now getting it started," Matt said. He crossed over to sit next to the lieutenant. "I want to know what you've done so far to find her."

Hamilton raised a brow and glanced across at Pierce. "He thinks he can figure out where she is when half my police force hasn't had any luck?"

"Apparently he does." Pierce smiled his first smile since Madison's disappearance.

Matt went into the front room and grabbed the map off the table. He came back in the family room and plopped down again. "What are all these red circles for?"

Hamilton eyed him much like he would a rattlesnake, but he answered Matt's questions.

Alex sat beside Pierce. "I told them the police probably wouldn't want anyone in the backyard with everything going on, but I think they all feel a bit helpless. If they can work on the renovations, it will make them feel needed."

"I don't see any problem with them working out back, as long as they stay out of everyone's way. The police are finished back there."

"Let me know if there's anything you need." He stood. "Come on, boys. It's time to teach an old lawyer how to dig footers."

## Chapter Seventeen

AT THE NOON hour, Braedon ordered boxed lunches to be delivered from a local café. After everyone wolfed down their sandwiches, they headed out again on their assigned search routes. Work continued on the footers in the backyard, but even though the footers were being dug at a record pace, nothing of interest had turned up. No clues about why someone was so determined to stop the renovations, if that was even the case.

Pierce rounded the house from checking on his brothers in the backyard and was about to head inside when Hamilton drove up. Pierce waited for the lieutenant to join him before going inside.

"Finally got a few hours sleep?" Pierce asked.

"Had to," Hamilton said. "It's hard to keep the respect of your troops when they wake you up in a puddle of drool on the coffee table."

Pierce slapped him on the back. "Tessa just got here. She said she has some news."

"Any news has got to be better than the big zero we have right now."

Pierce wasn't so sure he agreed. Tessa had flatly refused to give him any information on the phone, and she hadn't sounded enthusiastic about what she'd found. Instead, she'd sounded downright grim.

Tessa glanced up from her seat on the couch when they came inside. "You're not going to like this."

"I didn't think you'd come here to deliver good news." Pierce sat down on the other couch. Hamilton took one of the chairs.

Tessa set a file on the coffee table. "We can go over this in more detail later. I'll just give you the highlights. As far as the motel is concerned, the woman in those photographs is definitely not under any duress. I see no signs of coercion, and I interviewed three witnesses that saw her and the man she was with entering the motel room. All three were positive, without exception, that the two were an amorous couple."

Pierce scrubbed his face. "And you believe the woman was Madison."

Tessa nodded. "I believe the facts. None of the facts support the conclusion that it's not her."

"We'll come back to that later. What else do you have?"

She flipped the folder open and spread out a stack of faxes and printouts. "This is the dossier Casey—" she stopped, glancing up at Hamilton, as if she'd just realized she'd said something she shouldn't have said.

He rolled his eyes. "Like I didn't suspect Agent Matthews was helping you two. I'm sure he's focusing on the 'Simon says' case too. Go on." He waved for her to continue.

She nodded her thanks. "Casey dug as much as he could on Damon McKinley. The man is a saint. He doesn't have a criminal record, not even a speeding ticket. He was born and raised in Montana, was well-respected in his community. The only negative about him that I could find is that he had a lot of health problems, and he didn't seem to allow anyone to get close to him. He was reclusive, no friends, no family. No one knew him all that well, but he was generous with local charities and had an excellent reputation as a philanthropist in his community back in Montana."

"How far back did you go?" Pierce asked.

"All the way . . . birth."

That feeling of unease was starting up inside Pierce again. "That's not the picture Madison painted of him."

"He was an entrepreneur, like she said. He made a lot of money, but he gave away half as much as he earned."

Pierce stood and paced behind the couch. "Why did he move to New York if he was such a respected saint in his hometown?"

"That I can't answer. My theory is he got bored, wanted new challenges, new territory to invest in and build his wealth. I'm sorry, Pierce, but this man doesn't sound like someone who would fake his death and stalk his former wife."

Pierce stopped behind her. "Are you telling me you can't find one single bad thing on him?"

"Not so far."

The front door opened and Matt stepped inside. When he saw Tessa, he frowned and strode over to the couch.

Tessa barely spared him a glance. She looked over at Hamilton, who was following the conversation with fascinated interest. "On paper at least, Damon McKinley was a model citizen who had nothing to gain by faking his death. Madison, on the other hand, had everything to gain. She didn't become wealthy in her own right until after she inherited her father's money. Her husband had a million dollars in the bank when he died, money that went straight to Madison."

Pierce looked between Tessa and Hamilton. "You're both so convinced Damon is a good guy."

"I'm not." Matt crossed his arms and glared at Tessa.

"*Was* a good guy," she said, ignoring Matt. "He's dead."

"I'm inclined to believe a woman knows her own husband," Pierce said. "Madison said the man in the park was her husband. I believe her."

"You didn't seem so sure when she first went missing," Hamilton said.

"I'm sure now."

"Why? What's changed?"

"Twenty-four hours, that's what's changed. Something has happened to her or she would have called. She wouldn't put me through this type of hell on purpose." As soon as the words were out, he snapped his jaw shut. The look of pity on Tessa's face had him wishing he'd never asked for her help.

"Why would Damon stalk her?" Tessa's voice was

soft, hesitant, as if she were afraid he was on the verge of breaking down.

"I don't know, not yet. What I need you all to do is keep a few things in mind. First, on paper, Madison is just as innocent and as much of a model citizen as Damon appears to be. There's no reason to assume she's the bad guy in any of this." He looked directly at Hamilton when he said that.

Hamilton gave him a reluctant nod. "Agreed."

"Second, if you turn this around and assume Madison is right—that it really is Damon behind everything that's been happening since she came to Savannah—then he has some kind of motive you haven't discovered yet. There's more to this than you're seeing, than we're seeing. Think about the inconsistencies. There aren't any pictures of Damon. How do you know the man you researched is really Damon without having photographs?"

"I'm still working on that," Tessa said.

"You mentioned he had health problems." Pierce said.

"Damon had several medical problems. Nothing too serious, but one of the articles done about him in his hometown paper said he saw doctors regularly and took meds."

"Madison never mentioned that."

Tessa frowned. "She didn't?"

"No. Did you find his medical records in New York?"

"Not yet. I don't have anything worthy of a search warrant, so I may not even be able to get anyone to admit they *were* his doctor."

"Can I get a copy of that folder?" Hamilton asked.

"Absolutely."

"This isn't getting us anywhere closer to finding Madison," Pierce said. "Are you sure you followed up all the leads at the motel? Someone had to see Madison's car leave the parking lot. What direction did it go?"

"I'm drawing a blank there. I can't find a single person who saw the car leave, which seems bizarre since it's such an eye-catching color."

"And yet, you have several witnesses who saw the car arrive, and it was caught arriving on camera—conveniently showing the license plate as well," this from Matt.

Tessa looked up at him, her eyes half-closed as if she were only tolerating his presence because she had to. "I admit it seems like someone wanted witnesses to think Madison was at that motel."

"Right," Pierce interrupted. "But when the car left the motel, it left in some obscure way—perhaps down a back alley, to avoid witnesses and cameras."

"A set-up," Matt said.

"Seems that way to me. Madison has been with me for several days. She's had no opportunity to be alone, to arrange some clandestine meeting with some man in a motel. And she's not exactly the type to sneak around. If she wants to do something, she does it."

"Now, that I'll agree with," Hamilton said. "I've seen no signs of meek and mild in Mrs. McKinley."

Pierce raised a brow. "You're on my side now?"

"I've never *not* been on your side. I just want the truth."

"So what's the next step?" Tessa asked. "We're out of leads."

The front door slammed and everyone glanced up.

Logan Richards stood in the entryway, his usual crisp, polished appearance only a distant memory. He needed a shave as badly as Pierce did, and his suit was rumpled, as if he'd slept in it. He saw Pierce and strode toward him.

Pierce rose to greet him, but his words died on his lips when he saw the anger flashing in Logan's eyes.

"I asked you to check on my sister." Logan's deep voice boomed through the room. "And now she's missing." He shoved Pierce, forcing Pierce to take a step back. "What the hell are you doing to find her?"

"Now wait just a minute." Matt tried to shove his way between them.

Logan knocked him flat on the couch without even looking at him.

"Don't," Pierce said to Matt, when he jumped up with his fists curled in front of him. "Logan has every right to be angry. I should have protected Madison. It's my fault she's missing."

"Damn right it is," Logan said.

Matt ignored Pierce's warning and pushed between them again. "Arguing isn't going to help us find her any faster."

Pierce froze and blinked in disbelief as he stared past Logan. Logan turned and they both stood in stunned amazement to see who was standing in the open doorway.

*Madison.*

## Chapter Eighteen

"I TOLD YOU. I'M fine. Please stop fussing over me." Madison pulled her arm back from the EMT and rubbed where he'd just drawn blood.

Pierce sat on the couch across from her, unable to look at her. He was too afraid she'd see the doubt in his gaze. Instead, he focused on everyone else in the room while he tried to make sense of the story she'd just finished telling them about her abduction.

Her *alleged* abduction.

"We have to make sure you're okay." Logan put his arm around her shoulders.

"By poking me with needles? Gee, thanks."

Pierce looked down as she looked across the coffee table that separated them. She'd been abducted, by someone no one else saw. And she'd supposedly awakened this morning sitting in her car a few miles away. With the keys in the ignition. She'd simply started the engine and drove home.

It was perhaps the strangest story he'd ever heard. And he couldn't wrap his mind around it. He desperately wanted to believe her. But nothing she was saying made sense. Why would someone abduct her and not hurt her, not make any demands, and not make a ransom request, then just let her go?

"You didn't want to go to the hospital," Logan said, matter-of-factly. "And we have to be sure you don't have any drugs still in your system to worry about."

The EMT capped the blood vial and handed it to Lieutenant Hamilton, who in turn put it into a plastic bag and handed it to a uniformed police officer.

"The cloth he used smelled sweet," Madison said.

The EMT glanced at her. "Chloroform probably. It has a sweet smell. Do you need me for anything else, Lieutenant?"

"No, thanks for coming."

The EMT nodded and headed toward the front door with the policeman who had the vial of blood.

"You said he shoved a note under your door," Hamilton said.

"Yes." She shivered and rubbed her arms. "It said, 'Your punishment is about to begin.'"

"But you don't have the note. Or any of the pictures you said you saw."

Her face reddened slightly. "I wasn't exactly in a position to grab them and take them with me since I was drugged and knocked out again."

He didn't respond to her sarcasm. "You're sure you can't describe anything about your abductor? Hair color, eye color, height?"

"I only saw him once, when he opened the trunk of the car. But it was only for a split second, before he put the cloth over my face again. The sun was behind him. I didn't see any details. But . . ."

"Go on," Logan encouraged. "What else?"

"My gut tells me it was Damon. Maybe that famous gut of yours runs in the family."

Pierce heard the smile in her voice.

"Am I missing something here?" Hamilton asked. He turned to Pierce. "Do you know what they're talking about?"

He shrugged. He knew what Madison was talking about. Logan's gut was famous, among the men he worked with anyway. Following his instincts had solved many cases others had given up on, and had saved lives, including his wife Amanda's.

"Why won't you look at me, Pierce?" Madison's voice was soft and shaky. "Why won't you say anything?"

He lifted his gaze to hers, then quickly looked away. Logan glared at him and pulled Madison close to his side.

"Don't worry about him," Logan said, anger clear in his voice. "What else do you remember?"

"Not much. Just . . . the pictures. That horrible room."

While Madison talked about the photos again, Pierce listened intently, alert to the inflections in each word. She didn't sound like she was hiding anything, but she'd been supposedly held against her will for more than thirty hours. And there wasn't a mark on her. Not a bruise, not a scratch. Nothing to suggest she'd just been through a harrowing experience.

She'd said her hands and feet were bound with cloth, thus no ligature marks.

*Convenient.*

He didn't want to doubt her, but from the moment she'd walked through the door, as if nothing had happened, the doubts had slammed into him so hard they'd stolen his breath.

"How sure are you that the man who took you was your former husband?" Hamilton asked, from the chair on the other side of Logan.

Pierce raised his gaze to watch her when she answered. She was staring directly at him as she spoke. "If I had to swear to it, I couldn't. But I feel very strongly that it was Damon McKinley who drugged me and locked me in that room."

"Did he take you to a motel outside of town?" Pierce asked, unable to keep silent anymore with his doubts.

She seemed relieved that he was talking to her now, but then her blue eyes clouded with confusion. "Motel? You think the room I was in was in a motel? What kind of motel has bars on the window, and no furniture?"

"Before that," he said. "When you first left the house. You went to a motel."

She shook her head, her brow wrinkling. "What are you talking about? I was in my kitchen. Someone grabbed me from behind, held a cloth over my face. When I woke up, I was in the trunk of a car, tied up. He put the cloth on my face again, and the next time I woke up in that room."

"And then you woke up in your car. Right. During all of that, you never clearly saw the man you were with and he never spoke?"

"I wasn't *with* him." She spoke very slowly and clearly as if she thought he'd suddenly developed a problem with his hearing. "He grabbed me. I didn't go willingly."

"No bruises. No scratches."

Her mouth fell open. "You think I *wanted* to go with him? That I'm making all of this up?"

"Mrs. McKinley," Hamilton spoke up. "We have photos of you, or a woman matching your description, and your car, at a motel with some man. We're just trying to put all the known facts together and figure out what happened."

She frowned and rubbed the side of her head as if she was developing a headache. "I don't understand any of this. I was never at a motel."

"Why did he let you go?" Pierce asked.

Her eyes flashed with annoyance. "I. Don't. Know." Her eyes widened as if she'd just thought of something. She grabbed Logan's arm. "Mom, Amanda—he had pictures of them. That has to be some kind of a threat. You need to—"

He patted her hand. "Already done. Special Agent Tessa James made the necessary phone calls as soon as you told us about the photographs. They're safe."

She nodded with relief and relaxed against him.

"If Damon was your abductor," Pierce continued, "wouldn't he have asked for money?"

She crossed her arms. "I don't know what game Damon is playing. I can't speak for what he should, or shouldn't, have done."

"If he hadn't faked his death, he would have had plenty of money," Pierce said. "Especially after your father died. Why would he fake his death?"

"I don't know. Why don't you go find Damon and ask *him* instead of grilling me?"

Logan kissed the top of his sister's head and stood. He looked directly at Pierce. "Basement. Now." His voice was deathly quiet. He headed toward the back hall to the basement entrance, not bothering to turn and see if Pierce would follow.

PIERCE CLOSED THE door behind him and headed down the basement stairs. When he reached the concrete floor, he didn't even have time to duck.

Logan slammed his fist into his jaw. "That's for not protecting my sister."

Pierce stumbled back a few steps, his jaw throbbing.

Logan stepped forward and slammed his fist into Pierce's stomach, doubling him over. "And that's for being an ass. What the hell were you doing upstairs, treating her like a criminal?"

Pierce gritted his teeth and lunged forward, slamming his fist into the side of Logan's thick skull. Logan spun around, staggered, but kept his feet underneath him. "That," Pierce growled, "is for playing matchmaker and interfering with my life."

He ran forward and punched Logan again, slamming him up against the wall. Logan let out a vicious stream of curses and threw himself at Pierce. He wrapped his arms around Pierce's chest in a crushing grip, and they both went crashing to the floor.

Sharp, fiery pain shot through Pierce's chest. He gasped and twisted in Logan's hold, breaking away from him and throwing an uppercut to his jaw.

Logan's head snapped back, and Pierce smacked him in the side of his head with his elbow. They both grappled for control, falling to the floor, rolling and twisting as they fought to get in more punches. They knocked over a lamp, its light bulb exploding into a hundred jagged pieces that tinkled across the concrete.

They broke apart and staggered to their feet. Pierce blocked one of Logan's punches and took one of his own, spinning Logan around. Logan pushed off the wall and slammed his fist into Pierce's bruised ribs.

The pain was immediate, intense. Hot fire slashing through his chest. He doubled over, turning his injured side away as Logan rushed him.

Pierce grunted as he slammed against the wall.

Suddenly Logan let go, straightening and staggering back several feet. His chest heaved as he gulped deep breaths of air. "You've gone soft. That was way too easy."

Pierce threw a few choice curses at his friend. "I did pretty good considering I got shot a couple of days ago. I'd have had you on the ground again if you hadn't sucker punched me in my bruised ribs."

Logan raised a brow. "That's explains the bleeding."

"Ah, hell." Pierce looked down at his shirt in disgust. Blood was soaking through and spreading toward his pants. "That was my best shirt."

Logan stepped over to the dryer snugged up beneath the stairs and grabbed a small towel folded on top. He tossed it to Pierce.

He caught it, nodding his thanks as he pressed it against his stitches and slid to the floor. He leaned his head against the wall, taking in slow deep breaths as the fire in his ribs began to fade. "Just give me a minute. Then I'll get back up and whip your ass."

"Not in this lifetime." Logan chuckled and slid down to sit beside him. He waggled his jaw back and forth, running his fingers along a bruise that was already starting to form. "What's going on around here? You were supposed to take care of my sister, and here you are her worst enemy, basically accusing her of making everything up."

"Hell if I know. Maybe I've been talking to Lieutenant Hamilton too long. Nothing adds up."

"That's because you're looking at everything the wrong way. There are always patterns. But you have to have an open mind to see them."

"I'm trying."

"Try harder."

Pierce blew out a long breath.

"Tell me what happened," Logan said. "From the beginning. Don't leave anything out."

Pierce related the details of the shooting, the notes, the phone call. He told Logan about the missing yardman, the vandalism in the backyard. He even told him what Madison had said about the divorce coming through after Damon's death. He ended with Tessa's rendition about what happened at the motel. He pulled the towel away from his ribs. The bleeding had slowed to a trickle, so he tossed the towel on the floor.

"So, she divorced the bastard, huh."

"Bastard? You knew what a jerk he was, and you didn't do anything about it?"

"Not much I could do except make sure Madison knew she had someone to turn to if she'd ever admit she'd made a mistake."

"Tessa painted Damon out to be some kind of saint."

Logan snorted. "On paper, sure. But in person, there was always something slimy about him." He rolled his head on his shoulders and looked at Pierce. "I thought you cared about her?"

He stiffened. "My feelings for your sister are irrelevant."

"They're relevant to me. I want to know your intentions where she's concerned."

"My intentions?" he asked, incredulously. "My intentions are to keep her out of jail, to straighten out this mess, to find the truth."

Logan waved his hand in the air, much as Madison tended to do. "I'm talking about personal stuff here. Do you still care about her or not? Because the way you were acting upstairs, I have to say it doesn't seem like you care one damn bit."

"I took a bullet for her. That's all the answer you need."

Logan sat silently for several minutes. "I need to know she has an ally on her side when I leave."

"Leave? You just got here."

"Yes, but I can help her more by going back to New York, maybe even to Montana where you FBI guys traced Damon's roots. Unlike you, I've never doubted my sister. If she says Damon abducted her, then Damon abducted her. The only way to clear up this mess is to figure out why he faked his death, see what game he's playing. To figure that out, I need facts, more puzzle pieces."

"You and your puzzles."

Logan shrugged. "That's my talent, figuring things out. You're more the bull in a china shop kind of guy. If I can trust you to look after her, then I can focus on my own strengths."

He raised a brow. "I thought you said I was treating her like an ass."

"You were. That's why I reminded you of your manners." He climbed to his feet and offered Pierce a hand.

Pierce took it, grimacing when his ribs squeaked in protest.

"You have to protect her, keep her safe," Logan said.

"She owns more guns than I do. I doubt she'd like the way you're portraying her like she needs me."

"She does, you know . . ."

"Does what?"

"Need you." Logan headed toward the stairs. He stopped on the third step. "Only God knows why, but she seems to care about you." He headed up the stairs, then slammed the door behind him.

Pierce laughed, a harsh, hollow sound in the now empty basement. Right. Madison needed him. That's why she'd dumped him. That's why she'd lied to him more times than he could count.

He shook his head. Logan was wrong. But, unfortunately, the reverse was true. He needed Madison, or at least, he needed to make sure she was safe. It had nearly destroyed him when she went missing.

He'd survived the twenty-nine hours and thirty-two minutes that she'd been gone by refusing to let himself dwell on the terrible things that could have happened to her, by clinging to the hope that maybe Tessa was right and Madison really had run off with someone. At least that way, she would have been unhurt.

Even now, in spite of all the lies between them, all he could think about was going upstairs to reassure himself that she was really okay. Too bad his ribs hurt like hell; he could barely breathe.

He drew in several shallow, quick breaths, and hauled himself to his feet.

*Chapter Nineteen*

---

"I DID NOT GO to a motel with Damon, or anyone else." Madison crossed her arms and sat back against the couch, glowering at Lieutenant Hamilton sitting across from her. Everyone else had left on various assignments. Hamilton was pulling the typical cop routine of asking the same questions over and over, obviously trying to trip Madison up.

The sound of footsteps had her glancing up to see Pierce coming down the stairs where he'd gone after his "meeting" with Logan in the basement. His face was paler than it had been since the day of the shooting.

In spite of the cruel way he'd acted earlier, she couldn't resist the urge to go to him. The memory of his face, twisted in pain in the photograph on the ceiling of her prison, the blood seeping through his shirt, had her desperate to see him, to touch him, to reassure herself he was okay.

She jumped up and ran to meet him at the bottom of the stairs.

"Are you okay?" Her voice was low so it wouldn't carry to the lieutenant.

"Of course. Why wouldn't I be?"

"Oh, please. Logan had a bruise coming up on the side of his face, and he was grinning like a twelve-year-old who'd just caught his first fish when he came up from the basement. I know you two had a tussle."

The corner of Pierce's mouth tilted up. "A tussle?"

She waved her hand in the air. "A fight, whatever. Totally childish." She stepped closer, tapping her finger against his stomach. "You shouldn't have called him. You ruined his honeymoon."

He grabbed her hand and held it in his. "He's your brother. He had a right to know you'd been abducted."

"So . . . you believe me now?"

His look turned tender, and his eyes filled with regret. "Yes, I'm sorry for being such a jerk. I believe you. I have no idea why, because your story has holes big enough to drive my GTO through it, but I believe you." He reached out and pulled her to him, resting his cheek against the top of her head.

She clung to him, reveling in the feel of his arms around her, the familiar smell of soap and cologne in the fabric of his shirt. She had no idea what had caused his change in attitude so quickly, or why he was hugging her without caring that Hamilton could see them, but she wasn't going to question it. She was so relieved he was okay, and she'd needed this hug so desperately.

When he pulled back, he pressed a soft kiss against her forehead, then hauled her against his uninjured side. He pulled her along with him, nodding to Hamilton as he stopped with her beside the empty couch.

"Where's Logan?" He glanced around the room, then looked down at her expectantly.

"He's gone. He left you a note, said he had to leave fast to catch a flight to New York. Tessa drove him. Logan wanted her to fill him in on everything she and Casey had researched. He's trying to figure out what Damon is up to. For some reason he thinks going to New York will help him find out what he needs."

He nodded. "That's where I'd start too, if I didn't have to stay here to babysit you."

She pushed at him, trying to get him to let her go.

"Knock it off. I was teasing, and you know it." He hauled her up against him again, as if he was reluctant to let her go.

She quit trying to pull away. It felt too good being held by him to bother fighting. After all, she was exactly where she wanted to be.

She picked up the note Logan had left on the coffee table and handed it to him as they both sat down. "He insisted on sealing it in an envelope for some reason. I have no idea why."

He tore the envelope open and quickly read its contents, then shoved it into his pocket.

"Well?" she asked. "What did he say?"

He put his arm around her shoulders, and leaned

down to whisper in her ear. "He said to keep you close, so that's what I'm doing."

Her face heated, along with the rest of her.

"Hamilton, I've been thinking about the woman in those photos at the motel," Pierce said. "I wouldn't be surprised if she's a prostitute Damon hired to play a role."

"I hadn't considered that angle. That's something I can investigate fairly easily. I'll put the word out on the street to check with our usual sources, see if any of the regulars fit Mrs. McKinley's physical description."

"If there's nothing else for now, I'm taking Madison home."

Madison's heart skipped at the word "home," as if they were a couple and his house was her house.

Hamilton looked at him apologetically. "Sorry, Pierce. I want her close by, in case I need to ask her more questions. Can you take her to a motel here in town?"

Pierce looked at Madison.

She sighed. "All right. I'll go upstairs and pack *another* suitcase." She stood and headed to the stairs.

"Mads?"

She nearly melted into a puddle on the first step. She clung to the bannister and turned to face him. "Yes?"

"Don't booby trap the suitcase this time. You know I'm going to search it."

She turned away, before he could see her smile. There was more than one way to hide a gun, or two, or even three . . . and a couple of knives.

MADISON RAN HER fingers across the fluffy white comforter on the queen-size bed while Pierce set her suitcase on the floor next to the closet. The bed-and-breakfast he'd chosen was one she'd always wanted to try out, but not under these circumstances.

He made a circuit of the room, checking the locks on the lone window, checking out the closet, the bathroom, then going into the adjoining bedroom and doing the same security check in his room.

When he came back, he said, "You mentioned on the drive over that you wanted me to take you back to the place where you woke up in your car. I know you want to see if you can backtrack and figure out where Damon kept you. I'm okay doing that, but it's too dark right now. We can head out first thing in the morning."

She nodded her agreement.

He looked surprised. She couldn't blame him. She'd argued with every word of advice he'd ever given her. She sighed. Trying to control her temper, think things through, and accept his help was a lot harder than she'd thought it would be. But she was definitely going to try. The man had been through so much for her. She owed him that.

"Are you hungry?" he asked.

"I could eat. The sandwich I grabbed at my house before we left was the first food I've had since . . . well . . . since I can remember."

His jaw tightened, and he crossed the room to her, pulling her into his arms again. He'd hugged her several times since she'd gotten back, as if he couldn't quite believe she was here, safe.

He pulled back and looked down at her. "It's too late to catch supper downstairs. But there's a bar and grill around the corner."

"I don't care where we go, as long as the food is hot. I'll grab my purse."

He frowned, as if he'd just thought of something. "I'll get it." He crossed to the side table where she'd tossed her purse when they came into the room. He opened it, sighed heavily, and took out her Glock, along with her two magazines of bullets.

She frowned. "How am I supposed to protect you if Damon finds us?"

He shook his head in exasperation. "I'm the protec*tor*. You're the protec*tee*."

She shrugged and grabbed her jacket off the back of a chair.

He narrowed his eyes at her. "That was too easy. Hand it over." He held out his palm.

"Hand what over?" She tried her best to look innocent.

"The gun tucked inside your coat."

She grumbled and unzipped her jacket pocket, then slapped her other Glock onto his palm. "How did you know?"

"I didn't. I just know *you*." He strode into his adjoining room. He returned without her guns. "Now we can go."

"Madison, wake up."

She bolted up in her bed at the sound of a voice next to her ear.

Pierce grabbed the gun she was holding and yanked it out of her hand. "Good Lord, woman. You're going to shoot someone one day."

"That's kind of the idea." She rubbed her eyes and stretched while he unloaded the clip from her 9mm.

"Where in the world did you hide this one? It wasn't in your suitcase. I checked."

She shot him a glare as she reached for the bedside clock to see what time it was. "What did you do? Go through my things after I went to bed?"

"Damn straight. I didn't want to wake up with a three fifty-seven pointed in my face."

She cursed. Damn, she'd hoped he hadn't found that one. She'd sliced the bottom panel of her suitcase and had tucked the gun inside. She shrugged, pretending she didn't care.

"I also didn't want a Colt forty-five staring me in the face."

"Damn *it*." She curled her hands against the sheets.

"For you to be that mad, I must have found all of your guns. Now I can rest in peace."

She raised a brow. " 'Rest in peace.' Interesting choice of words."

He gave her a warning look.

"Good grief." She blinked at the clock, finally able to focus her bleary eyes. "It's only seven in the morning."

She plopped back down on the pillows and closed her eyes. "Why did you wake me up so early?"

"Braedon called. There's been some trouble at your house."

Her eyes flew open. "*Again?* I swear I must be cursed. What else could possibly go wrong? Did it burn to the ground or something?"

"Or something. Get dressed. You've got twenty minutes. We'll go through a drive-thru for breakfast on the way." He grabbed her arsenal of weapons and headed toward the adjoining door.

"Wait." She scrambled out of bed after him.

He turned, his gaze immediately dipping down to her legs.

She belatedly remembered she was only wearing a thong and a T-shirt. Well, let him look. He'd seen it all before anyway. She snapped her fingers in front of his face. "Pay attention."

"I *am* paying attention."

"To my face, bucko. What happened at my house?"

He swallowed, hard, then dragged his gaze up to meet hers. "Your house?"

She thumped his stomach. "You said Braedon called."

He scrubbed his hand across the stubble on his cheeks. His gaze slid back down her T-shirt again, pausing on her breasts, before sliding further south. He cursed beneath his breath and headed through the adjoining door. "Nineteen minutes." He slammed the door shut between them.

She stomped her foot in frustration. She hated getting

up early, hated being ordered around, and hated that he'd taken her guns. Well, most of them anyway. She headed into the bathroom to get ready, and to pull the plastic bag out of the toilet tank where she'd hidden her last remaining gun—a Colt .380—along with two of her favorite knives.

It was amazing what you could duct-tape inside a Wonderbra.

FOR ONCE, PIERCE didn't argue with Madison when she asked him to let her accompany him to the backyard to see what was going on. He grabbed her hand, hauled her out of his car, and tugged her after him toward the backyard.

There were just as many policemen, if not more, running around her yard and parked on the street as there had been when she'd been abducted. Then she caught sight of another vehicle, parked farther down the block.

"Oh no," she whispered.

Pierce glanced at her, then followed her gaze. "I know," he said. "Come on. You're not leaving my side."

She looked away from the medical examiner's van, feeling much less enthusiastic now about seeing what Braedon's crew had found in her backyard.

As they rounded the corner, Hamilton saw them. He was standing with Tessa and a group of officers beside a hole in the ground. He frowned and hurried over.

"She shouldn't be here."

"Where I go, she goes."

"She doesn't come inside the yellow tape," he said, referring to the crime-scene tape surrounding a portion of her yard, up near the house's foundation.

Pierce motioned toward Braedon, who was standing near the back fence along with his other brothers.

"Braedon, keep Madison with you guys until I finish talking to the lieutenant."

"No problem." Braedon smiled and held out his hand. "Morning, darlin'. Would you mind coming with me, please?"

She raised a brow and took his hand. "It's nice to see at least one of the men in your family knows how to ask, instead of giving orders."

Pierce rolled his eyes and headed toward the crime-scene tape with Hamilton.

"LOOKS LIKE WE found our missing yardman." Hamilton held a wallet between his gloved fingers and showed it to Tessa, before showing Pierce the driver's license inside.

Pierce watched the medical examiner studying the remains that had been placed onto a plastic sheet beside the hole in the ground.

"Now we know why the perp didn't want my brothers digging the foundation," Pierce said.

"How long has the vic been dead?" Tessa asked the medical examiner.

"Too long to give you an exact time, or even date. He's been in the ground for weeks, maybe longer."

Hamilton threw out a date. "Was he killed before or after that?"

Pierce stiffened. That was the date when Madison had moved to Savannah. "What are you doing, Lieutenant?"

"My job."

Tessa glanced back and forth between them. "Something I should know here?"

"He died right around that time," the medical examiner said. "Could be a week before, a week after. The insect activity should help narrow it down, but that's the best guess right now."

Hamilton motioned toward a uniformed officer, calling him over.

"Don't do it, Lieutenant," Pierce said.

"Back off, Agent Buchanan. You're interfering with a criminal investigation. I'll have you arrested."

Tessa grabbed Pierce's arm. "What's going on?"

He gently removed her hand. "Hamilton's going to arrest Madison for the yardman's murder." He started to follow the lieutenant and uniformed policeman across the yard toward Madison, when one of the crime-scene techs collecting evidence in the grave yelled out.

"Lieutenant, I need you over here."

The lieutenant and officer stopped, then hurried back to the hole in the ground.

"Did you find the murder weapon?" Hamilton asked.

Pierce squatted down beside the yardman's grave. His stomach lurched with dread when he saw what the technician had seen. Madison's quip about being cursed might very well be right. "He found a hell of a lot more than that." He glanced up at the lieutenant. "He found another body."

## Chapter Twenty

Pierce double-parked his car in front of the police station. He didn't give a damn if he got towed. Hamilton had refused to let him ride in the patrol car with Madison, and Pierce wasn't about to let her go into the station without an ally.

He'd encouraged her not to talk to Hamilton without an attorney. But she'd argued that since Hamilton hadn't arrested her yet, she might be able to answer his questions and get out quickly. Pierce thought that was a horrible idea, and he was still determined to make her listen.

He put his pistol in the glove box, then jumped out of his car and headed over to where Hamilton had parked against the curb.

When the uniformed officer opened the back door for Madison, Pierce shoved past him and held his hand out to help her out of the car.

"Sir, you need to back up," the officer said.

Pierce flashed his FBI badge. "I suggest you stay out of my way."

Hamilton slid out of the other side of the car. "It's okay officer. Let him escort her inside. Then we'll take her to interrogation."

Pierce took Madison's hand, bracing himself for the fear he knew he'd see in her eyes. She held on to him, stood, then looked up.

She wasn't afraid. She was furious. Her brows were dark slashes, and her blue eyes had turned almost black.

"When this is over," she said, "I'm going to go all high school on Hamilton."

Some of the tightness in his chest eased when he saw she still had her flash and fire. "What exactly does 'go all high school' mean?"

"Give me a dozen eggs and a roll of toilet paper, and I'll show you."

He laughed and turned with her toward the station.

Hamilton was frowning as he watched them.

Madison blew him a kiss.

"For the love of . . . stop baiting him," Pierce whispered harshly. "You need to take all this a bit more seriously."

"Oh, I am. Trust me. I am seriously considering all the ways I can make Hamilton's life hell when I get out of here."

He shook his head, at a loss for words. Madison was like a force of nature, and he still hadn't figured out how to contain her.

Hamilton and the uniformed police officer reached them just as Pierce held the door open for Madison.

She started to go inside, then her eyes widened, and she backed up, pulling Pierce with her.

"Mrs. McKinley," Hamilton said, "you have to—"

"Give us a minute," she said. "Just one minute." She took a deep breath and smiled. "Please."

He crossed his arms. "Make it quick."

She tugged Pierce over to the shrubs a few feet from the front door, and turned her back on the police.

"What's going on?" Pierce asked.

Madison looked over her shoulder, then shifted so her back was directly to Hamilton. She reached up and pulled Pierce's head down to her. "There's a metal detector in there," she whispered.

"Well, yes, of course. Why do you . . . ah hell. You have a gun don't you?"

"A girl has to protect herself."

"Where is it?" he growled.

She reached into her bra and pulled out a Colt .380 with a piece of silver tape on it.

Pierce couldn't help but be impressed. "Duct tape. Clever. I should have thought of that." He grabbed the gun and shoved it into his pants pocket. "Do you have a machine gun in there too?"

"No, but I do have a knife . . . or two. Give me a second." She started unbuttoning her blouse.

"Oh, for the love of . . . you're going to be the death of me woman." He opened his jacket and stepped in front of her to shield her from anyone watching from the street.

"Hey, what's going on?" Hamilton took a step toward them just as Madison pulled two pieces of duct tape from the inside of her blouse, concealing two small pocket-knives.

Pierce grabbed them and shoved them in his other pants pocket just as Hamilton reached them. He stepped around her, blocking Hamilton's view while Madison buttoned her shirt.

She turned around and pressed her hand lightly against Pierce's chest. "Don't mind us, Lieutenant. We were just saying good-bye." She leaned up and tugged his head down so she could press a kiss against his cheek. "See you inside."

Hamilton looked thoroughly confused as Madison swept past him.

"Want to explain what that was all about?"

Pierce shook his head. "Actually, no, I *really* don't."

Hamilton opened the door. "Are you coming?"

"I'll catch up in a few minutes."

He shrugged and went inside.

"What did I miss?" Casey called out, hurrying up the front walk toward Pierce.

"It's about time. I called you half an hour ago."

"Excuse me. Been a bit busy with the 'Simon says' case."

"Any leads?"

"Not that have panned out. When you're finished with this stalker business, maybe I can bribe you to work one more serial-killer case." He glanced around. "Where's Mrs. McKinley? You said Hamilton was arresting her?"

"I talked him out of arresting her, for now, but only if she'd answer a few questions. I wanted her to wait for a lawyer, but she's convinced she can talk Hamilton into letting her go."

"Big mistake."

"Tell me about it."

"So, she's inside?" Casey started toward the front door.

"Hold on a minute." He reached into his pockets and grabbed the Colt .380 and knives. "Here, hold these." He shoved the weapons into Casey's hand, and tossed him his keys as he ran toward the door. "Mind moving my car? I'm double-parked."

He didn't wait for Casey's answer.

"YOU'RE LUCKY I didn't let your car get towed after that stunt." Casey stepped into the interrogation booth, joining Pierce.

Pierce watched Madison through the two-way glass. "She waived her right to an attorney. I couldn't convince her otherwise. You'd think the sister of a cop would know better. She's too stubborn for her own good. She thinks that because she hasn't done anything, she shouldn't be worried."

Casey raised a brow. "Theoretically, she's right. Innocent until proven guilty."

"Tell that to all the innocent people in prison." He turned back to the glass, then grimaced at one of her sarcastic responses. "If she doesn't really kill someone by the time this is over, it will be a miracle."

Madison clasped her hands together beneath the scarred wooden table. It was either that or slug the detective sitting across from her. Since her goal was to stay *out* of prison, hitting him definitely didn't seem like the way to go.

No matter how satisfying hitting that smirk off his face would be.

Lieutenant Hamilton had already questioned her. Now she was sitting across from another detective answering the same questions over and over.

Her patience shredded a little more with each repeated question. She was beginning to understand how someone could confess to a crime just to end an interrogation, even if they were innocent.

She glanced at the dark rectangle of glass that took up half the wall behind the detective. Was anyone behind that glass watching her? Probably, and if she had to guess she'd bet it was Lieutenant Hamilton, watching her every move. He hadn't tried to hide the fact that he didn't believe her story.

"Mrs. McKinley? Would you answer the question please?"

She squeezed her hands together so hard her knuckles throbbed. Forcing a smile, she focused on the young detective in front of her. "I'm sorry. What was the question?"

"I asked how long you've been a widow. When did your husband die?"

Her stomach jumped at this new line of questioning. "How is that relevant?"

"Background questions. Standard procedure, ma'am."

She drew a deep breath. "Over a year now, almost a year and a half."

He scribbled on the notepad in front of him. "How did he die?"

She glanced at the bottle of water in front of her. Her mouth was dry from all this useless talking, and she longed for that water. But she didn't want to fall into the trap of needing a bathroom and not being allowed to use one. She crossed her arms and offered him a tight smile. "Damon died in a tragic car accident."

"Tragic? How so?"

"I would think any death is tragic, Detective. My husband was only thirty-five years old. He lost control of his car on a curve and went off the road. There was a fire." She shivered, remembering the policeman standing in her doorway, telling her about the accident.

*And her overwhelming relief that Damon was dead.*

"Tell me the identity of the second body found in the shallow grave behind your house."

She looked at him incredulously. "I told Lieutenant Hamilton, and I've already told you, at least two times. I don't know. How about you answer a question for me? Why would I hire a company to dig up my yard if I'd buried a couple of bodies back there? Doesn't that sound idiotic to you?"

He tapped his pen on the piece of paper. "Maybe you didn't realize how deep the construction company would have to dig for the foundation. Having a slab of concrete poured over a grave is a great way to keep anyone from discovering the bodies buried there."

She tapped her foot impatiently. "Tell me something. Has anyone even *tried* looking into my abduction? Did they trace back from the place where I woke up in my car when Damon let me go? Please tell me someone is actually doing some real police work, that you aren't all sitting around hoping I'm going to suddenly confess to killing whoever was buried in my backyard. Because, hey—guess what—not going to happen. I haven't killed anyone. I'm the *victim* here."

"I'm not at liberty to discuss the details of the investigation, ma'am. Just answer my questions please."

She clenched her fists together. "Did you ask me another question, and I missed it?"

He blinked at her, obviously not appreciating her sarcasm. "What's the identity of the second body buried in your yard?"

She shoved back from the table and stood.

"Sit down, Mrs. McKinley. We aren't finished."

"Am I under arrest?"

"No."

"Then we are most definitely finished." She strode toward the door, but the detective jumped up and grabbed her arm.

The door burst open. Pierce stood in the doorway.

"Let her go."

The detective released Madison and swallowed hard, his Adam's apple bobbing in his throat as he looked up at Pierce. "The interview isn't over."

"Sure it is." He guided Madison out the door.

"What are you doing?" Casey whispered furiously as he followed them.

"What I should have done in the first place." He turned to Madison. "Do not say another word without an attorney."

Hamilton came running up to them, shaking his head in disgust at the detective. "She's not leaving yet. We aren't finished asking questions."

"Yes, you are." He led Madison to the reception area, with Casey and Hamilton following close behind.

"I can hold her overnight without arresting her, Agent Buchanan."

Pierce turned around. "You'd better decide right now how you want to play this. If you hold her, the front-page story in tomorrow's newspaper will be about Savannah-Chatham Metro PD's harassment of a young widow and how they threatened to arrest her when she called the police for help—three times—because a man was stalking her. The story will explain that you're blaming that same widow for the crimes of the very man who abducted her. Shall I continue?"

Hamilton's face turned bright red. "You're being entirely unprofessional."

"I might say the same about you. You're taking the easy way out, instead of investigating these crimes the way you should."

"Go on, get out of my station. Make sure you get her a good lawyer. I promise you. She's going to need it."

MADISON HAD TO practically jog to keep up with Pierce and Casey's long strides as they exited the police station. She was really, really tired of all these long-legged men making her run all the time.

"You just stirred up a hornet's nest." Casey tossed Pierce's car keys to him.

"It was either intimidate the man or let him railroad Madison into jail. We have to act fast. He's not going to drop this."

"Act fast how?" Madison asked.

He didn't seem to hear her. He and Casey continued to talk about the case while they walked through the parking lot, as if she weren't there. The only way she knew Pierce hadn't forgotten about her was that his hand was on the small of her back.

That hand might as well have been a leash for as much attention as he was giving her.

"Guys, I'd like to be included in any plans you're cooking up. It is my life after all."

Pierce opened the passenger door and handed her the car keys. "Turn on the heater and lock the door. I'll be right back."

"Wait, I want to—"

He closed the door, shutting her inside. She slapped her hand against the window in frustration as he walked between some parked cars to another aisle, apparently to Casey's car.

She tried to sit patiently, but the more time that passed, the angrier she got. It was her freedom, her life at stake. She needed to get going, find Damon. And she knew just where to start.

She shoved the keys into the ignition.

AFTER TALKING TO Casey, and getting Madison's knives and gun from him, Pierce headed back toward his car. He was tempted to start calling Madison "trouble" like her brother did. She'd certainly caused *him* a lot of trouble today, and it wasn't even lunchtime yet.

He and Casey had brainstormed on what to try next. Casey was going to head over to the medical examiner's office to see if he could get any information on the second body found in Madison's backyard. Pierce was going to go ahead and take Madison up to the spot off the interstate where she said she'd awakened inside her car after the abduction. He didn't know why it was so important to her to go there when the police had already combed the area, but if it made her feel like she was doing something to help with the investigation, he'd take her.

Besides, if he didn't take her, he figured she'd probably go there by herself.

His cell phone rang just as he crossed into the next aisle in the parking lot and saw the empty space where Casey had parked his car. Without looking at the phone's screen, he took off running for the parking lot entrance to catch Casey before he drove away.

"Hello," he yelled into the phone, as he flagged Casey down.

"I got tired of waiting while you and Casey discussed

my future," Madison said. "Don't worry about me. I found your gun in the glove box. I'll meet you back at the b-and-b later tonight." The line went dead before Pierce could respond.

Casey pulled up beside him and rolled down the passenger window. "What's going on?"

Pierce opened the door and hopped in. "Madison stole my car."

Casey started laughing. "I suppose that was her on the phone."

Pierce shoved his phone into his jacket pocket. "Take me up to the spot off I-95 where the police searched for Damon."

"Is that where she said she was going?"

"She didn't bother to tell me where she was going. But I'm sure that's where she went."

Casey pulled out into the street and headed toward the highway. "What are you going to do when you find her?"

He tightened his hands into fists. "I'm going to very patiently explain to her the dangers of going off alone right now, of course."

Casey laughed. "Of course."

THE INTERSECTION OF the two rural highways a half mile from I-95 looked like any other highway intersection. There was nothing dark or sinister to suggest that Damon had been here yesterday morning, putting Madison's body into her car.

She shivered at the thought of him touching her while she was unconscious. The days when she'd fancied herself in love with him were so long ago, and buried under so much hurt, she couldn't even remember what had attracted her to him anymore.

Thoughts of Damon had her glancing around, nervously searching the shadows in the trees on the side of the road. Had she really thought she'd be able to find something by coming up here? There wasn't a spark of memory, no images in her head telling her what direction Damon might have gone.

She shivered in the chilly air and hugged her jacket to her. Having the weight of Pierce's 9mm in her jacket pocket was comforting, but she still felt too exposed and was seriously doubting the wisdom of coming here by herself.

The sound of a car coming up the road had her stepping onto the shoulder, behind Pierce's car. The other car was coming up fast, a car she didn't recognize. She stepped farther back, and wrapped her hand around the butt of the gun as the car pulled to a stop just a few feet from the rear bumper of Pierce's GTO.

She released the gun, relief flooding through her when she recognized the driver—Agent Casey. She waved a greeting.

He waved back, an amused smile flashing across his face.

The passenger door flew open and suddenly Pierce was storming around the car toward her. "Adding grand theft auto to your rap sheet is not a good way to prove your innocence."

She opened her mouth to explain, then squeaked in surprise when he didn't slow down. He just grabbed her hand and hauled her toward his car.

Madison looked back at Agent Casey, but he was no help. He gave her a cheeky wave and did a U-turn in the middle of the highway, heading back toward town.

"What are you doing? Let me go," she insisted as Pierce opened the passenger door and pushed her inside. She tried to shove back out of the car when something hard and cold fastened around her wrist, followed by a loud click. She gasped in outrage when she saw that he'd handcuffed her to the inside of the car.

*Again.*

She cursed viciously, calling him every name she could think of as he reached into her jacket pocket and pulled out his gun. He put her seat belt on, slammed her door shut, and strode to the driver's side. He took off so fast the wheels spun in the dirt beside the highway, throwing up a cloud of dust around them.

"Unlock these cuffs." Madison futilely jerked on the chain.

Pierce's jaw tightened. He sped around a curve, then braked hard and swerved down a side road.

She jerked the cuffs again.

"Stop it before you hurt yourself."

"So I took your car," she spat back. "Big deal. You knew I'd return it. Why are you so angry?" She waited for him to respond, but apparently he wasn't going to.

He slowed for another curve then punched the gas again. Every line of his body was rigid.

She was starting to think maybe she'd pushed him too far this time. She glanced nervously out the side window at the trees rushing past. She frowned, not recognizing the road. "Where are we going?"

"Short cut."

"Short cut to where?"

He didn't answer. A few minutes later, he slowed the car and turned up the familiar bumpy drive that ended in front of his cabin. He braked hard, nearly running into the house.

As Pierce got out of the car, Madison glanced at the keys dangling in the ignition and debated how far her arm could stretch. Could she slide over into the driver's seat with the cuffs on?

Too late, her door was flung open and Pierce leaned inside. With lightning speed he unlocked the cuffs, released her seatbelt, then—instead of helping her out of the car—he grabbed her and threw her over his shoulder.

Her breath left her with a surprised whoosh, and she bounced up and down on his shoulder. He took her inside the house, slamming the door shut behind him as he turned off the alarm. Madison's world tilted crazily as he set her on her feet.

She took one step back toward the door when his hand clamped around her wrist and he tugged her back.

"Oh no you don't. You're not running away this time. You're going to stand here and listen for a change."

She stiffened. "I wasn't running away. I just choose not to be here."

He tugged her toward the couch. He plopped down,

and yanked her arm so that she fell onto his lap. She wiggled to free herself. He drew in his breath sharply and grabbed her around the waist.

"Be still."

She froze at the pained grunt he made, immediately feeling contrite. "I hurt your ribs again. I'm sorry. Are you bleeding?" She tugged one of his buttons loose and ran her hand down inside his shirt.

He grabbed her hand and pulled it out, holding it down to her side. "My ribs are fine. It's another part of my anatomy that's in pain from all your wiggling. Now be still."

Her eyes widened as she realized what he meant. "Well, if you let me off your lap, that won't be a problem."

"If I let you go, do you promise not to run?"

She glanced at the door.

"That's what I thought." He sighed heavily. "Why didn't you wait for me at the police station?"

"I did wait. But you took forever, and I wanted to go check out that intersection."

"I was gone for five minutes."

"You and Casey were discussing me like I wasn't even there. I kept trying to ask you about going out to I-95, but you wouldn't listen."

"The police had already checked out that intersection. There was no reason for you to go there."

"Well, you didn't tell me that. See? You *can* talk to me if you try. You don't have to ignore me after all. I do prefer a conversation instead of you ordering me around like a child."

"Trust me," he said, grimacing and shifting beneath her. "I don't think of you as a child."

The growing pressure against her bottom had her belly tightening in response. She licked her lips as her gaze dipped to his mouth.

"Stop it," he said.

She licked her lips again, and purposely shifted. "Stop what?" she asked innocently.

He plucked her off his lap. He set her on the couch and stood. "Is everything a game to you? I'm trying to be serious here, and you're acting like a cat in heat."

She gasped in outrage and jumped up. With him this close, she could only see his chest, and she had no room to back up. She climbed onto the couch and stood on the cushion facing him with her hands on her hips. She poked him in the chest, careful not to touch the side where his hurt ribs were. "You . . . are an ass."

He leaned forward, his eyes blazing. "You are a spoiled brat who doesn't care who she hurts to get what she wants."

"That's not fair. It's not my fault you got shot."

"I'm not talking about getting shot. You don't need bullets to wound someone. All you need is that sarcastic mouth of yours. If you could have had a calm conversation back at the police station, you might have been able to settle that detective's concerns and Hamilton would have moved on to some other suspect. Instead, you had to put your royal airs on and get everyone's back up. Now Hamilton is gunning for you, and you just might find yourself in jail before long."

"My royal airs? I'm not the one going all caveman and ordering other people around. You treat me like I don't have a brain and can't make my own decisions."

"Oh, you have a brain all right. You just don't use it because you're too busy having temper tantrums when you don't get your way."

"Oh . . . you . . . you . . ." She was so angry she sputtered into silence.

"Yeah, go ahead. Curse at me like usual. I've heard it all before. Let me know when you come up with some new insults."

She snapped her mouth shut and hopped off the couch. She marched to the door.

"Ah, the predictable Madison. Running away again instead of facing her problems."

She stopped in front of the door and whirled around. "What do you want from me?" She flung her hands in the air. "What am I supposed to do? Sit around while you decide what's best? Pretend I don't have an independent thought of my own?"

He strode toward her and bent down so that his face was even with hers. "Is it really too much to ask that you trust me? I'm a federal agent. I have experience with abductions and murderers and stalkers. It's what I do."

He reached out and pressed his hands against the sides of her face, his thumbs lightly stroking her skin as his eyes filled with concern. "You might not care about me anymore, but I realized something when you went missing. Whether I want to or not, I still care about you. I couldn't bear it if you were hurt. All I want is for you to trust me and let me handle this investigation. Is that really too much to ask?"

Sorrow and regret filled her. "Oh, Pierce. Haven't you figured it out yet? I do care, too much. I always have. That's why I ran away. This . . . " she waved her hand in front of her. "Whatever it is that we have, this bond, it scares me."

His eyes darkened, and he leaned closer. "Why does it scare you?"

"Because it's all flash and fire. It can't be real; it can't last."

He moved even closer, his hips cradling hers as he dipped down and pressed a whisper soft kiss against her lips. He shuddered against her and kissed her again. "What we have"—he kissed her again, sending butterflies dancing in her belly—"is special. It should be treasured, enjoyed. There's no reason to think it won't last."

She moved against him, heat flashing through her veins as she wrapped her arms around his neck and sank into his kiss. The fear that was always there, in the back of her mind, began to fade. His mouth moved against hers with a sensual heat that sent her thoughts and fears flying away. Like a drug, it created a hazy fog, heating her skin, making her desperate for the feel of him against her.

He broke the kiss and moved his lips to the side of her neck. She arched against him, stretching on her tiptoes to fit her body more perfectly against his. "When you hold me like this, the fear fades."

"Fear?" he whispered, his hot breath making her shiver as he pressed a kiss against her collarbone.

She shivered again, the fog growing thicker in her mind. "Um," she murmured. "Seems so silly right now to worry that I was so head over heels for Damon when we first met too." She pressed an answering kiss against his neck.

He froze, then jerked back, his hands on her hips as he stared down at her. "Damon? You're comparing me to the man you think is trying to kill you?"

She frowned and tried to pull him close. "I'm not saying that at all. I'm just saying . . . I was frightened. We fell too hard, too fast. It scared me."

"Because you fell hard and fast for your former husband too?"

"Exactly."

"That's why you left me? You were worried I'd turn out like him?"

"Yes . . . wait, no, that's not what I meant . . . " She waved her hand in the air. "That's not what I meant at all."

He yanked her away from the door, then opened it and tugged her outside.

"Wait, stop, what are you doing?"

He hauled her to the car and threw the passenger door open. "I'm leaving you with Alex and my brothers to watch over you. I'll get our things from the b-and-b. And then I'm going to resolve this case. After that," he leaned down so his blazing eyes were inches from hers. "You'll never have to worry again that I might turn into the type of man your husband did."

Her eyes widened. "No, that's not what I meant. Let me explain."

But he'd already turned away.

*Chapter Twenty-One*

By the time Pierce left Madison with his brothers, he'd calmed down considerably and was feeling a bit like the ass Madison had called him earlier. She'd apologized over and over for comparing him to Damon, saying she hadn't meant it that way. And now that he thought about it, she was probably telling the truth—that she'd been afraid of her own feelings, not his, and she wasn't saying she thought he'd ever turn out to be like Damon.

But he'd ignored her, because he'd wanted to hurt her like she'd hurt him. And the one thing he knew she couldn't stand was silence. Predictably, the more he ignored her, the more she talked.

And the madder she got.

When he'd turned the spitfire over, Braedon had actually blushed at the curses coming out of Madison's mouth.

Pierce didn't even know his brother *could* blush.

He turned down another street in the historic district on his way to the bed-and-breakfast. Madison's parting shout was still ringing in his ears, ordering him to make sure he got her make-up from the b-and-b's bathroom. Only God knew why he was doing her bidding. It certainly wasn't because of the pleasure of her company. Not when she was yelling like a shrew.

His phone rang as he stopped at a traffic light. When he saw it was Casey, a sinking feeling settled into his stomach.

"Please tell me this is good news this time," Pierce said when he answered the phone.

"Sorry. I told you that you'd stirred up a hornet's nest with Hamilton. He's on a rampage. He convinced a judge to give him a very broad search warrant. His men are at Madison's house right now, turning the place upside down. They're not stopping at computers and printers this time."

"Do me a favor. Call Alex. I think Madison is going to need a lawyer."

"Already did. He took Austin to some doctor. Said he'll be back in a few hours."

"Thanks." He snapped the phone shut and gunned the engine, hurrying back to East Gaston Street.

Madison's side yard was full of police cars and evidence tech vans.

Pierce yanked the car door open and headed across the lawn and through the open front door. A policeman in the foyer with a clipboard stopped him.

"Badge, please," he said.

"Special Agent Pierce Buchanan," he said, holding out his badge.

"Sorry sir. This is a crime scene. Only Savannah-Chatham Metro PD allowed in at this time."

"Let him in, officer." Lieutenant Hamilton stepped forward. "Pull any stunts like you did earlier at the station, and I'll have you in cuffs."

Pierce nodded and offered his hand. "I'm sorry about that. Mrs. McKinley tends to make me forget my manners."

Hamilton shook his hand, giving him a stiff nod. "You're here to see the warrant I suppose. Is Mrs. McKinley with you?" Hamilton looked past him.

"No."

"Where is she?"

"The warrant?" Pierce held out his hand.

Hamilton dug it out of his pocket and handed to him.

Pierce frowned as he read it. "What game are you playing now?"

Hamilton motioned toward the front room and led Pierce over toward the window to get out of the way of the techs crawling all over the house. "We've had a couple of developments today. Remember the printer we took out of this room?"

"Yes."

"Seems that's the same printer that the so-called threatening notes were printed from. The ones she said were from her stalker."

A sick feeling flashed through Pierce's gut. "Same brand?"

"Same *printer*. The exact same machine. The techs said there's something called metadata they can use to identify the exact machine that printed out the note. Mrs. McKinley's printer is a match. And that's not all we found."

"You know that doesn't make sense that she'd print out the notes. Someone else, the same person who abducted her, had to have had access to the house and used her printer."

"Why would they risk discovery by sneaking into her house to print something?"

"I haven't figured that part out yet. What else did you find?"

"Out techs were able to recover several interesting files from Mrs. McKinley's hard drive, files she thought she'd deleted. That's why we have a warrant. Turns out, Mrs. McKinley performed several Internet searches and kept files about a certain toxic substance called Maxiodarone and how it can simulate a heart attack. We looked into her past and lo and behold, her daddy died of a heart attack. The same father who left her millions. I also got a warrant to exhume her father's body to see if he really died of a heart attack. His body is already on its way to the New York City OCME.

Office of the Chief Medical Examiner—OCME. The sick feeling in Pierce's stomach grew. This was so much worse than anything he'd imagined might happen. "I know Mrs. McKinley, and her family. She's not a murderer. And her father had a history of heart disease."

"Okay, I'm a reasonable man. Give me a theory that

makes sense. Give me something I can sink my teeth into. What explains those files? What explains the printer? The bodies in the backyard?"

Those infamous puzzle pieces Logan was always talking about started clicking into place. "I know it sounds crazy, but I think Damon is trying to frame his former wife. For some reason, he wants her in jail."

"Why would he want her in jail?"

"I don't have all the answers yet."

"Well, until you do, I have to go with what matches the evidence. Right now, all the evidence is telling me that the woman you're working so hard to protect is a black widow."

"What? Where did that come from?"

"She searches for how to fake a heart attack and her father dies of a heart attack and leaves her a fortune. Her husband dies in a car crash a week later and leaves her a million dollars. Do the math."

"Where does the stalker fit in to all this? If he's not Damon, then who is he?"

"The only evidence I have about a stalker is a couple of notes printed on Mrs. McKinley's printer. The shooting was self-defense, unrelated, as far as I can tell. I've got no evidence to tell me otherwise."

"And the abduction just never happened, is that your stance?"

"The lab results came back from the blood the EMT drew after Mrs. McKinley's abduction. Want to guess whether they came back negative for chloroform?"

Pierce narrowed his eyes. "There are other drugs

equally capable of knocking her out, fast-acting drugs that could have been out of her blood by the time the sample was drawn."

"True," Hamilton agreed. "But we've all seen the photos from the motel. Mrs. McKinley is having an affair with someone, probably a married man who doesn't want anyone to know about it. She had to lie when she returned, because the police were here, and she couldn't let her lover's identity get out."

Pierce shut his eyes and drew a deep breath before opening them again. "Everything you said can be explained without marking Mrs. McKinley as a suspect in any crime."

Hamilton shrugged. "That's how circumstantial evidence works. Each piece, by itself, can be explained away. But put them all together and you have a mountain of evidence that points to only one logical conclusion. Mrs. McKinley has been lying to the police all along, and could very well have murdered both her father and her husband. And once I get the medical examiner's report on those bodies in the backyard, we can add two more murders to the charges against her."

"Charges? You're actually going to arrest her?"

"Not yet, not until I have some physical evidence to back up my theories. I'm not an unreasonable man, Agent Buchanan."

Since Pierce knew Madison hadn't killed anyone, he relaxed, if only a bit.

One of the technicians stepped into the room, holding a clear plastic bag. "Lieutenant?"

Hamilton waved him over, and even before the tech showed Hamilton the bag, Pierce knew things had just gone from bad to worse.

Hamilton read the label on the pill bottle inside the baggie. "Maxiodarone, the same drug that came back on several of Mrs. McKinley's searches on how to make a death look like a heart attack." He handed the baggie back to the technician.

"Where is Mrs. McKinley?"

MADISON HELD HER hands down on the glass plate while the scanner read her fingerprints. "Hey, at least I won't get any ink on my fingers this way."

The policewoman taking her prints didn't even crack a smile.

Madison took a deep breath, trying to still the tremors that kept going through her. She felt like her insides were shaking so hard her teeth would start rattling any minute.

Other than the day her father died, this had to qualify as the worst day of her life. And the way things were going, she was worried the coming days might even top this one.

"Step over here, please. Face the camera. Don't smile."

Smiling hadn't even occurred to Madison, not when she was being arrested and processed for murder.

The policewoman clicked the camera sitting on the tripod. "Turn to your right please." Click. "Now to your left." Click.

"Follow me please."

She swallowed hard and followed the policewoman down a narrow hall. The officer stopped in front of a door with a thick glass inset and slid a card through a card reader. The door buzzed and clicked open.

"Step inside, please."

Madison's heart was pounding so loud she felt light headed. She moved into the tiny cell, then jumped at the sound of the door buzzing closed behind her. Alone, in a six-by-eight room with no windows, she gingerly sat down on the tiny cot attached to the wall and drew her knees up to her chest.

She still hadn't seen Pierce and didn't even know if he knew she'd been arrested. An hour after he'd left her with his brothers, two police cars had roared up the driveway with lights flashing. She hadn't even been given a phone call yet.

Trapped. The walls felt like they were closing in. Panic bloomed in her chest. The feeling of being locked up, no windows, no way out, reminded her of how she'd felt when she'd been abducted.

She closed her eyes and tried to block out everything around her. She pictured Pierce, handsome and smiling in his gray Italian suit, her favorite—exactly the way he'd looked the first time she'd met him.

Before she'd hurt him so badly that he could no longer stand the sight of her and he'd dumped her at Alex's house.

THE BUZZER SOUNDED on the door, startling Madison. She looked up as the door opened.

*Pierce.*

She jumped up and launched herself at him. He caught her against his chest and wrapped his arms around her.

"I'm so glad you're here." She hugged him tight, then belatedly remembered his bruised ribs and pulled back. "I'm sorry. Did I hurt you?"

He tightened his arms, pulling her back against him as he kissed the top of her head. "I'm fine." He eased her back and anchored her against his side. It was then that she noticed who he'd brought with him.

Alex Buchanan.

He looked far more serious and grim than when he'd threatened her on the back deck of his house the night she'd met him.

"Why is he here?" she asked.

"Pierce," Alex said, motioning toward Madison, "give Mrs. McKinley a dollar."

Pierce pulled out his wallet, extracted a dollar, and handed it to Madison.

She blinked at the money in her hand. "What is this for?"

Alex held out his hand. "Give me the dollar, please."

She frowned in confusion, but handed him the money.

He shoved it into his pants pocket. "Congratulations. You just hired yourself a lawyer."

"You? Why would you want to help me? You don't even like me."

"Madison—" Pierce said.

Alex held up his hand. "She has a valid question, and a valid point." He lowered his hand. "I don't trust you, but Pierce does. He thinks you're innocent, and he wants me to help you. That's good enough for me."

"Do you . . . think you can help me?"

"That depends."

"On?"

"On whether you tell the truth." He turned and opened the door, then stepped out into the hallway.

"Come on." Pierce put his hand on the small of her back.

"Am I getting out of here?"

"We're just going to a conference room. As for getting you out of jail entirely, that depends on the answers you give us, and how many strings we can pull."

"We?"

"Alex, Casey, and me. Alex isn't the only one with influence in this town. Casey has his share, and I worked a few cases back in my time that left me with some pretty hefty favors to call in. Between us three, we have dirt on half the judges in Savannah."

"WE NEED MADISON'S computer." Pierce rested his crossed arms on the conference room table. "Hamilton has it in evidence. Madison said she has files on there she copied from her husband's computer. We need to look at those. And Casey has some fake contracts Damon apparently created. I can get you those."

Alex shook his head. "None of that does us any good unless Damon McKinley is really alive and involved in all of this somehow."

"He's alive, and he's most definitely involved," Madison said.

Alex didn't respond to that. He sifted through the folder of notes sitting on the conference room table. "They've already identified the woman's body that was buried in your yard. Her name was Leslie O'Neil. She's from New York. Ever heard of her?"

Pierce watched her closely to gauge her reaction.

She shook her head. "No, the name isn't familiar."

She seemed to be telling the truth. "How did they identify her?" Pierce asked.

"She had a pacemaker. The police traced it through its serial number. Looks like Miss O'Neil was divorced, estranged from her family, so no one ever reported her missing."

"Just like the yardman," Pierce said. "Was she wealthy?"

"No, although she did have a fairly healthy bank account, at one time. She was a career woman. Started out in computers, then later became a pharmacist. Her ex-husband said she'd been laid off from her job shortly before the last time he saw her. He assumed she'd moved somewhere else for a job opportunity and never thought anything of the fact that he didn't see her again."

"She had a healthy bank account *at one time*?" Madison asked.

"There were substantial withdrawals over a period of about twelve months, beginning almost a year and a half ago and stopping right around the time of her death—which has been placed as about four months ago."

Pierce glanced at Madison. "The same time you purchased your house."

She nodded, wrinkling her brow in confusion. "What does this mean?"

"My guess," Pierce said, "Is that when Damon disappeared he took up with Miss O'Neil to use her as his meal ticket. It probably took him a few months to get in good with her, and then she opened her bank account to him. When the money started running out, he began to resent that you had inherited so much money and he was probably close to being broke. He eliminated Miss O'Neil because she had no more value to him. He may have been keeping tabs on you, maybe in the hopes he could get some of his money back someday. When you bought that house, and didn't move in, he might have seen an opportunity. He was living there, maybe to make it look like he was upper crust in Savannah, so he could blend in with the wealthy."

Her eyes widened. "He was looking for another target? Someone else to con so he could get their money?"

Pierce nodded. "Makes sense."

"But when I moved here, he was forced to leave the house."

"Right, and his entrée into society. You ruined his get-rich-again-quick plan. He probably thought he could make your life difficult so you'd leave rather than face the problems. Then he could go back to his original plan, find a new rich person to con, and his money problems would be solved."

She winced at his "leave rather than face the problems" statement. He took her hand in his and gave her a reassuring squeeze.

Alex flipped the paper over. "Those are decent theories to pursue. But why wouldn't your husband just kill you if he wanted your money, rather than try to scare you away?"

"I don't know."

"The police have already exhumed your father's body and should have lab results any time."

She blinked and held her hand to her chest. "They dug up my father's body?" Her voice was a shocked whisper.

"You didn't tell her?" Alex asked Pierce.

"I haven't had a chance yet." He watched her closely. The blood had drained from her face, leaving her deathly pale.

He got out of his chair and crouched down beside her. He gently pushed her dark hair back from her face. "Are you okay?"

She squeezed her eyes shut. "This is a nightmare."

"We'll get through it." He squeezed her hand again. "I'm not going to let you go to prison for something you didn't do. Okay?"

She nodded, but he could tell she didn't believe him.

She tugged her hand away. "I'll be okay. Let's get this over with. Tell me everything."

Pierce sat back down in his chair next to her, across the table from Alex.

"The chief medical examiner in New York is reviewing your father's case right now," Alex said. "Your father had congestive heart failure. He was on Digoxin?"

"Yes."

"The medical examiner said your father's EKG from the hospital had a specific pattern called torsade de pointes. He said that's something he'd expect to see if there was some kind of drug interaction."

Her brow wrinkled in confusion. "Wait . . . that's not . . . are you saying my father's doctor made some kind of mistake? He gave my father medicine that caused his heart attack?"

"I'm not saying that at all. I'm just stating what the report says. The medical examiner is reviewing the records and performing tests on your father's body. We'll find out more once he's finished with his review." He flipped a page. "Now, onto the next item. Metro PD has some fairly damning circumstantial evidence against you, but as long as the medical examiner rules your father's death was indeed by natural causes, you have nothing to worry about, at least as far as that particular charge goes."

Pierce studied Madison's every reaction, paying close attention to her body language. There was no sign of relief in her expression. If anything, she looked more worried than she had a moment ago. This was not the look of a woman who just heard that the medical examiner's ruling would clear her of a murder charge.

"What circumstantial evidence?" she whispered, staring down at the table.

"It seems that someone performed searches on your

computer for a drug called Maxiodarone, a derivative of . . ." He squinted down at the paper. "Amiodarone." He looked up at her. "A search warrant was executed against your home earlier today. The police found a bottle of Maxiodarone. When the medical examiner was asked about that drug, he said if it were mixed with Digoxin, it could cause the EKG pattern he saw. And it could cause a heart attack." He put the paper down that he was reading. "Your fingerprints were found on the bottle."

Pierce waited for Madison to get mad, to jump up and argue about planted evidence, but she remained silent. She squeezed her hands together in front of her and wouldn't meet his gaze.

*What the hell was going on?*

"If you have any theories to explain those computer searches or your prints on that bottle, that might speed things up." Alex took out a pen and waited.

Pierce watched her, alarm bells going off in his mind the longer she remained silent. "Alex," he finally said, "give us a minute alone."

Alex glanced at his watch. "We don't have a lot of time if we're going to try to catch a judge today—"

"Five minutes."

"All right. Five minutes. No more."

Alex got up, and closed the door behind him. Pierce continued to watch, and wait.

Finally, Madison lifted her head. Her eyes were bleak, her skin still deathly pale. "I *did* perform those Internet searches. And the fingerprints on that pill bottle are mine."

## Chapter Twenty-Two

OF ALL THE outrageous things that Madison could have said, Pierce never would have expected this. He stared at her incredulously as she sat next to him at the conference table. Could he have heard her right? He had to have misunderstood, but the sick feeling in his gut was telling him otherwise.

He turned in his seat to face her directly, his knees bumping against the side of her chair. "What did you just say?"

At first, she wouldn't look at him. Then, she swallowed and scooted her chair back so she could face him too. They sat with their knees touching, and when she looked into his eyes, he felt a jolt of true fear shoot through his body—fear for Madison and her future—because he already knew from the bleak look on her face that he *hadn't* misunderstood her.

"The fingerprints are mine. I'm the one who performed those Internet searches."

A hundred questions raced through his mind, but it all boiled down to one, a question so terrible, he couldn't even voice it.

*Did you kill your father?*

As soon as he thought the words, he rejected them. He shoved them to the darkest recesses of his mind, locked them away, never to take them out again. He wouldn't ask her that, couldn't ask her that. It would hurt her too much, and he didn't need to ask, because he already knew the answer.

The love that shined through her eyes, that softened her voice whenever she spoke about her "daddy," wasn't the love of a daughter who could kill her father. There was another explanation.

*There had to be.*

Unshed tears made her eyes bright, and her jaw clenched as she looked at him. "Aren't you going to ask me if I killed him?"

Her voice was defensive, accusing, but he heard the thread of pain underneath, the fear that he would believe something like that about her. He couldn't blame her for worrying, after the way he'd treated her yesterday, doubting her story, throwing accusing questions at her.

"I'm not going to ask, because I already know the answer. You didn't kill your father."

The look of surprise and relief that crossed her face had him feeling even more like an ass for how he'd treated her.

"Mads, you've lied to me, and you've hidden things from me since the moment this all began. I want to help you. But I can't, unless you're honest with me. This is it. You've got to tell me everything. It's the only way we can beat this."

Her lower lip wobbled, and she closed her eyes. A minute passed, and she still wasn't talking.

He reached out, gently forcing her chin up so she'd open her eyes and look at him. "You could go to prison. Do you get that? You have to tell me what happened. How did your fingerprints get on that bottle?"

She swallowed hard, and took a deep gulping breath. Wrapping her arms around her middle, she seemed to curl into herself, like a wounded animal. "I told you that Damon had disappeared after we fought, and that he showed up again when my father was in the hospital. When daddy . . . died, Damon was so . . . odd, so . . . smug. A horrible suspicion went through me, that maybe he'd done something to my father. That he'd . . . somehow . . . caused his heart attack. I didn't even know if that was possible."

She twisted her hands together. "I couldn't shake that awful suspicion. He was at the funeral, and he kept watching me. Every time I looked up, he was there. I avoided him, refused to talk to him, even though he tried, several times. A few days later, I was digging in my purse, and I found that bottle of pills. I swear I'd never seen them before. They weren't mine."

"I know. Go on." He tried to put as much encouragement in his voice as he could, letting her know he believed her. That seemed to calm her, and after a few moments, she continued.

"My father's name was on the label, but I knew all the meds he was taking, and I'd never heard of that one . . . Maxiodarone. I knew, somehow I knew, that Damon had put those pills in my purse, and that he'd used them to cause Daddy's heart attack. I searched on the Internet about the drug itself, and how to fake a heart attack." She swallowed again. "That's when Damon called, while I was looking things up on the Internet."

"You were at home when he called?"

"Yes. He was standing right outside, calling on his cell." Her voice was thick with unshed tears, her eyes watery. "I shouldn't have let him in, but I was distraught, and so angry. I'd just found the pills, and I had to know . . . had to know if he was the one who'd put them in my purse, and why, and if he'd killed . . ." She shook her head. "I let him in. We argued. I showed him the pills. I told him I thought he'd done something to cause my dad's heart attack. I accused him of murdering my daddy. He . . . saw my computer screen, and he knew what I'd been doing."

The thought of her alone with Damon, telling him she believed he was a murderer, had cold chills running up his spine, just thinking about what could have happened to her. "What did he do?"

The tears she'd been trying to hold back started running down her face. "At first he denied it, but when he realized I didn't believe him . . . he was furious. He said I'd ruined everything. He admitted the pills were his, that he'd thrown them in my purse because someone saw him with them, and he'd hoped to get them back later, but I'd refused to see him."

She beat her fist against her thigh. "He admitted he'd killed my father, as if it was nothing, as if he was discussing a new suit he'd just bought."

Her eyes squeezed shut, and she let out a choking sound.

Seeing the pain on her face made Pierce want to pull her into his arms, but he didn't have time for that now. The best way to help her was to get her to tell him everything. He gently brushed her hair out of her eyes. "Did he explain what he meant when he said you'd ruined everything?"

"No."

"Go on, Mads. Tell me the rest. What happened after that?"

"It was cold that day, and he was wearing gloves. I didn't think anything about that, until he grabbed the bottle of pills from me. I never saw that bottle again. But I . . . I knew what he'd done. My fingerprints were on the bottle of pills used to kill my father, my prints, no one else's. I couldn't tell anyone, especially Logan, because if I did . . ."

"You actually thought he'd think you'd killed your father?" he asked, unable to hide the surprise in his voice.

Her brows scrunched together and she shook her head. "No, no, of course not. Logan would never think that of me. But he was already grieving my father's death. I didn't want him to go through the pain I was going through, knowing his death could have been avoided, knowing the evil man I'd brought into our lives was the one who killed my dad."

"Mads, you can't blame yourself. And you should have told Logan. He would have helped you."

"How? How would he have helped me? By trying to bury the evidence if that bottle ever showed up? I honestly don't know if he would do that, even if he could, but I couldn't take that chance. Law enforcement is his life. It would have killed him inside if he turned against everything he believed in and suppressed evidence. I couldn't do that do him, couldn't force him to choose between his integrity, and protecting his sister."

She shrugged, looking defeated. "Not that it matters anymore. The police have the bottle, and my computer. There's nothing anyone can do now. I'm going to prison, and the man who killed my father is still out there, free to destroy another family the way he destroyed mine." She choked on the last word and buried her face in her hands.

Unable to bear seeing her in so much pain, Pierce reached for her and pulled her onto his lap. He hugged her tight, rocking her against him until her shaking began to ease. "Why didn't you tell me this from the beginning?" he whispered.

"After the way I'd hurt you, I didn't know if I could trust you. I thought you'd tell Logan everything. I couldn't risk that."

A week ago, he might have told Logan everything. But now . . . hell, he wasn't sure what he would have done today. That choice had been taken away from him the moment the police found that bottle of pills.

The door opened, and Alex stepped into the room.

Pierce glanced at his watch. "Has it been five minutes already?"

"It's been ten." He pulled out his chair and sat down. As if suddenly noticing the tension in the room, he looked back and forth between them. "Did you need more time?"

Pierce looked down at Madison, raising his brow in question.

She opened her mouth, as if to say something else, but then she pressed her lips together and shook her head. She moved to her own chair and sat ramrod straight, staring at the far wall.

What had she been about to say? Was it possible there was still something else she hadn't told him? He'd have to ask her, later, when they were alone—and when she was ready to answer questions again. Right now she looked so fragile, brittle, as if she were ready to break.

Alex skimmed the page in the open folder on the table, then looked up at them. "I'm going to assume your husband did the searches on the computer, and somehow planted your prints on the bottle, or maybe changed the label and switched with another bottle of medication you'd handled for your father." He wrote some notes down. "That makes sense in light of the abduction. The abduction proves he had access to your house. He could have used a locksmith one day while you were out and had another key made, something like that. You'd be surprised how many locksmiths will make a key without verifying proof of address. We'll have the alarm company check out the door to the basement. Maybe your husband disabled the alarm on that one door so he would have full access to the house."

"The alarm was turned off the day of her abduction," Pierce said, "because the police were going in and out. But you're right, the alarm company needs to come out and perform a complete security check to see if all the entry point contacts are working. I hadn't thought about that."

Madison looked at him, and he could tell she was wondering if he was going to tell Alex the truth about her prints on the bottle, and the Internet searches. Of course he was. How did she think he could protect her, help build a defense, if they didn't tell her attorney the truth?

But for now, he'd rather keep it to himself. He wanted to think about what she'd told him, and see how everything played out. He also didn't want Alex to decide not to help her. Alex had never been the kind of defense attorney who would defend someone if he thought they were guilty. He was giving Madison considerable latitude, not because he believed her story, but because he was supporting Pierce.

"Let's discuss the known facts about your father's death." Alex looked expectantly at Madison.

"He had congestive heart failure. He was getting worse, so they put him in the hospital."

"Was he having surgery? Or being treated with medication?"

"Medication. He improved right away after he was admitted. I thought he'd be going home the next day. I had breakfast with him in his room and he was joking around. Weak but feeling better."

"Then what?" Alex asked.

"I left for a consultation with his doctors. When I came back, he was sleeping. Thirty minutes later," she swallowed and cleared her throat. "The alarms started beeping."

"He had a heart attack?"

"That's what the doctors said. People ran into the room, tried to revive him. But it was too late. He was . . . gone."

Alex tapped his pen on the sheet of paper. "So, you were the last person to see your father alive?"

She frowned. "I guess so."

"Hmm."

Some of the paleness left her face. "What's that supposed to mean?"

"Just that it's hard to prove your husband killed your father when you were the last person in the room with him."

She started to get up, but Pierce wrapped his arms around her shoulders and anchored her to the chair. "We have to fight this, together. You can't run from this, not anymore."

Pain flashed across her face, but she relaxed in his grip.

Alex poised his pen over his paper again. "Did Damon stop by to see your father that day?"

"Yes, earlier that morning."

"What time?"

"I'm not sure. Eight, maybe nine. It's probably in the log. We had to sign in to go into his room."

Alex wrote down some more notes. "You said you had a consultation with the doctors. Do you remember what time that was?"

"Around noon, I guess. Right after lunch."

He wrote that down, then shut his folder. "I'll drum up a toxicology expert, and subpoena the hospital records. In the meantime, I called in a favor and arranged bail. Settle your bill with the cashier, and you're free to go—with the stipulation that you remain with Pierce. The judge is counting on him, as a federal agent, to keep an eye on you.

## Chapter Twenty-Three

RATHER THAN TAKE Madison back to the bed-and-breakfast, Pierce decided to take her to his house. She was far too shaky and pale for him to want to answer any concerned questions from the innkeeper owner when he saw her.

He opened the front door of his house for Madison and stood back for her to go inside. She stood frozen, as if in a trance, and he had to gently push her to get her to move. His heart ached for the desolation on her face. She looked lost.

"Have a seat." He nodded toward the couch, and carried the Chinese take-out food he'd grabbed back in town to the kitchen countertop. He set out two plates and some silverware, and put some ice in some glasses. He turned to ask her what she wanted to drink, and frowned when he saw she was still standing where he'd left her.

He stepped over to her and tugged her hand to get

her to sit on the couch. She sat, staring out the front picture window. He was pretty sure she wasn't looking at the acres of trees that lined his property. She was looking somewhere he couldn't see right now.

"It's way past lunchtime. You haven't eaten since this morning. Are you hungry?"

She shrugged, continuing to look out the window.

He tapped his fist against his thigh and stood in indecision. He knew Madison's forceful personality tended to rub people the wrong way, and in the middle of an investigation her temper and lack of tact was frustrating, to say the least. But seeing her like this, so quiet, so meek, had him worried. She was so strong. He never would have thought anything could affect her this way.

"I'll get you some lo mein and fried rice. How about an egg roll? You like those, right?"

She didn't respond. She just stared out the window.

He looked around in desperation. He knew Madison wasn't much for watching TV, but she needed something to help pull her out of the funk she was in. He crossed to the bookshelf on the far wall and turned on the satellite radio sitting there. Madison was a free spirit who loved anything artistic, including music of all kinds. Pierce scanned until he found an upbeat popular tune and turned it up.

He glanced back at her, but she hadn't even reacted.

Shoulders slumping, he headed into the kitchen to make her a plate. When he came back out, one of her favorite songs was playing, but she wasn't even moving to the music.

After setting the bottles of water and plates down on an end table, he plopped down on the couch beside her. He reached over, lifted her up, and placed her on his lap.

She blinked as if only now noticing him. "What are you doing?"

"Feeding you. You need to eat."

"Not hungry."

He grabbed one of the plates and held a forkful of noodles beneath her nose. "It's your favorite, pork lo mein, extra soy sauce. Come on, try it."

She sniffed and looked down at the fork.

"Take a bite," he said. "Do it for me."

He lightly held the fork of lo-mein against her lips.

Letting out a small sigh, she opened her mouth.

A few hard-won bites later, he said, "Come on, I went to a lot of trouble putting all that soy sauce on there. The least you can do is tell me how fantastic it is."

The halfhearted smile on her face was far from convincing. "It's great."

After he hand-fed her several more bites, she turned her head, refusing to eat anymore.

She took a drink of water when he offered it, then pushed the bottle away. Pierce set the bottle down on the table and sat holding her, wondering what else he could do to get the old Madison back. He needed to tease her. Or make her mad, anything to bring back that spark that was Madison.

An idea shot through him, an idea that would either work, or get him slapped. He was willing to risk it. He sank his fingers in her hair and pressed his mouth against hers. He'd only meant to shock her into awareness, but the moment his lips touched hers he couldn't pull back. Not yet. He deepened the kiss, tasting the rich soy sauce, tasting *her*, teasing her until she parted her lips on a soft sigh.

He swept his tongue inside, and pulled her closer. At her lack of response, he finally pulled back in frustration. She stared up at him, blinking like an owl.

Then she burst into tears.

"Ah hell." He pulled her against his chest, feeling like a jerk. "Not exactly the reaction I was going for." He rocked her against him, not sure what to do. He'd never, not once, seen her cry like this. Even the tears she'd shed back at the police station didn't compare to the flood of tears streaming down her face now, as she took in big gulping breaths between sobs.

The whole idea of her breaking down like this seemed foreign. She was a rock. If anything, she seemed too strong sometimes. He didn't have a clue how to comfort her.

A slow song flowed out of the speakers across the room. In desperation, he stood with her in his arms, kicked the coffee table out of the way, and set her on her feet. He put his arms around her, hugged her against his chest, and started swaying to the music.

Relief swept through him when she started swaying too. He took one of her hands in his and moved around the room in slow circles. Her sniffles gradually quieted until they finally stopped.

When another slow song came on, she tugged her

hand free and reached up to lock her arms behind his head. Her eyes had lost their glassy look and were focused on him now, as she moved with him.

"I didn't know you could dance," she whispered.

"I can't. I'm totally faking it and hoping you won't notice."

Some of her spark was coming back into her eyes as she gave him a small smile. "Oh, I don't know. I sense some raw talent here. You're better than you think." She sniffed again, and lowered her head against his chest.

Her fingers started playing with his hair, stroking his neck, sending heat racing down his spine. He cleared his throat and tried to concentrate on the music so that he wouldn't step on her feet.

She moved closer to him, the heat of her belly cuddled against his groin. He stumbled but quickly recovered, trying to think of something, *anything*, but the warm woman pressed against him. The dancing had calmed her, and woke her up from that scary trance she'd been in earlier. He didn't want to do anything that might make her go back to being the quiet, lost woman she'd been a few minutes ago.

*Because that had scared the hell out of him.*

One of her arms slowly slid from around his neck, her fingers brushing down his chest, across his abs. He sucked in a breath when she hooked her fingers in the waistband of his pants.

A trickle of sweat ran down the side of his face, even though the room was on the chilly side because he'd forgotten to turn up the heat when they came in. Madison couldn't possibly know the effect she was having on him, could she?

"Are you okay?" Her lips moved against his shirt, her hot breath washing through the opening between the buttons and rasping across his skin.

He tensed and held his breath before slowly letting it out. "Of course." His voice came out rough and raspy. He cleared his throat. "Why?"

She slid her finger through his shirt opening and touched his skin. "Your heart's racing a lot faster than it should for a slow dance."

"It's a bit warm in here. I'll check the thermostat." He pulled back.

Her hand tightened around his waistband, and she tugged him back against her. "Here, I'll take off your shirt. That should cool you off." An impish light gleamed in her eyes.

He grabbed her wandering hands as she started unbuttoning his shirt. "Mads, don't."

She frowned. "Why not?"

He swallowed, hard. "Because you're not thinking clearly right now. You're under a lot of stress."

Her mouth curved up in a delighted grin. "I know a great stress reliever." She grabbed the edges of his shirt and yanked it open, sending the buttons flying.

Now *this* was the Madison that Pierce remembered.

Grabbing her hands, he stopped swaying to the music. "I'm very glad the real Madison is back, but I'm not going to do something you'll regret later." He leaned down and kissed the top of her head. "No matter how much I want to."

He retreated several more steps, but she followed him, her hips gyrating as she stalked him across the room.

He grunted when he backed up against the wall.

Her fingers feathered mercilessly down his chest. "You don't have to worry about regrets. I won't have any. I want you. Now." She started undoing his belt.

The way she wiggled against him had his traitorous body throbbing in response. He grabbed her hands.

She grinned and wiggled again.

"Stop it," he croaked, sliding his hips to the side and stepping away from her. "Behave."

Refusing to show him any mercy, she grabbed the hem of her shirt and yanked it off over her head.

His mouth went dry as his gaze dipped down to her generous breasts encased in a scrap of lace that didn't deserve to be called a bra. He didn't want to look, but he couldn't help it. "This was a bad idea coming here. I'll take you back to Alex's house."

Her hands moved down to her jeans and she flipped the button open. "The only place I want to go right now is your bedroom. With you." She yanked her zipper down, then shimmied out of her jeans.

For all that the mouth-watering thong covered, she might as well have not been wearing anything. Pierce groaned and closed his eyes. "I mean it, Mads. This isn't going to happen. You broke up with me for a reason. There's no point in going down that road again."

"Open your eyes."

"No."

"Now who's the coward?"

He opened his eyes and nearly stumbled to his knees. She was standing in front of him in all her naked glory. The woman was perfection personified, and Pierce's willpower was rapidly fading. He swallowed against his thick tongue, and totally gave up trying to look her in the face. His hungry gaze caressed every inch of her golden skin.

"Why the hell don't you have any tan lines?" he growled.

Her hips rolled seductively as she took a step toward him. "I want you. And you can't exactly lie and say you don't feel the same way. The more than generous proof is right in front of me."

He cursed and took a step back down the hall, away from the temptation of her body.

Like a sex goddess, without a hint of modesty or embarrassment heating her naked flesh, she pursued him.

When Pierce bumped up against his bedroom door, Madison stopped directly in front of him, her breasts pressing against his chest. She reached up and captured a drop of sweat running down the side of his face and sucked it off the tip of her finger.

"Um, salty."

His body jerked and he groaned. "You're not playing fair."

Her smile disappeared and for the first time since she'd started this little striptease, her face turned serious. She lifted her arms around his neck and pulled his head down.

"I'm not *playing*. I'm scared. I don't know what's going to happen when we leave here. I don't want to think anymore. I just want to feel. I want to know that someone cares about me. I want to forget, to pretend that none of the bad things ever happened. For just a few hours, I want to love and be loved. Is that really such a bad thing to ask?" She reached up on her tiptoes and pressed her lips against his in a kiss that was so sweet it made his heart skip a beat.

When she pulled back, her eyes were wide and searching. "Love me. Please?"

He knew it was wrong. He knew she'd regret this later, as would he. He didn't want to be her temporary reprieve from the pressures of the world. But looking into her sad eyes, hearing the pleading tone in a voice he'd never heard plead before, all his noble intentions died in a heap of ashes.

He opened the bedroom door behind him, then bent down and lifted her against his chest and carried her inside.

Now that he'd given up trying to resist her, he couldn't seem to slow down. He hadn't been with anyone else since she'd broken up with him. And he'd never been the celibate type.

She was under his skin, in his blood, and he didn't know how he'd survive again without her after tasting her again. He shoved that bleak thought away and focused on her, only her.

He quickly shed his clothes, leaving them on the floor beside the bed.

They twisted against each other, their arms and legs tangling together as they fought to get closer. The familiar scent of jasmine rose from Madison's heated skin. She shoved Pierce onto his back and covered him with her body, positioning him at her entrance then lowering herself on him in one quick stroke that had him arching off the bed.

Never one to worry about foreplay, Madison rode him with fervor, her hips arching up and down. Pierce grabbed her waist and ground himself against her, pushing deeper, faster.

Suddenly she cried out and tightened around him. He thrust upward two more times and joined her, shouting her name as he climaxed inside her.

She shuddered and fell across his chest, limp, sweaty, her breath coming out in choppy pants.

He grimaced at the tug on his stitches, but he didn't care. Being with Madison had always been this way, explosive, incredible, totally satisfying in a way no other woman had ever satisfied him. She loved to take charge in the bedroom like she tried to do outside the bedroom, and he didn't mind letting her.

*The first time.*

He'd give her a few minutes to recover. Then he'd love her the way he wanted to love her, slowly and thoroughly, tasting every delectable curve until she tightened around him and cried out his name.

And then he'd love her again.

WHEN DAWN BEGAN to make its way across the sky, its first rays fell through Pierce's bedroom window, dusting gold across Madison's flawless skin, marred only by the tiny dragon tattoo that he knew was on her left buttock. She lay splayed out across his chest like a blanket, snoring like a lumberjack.

He grinned and gently eased her hair back from her face. There were dark circles under her eyes from the makeup she hadn't taken off, and from lack of sleep. Neither of them had been able to keep their hands off each other last night.

His cell phone chimed, letting him know he had a message. He gently eased Madison to the side onto the mattress. She snorted and rolled over, facing away from him, giving him a delightful view of her curvy little backside, and the tattoo. Unable to resist, he leaned over and gave her a kiss on that little splotch of color.

The cell phone chimed again. He wished he could ignore the world right now, but he knew he couldn't. He leaned over the edge of the bed and grabbed the phone out of the pants he'd discarded on the floor. The message was from Alex. Lieutenant Hamilton wanted Madison to come to the station. Alex didn't know why, but he didn't think it was good news.

Pierce glanced at the time on his phone. They needed to be at the station in an hour. He hated to wake Madison up, but there was no way to avoid the real world any longer.

He set his phone down and rolled over, spooning his

hips behind her. He placed a soft kiss against the nape of her neck. "Wake up, sweetheart."

She snored louder.

After three more tries, he gave up the sweet, easy way of waking her up. Lord help her if there was ever a fire, because he didn't think a host of smoke alarms would wake the woman when she was this tired.

He padded into the bathroom, took care of his needs and brushed his teeth. Then he turned on the shower. Once it was warm, he went back into the bedroom and scooped Madison into his arms.

"Um." She snuffled against his chest, still asleep.

He kissed her soft, pink mouth, and carried her into the shower.

Her eyes flew open when the water hit her. She pressed against him and turned her face away. "Need to pee and brush my teeth."

He laughed and stepped back out of the shower with her. He slapped her bottom and went to the door. "Hurry. I'm not going to wait very long."

She cursed and grabbed the nearest object she could find to use as a weapon. The hairbrush went flying. Pierce ducked, laughing as he hurried out of the room and shut the door behind him.

When Pierce stepped back into the bathroom a few minutes later, Madison was already in the shower, washing her hair. Her eyes were closed, so he quietly stepped in the tub, leaned down, and drew her nipple into his mouth.

Her eyes opened wide, and she cursed again, but this time she pulled him closer.

IN THE PAST, police stations had always felt like home to Madison. Her brother had been in law enforcement for as long as she could remember, and he'd enjoyed giving her tours, introducing her to his friends. She'd never expected to feel intimidated in a police station like she did today, not knowing why Hamilton had called them.

The feel of Pierce's hand on the small of her back as he led her to the conference room helped comfort her, but she was still shaking inside. She had no idea what they were meeting about, but Alex had assured her the bail hadn't been revoked.

*Yet.*

Pierce opened the door, and Alex, who was already inside waiting, stood and shook both of their hands.

"What's this about?" Pierce asked.

"No idea. Hamilton told me what he told you—to get here quick because he had some news to share about the investigation."

Madison declined the seat Pierce pulled out for her. "I'd rather stand."

He leaned down next to her ear. "I'd rather you sit. That way I can grab you if you start to slug Hamilton."

She narrowed her eyes at him and leaned against the wall beside the window.

Mimicking her pose, he crossed his arms and leaned against the wall beside her. He grinned and gave her a sexy wink.

Seeing this teasing side of him had the anxiety inside

her loosening its hold. If he could smile and tease her, maybe she shouldn't be so worried.

The door opened and Lieutenant Hamilton stepped inside, along with Casey and Tessa.

Pierce straightened away from the wall, his face mirroring his surprise. "What are you two doing here?"

"One of our agents on another case stumbled across some evidence that ties back to this case," Casey said.

Everyone except Pierce and Madison sat down. Hamilton plopped a manila folder on the table. He pulled out an eight-by-ten color photo and slid it toward Pierce.

Madison started to step forward, but Pierce moved in front of her, blocking her view. "What are you trying to pull, Hamilton? Turn the picture over. Now."

"You don't have to protect me," Madison said. "I have a right to see any evidence against me."

"That isn't evidence," Pierce said, his voice shaking with anger.

She shoved past him and grabbed the photograph. He swore behind her and joined her at the table, but he didn't try to shield her again or take the picture away.

Her gut wrenched at the look of terror frozen on the dead woman's face. But then her stomach twisted with a completely different emotion. She glanced up at Hamilton in surprise. "She's wearing my clothes, and she looks just like me. Who is she? What happened to her?"

"Her street name is Misti," Hamilton said.

"Street name?"

"She's a hooker, was a hooker," Casey explained. "Her

body was found in an alley not far from the motel where you were supposedly caught on camera the day you went missing. An undercover agent found her, and when I saw the picture, I knew we were on to something. She could practically be your twin, and it can't be a coincidence that she's wearing the same outfit you were the day you were abducted."

Pierce raised a brow. "So, now you believe her story?"

"Hard not to. Even Hamilton is coming around, aren't you, Lieutenant?"

"I'm stubborn, not stupid. Even I can't deny what this looks like. Damon McKinley, or whoever abducted you, may very well have used this woman to pretend to be you at the motel. The only motive I can think of is the one written on the note you said you saw when you woke up in that room where your abductor held you. He wants to 'punish' you. I sure wish I had that note," he grumbled.

Since his voice sounded disappointed rather than suspicious, Madison wasn't sure what to think.

Tessa pointed one of her perfect fingernails to the dead woman's cleavage. "See that mole? We studied the motel photographs and found the same mole in an overhead shot when her shirt was gapping open. All of us—Hamilton, Casey, and me—believe this is the woman who was in your car at the motel. Unless you have the same mole, this is corroboration for your story that you weren't at the motel."

"She doesn't." Pierce's eyes widened and his face flushed light red, as if he'd just realized he'd spoken out loud, and hadn't meant too. He cleared his throat. "Go on, what else do you have."

Casey looked like he was stifling a grin.

Alex frowned at Pierce and leaned forward, his hands crossed on the table. "Lieutenant, this is great news, but I got the impression on the phone there was something more you wanted to tell us."

Hamilton loosened his tie and suddenly looked uncomfortable. "We've had some developments with the toxicology regarding your father," he said, addressing Madison.

Feeling she might need to sit to hear this, Madison pulled out a chair and sat down, clasping her hands together in her lap. Pierce moved to stand behind her chair and rested his hands on her shoulders. She didn't know if he was trying to comfort her or keep her from slugging Hamilton when he said whatever he was going to say. Either way, she was glad for his support. She leaned slightly back and he squeezed her shoulders reassuringly.

Hamilton pulled out another sheet of paper from the folder and passed it to Alex. "As you can see, the tests confirmed a lethal dose of Maxiodarone was in Mr. Richards' body. He was definitely murdered."

Madison tensed and Pierce tightened his hands.

"The interesting thing about Maxiodarone is that, even though it's lethal, it's slow-acting. The expert estimates the poison was administered two hours before your father died."

Casey pointed to the paper Hamilton had given to

Alex. "This is a log from your father's doctors, showing that you were in the middle of a consultation with them during that time. You have a solid alibi. You couldn't have murdered your father."

Hamilton cleared his throat. "Given the lack of physical evidence, and just how freaking fishy all this looks, I no longer believe you had anything to do with the murders of the two people found in your yard either."

Alex tapped the paper and handed it back to the lieutenant. "I'll expect all charges to be dropped immediately."

"Done." Hamilton stood and held out his hand toward Madison. "Mrs. McKinley, on behalf of the Savannah-Chatham Metro Police, I'd like to apologize for putting you through this harrowing experience. All charges against you are dropped, and we're proceeding forward with an intense investigation into your abduction and those stalking charges. You're free to go."

Madison was stunned. This was the last thing she'd expected when she'd come here. She shook his hand and frowned. "What about my father? Are you investigating his murder? You have to know Damon is the one who killed him."

"That's out of my jurisdiction. The New York district attorney has been made aware of our findings. It's up to him now to pursue that investigation."

"What does that mean? Are they pursuing it or aren't they?" she asked, rising from her chair.

"Don't worry," Agent Casey assured her. "The FBI is now officially in the game. Hamilton invited us to review the case. And, at my urging, the New York police invited us to investigate your father's death. We believe Damon McKinley could be part of some major crimes over several decades with many potential victims. We can't ignore that. We want to know what's going on just as much as you do.

"Thank you," she said, amazed at how things were turning out.

He nodded. "I apologize for not believing you before. I hope you understand. In my business, it's all about evidence."

"Come on, let's get you out of here," Pierce said. "We can call Logan and let him know the charges have been dropped."

Madison smiled her first smile in days and stepped out of the conference room. Pierce put his hand on the small of her back again, invoking images of the shower they'd shared earlier, heating her skin and tightening her belly. She was suddenly anxious to get him alone where she could do all the things she'd wanted to do to him last night but was too exhausted to do by the time he'd finished with her.

She was far from finished with him.

She grinned up at him and gave him a saucy wink.

He gave her an admonishing look, but she could tell he wasn't all that worried.

"Well, hello there."

Madison stumbled to a halt, a shiver of dread running up her spine. No, it couldn't be. She whirled around, her heart in her throat as she stared at the man sitting at a desk with a detective.

Pierce put his arm around her shoulders. "What's wrong?"

Words couldn't seem to get past her constricted throat, so instead she pointed at the man.

He smiled at Pierce. "You must be Special Agent Buchanan. What a pleasure to finally meet you. I'm Damon McKinley."

Pierce shoved Madison behind his back. "Hamilton, you've got enough evidence to justify a forty-eight hour hold on this man."

"Absolutely." Hamilton strode forward, yanking out his cuffs as he stepped around the desk. But instead of handcuffing McKinley, he stopped, his face mirroring shock.

Pierce frowned. "Why aren't you cuffing him?"

Hamilton shook his head. "There's no way this man is the stalker. He's not the man Mrs. McKinley chased in the park. He's And he couldn't have abducted anyone."

The look of satisfaction on Damon's face made dread shoot through Madison.

"Why not?" Pierce demanded.

Damon eased around the desk.

*In his wheelchair.*

## Chapter Twenty-Four

EVERYONE STARTED TALKING at once.

"He's faking it," Madison insisted. "He's the one I chased in the park. He shot Pierce, and abducted me. He's no more paralyzed than I am."

"Tsk, tsk." Damon clucked his tongue. "Is that any way for a wife to treat her long-lost husband?"

She took a step forward.

Pierce grabbed her and pulled her back. "Mr. McKinley, how long have you been in that chair? Looks new to me. Did you buy it right before you wheeled in to the station?"

Damon glanced down at his chair and wiped his thumb across one of the stainless steel bars, making a play of rubbing a smudge out of it. "I take good care of my equipment." His face turned sad. "After all, without it I'd be at the mercy of others."

"How is it that you're here and not dead?" Hamilton asked.

"Well, now, that's a long story. One I'm happy to share with you, officer." He turned his steely gray gaze on Madison. "After I speak to my wife. In private."

"That isn't going to happen," Pierce growled.

"I have a feeling Madison won't agree with you," Damon said.

"I've got nothing to say to you," she spat. "You're a murderer. You killed my father. And you killed that poor woman they found buried in my yard, along with the yardman."

He placed his hand on his heart. "Accusing me of murder, my dear? How shocking. I am, of course, quite innocent of these terrible charges."

Agent Casey stepped forward. "Who died in your car in the accident in New York? Who created those fake contracts, signed with your name, as part owner in businesses who all insist the contracts aren't real?"

"Contracts? I assure you, I don't have any idea what you're talking about." He sighed heavily. "Let me guess. My dear wife provided them to you. Has she become a forger now in addition to her other . . . skills?"

Madison tried to shove past Pierce, but he grabbed her and held her back.

"And the man who died in your car in New York?" Casey asked.

Simon clucked his tongue again. "I was carjacked, mugged. Terrible business, that. He took my wallet, my car, even my clothes. I had short-term memory loss from my injuries. It took a bit of time before I realized what had happened, and who I was."

Pierce snorted. "Right. And then, instead of going home, you let the world believe you were dead. I'm not buying it. You were running from something, or to something. Why did you fake your death?"

"I didn't fake my death. But once I realized everyone believed I was dead, I had a very good reason to allow that belief to stand." Again he looked at Madison, who was peering around Pierce. "Madison, I'm sure you'll want to speak to me, alone, before I answer any more questions about the last time we saw each other. Don't you agree?"

Pierce shot a glance at Madison. Her pale face and wide eyes told him they were in trouble here. He'd been worried yesterday, when Alex interrupted their conversation, that she was still holding something back. He'd meant to ask her about it. But he'd gotten a bit distracted after he took her home.

What else could Damon possibly be holding over her?

He turned back toward Damon. "You're not getting anywhere near her." He shoved Madison behind him again, and this time she didn't resist. "And don't expect me to believe for one second that you're really paralyzed. You're the man who shot me in the park."

Damon rolled his eyes and let out a long, deep breath as if he was bored. "Why don't we just clear up that little misconception right now." He suddenly leaned over the desk beside him and grabbed a letter opener.

Hamilton lunged toward him, clearly worried that

Damon was going to hurt someone. Before Hamilton could stop him, Damon raised the letter opener and plunged it into his thigh.

EVERY EYE IN the squad room stared in shock at Damon McKinley. He hadn't moved, not even a flinch, when he stabbed his leg.

He stared at Pierce as he calmly set the letter opener on the desk. It had only gone in about a quarter of an inch, but that was enough to get his point across.

"Good grief, he's bleeding all over the place." Hamilton snapped his fingers at a detective. "Get some paper towels or napkins. Has anybody got an extra shirt, something to stop the bleeding?"

The detective whose letter opener had just been used was pale and wide-eyed, but he opened his drawer and pulled out a towel. "From my gym bag." He handed the towel to Hamilton. "It's clean."

Hamilton grabbed the towel and pressed it over Damon's wound.

"The bleeding is already stopping, Lieutenant," Damon said. "No big deal, truly. Allow me." He pushed Hamilton's hand away and held the towel against his leg, all the time aiming a smug smile at Pierce and Madison.

Hamilton gave Pierce a disgusted look. "I suppose you think he just faked that?"

Pierce didn't answer. He didn't know what to think at the moment.

"Mr. McKinley," Hamilton said, "you need to get to a hospital."

"No, no. I told you. I'm fine. I am a bit tired, though. I'd like to go ahead and answer any questions you have, of course, but again . . . I really must insist that I speak to my wife first. It's been quite some time since we've seen each other—"

"Not very long at all," she said, her voice shaking with anger. "The last time I saw you, you were shoving a threatening note under the door at me, in the room where you held me prisoner."

Damon shook his head sadly, as if he doubted Madison's sanity.

"Let's straighten this mess out." Hamilton motioned to the detective at the desk beside Damon. "Take him to the main conference room. We'll be right there."

As the detective wheeled Damon across the room, Hamilton glared at Pierce and Madison. "Mrs. McKinley, I've given you the benefit of the doubt from day one."

She snorted and rolled her eyes.

He gritted his teeth. "And, I've tried, very hard, to believe your outlandish stories. But the lies have to stop, now, today. I want the truth."

"The truth," she said, "is that my former husband obviously faked his death. Someone else died in his place. I should think you'd be concerned about who he killed to make that happen."

"Once again, based on the obvious physical evidence he just presented, I'm inclined to believe his version, that someone mugged him and took his car. I have no reason to believe otherwise."

"Oh, and I suppose him not showing up for a year and a half doesn't seem suspicious to you?"

"Of course, it does. I intend to ask him about that. Which brings up another point. What, exactly, does he have on you?"

"What?"

"He mentioned the last night you two saw each other. He seemed to imply there was something significant, something you wouldn't want others to know about. So, what happened?"

Her face clouded with anger. "We argued, as we always did. I told him to leave. When he wouldn't, I—"

Pierce grabbed her and anchored her to his side. His abruptness caught her by surprise, making her stop mid-sentence, just as he'd hoped. He didn't like the look on her face when she was answering Hamilton, and he'd been very worried that the next words out of her mouth were about to put her from the proverbial frying pan into the fire.

Or back in jail.

"Lieutenant, I need a moment with Mrs. McKinley," Pierce said.

Madison tried to shove away from him. "I'm not done."

"Yes. You are."

"No, I'm—"

He clamped his hand over her mouth.

"Do not, under any circumstances, say another word."

Her face reddened even more as she tried to pull his hand away from her mouth.

He leaned down and whispered in her ear. "I swear to God, if you say one more thing before I get you in a closed room away from the people who want to put you in prison, I will throw you over my shoulder and carry you out of here. Got that?"

Her eyes narrowed, but she nodded.

He lowered his hand. "We need a minute, Hamilton."

"What you need is to come to the main conference room so we can talk this out."

Alex had been watching all the commotion without comment until now. He stepped forward, stopping in front of the lieutenant. "You forget that you formally dropped all charges against Mrs. McKinley. If you're reinstating those charges, keep in mind she already posted bail. So, unless you're prepared, right now, to press *new* charges, she's free to go. If you aren't going to arrest her, then I suggest you give Pierce and Madison some privacy. Otherwise, I'm advising my client to leave without making any more statements."

"All right." Hamilton didn't look happy at all, but he waved toward the back corner of the room. "Take my office. But make it quick. I want answers."

As PIERCE LED Madison into Hamilton's office, he reminded himself that this was the woman he'd made love to last night and this morning. This was the woman who'd crept into his heart even though he didn't want her to. He cared about her.

He reminded himself of that again.

He cared about her.

*Therefore, he should not strangle her.*

The moment the door to Hamilton's office closed, Madison wheeled around, practically shooting sparks from her eyes. "Do not, ever, put your hand over my mouth and tell me to shut up again."

His jaw tightened. "Save the histrionics for someone you can intimidate. Now that we're not in the middle of a room full of cops wanting to arrest you at the slightest provocation, tell me what you were so hot to tell the lieutenant."

Some of the anger left her, and she started to look worried. "There might have been one tiny little thing I haven't told you yet. It's not that big a deal, really. But I'm pretty sure I know why Damon wants to talk to me."

"Go ahead. Enlighten me on this *tiny little thing* that's no big deal. Please. I'm all ears."

She plopped down on one of the chairs in front of Hamilton's desk. Pierce sat in the chair across from her and rested his forearms on his knees.

"The last night Damon and I were together," she said, "we fought, just like I said. When he wouldn't leave, I . . . well . . . I grabbed one of my guns to make him leave. I might have . . . well . . . shot him."

Pierce dropped his head into hands and counted to five before he looked back up at Madison.

She was chewing her bottom lip, looking worried for the first time since Damon had wheeled around the desk. "I guess that didn't sound so good once I said it out loud."

"You think? I don't suppose you shot him in the back? Because that might explain the wheelchair." He didn't bother to hide the sarcasm in his voice.

She huffed and crossed her arms. "Of course not. I shot him in the shoulder. He was perfectly fine when he ran out the door. That wheelchair thing is recent, a ruse. I have no doubts about that."

"Well, it's good to know someone around here has no doubts," Pierce grumbled. "I'm a little slow here, so bear with me. You shot him . . . by accident?"

She shook her head. "Oh no. I meant to shoot him."

This time he counted to ten. "Can you please remember, for one second, that I'm a federal officer? Please tell me you were *not* trying to kill him."

She frowned, looking as if he'd just insulted her. "I always hit what I aim at. If I'd wanted to kill him, he'd be dead. I would have double-tapped him in the head."

He blinked. "Double-tapped?"

She nodded. "Two quick shots, one, two . . . right between the eyes."

Counting wasn't helping his temper, but he tried it again. He counted to twenty this time.

"Mads, what do you think would happen if you told this to Lieutenant Hamilton? He'd arrest you for attempted murder. You can't tell him."

"But I wasn't trying to kill Damon."

"Hamilton wouldn't believe that."

She chewed her bottom lip again. "I didn't think about that."

"No kidding."

She narrowed her eyes.

He continued, before she had a chance to argue. "You think Damon wants to confront you, hold that over you. Why, as blackmail? To get money?"

"Probably. But there's no proof, so he doesn't really have anything to hold over me."

"Don't underestimate him. From what I've seen, he's very resourceful. Hell, he probably saved the bullet. I don't suppose you were thoughtful enough to keep the gun, so Hamilton could run ballistics against it and prove where the bullet came from?"

Her wide-eyed look answered that question.

He shook his head and tapped his hands on his thighs, deep in thought. He studied the problem from every angle, and he kept coming back to the same thing. He needed to know what game Damon was playing.

And there was only one way he could figure out how to get that information.

"You're going to have to give Damon what he wants," he said.

"What do you mean? Money?"

"No. I want you to talk to him. Alone."

DAMON SAT IN his wheelchair in the middle of the court-yard behind the police station, while Madison sat on a wrought-iron bench across from him. Damon had refused to speak to her inside the police station, because he didn't want anyone to overhear their conversation. This courtyard was the only place all parties would agree to.

And he'd insisted on having Madison open her blouse to prove she wasn't wearing a wire, something Pierce had violently objected to. In spite of his protests, she'd whipped her blouse open, turning around in front of Damon to prove she wasn't wired, before buttoning it back up and sitting down on the bench.

Pierce, Lieutenant Hamilton, and half a dozen police officers stood guard thirty feet away. Damon held up his handcuffed hands, which had a length of chain running from them to his wheelchair.

"Your boyfriend is a bit paranoid, don't you think?"

Pierce was definitely paranoid. He'd left nothing to chance. In addition to cuffing both Damon's hands and legs to the wheelchair, Pierce had cuffed Madison's hands to her bench.

As she stared at the man who had taken so much from her, she had to agree that Pierce had been wise to cuff her. Because right now all she wanted to do was leap across the clearing and strangle her former husband.

The sunlight glinted off the ring on Damon's left hand, making Madison start in surprise. It was a wedding ring—the ring she'd given him.

He noted her interest, and held up his hand, a sardonic smile on his lips.

"Why?" she asked.

"I take my vows seriously." He leaned slightly forward. "Until death do us part. Neither of us is dead. Yet."

She glanced sharply at Pierce, positioned well behind Damon. He nodded reassuringly. She drew a deep breath. "Why did you kill my father?"

Damon raised a brow. "Now, why would I kill my esteemed father-in-law? Shame on you for even thinking that."

She yanked her fist, but the chain kept her from moving more than a few inches.

He laughed. "You still haven't learned to control your temper. That's going to get you killed someday."

"Is that a threat?"

"With all these guns trained on me? Of course not. I have far more self-control than that."

"You wanted to talk. So talk."

His grin faded as he leaned forward as far as the chains would allow. "You want me to get right to the point? Fine. I left you with a million dollars of my money. Honestly, at the time, I had other resources and thought you might need the money, at least until your father's money came through. But things have changed. I want it back." He spoke in a low voice, so low that she almost couldn't hear him.

She leaned forward too. "You aren't getting a single penny. I'm not paying my father's murderer."

He glanced at the policemen watching them. "I suggest you lower your voice, my dear, and be very careful what you say. I didn't roll in here without making sure I held all the cards. What did you think all those photographs meant when I held you in that room?"

She curled her hands together in frustration. Damon was openly admitting he'd abducted her, and no one else could hear him. "You can't hurt my family. They're all in protective custody."

"How *is* that wonderful mother-in-law of mine?" he asked. "And my new sister-in-law. Amanda, isn't it? She's quite the stunner, if you only look at her from the left side of course." He winced. "That jagged scar down the right side of her face is a bit off-putting, but I suppose I could warm up to her in a pinch."

Madison jerked against her restraints. "What do you want?" she hissed.

"One million dollars."

"I'm not paying my father's murderer," she repeated.

"Either pay, or your mother dies, along with her new husband. Then Amanda. And, lastly, that precious brother of yours. They can't stay in protective custody for the rest of their lives." He smiled. "Then again, maybe they will. Because the minute they're out of custody, their lives are over. Unless you pay me."

"Why are you doing this? Why did you choose me as your target? Did you ever care about me at all?"

"You were struggling middle-class when I met you. Of course I cared about you or I wouldn't have bothered with you. But the money started to run out. I had to make alternate plans. The only reason you're still alive is *because* I care about you. I could have killed you and kept your money, all of it. A million dollars isn't much to ask when you have far more than that, and your life, because I allowed you to keep both."

She squeezed her hands together. "And my father? Why did you kill him?"

He frowned. "Lower your voice."

"Tell me, please," she whispered. "I need to know."

He glanced back toward Hamilton and seemed to consider. "If I, hypothetically, were involved in your father's death, it would have been because I knew you would come into millions when he died." His face twisted into a snarl. "But you were suspicious, even back then. You couldn't leave well enough alone, and you confronted me with your damned suspicions. Because of you I had to run." He rolled his shoulder. "I should pay you back for that little nick you gave me. Hurts like hell in the winter."

She gritted her teeth. "I'd shoot you again if given the chance. And this time I wouldn't aim for your shoulder. If you didn't want to kill me, and that's why you left after I confronted you, then why fake your death?"

"I didn't want you to convince your cop brother to go on a hunt for me. I knew you'd tell him your suspicions if I stayed. I have an aversion to prison my dear. Been there, done that. I'm not going back again, no matter what."

"You've been in prison?"

His nostrils flared. "Well, I didn't exactly mean to tell you that, but yes."

"Why are you back now? You faked your death. Now you're faking your injury. Why announce to the world that you're not really dead? Especially if you're concerned my brother would go after you to prove you killed my father."

He shrugged. "Simple. My money ran out. You forced me to leave New York before I was ready. I tried to look you up several months ago and tracked you, along with your *lover*, to Jacksonville. Later I followed you to Savannah, where you bought your very nice house. Then you were accommodating enough to go back to New York, leaving that luxurious house empty for me. I decided to give you another chance. Instead of killing you, I moved in."

He tapped the arm of his chair. "I must say, I was thoroughly enjoying my . . . pleasures here, when you decided to come back, and ruined everything. So it's only logical that I get my money from you. You want to live here in Savannah—fine. I'll go somewhere else, but I will not be a pauper again. I left you sitting pretty with my own money, not to mention what you got from your father. I think you should be grateful that I'm only asking for *my* portion of the money. I could demand *all* of your money."

She frowned. "What do you mean, you had to leave New York before you were ready? Have you done this before? Ruined someone's life the way you ruined mine?"

He scrunched his mouth together and glared at her. "I've changed my mind. The first to die won't be your mother. It will be your new boyfriend. Get a cashier's check today and meet me tonight at your house. If I see any cops, I'm gone and your boyfriend dies."

She shook her head. "No. I won't do it. And you can't hurt Pierce. He can take care of himself."

He arched a brow and snorted. "Really? How sure are you he can protect himself twenty-four hours a day? You aren't the only one who's an excellent shot. I happen to be quite lethal with a rifle. I can reach your boyfriend from a long ways a way. I promise you. If I want to kill him, he's as good as dead."

She started shaking so hard her handcuffs rattled against the bench.

The sound of footsteps against concrete had Madison and Damon both looking back at Pierce. He stepped over to Damon's wheelchair. "This meeting is over."

Damon smiled up at him. "I got what I wanted." He held up his hands. "Now take these wretched cuffs off."

Pierce ignored him and took Madison's cuffs off first. He led her over to one of the uniformed police officers. "Take her inside." To Madison, he said, "Wait for me." Then he turned around and strode back to Damon.

"WHAT DID YOU say to her?" Pierce demanded as he sat on the same bench Madison had been sitting on a few minutes ago.

Damon raised a brow. "That's between me and my wife."

"She's not your wife. She divorced you, right after you killed whoever died in that car in your place. So if your plan was to frame her and put her in prison so you could get the courts to award you her money, think again. You'll never see a dime."

Damon blinked, his face reddening. "She divorced me? Truly?"

Pierce nodded.

Damon cleared his throat and shrugged, back in control. "Doesn't matter. My plans, whatever they may be, are not affected by the state of my marriage." He yanked on one of the handcuffs. "I have nothing more to say to you. I suggest you release me, now, before I call a lawyer and sue you and everyone else in this station."

Pierce gave a harsh laugh. "I don't think your background can stand up to the scrutiny of a drawn out lawsuit. If you want to try, go ahead." He leaned forward. "I don't know what game you're playing, but it ends here. If I ever see you anywhere near Madison, I'll throw your ass in jail."

Damon gestured to his chair. "Come now. What could I possibly do to hurt my dear sweet wife? And why would I want to?" His lips curved up in a taunting smile. "Maybe I'll strike up our relationship where we left off. She really is a little firecracker in bed, as I'm sure you know. I wouldn't mind having some of that again."

Pierce jumped off the bench and grabbed Damon's shirt, lifting him out of the chair as far as the handcuffs would allow.

"Let him go!" Hamilton and two other police officers grabbed Pierce and tried to pull him back.

Pierce shrugged them off. "Stay away from Madison." He let Damon fall back into the chair.

Hamilton grabbed Pierce's arm. "Get your temper under control before I arrest you for assault."

"Get your hands off me. Now."

"Only if you promise not to touch Mr. McKinley again."

"Scouts honor," Pierce gritted between his teeth, not bothering to mention that he'd never been a scout.

"I've changed my mind about speaking to you any further, Lieutenant," Damon said. "I insist you let me go, or I will sue you and your department for assault. I'm ready to leave."

Hamilton glared at Pierce and motioned to one of the police officers. "Un-cuff him, and get him out of here."

"What are you doing?" Pierce demanded. "You can't let him go."

Hamilton waited until Damon had been wheeled back into the building.

"I don't exactly owe you or Mrs. McKinley anything, not after being lied to for so long. I'm not going to put myself on the line for either of you when I don't have any physical evidence against Damon McKinley. The FBI will have to take it from here, see if they can build a case. However, I have already instructed my men to keep him under surveillance. When Casey has enough evidence for a warrant, I'll haul McKinley back in, but not before then."

"You've already got probable cause to hold him on any number of crimes."

"I can only hold him for forty-eight hours. If I don't have forensic evidence against him by then, he's out."

"He's out anyway."

"You want me to hold him, then help me. Explain how a paraplegic could have abducted Mrs. McKinley and placed her in the trunk of her car like she said? She never mentioned a wheelchair when she talked about her abduction."

Pierce raked his hand through his hair. "He has to be faking the paralysis."

"How? Why?"

"The *how* is beyond me, for now. But the *why* will be clear as soon as we talk to Madison and find out what Damon said to her. " He strode past Hamilton toward the building.

He yanked the door open and headed inside. When he reached the squad room it didn't take him long to realize that Madison wasn't there. He stopped at the desk of the detective whose letter opener Damon had used earlier.

"Where's Mrs. McKinley?"

"She said she had to run an errand."

"You let her leave? Knowing Damon McKinley is out there?"

The detective's eyes widened. "Was I not supposed to?"

Pierce swore and sprinted through the squad room to the elevator. What was Madison up to this time? He prayed he caught up to her before she caught up to Damon.

## Chapter Twenty-Five

MADISON PULLED UP short when she stepped out of the bank and saw Pierce lounging against the side of his car, illegally parked. His arms were crossed over his chest, and he looked like he wanted to strangle her.

"Explain." One hoarsely uttered, clipped word.

She clutched her purse as she stopped in front of him. "I had to get out of the station, clear my head. And it dawned on me, that with all the craziness going on lately, I hadn't made my mortgage payment this month."

He looked up at the sky, as if he were praying for divine guidance. "You went to the bank to pay your mortgage. You expect me to believe that?"

"Of course. It's the truth."

He held out his hand. "Give me your purse."

"Excuse me?"

He raised a brow. "If all you were doing was making your mortgage payment, you've got nothing to hide."

"If you want it that badly, take it." She slapped the purse into his hand. "But it's really not the right color for your outfit."

He rolled his eyes and plopped her purse on the hood of his car. When he found her mortgage payment receipt inside, he looked at her in surprise. But when she held out her hand for her purse, he ignored it and finished his search.

Once he was done, he shoved everything back inside and held the purse out to her. "My mistake. I thought Damon might have asked you for money, and you got a cashier's check for him. *Did* he ask you for money?"

Her pulse leaped in her throat. "Yes, he did. He wants a million dollars. But I'm not paying him. I will never pay the man who murdered my father. Not one cent."

The anger faded from his eyes, replaced by a look of approval, and relief. He gave her a tight nod. "Good to know. You can't bargain with people like him. Any agreement he made he'd back out on. He's dangerous. The only way to deal with him is to get evidence and put him away. Speaking of which, Logan called. He's in Montana and has some news to share on the investigation he's been conducting into Damon's past."

Once Madison was inside the car, Pierce crouched in the doorway. He gently pushed her hair out of her eyes, his fingers lingering on her skin in a gentle caress. "You scared years off my life when I thought you'd gone chasing after Damon. What else did he say to you back at the station? What had you looking so scared?"

The memory of Damon's threats, the calm certainty in

his voice, had her curling her fingers against the edge of the seat. "He said . . . he'd hurt my family . . . and you . . . if I didn't pay him."

His gaze softened. "I won't let that happen. Your family is safe. A private security firm is watching over them."

"Including Logan? What about you? Who's protecting you?"

"Logan and I can take care of ourselves."

Moisture filled her eyes. She swiped the tears away and shook her head. "You can't watch over your shoulder all the time. What if he . . . has a rifle or something."

He tenderly cupped the side of her face. "Don't worry. This will all be over soon. I have a feeling that whatever Logan is going to tell us will be good news. If he's found something we can use to put Damon away, then everyone will be safe."

Since he seemed to be waiting for her agreement, she nodded. But she very much feared he was wrong. Pierce didn't know Damon the way she did. And he hadn't seen the look of pure evil in Damon's eyes when he'd promised to kill everyone she loved if she didn't pay him.

After pressing a whisper soft kiss on Madison's lips, Pierce closed her car door and headed around the front of the car toward the driver's side. Madison desperately hoped he was right, that Logan had discovered something that would help them put Damon behind bars. Because if he hadn't, she would have to fall back on plan B—the million dollar cashier's check hidden inside her bra.

"WE'RE HERE, LOGAN—Madison, Lieutenant Hamilton, and me," Pierce said. "Casey and Tessa had to go back to the office. I'll fill them in later." He turned the computer monitor around on the conference room table. He centered it so the built-in Webcam would hopefully capture all three of them. "Can you see and hear us okay?"

"Yes." Logan looked at Madison. "How are you holding up, trouble?"

She squeezed Pierce's hand beneath the table. "Pierce is taking good care of me."

"Good. I don't want to have to teach him his manners again when I get back." The teasing expression on his face turned serious. "You should have told me about Dad."

She nodded, blinking her eyes rapidly as if to hold back tears. "I know. I'm so sorry."

"What do you have for us?" Hamilton asked, sounding impatient.

"More than I expected, but it took some trickery to get the information. Bigfork is a tight-knit community, and no one wanted to share anything about their former benefactor. I told them Damon had died in a car accident in New York, and that I was trying to find out if he had any family or friends that needed to be notified. They suddenly became quite friendly."

"I'll bet," Pierce said. "They were hoping for a cut of his estate."

"I've already e-mailed softcopies of this information to Lieutenant Hamilton and you. I'm overnighting the hardcopies, which are mostly pictures."

Logan shuffled some papers on the table in front of him. "Damon was born here and had few friends, but he was generous to the local community. They named a high school, and even this library after him"—he waved toward the building he was sitting in—"because of a large donation. But he was sick, a lot. He had failing health for the last couple of years that he lived here. No one seemed quite sure what his diagnosis was. The local doctor refuses to give me any information without a warrant. He had a full-time nurse during most of those two years. Then, all of a sudden, he picked up and moved away. He had the house sold and liquidated all his assets in Bigfork. That was around the time he went to New York."

Madison frowned. "Damon was always healthy. I can't remember him ever being sick."

Logan's lips thinned. "That thought occurred to me too. The man I heard about didn't sound like the man I'd met."

He held up a picture in front of the camera. "Trouble, tell me if you recognize this man."

Madison studied the black-and-white photo of a man sitting on a bench in a garden. His hair was dark, streaked with gray, and his eyes were slightly sunken in as if he was ill. She shook her head. "He doesn't look familiar. Should I know him?"

"I would think so. Since you married him."

"What?"

"This is Damon McKinley, the real one," he said, picking up another photo and holding it up. "And this is the male nurse who used to take care of Mr. McKinley."

Madison made a choking sound and pressed her hand against her throat. "That's Damon," she whispered.

Logan put the picture down. "No, that's Simon Rice, the man I believe stole Damon McKinley's identity and married you."

"Simon?" Pierce and Hamilton both said at the same time.

"I thought you'd catch that," Logan said. "What are the odds he's your 'Simon says' killer too?"

Madison held her hand against her mouth, as if she were trying not to throw up.

Pierce put his arm around her shoulders. "We had always assumed the 'Simon says' killer was actually named Simon, making it easy to rule Damon out . . ."

"What was the point of leaving those notes?" Madison asked, her voice barely above a whisper. "And killing all those people?"

"To throw us off track," Hamilton said. "And to keep my men busy, to distract us from following up on your stalker."

"I disagree," Pierce said. "I've worked enough serial killer cases to know how their minds work. If Damon is this 'Simon says' killer, it's a compulsion. He's a psychopath. He kills for the thrill. Even if part of his plan was to distract the police, he killed because that's just what he does. He can't stop. I'll bet if we look for similar cases in New York, we'll find he killed others while he lived there."

"While he was married to me," Madison said, her voice breaking. She was so pale Pierce wrapped his arm around her shoulders, afraid she might faint. But she drew a deep breath, and seemed to brace herself. "Go on," she said to Logan. "Finish this. What else did you find out?"

"The real Damon McKinley is missing," Logan continued. "Unfortunately, without a body, we don't have anything against Simon, not even identity theft."

Hamilton frowned. "What do you mean? Seems pretty cut and dry to prove that he passed himself off as McKinley."

Logan held up another document. "He legally changed his name to Damon McKinley when he moved to New York. The man crossed every t, dotted every i. There's nothing illegal about changing your name."

Madison clutched Pierce's hand beneath the table. "But, what about the money? He only had a million dollars left when he supposedly died in the car crash, but when we first got married, he had several million dollars. He had to have stolen that money from the real Damon McKinley."

"I'm sure you're right," Logan said. "But we have no proof, and there's no dead body to prove he killed the real McKinley. The real McKinley apparently transferred all his money to Simon Rice before leaving Bigfork. Naturally, I assume it was either done under duress or fraudulently by Rice. But, again, I have no proof. I think the FBI needs to dig in on that, but for now, we have nothing."

Pierce leaned forward. "You said Rice was a nurse?"

"Yes."

"Then it's not much of a stretch to think he'd have

knowledge of what drugs to use to cause temporary paralysis if he wanted to fake an injury. I assume that could be done."

Madison grabbed his arm. "It can. I remember Austin telling me the drugs his doctors have him on right now cause temporary paralysis. If Damon . . . "—she swallowed and cleared her throat—"or *Simon*, was a nurse, he would have known what to use."

Logan frowned. "What are you talking about?"

"Damon was here, at the station today," Pierce said. "In a wheelchair, pretending to be paralyzed."

"Clever," Logan said. "Got to admit, that's a first in my experience."

Pierce nodded. "Mine too. As a former nurse, he'd also have a thorough understanding of the kinds of drugs, and timelines involved to fake a heart attack. Heck, he might have kept all the drugs he used while taking care of the real McKinley and has his own little pharmacy of meds to use if he wants."

Hamilton shook his head. "Or he got them from the woman he killed and buried in Mrs. McKinley's backyard. She was a pharmacist."

Logan looked grim. "You're probably right. He had the opportunity to kill my father, and the knowledge. I can't think of a motive though, why he'd want to kill him. If it was the money Madison would inherit, then why would he fake his death and disappear when he could have stayed and had millions more?"

Madison swallowed hard. "Damon said he left because I was suspicious about Daddy, and that he knew I'd tell you if he stuck around. Supposedly, the only reason he didn't kill me . . . was because he loved me."

"When did he tell you all this?"

"Today, when he came to the station."

A knock sounded on the door.

"It better be important," Hamilton said, as a police officer opened the door and stepped inside.

"Yes, sir." He looked at the others and hesitated.

"Don't worry about them. What's up?"

"There's been a murder, sir, outside of town off I-95. The man's name is Joshua MacGuffin."

Madison gasped and stared at the policeman in horror.

"Do you have any more details?" Hamilton asked.

"The medical examiner is on the scene, says the C.O.D. is most likely strangulation. Mr. MacGuffin has been dead for several days. And, Lieutenant, we found a room in the basement of his house with a mattress. The ceiling had all kinds of pictures on it. One of the officers on the scene said he e-mailed some snapshots to you from his phone."

Hamilton clawed for his cell phone and opened up his e-mail. He turned the phone around toward Madison. "Are these the pictures you saw when you were abducted?"

She nodded, her heart breaking at the thought of poor Mr. MacGuffin being killed just because he'd wanted to help her. "Yes," she whispered. "Those are the pictures I saw."

Hamilton shoved the phone in his jacket. "Thanks, officer. I'll head out there in a few minutes."

The officer nodded and closed the door.

"Several days," Pierce said. "I bet he was killed the night he called to tell Madison he'd seen her husband. When he saw Damon in the restaurant, he must have reacted somehow, and Damon realized the man had recognized him."

Madison blinked back tears. "Mr. MacGuffin was so nice to me, so concerned about me."

"Hamilton," Logan said, from the monitor. "I heard you have Madison's computer. We'll need a look at that, to see if the files she had on Damon can help us prove his crimes."

"Of course."

"And," Logan continued, "you need to have Damon tested to prove he's faking the paralysis. That will take away his main defense, and you can investigate from there."

It was Hamilton's turn to redden slightly as he shifted in his chair. "I'm afraid that's not possible."

"Why not?" Pierce and Logan asked at the same time.

"I had a tail put on McKinley when he drove off in his van. But I think he must have realized he was being followed. He shook the tail. I don't know where Damon McKinley is."

MADISON RUBBED HER hands up and down her arms and paced the length of Pierce's bedroom. They were back in the bed-and-breakfast, because once again Pierce had wanted to stay in town to be close to the investigation, and the search for Damon.

He quietly watched her from his bed. The cashier's check pressed against Madison's chest like a heavy weight, reminding her of the lie she'd told him.

Reminding her of the choice she had to make.

"Hamilton dropped all the charges against you," he said. "You should be relieved."

"I know. I am. But—"

"But you're still worried about Damon. I won't let him hurt you."

She stopped pacing at the foot of the bed and put her hands on her hips. "You may be tall, dark, and handsome, but you're not Superman. You still bleed. You can still die."

He slid off the bed and stood in front of her. He put his arms on her shoulders. "I may not be a superhero, but Damon isn't a supervillain either. He's just a man. I'll find the evidence I need to put him away for a very long time. I'm good at what I do. I *will* put him behind bars."

She shook her head. "You don't understand. He's sneaky, and smart, and . . . and . . . he doesn't have a conscience. You heard the lieutenant after that call with Logan. He said he still doesn't have enough evidence to take to a grand jury. There's nothing he can do."

"There's nothing he can do *yet*. Casey's working on the case. Logan's still trying to dig up evidence. Hamilton's looking into it. It's just a matter of time."

Shaking off his hands, she paced across the room again. She wrapped her arms around her waist and faced him. "Can you promise me, swear to me, that you're one-hundred-percent positive you'll be able to get enough evidence together to put him away? Can you swear to me that he'll pay for killing my father? That he won't be able to hurt my family, or you?" Her voice broke on the last word.

"You know I can't swear to that. Do I believe I can find the evidence I need to put him away? Yes. Absolutely. Am I positive? Would I bet my life on it?" He shook his head. "No. But, I swear I'll do my best, and I'll keep you safe."

"What about my mom and her husband? Amanda? Logan? What about *you*? How will you keep all of them safe if Damon is free?"

He frowned. "I've never seen you this nervous. What's really going on?"

She closed her eyes tightly but a tear still slipped down her cheek. She almost never cried, but in the past twenty-four hours she couldn't seem to help herself. She was so scared, so worried about her family, about Pierce.

"Ah, sweetie. Don't cry." He dragged her against him and held her close.

She clung to him, willing her tears to stop as she breathed in the comforting scent of his aftershave, and allowed his welcome heat to seep into her. She loved him. The thought came to her with a startling clarity. Through all the months, all the doubts, all the worry that she couldn't trust her own feelings . . . she suddenly realized her doubts were gone.

She not only loved him, she knew, beyond any doubt, she would *always* love him. This wasn't a bright flash of love like she'd had for Damon when they'd first met. Her feelings for Pierce were totally different.

But it was too late for her epiphany. Pierce might believe he could keep her family, and himself, safe from Damon. But Madison couldn't bear to risk anyone she loved on the off chance that Damon might hurt them. She had to make sure he could never hurt anyone she loved ever again.

Tonight she would offer him a trade. One million dollars for his confession, a confession she would record. She couldn't let him go free. This time she had to protect everyone she loved.

Looking up at Pierce, for the first time she allowed all her love to shine in her eyes. She reached her hand up and cupped his face.

His brows wrinkled in confusion. "Mads? What—"

"Love me," she whispered. "Please."

Surprise flickered across his face. He started to step back, but Madison grabbed his arms.

"Pierce, love me."

He stopped and his gaze fell to her lips. "No. Not again. I'm not a 'friends with benefits' kind of guy. I want it all, Mads. All, or nothing." He stared down at her for several minutes, as if weighing an important decision. Then he reached into his jeans pocket and pulled out a ring. He held it up in front of her.

Madison stared at the pear-shaped diamond solitaire, but she didn't say anything. She couldn't. Her heart was already breaking. Again.

"This is yours, if you want it," he said. "If you want *me*. I love you. I have from the first sarcastic comment that came out of your mouth. I bought this ring a long time ago, for the woman I loved. I was going to propose. But you left."

Misery choked the words from her throat. She couldn't agree to marry him, no matter how much she wanted to, not when she was about to go face Damon . . . or Simon . . . and might very well not come back. She knew the odds weren't good, that she could be killed. She couldn't tell Pierce, and have him go with her, because Damon had already told her what would happen if she didn't come alone.

He'd kill her family. He'd kill Pierce.

She couldn't agree to marry Pierce and then leave him, not like this. But more than that, she knew if she said yes, that he wouldn't let her go. She'd be expected to be happy, to celebrate with him. There would be nothing she could say to him that would allow her to sneak out of the bed-and-breakfast to meet up with Damon.

There was no way she could say yes. She had to hurt him, again. And she knew, this time, there was no going back. He couldn't take that kind of abuse from her twice, and give her a third chance.

Hot tears streamed down her face as she realized Damon had already won.

*He'd taken Pierce from her.*

He took another step forward, watching her intently, waiting.

"I can't marry you."

His entire body went rigid. He stood for a full minute, not moving, just staring at her. Then his brows lowered, and he shoved the ring into his pocket. He was suddenly crowding her against the wall, using his body to trap her there. His legs were spread wide, one on each side of hers, and his palms flattened on the wall on each side of her head.

"What do you want from me?" Her voice came out a miserable whisper.

"I want the truth, for once," he whispered harshly. "Tell me what's going through that sarcastic, obstinate, frustrating . . ." He closed his eyes and rested his forehead against hers. He shuddered and drew a deep, shaky breath. "Tell me what's going on inside that beautiful, intelligent, wonderful mind of yours." He kissed her gently on the lips. "Not some made up lie about wanting to move on. I knew you were lying that day. Don't lie to me again."

She drew in a sharp breath. "You didn't know I lied about that until Austin tricked me into admitting it."

"Do you honestly believe that? I know you far better than you think I do. And I always know when you're lying."

Alarm shot through her. "That's ridiculous."

"Is it? Every person has things they do when they lie, a 'tell.' And I know all the signs when it comes to you. Go ahead. Test me. I'll tell you if you're lying or not."

"Stop it." She curled her fists in frustration. "Let me go. I don't want to be this close to you." She shoved her hair back from her face.

His expression softened. "Lie." He lifted his hand and stroked her cheek.

She shivered, hating that he was right. With him this close, feeling his heat, breathing in his tantalizing scent, all she wanted was to curl up against him.

"What happened to us, Mads?" His deep voice sent tendrils of fire curling in her belly. He ran a fingertip gently down the curve of her face. "We used to talk for hours. We laughed until you were hoarse. Do you remember all those late nights on the beach, watching the waves crash against the shore?" His gaze dipped to her mouth. "Making love?"

She shivered against him, remembering, longing for the past more than he would ever know.

"You were happy," he said. "We were happy. What changed that?"

She shook her head, digging her fingernails into her palms to keep from reaching out to him. "Two months. We knew each other for two months, and only dated for one. It didn't work out. That's all."

"What we had was a hell of a lot more than just dating. We were always good together." His finger burned a fiery path down the side of her neck. "In every way."

His voice had dropped to a husky note when he said those last three words, and she couldn't help the shiver of longing that swept through her. He caught that little shiver and his eyes turned hungry. He brushed his lips against hers. Once, twice, three times.

She was suddenly in his arms, unable to get close enough to him. He winced, reminding her of his bruised ribs, but when she tried to pull away, he wrapped his arms around her and pulled her closer.

His mouth ravaged hers, his tongue slipping inside, fanning her desire into an inferno so quickly it left her breathless. It felt so good to be in his arms, so . . . right.

Like coming home. But when his lips moved from her mouth to the side of her neck and her eyes opened, the logical part of her screamed that she had to stop him or he would think they could be together again, that there was a future for them. She didn't even know if she *had* a future after tonight.

Convincing him that she didn't care about him was the only lie that would ensure that he would leave her alone long enough for her to slip out and meet Damon.

"Don't." She pushed against his shoulders, careful not to touch his ribs.

He eased his hold but didn't let go. His eyes were dark and smoldering with heat.

"Why?" he asked.

Inside, she was dying, already aching for what she was about to do.

"The truth?" She clutched her hands together to keep from reaching for him. "I told you the truth when I left you all those months ago. You were fun, a lot of fun, especially in bed. I got what I wanted, and it was time to move on. I didn't want to be tied to one person. Just because I didn't find anyone else I was interested in dating since then doesn't mean it was a lie."

He jerked back as if she'd struck him. His eyes searched hers. He looked down at her hands, as if expecting her to move them. Pain streaked across his face. "So I'm just a good lay?"

She grimaced. "That's a crude way to put it, but yeah. We were great in bed, but that's pretty much it."

He stared at her for a long time. Then he let her go,

turned around and stood at the window looking out on the street.

Unshed tears clogged her throat. She headed back into her bedroom and closed the connecting door.

Five minutes later, she stepped into the hallway, armed with the two guns she'd retrieved from her house before going to the bank.

THE HOUSE ON East Gaston Street was dark, and Madison wasn't sure where Damon would be. Was he watching her now? Had he seen her creep down the street from around the corner? She was wearing the darkest clothes she had—dark jeans, a dark blue button-up blouse. Brown leather boat shoes weren't her fashion choice, but her white sneakers would have flashed in the meager light from the street lamps.

Concealed across the street behind some tall shrubs, she watched the front windows of her house. After half an hour, her patience was rewarded. A shadow, slightly darker than the rest, paused in front of the picture window in the family room. The gauzy curtains opened a few inches as the person behind them looked outside.

Remaining as still as she could, barely breathing, so she wouldn't give herself away, she waited. Finally, the curtains closed, and she let out a shaky breath. She gathered her courage and steeled herself for the meeting that was about to come.

Pierce didn't know how long he stood in his room, thinking about Madison, and kicking himself for being so pathetic as to offer his ring, his name, and his heart all so she could turn him down.

*Again.*

The bright numbers on the clock by the bed told him how late it was. Usually, he'd be asleep by now, but he doubted he'd be able to get any sleep tonight. He listened for the sounds from the other room that would tell him Madison had gone to bed, but all he heard was silence.

Silence? Madison wasn't the quiet type. Everything she did, she did with gusto. She wasn't the kind to tiptoe around a room. And when she slept, she snored. He should hear her, but instead, he heard . . . nothing.

As if she weren't even there.

A sinking feeling in his gut had him rushing across the room and throwing open the door to her bedroom. It only took a moment for him to realize the room was empty.

*Madison was gone.*

He grabbed his 9mm and shoved it in the holster he still hadn't removed. He threw his shoes on and rushed downstairs. The TV was blaring in the family room, but the innkeeper, Mr. Varley, wasn't in his usual spot in his favorite recliner. Pierce checked the kitchen next, softly calling out Madison's name. She wasn't there.

Where else could she be? He headed out the front door and ran to his car parked at the end of the block. As he hopped into his car, he tried calling Madison's cell phone. But after calling twice without an answer, he punched another number into the phone.

"Someone had better be dying for you to call me at this hour," the sleepy feminine voice grumbled on the other end of the phone.

"I need a trace on a cell phone."

"Nice to talk to you too."

"Tess—"

"Yeah, yeah. I'm sure you'll explain later. Give me a second to log into work." A moment later she said, "What's the number?"

He rattled off Madison's cell phone number and started the engine, waiting impatiently as he listened to Tessa typing on her keyboard.

"Tes—"

"Hold on. I've got it, Mr. Impatient. The phone is stationary. Looks like it's on Abercorn, near the intersection with East Taylor."

"Calhoun Square. Thanks Tessa. I owe you."

MADISON KNEW SHE was a coward. Pierce deserved to hear the truth from her, that she loved him. But she'd rather hurt him with a lie of omission than risk his life by allowing Damon to go free.

She crept toward the backdoor, hoping to catch Damon by surprise.

"I didn't really think you'd come."

Before Madison could react, Damon's arms were suddenly around her, crushing her back against his chest.

His hot breath tickled the hairs on the side of her neck, sending a shudder of revulsion coursing through her.

"Let me go. You don't have to hold on to me. I came here to see you of my own free will."

"True, you did. Surprised me quite a bit when I saw you creeping through the bushes out front. I didn't think it would be this easy to get you here. But that doesn't mean I trust you. Let's get inside."

She stiffened against him, and he laughed as he forced her through the door into the back hallway and into the mudroom.

When he let her go to shut the door, she dug into her pocket for the Colt .380 hidden there.

"Uh-uh-uh," he clucked as he wrestled it away from her. "I'll take this." He ran a hand across her body, making her squirm away in disgust when his hands squeezed her breasts.

"What's this?" he asked as his hand pressed against her midsection.

The electronic recorder she'd brought with her. She tried to wiggle out of his arms but he was too strong. He shoved his hand into her front pocket and pulled out the recorder.

He eyed it with scorn. "What did you hope to do with this? Wring a confession out of me and record it? Send me to prison?"

"It was a thought."

He grinned and held the recorder up to his mouth like a microphone. "I confess that I killed Madison's father." He shoved the recorder into his own pocket. "It doesn't matter what's on that recording. No one's ever going to hear it. Besides, I'm not the only guilty party here. You tried to kill me. You shot me, or don't you remember?"

"I wish I'd killed you that night."

"I'm sure you do. Good thing for me your aim was off. You only winged me."

He pushed her down the hall toward her home office. She balked, and he gave her a rough shove, driving her to her knees. Biting back a yelp of pain, she gritted her teeth and moved into the front room.

"How did you keep getting into my house?" she asked. "How did you get into it tonight, without tripping the alarm?"

He reached into his pocket and pulled out his keys. Attached to the key ring was a security fob, like the one she used to have that had broken.

"It pays to have friends in the security alarm industry," he said, "especially when the security company is the same one who changed your locks." He pocketed the key ring.

She glanced around the room, trying to play up her nervousness so that he wouldn't feel threatened by her. Inside she was seething, and yearning to yank her other gun out of her ankle holster. But unless Damon lowered his guard, he'd shoot her before she had a chance.

"Would you quit pointing that thing at me? You could accidentally shoot me."

"Like you shot me?" he sneered. He held the gun out in front of him, aiming it at her. There was no way he would miss at this range. "What? No pleading? You're not going to beg my forgiveness and tell me you didn't mean to shoot me?"

"Of course I meant to shoot you. You were trying to leave, and I wanted to stop you. I wanted you to pay for killing my father. "

"Tell me, dear wife, what did you think when my body was found—without a bullet in it? Did you realize I was still alive or did you just assume the bullet was lost in the fire?"

"I . . . wasn't sure."

He stalked toward her and leaned down in her face. "Does your boyfriend know you tried to kill your husband?"

"He knows I shot you. If I was trying to kill you, you'd be dead. I never miss what I aim at. Why did you marry me if it was all a lie?"

"I don't suppose you would believe I was in love with you." He shook his head at her disbelieving expression. "I didn't think so." He shrugged. "I don't know that I'll ever love anyone, but I cared about you, enough not to kill you like I've done every other woman in my life. I wanted you to be happy, and if your dad had died when he was supposed to all of this could have been avoided."

She shuddered at his reference to killing, in that matter-of-fact tone. She wondered how many people he'd killed over the years, and counted herself lucky she'd managed to stay alive this long, after actually marrying the man. Bile rose in her throat, and she had to force it down. Then it dawned on her what else he'd just said.

"What do you mean—'if my dad had died when he was supposed to?'"

"It's amazing what people know and don't realize they know. When I met you and you talked about your family, I immediately realized there was probably some money there, even though you didn't. It was easy to get your father to brag about his investments, man to man. He was so proud that he was providing for his family, that you'd all be taken care of in style when he was gone. We're talking millions of dollars. He'd lived a full, good life. If he'd died the first time I tried, you and I would probably still be together."

Shocked, she could do little more than stare at him.

"Poor little Madison. You really haven't learned much about me, even after helping your new boyfriend investigate me. What did he tell you? Did he figure out who I really am?"

"You mean, an identity stealer, a con artist, and a loathsome serial killer—*Simon*?"

He laughed. "Well, I'm all that—although I do think loathsome is a bit strong—and so much more. Your family was a means to an end. And eventually, when I tired of you, I'd have been set, a wealthy widower grieving the loss of his beloved wife. I could have lived off the money for years before I ran through it, or before I made a mistake and killed too close to home, forcing me to switch identities again." He cocked his head. "Enough reminiscing about old times. Where's the cashier's check?"

"I don't have it," she lied. If she gave him the money,

she was dead. The only reason she'd brought the check was to use it in exchange for his confession. But without her recorder, or her gun, the check in her bra was now a liability.

She needed to stall him, distract him, so she could go for her other gun.

"You wouldn't have come here without the money. Where is it?" he demanded.

"In the safe."

"Safe? What safe?"

"Over there." She waved toward the far wall.

He shoved her forward. "Go on."

She pulled a picture down, revealing the wall safe.

Damon ground the muzzle of his gun in her back. "Open it."

## Chapter Twenty-Six

PIERCE CUT HIS headlights and inched the car forward until he was fifty feet behind a parked car he didn't recognize, the only other car on Calhoun square. It had to be the car Madison had taken, but he didn't know where she'd gotten it.

What was she thinking to sneak out of the inn this late at night? Why had she gone to Calhoun Square of all places and parked on the darkest curb far away from the nearest street lamp?

He was going to give her hell just as soon as he was certain she was okay. He could see someone sitting in the driver's seat, a shadow among shadows. But something wasn't right. The shadow sat too high in the seat, with shoulders far too broad to be petite Madison.

A deep feeling of unease swept through him. He got out of his car and eased the door shut. Gun drawn, he crept forward. He crouched down when he neared the other car, careful to stay in the driver's blind spot. A few more feet, then he stood up beside the driver's window, gun and flashlight pointing at the occupant inside.

Startled, the driver jumped then threw up his hands as he blinked against the harsh light.

Pierce swore viciously as he recognized the man inside. "Open the door, Mr. Varley."

Varley, shaking so hard he could barely manage the door handle, finally unlocked the door.

Pierce shoved the door open and hauled Varley out of the car with a quick twist of his shirt collar.

Varley landed on the street. Pierce did a quick sweep of the car's interior. Empty. He turned his attention on the frightened innkeeper owner.

"What are you doing out here?"

Varley's eyes were as wide as an owl's. He held his hands in the air, his mouth opening and closing like a fish but making no sounds.

"Oh for the love of . . . put your hands down. I'm not going to shoot you." Pierce shoved his gun into his waistband and hauled the man to his feet. "Speak, before I change my mind about shooting."

The man stared at Pierce's gun for a few more seconds then finally managed to raise his gaze. "I was watching a late movie in the common room when Mrs. McKinley came downstairs. She told me a friend had called her, that she'd had car trouble and Mrs. McKinley was going to help her."

"Go on," Pierce urged him.

"I told her it wasn't safe to go by herself at this hour.

I insisted that she take you with her. She told me you were sleeping. She said she didn't want to wake you to get your keys, and asked if she could borrow my car. I . . . I couldn't let her go by herself, so I agreed to drive her. Once she got to this square she told me to wait for her, that she'd be back in a few minutes." He looked around as if he expected her to appear at any moment.

"She didn't tell you where she was going?"

"No."

"Did you at least see which direction she went?"

Varley scratched his head. "I'm not really sure. It's too dark to see anything out here." He shivered and looked around, as if he were afraid someone was going to jump out of the shadows at him.

Pierce gritted his teeth against the urge to shake him. Something wasn't adding up here. Tessa had triangulated Madison's phone to this car. "Where's her phone?"

"Her phone? I don't under—"

Losing patience, Pierce turned and conducted a more thorough search of the car. Just as he'd suspected, Madison's phone was inside. She'd shoved it down between the passenger seat and the middle console.

"Special Agent Buchanan, sir?" Mr. Varley was standing a few feet back from the open door, twisting the hem of his shirt between his hands.

"What?" Pierce growled.

"Do you think I should . . . ah . . . call the police or something? Do you think Mrs. McKinley is in some kind of trouble?"

"She's always in some kind of trouble."

Varley's brows crept up to his hairline. "Sir?"

"Just give me a minute." He tried to ignore the nearly apoplectic man standing beside him. He punched the screen on Madison's cell phone and the light came on, showing that a message was waiting to be read, a message she'd texted to her own phone. He opened the message.

*Pierce, I couldn't risk Damon being free to hurt anyone else. I went to get his confession. If you're reading this, I didn't succeed. I had to do this. I had to see it through to the end. And I couldn't risk your life, not again. I had to protect you, which is why I couldn't take that ring. I needed you to be angry enough to leave the room, so I could go home and meet Damon. Please forgive me. I have always loved you. I will always love you. Always.*

He cursed and threw the phone down on the seat. He glanced around the square, trying to get his bearings. Madison's house wasn't far from here, a short hike. She'd probably just walked there after leaving Varley sitting in the car.

Digging his phone out of his pocket, he punched up a quick message and pressed send, before handing his phone to Varley. "Call the number on that screen as many times as it takes to wake up the person on the other end. Ask for Lieutenant Hamilton and tell him to read the text message that I just sent him. Can you do that?"

"Well, uh, sure. I guess so. But why don't you call him yourself?" He held the phone toward Pierce as if it were a snake, and he was afraid of getting bitten.

*Because Hamilton will order me not to go in without backup.*

"You can drive back to the inn, but not before making that call. I know where Mrs. McKinley is, and she needs my help. Just promise me you'll make that call. It's vitally important. You could be saving Mrs. McKinley's life."

As Pierce had hoped, Varley puffed his chest out with self-importance. "Yes, sir. I can make that call." Just then the phone rang and Varley jumped in surprise. "Should I answer it?"

Pierce leaned over and looked at the screen. *Hamilton.* He'd gotten the text after all and he'd called the phone that had sent him the text.

"Yes, that's the man I wanted you to call. Make sure he sends help. I'm relying on you. Mrs. McKinley is relying on you."

"You can count on me, Special Agent Buchanan." Mr. Varley punched a button on the phone. "Hello?" He winced and held the phone away from his ear.

Pierce could hear the yelling coming through the phone. He shot Varley a sympathetic glance and ran for his car.

ONE MORE SPIN of the dial. Click. Madison pulled the lever and the safe opened.

Damon shoved her to the side and reached his arm into the safe.

Taking advantage of his distraction, Madison jumped up and kicked his wrist, sending his gun flying across the carpet. He whirled around. She ducked and rolled out of his way.

He lunged after her, but she came up with the gun from her ankle holster. He stopped inches away with the muzzle of her gun pressed against his forehead.

"Back off. Now."

He slowly backed away, his hands in the air. "You'd begrudge your husband a few lousy bucks?"

"Quit saying that. You're not my husband anymore."

"Sure I am. Until death do us part, sweetheart."

He suddenly dove to the side and came up with the other gun.

A shot rang out, deafening in the small room. Damon cried out as the gun sailed out of his hand. He screamed in agony, clutching his bloody hand to his chest. Pierce stood in the doorway, his own gun leveled at Damon.

He glanced at Madison. "Are you okay?"

"Yes, I'm . . . I'm fine."

Damon lunged for the gun on the floor, grabbed it, and ran through the archway, disappearing into the darkened house beyond.

"Stay here," Pierce ordered. "Hamilton is on his way."

The blackness swallowed him up as he ran after Damon.

DAMON HAD RUN into the closet to the basement stairs.

Pierce waited a few seconds to let his eyes adjust to the darkness, then he crept down the staircase, hunched down in case Damon got off any wild shots. When Pierce reached the bottom, he dove onto the floor and rolled behind some boxes. He crept through the dark to the light switch, and flipped it on.

Damon stood about twenty feet away, unarmed, clutching his hurt hand to his chest.

He laughed harshly. "Can you believe I dropped the damn gun while I was running down the stairs? Couldn't find the thing in the dark. I guess you got me." He slowly raised his hands.

Pierce eyed him suspiciously, not trusting him. "Raise your hands higher. Spread your legs. You're under arrest."

"No." Madison's soft voice called out from the stairs. "If you arrest him, he'll just get out again. We can't let him go." She slowly walked down to the bottom of the steps, all the while pointing her gun at her former husband.

"Madison, stay back," Pierce ordered. "Put the gun down."

She shook her head violently. "He killed my father. He threatened to kill you, my family. He has to be stopped."

"Not like this, Mads." Pierce lowered his gun and angled over toward her.

"Don't try to stop me. He won't go to prison. You said so yourself. Not enough *evidence*." She practically spit that last word.

Damon laughed. "That's right. I'm not going to prison. Because, hey, I'm innocent." He grinned.

The gun jerked in Madison's hand.

"Shut up, Damon," Pierce said. "If you value your life, shut up."

Damon looked at the gun in Madison's hand, then his gaze raised to her eyes and his grin faded.

Pierce slowly reached a hand toward Madison. "Give me the gun, sweetheart."

She stepped away from him, keeping her gun trained on Damon. "No. Don't you understand? I have to kill him. To keep my family safe. To keep you safe. For *Daddy*."

"Would your father want you to go to prison?"

Her lips thinned into a hard line. "I don't have a choice. Damon is going to kill you, or the rest of my family. I have to kill him, to keep you safe. And he deserves to die for killing my father. If bringing his killer to justice means I have to go to prison, so be it."

"What about Logan? Your mom? They've already lost your father. They won't want to lose you too."

Her lower lip trembled. "Damon has to die."

The bleakness in her voice touched something deep inside him. He sighed heavily and trained his gun on Damon again. "All right. If it means that much to you, fine. But I'll do it. The paper work is easier that way."

"What are you doing?" Damon hissed.

Madison's gun wobbled, and she blinked in surprise. "You can't shoot him."

He raised a brow. "Why not? If it's okay for you to shoot him, then it's okay for me. No one else will care if he dies. He's a lowlife. A murderer. He deserves it." He carefully aimed his gun. "Say your final prayers, McKinley. Make it quick."

Madison's arm dipped. "You can't just shoot him."

"Why not? Hurry up, McKinley. I don't see you praying."

She glanced back and forth between Damon and Pierce, confusion etched on her brow. She lowered her gun, and stepped forward. She put her hand on Pierce's arm. "I can't let you do this."

"You said it yourself. He deserves it."

She blanched white. "Yes, he does. But killing an unarmed man would destroy you. All you care about is the law."

"No, all I care about is you. I can't let you shoot Damon. I can't let you bear the burden of that guilt. But if it's what you really want, then I *will* kill him. Just say the word."

He watched her intently, waiting for her decision.

She glanced back and forth, from him to Damon, and back again. Finally, she let out a sob. "No, no, you can't kill him. I can't let you do that."

"What about justice for your father? It ends here, Mads. One way or the other. You have to make a choice."

"He'll come after you. I can't let him hurt you," she cried.

"Trust me. I won't let him hurt me, or anyone else. Trust me," he repeated.

Her face crumpled. "Let him go."

Pierce lowered his gun.

Lieutenant Hamilton stepped through the opening into the basement, his gun at his side. "I thought for sure you were going to shoot him."

"How long have you been standing there?" Pierce asked.

"Long enough." He glanced at Damon before looking back at Pierce. "That was a hell of a chance you just took, bluffing with Mrs. McKinley like that."

Pierce raised a brow. "What makes you think I was bluffing?"

Hamilton cocked his head. "I guess I'll never know for sure. Mrs. McKinley, you don't have to worry about your former husband coming after you again or getting away with murder. Your brother has been working hard on your behalf and has uncovered a wealth of information in Montana. We have enough evidence now to arrest Damon McKinley for the murder of the *real* Damon McKinley. And before the week is out, I expect I'll be able to arrest him for the 'Simon says' murders too. He's going away for a long, long time."

A shout of rage had all three of them turning back toward Damon. He dove to his side and grabbed the gun he'd dropped earlier. Gunshots filled the air as Madison, Pierce, and Hamilton raised their guns and fired.

FLASHING LIGHTS FROM the police cars outside lit up Madison's family room, shining through the front windows of the adjoining home office. Madison waited beside the couch with Agent Casey, where the lieutenant had directed her to stay out of the way. He and Pierce and a dozen police officers were in the basement, dealing with the aftermath of Damon's ill-fated attempt to blast his way to freedom.

*Damon would never hurt anyone else ever again. Her father's murderer was dead.*

Finally, the lieutenant and Pierce appeared in the back hallway and walked into the family room. Pierce looked around, his gaze lightly touching on everyone there until he spotted Madison. He strode across the room, grabbed her hand, and didn't even slow down as he tugged her behind him out of the house.

He didn't stop until they reached Forsyth Park a few blocks away. He plopped down on a bench and pulled her onto his lap. Then he buried his face against her hair. It was only then that she realized he was shaking.

"Pierce," she whispered against his chest. "Are you okay?"

He pulled back and the fury in his eyes took her breath away.

"Pierce?"

"What the hell were you thinking meeting Damon alone? You could have been killed." He pulled her against him again, and stroked her hair. "Don't ever scare me like that again."

She stiffened and pulled back from his embrace. "What do you mean, *again*? You can't possibly want to ever see me after this. I was horrible to you. Twice. I said the most awful, cruel things."

"Yes, you did. But then I read your text."

She let out a shaky breath. "I'm so sorry I hurt you."

He gently smoothed her hair back. "Say it."

"I'm sorry."

"Not that, say what you said in the text."

She frowned, then understanding dawned. "I love you," she said, as if she was confessing a terrible secret.

"It's about damn time you admitted it. How about we try this again?" He stood and fished in his pocket, then dropped to his knees.

She stared in disbelief at the solitaire diamond ring he held. "You can't be serious, after what I did to you."

"It's my duty," he said. "Someone has to take you in hand, and protect the world from you."

Her throat thickened with the urge to cry. "That's the sweetest thing anyone has ever said to me."

He laughed and leaned forward, kissing her cheek, gently smoothing her hair out of her eyes. "I love you, Mads. Is that really so hard to believe?"

"But . . . you let me go so easily, when I broke up with you. You never came after me. I never thought you cared for me as much as I did you."

"I knew you were lying when you told me you were bored and ready to move on. You needed time. I knew you were working through something. I didn't know what you were working through, but I knew you weren't ready. I have to admit, after a while, when you didn't come back, I pretty much thought I was an idiot and had imagined the way you'd looked at me, the way you touched me or said my name in your sleep. I began to think I might be wrong about how you felt."

She shook her head. "You knew I'd lied?"

He nodded.

"How? You always know when I'm lying. You said I do something when I lie. What do I do?"

He grinned and brushed her hair back behind her ear. "If you haven't figured it out, I'm not telling."

She started to argue, but he pulled her to him and kissed her thoroughly until she was quite breathless.

When he pulled back, she looked at him in wonder. "Will you marry me, Pierce?"

He burst into laughter and slid the ring onto her finger. Then he grabbed her by the waist and literally swept her off her feet.

## *Epilogue*

LOGAN GLANCED DOWN at his shirt and wrinkled his nose in distaste. "Why the hell are we wearing pink?"

Pierce grinned. "The same reason we wore purple on *your* wedding day. That's what the bride wanted."

Logan sighed heavily. "Point taken." His face wore a resigned look as he waited for his wife, Amanda, to make her appearance as the matron of honor.

Pierce stood next to him, not minding at all that he and Logan were wearing pink shirts, pink cummerbunds, and pink bow ties with their black tuxedos—as long as it made Madison happy. He didn't even mind that Madison had chosen to get married outside in the blustery wind in Whitefield Square, standing in front of a gazebo, where all the tourists could gawk at them.

What he did mind was that the men he worked with were sitting in the rows of white folding chairs on the grass a few feet away, hiding their smiles behind their hands.

Taking pictures of him.

*Wearing pink.*

He didn't bother to lower his voice when he stared at one of the agents in the front row, snapping picture after picture with a huge grin on his face.

"Did you bring your gun?" he asked Logan.

"Of course."

"I'll need to borrow it after the ceremony." He narrowed his eyes at the agent.

"Is there a problem?" Logan asked.

The agent paled and lowered his camera.

Pierce grunted in satisfaction. "Not anymore."

He looked over at his brothers, sitting on the groom's side on the front row. He nodded in response to Braedon's grin and his thumbs up signal. Devlin was next to him, looking bored. Austin was sitting in the last seat. Today was one of his good days. No wheelchair. Just a cane.

Pierce couldn't help but grin when he saw where Matt was sitting—next to Tessa on the second row, with a dark frown on his face, as if he'd been forced to sit by her and didn't want to. Tessa was pretending to ignore him, but doing a poor job of it since she kept glancing at him beneath her lashes when he wasn't looking. Pierce had a feeling he and his family would be seeing a lot more of her in the near future, once she and Matt decided to quit fighting their obvious attraction for each other.

Logan leaned in close and spoke in a whisper. "Does

my sister know what *really* would have happened in that basement if she hadn't butted in?"

Pierce stiffened. "I'm sure I don't know what you mean."

"You can't tell me you wouldn't have killed Damon, if you thought for one second he might not go to jail, that he could be a threat to Madison in the future."

"I *did* kill him."

"You know what I mean. If Hamilton and Madison hadn't been there, if it had only been you and Damon, there's no way he'd have left that basement alive."

Pierce crossed his arms. "I guess we'll never know."

Logan grinned. "Yeah, I guess we won't. But I'm certainly not shedding any tears for the bastard." His breath hitched as he looked down the middle aisle.

His wife, Amanda, slowly waltzed up the path in a long-sleeved, floor-length, pale pink dress that shimmered in the sunlight. She and Logan seemed lost in each other's gazes, as if this were *their* wedding day all over again. Pierce was in awe of the love that shone between them, and he was more than a little pleased that he'd had a small hand in getting them together all those months ago, when Logan had been too stubborn and proud to realize what he was throwing away.

Amanda crossed onto the brick path in front of the gazebo. She nodded respectfully at the preacher standing on the top step as she took her place across from Logan.

Logan looked back down the aisle and started laughing.

Pierce followed his gaze and promptly elbowed him in the ribs. "Knock it off."

"I hope you like cotton candy." Logan choked back his laughter.

Pierce grinned at the delightful pink confection otherwise known as Madison. "As a matter of fact, I do."

Madison's answering smile beamed out at him as she stood at the end of the grassy aisle, holding onto Alex's arm. Her gown was anything but traditional. It suited her perfectly. The hot pink top hugged her curves and the dress flared out over her hips. He had no idea what the skirt was made of but it hung down in long, thin strips in various shades of pink, floating and swirling around her in the breeze. On her feet were shiny, flat pink slippers like a ballerina would wear.

Rather than walk Madison down the aisle, Alex kissed her cheek and stood to the side. Madison had chosen to go down the aisle by herself, saying her daddy in heaven would walk beside her.

She'd insisted on not having any music, and Pierce could see why. She was a bundle of energy and never could have managed the slow walk of a wedding march. Instead, she pranced—there was no other word for it—up the path until she stood next to him. She gave him a saucy wink and an outrageous leer. Then suddenly she was in his arms pulling his mouth down to hers.

Pierce ignored the catcalls and laughter coming from their small audience and gave back as good as he got. But when the preacher cleared his throat, Pierce reluctantly broke the lusty kiss.

Madison gave Pierce another quick, hard kiss. "I'm going to marry you," she whispered.

"I certainly hope so," he whispered back.

They joined hands and faced the preacher. As the laughter subsided, the preacher wiped his forehead and adjusted his collar. His face was an unusually bright shade of red as he cleared his throat. "Dearly beloved . . ."

Keep reading for an excerpt
from Lena Diaz's thrilling

## *He Kills Me, He Kills Me Not*

Available now from Avon Impulse

# Chapter One

THE SWEET MUSIC of her screams echoed in his mind as he inhaled the lavender-scented shampoo he'd selected for her. He sat cross-legged on the carpet of pine needles, stroking her hair, his fingers sliding easily through the silky brown mass he had washed and brushed.

Underlying that scent, the metallic aroma of blood teased his senses. He traced his fingers across her naked belly to the sweet center of her. The temptation to linger was strong, but the ritual wasn't complete.

He picked up the blood-red rose and tucked its velvety petals between Kate's pale, generous breasts. Molding her cool fingers around the stem, he pressed her palms together, embedding the single remaining thorn in her flesh. As he stood, her sightless pale blue eyes stared at him accusingly, just like they had in Summerville the first time he gave her a rose.

Let her stare. She couldn't hurt him anymore, not today.

A rhythmic pounding noise echoed through the trees, an early morning jogger trying to beat the impending heat and humidity of another scorching summer day. The sun's first rays were starting to peek through the pine trees, glinting off the rows of swings and slides.

Thump. Thump. Closer. Closer. A cold sweat broke out on his forehead as he listened to the jogger approach. Was Kate coming for him again, already? No matter how many times he punished her, she always came back. He'd walk around a corner and there she was, condemning him with a haughty look, taunting him with her sinfully alluring long hair.

He risked a quick glance down and let out a shaky, relieved breath. She was still lying on the ground. She hadn't come back to torture him.

Not yet.

After one last, longing glance at her body, he slid between some palmettos and followed his makeshift path through the woods. He emerged at the parking lot of Shadow Falls' only mall, next to a row of dumpsters. Exchanging his soiled clothes for the clean ones he'd hidden in a plastic bag, he quickly dressed. Then he stepped around the dumpsters, pitched the bag into his trunk, and got into the patrol car.

LOOSENING HIS TIE in deference to the already sweltering eighty-degree heat, Police Chief Logan Richards did his best to blend into the shadows beneath the moss-covered live oak tree. Several feet away, Officer Karen Bingham interviewed the young female jogger who'd discovered the body. Logan had offered to help, but Karen had informed him the young woman didn't need an NFL linebacker hovering over her when she was already terrified.

He'd never been a professional football player, but he conceded the point. His size intimidated people. That had served him well when he'd worked as a beat cop here in Shadow Falls, and later as a detective in the roughest precincts of New York City. But intimidating this young witness was the last thing he wanted to do.

She sat on a wooden bench a few feet away, sheltered from the press's cameras by a stand of pine trees. Her freckled face was pale and her shoulders hunched as she wrapped her thin arms around her abdomen, shaking as if she were in the middle of a snowstorm instead of the Florida Panhandle in July.

Someone called Logan's name. He looked toward the obscenely cheery yellow tape that cordoned off a section of the park, contrasting starkly with the macabre scene within its borders. Medical Examiner Cassie Markham was waving at him, ready to share her initial findings.

Logan crossed to the tape, ducking beneath it, careful not to step on any of the bright orange tags his detectives were using to mark off their search grid.

Cassie was kneeling next to the body, sliding a brown paper bag onto the victim's hand. One of two Walton County medical examiners who rotated on-call duties for Shadow Falls and the neighboring communities, Cassie rarely had the need to visit this small rural town in her official capacity. Logan had only met her once before, about six months ago when she'd handled a domestic violence case, right after he'd moved back to take the job as chief of police.

"Hell of a way to spend a Sunday morning," he said when she looked up at him.

"You got that right." She tossed her head to flip her short blonde bangs out of her eyes. "Is she your missing college girl?"

He gave a short, tight nod. "Carolyn O'Donnell."

"How long was she missing?" Cassie picked up another brown bag and gently lifted the victim's other hand.

"A little over three days. She disappeared late Wednesday night, from this same park."

"I'm guessing a young woman her age wasn't playing on the swings. Neighborhood hangout?"

"So I hear." An uneasy feeling gnawed at the pit of his stomach as he noted the way the body seemed posed, her legs spread for maximum shock value. Ligature marks darkened her wrists and ankles. Stab wounds riddled her abdomen and extremities. Many of her bruises were deep purple or black, indicating they'd begun to heal before she was killed. Dreading the answer, he asked, "How long has she been dead?"

Cassie finished securing the paper bag before answering. "She's not in full rigor yet. Liver temp indicates about six hours, but it's hard to be specific in this heat. Might be longer."

Logan scrubbed his hand across his brow to ease the dull ache that was starting to bloom. While he and his men had been searching door-to-door, the killer was sadistically torturing this young woman. Where the hell had he stashed her? And where was he now? Was he already searching for a new victim? Logan blew out a frustrated breath. "Tell me what you have so far."

"Not much beyond the obvious." She peeled off her gloves and stowed them in her kit, then stood up beside him, her head barely reaching his shoulder. "The amount of blood doesn't fit the injuries. She was killed somewhere else and washed down before he dumped her."

Logan nodded, having reached the same conclusion. "Trace?"

"A few cotton fibers, nothing remarkable or distinctive. No hairs. No bite marks. He sliced off her fingertips. I figure she scratched him and he wanted to make sure we couldn't get his DNA from under her nails."

The perp was aware of forensic techniques. Then again, who *wasn't* these days, with all the crime scene investigation shows on TV? Logan didn't ask if the victim had been raped. The answer was painfully obvious. "Semen?"

"I'll take swabs but I doubt we'll find anything. As careful as he was not to leave any other evidence, he probably wore a condom. There's bruising on her neck, petechial hemorrhaging in her eyes."

"He strangled her."

"Yes, but I suspect that was the killer's version of 'love play'. I can't be sure until I perform the autopsy, but I'm leaning toward exsanguination as cause of death. She has deep puncture wounds in her abdomen. She would have bled out in minutes."

"What about her face?" A deep, ragged wound splayed her open from temple to jaw. Logan hoped to God she was already dead when the killer cut her.

"That's unusual, isn't it?" Cassie said. "It would have bled all over the place. Not enough to kill her, but it would have hurt like hell."

Logan's hands curled into tight fists as he struggled to tamp down his anger. Ten years ago he'd allowed his emotions to control him, and he'd made a tragic, rookie mistake that allowed a killer to go free. How many other women had suffered and died at the hands of that killer because of Logan's screwup? That question haunted him every day. The whole mess was the reason he'd fled Shadow Falls so long ago and had gone to New York City.

He'd worked in the toughest precincts to be the best detective he could be, so he'd never make that kind of mistake again. No matter how much he wished he could wrap his hands around the throat of the animal who'd tortured Carolyn O'Donnell, he couldn't let his anger cloud his judgment. Other women's lives hung in the balance if he made any mistakes with this investigation.

"Did you hear about the rose?" Cassie asked, breaking into his thoughts.

"The responding officer said Carolyn was holding a long-stemmed, red rose."

"That's right. The rose bud was nestled between her breasts and the stem was stripped clean of all but one thorn, which he embedded in her right palm, postmortem. Creepy."

Definitely creepy, but if Logan's suspicions were correct, that rose might be part of the killer's signature, his pattern. Everything about the scene told Logan this was the work of a killer who'd killed before—and would kill again.

Cassie motioned for her assistants to bring the gurney. "When I finish the autopsy, I'll overnight the samples to the state lab."

"Hold onto the samples. I want to give the Feds first crack at the evidence."

Cassie nodded, her relieved expression telling him she was just as anxious as he was to get help with this case. Shadow Falls was a small town with limited resources. And although Logan had worked on several serial killer cases in New York, no one else in the Shadow Falls Police Department had that kind of experience. He couldn't do this alone.

Cassie gave him a friendly wave and turned to help with the removal of the body.

Once the body was carried outside the taped-off area, Logan crouched down to examine the footprints he'd noticed earlier. He followed the trail to a group of palmetto bushes. Some of the palm fronds were bent and twisted as if someone had recently passed between them. When he parted the leaves, he saw a narrow trail hacked through the woods. Someone had spent hours, maybe days, cutting this path. The killer? Had he also selected his victim ahead of time? Or did Carolyn O'Donnell just have the bad luck of being in the park when the killer made his move?

Looking back, Logan located his lead detective, David Riley. At thirty, Riley was only five years younger than Logan, but a lot less experienced. When Logan had taken the job as chief and inherited Riley as the lead, he'd assumed Riley was in that role just because the department was so small and there weren't a lot of candidates to choose from. But Riley had quickly proven his abilities.

He was smart and friendly, able to play good cop or bad cop, depending on the need. He could charm a confession out of a suspect before they'd even seen the trap he'd set.

Unfortunately, Riley was speaking to Randy Clayton, a well-seasoned officer with a mouth that never quit. Clayton, who'd already been a veteran back when Logan began his career, wasn't a bit pleased that the rookie he'd once taunted was now his boss. Logan only tolerated his smart-ass attitude because Clayton was due to retire in a few months.

Sighing in resignation, Logan motioned for Riley to join him and wasn't surprised when Clayton tagged along, his usual smirk firmly in place.

Logan ignored Clayton and addressed Riley. "Has anyone searched this area yet?" He parted the fronds, revealing the path between them.

Riley's brows rose in surprise. "We stayed out of this section, waiting for the medical examiner."

Logan drew his gun from the shoulder holster beneath his suit jacket. He stepped between the palmettos, careful to avoid their sharp tips, keeping to the edge of the path so he didn't tread on any of the footprints. "Let's see if we have company."

Riley and Clayton glanced at each other with wide eyes and drew their weapons. The three men followed the path through the thick brush. A few minutes later they emerged at the edge of the mall parking lot, next to a row of dumpsters.

Logan motioned to the others and they fanned out, checking possible hiding places. When he was sure there was no danger, he holstered his weapon. "I'll call for another team to tape off the area. Secure the scene until they arrive."

Clayton tugged on his pants to pull them up over his protruding belly. "Riley, doesn't this seem similar to that other murder when you were a street cop? About four years ago?"

A look of realization crossed Riley's face. "You're right. I should have thought of that."

"What murder?" Logan glanced back and forth between them.

Clayton scratched at the gray stubble on his jaw. "There was another girl that went missing, and then turned up in a cabin all cut-up a few days later. There was a rose in her hands too. I can't remember her name though, something like Diana, Deana—"

"Dana," Riley said. "Dana Branson. I should have thought of her as soon as I saw the body this morning. I wasn't a detective back then, but I heard the details, saw the pictures." He shuddered, his Adam's apple bobbing in his throat. "It seems like an obvious tie-in now, but I was at the convention when O'Donnell went missing, and didn't think about it when you called me, Logan. Maybe if I'd been here a few days ago, I might have—"

Logan waved Riley into silence, impatient to hear the details about the other murder. "Clayton, tell me what you remember about the other case."

"The vic was Caucasian, mid-twenties, long, brown hair, blue eyes. She, ah . . ." He cleared his throat, his face flushing red. "She was missing for three days before we found her. Just like O'Donnell."

Logan's throat ached with the urge to shout his frustration. He wished his men had told him about the earlier case when O'Donnell first went missing. Would it have changed how he'd directed the search? Maybe, maybe not. It all depended on the details of that first case and whether there were any clues to that perp's identity. Without knowing for sure, he wasn't about to lay that kind of guilt on someone else. He was the chief. Ultimately, he was responsible. "Who were the suspects in the original case?"

"There weren't any suspects. All the leads went cold," Clayton said. "But Branson wasn't alone. There was another woman with her."

Disbelief had Logan clamping his jaw shut to avoid saying something he knew he'd regret. How could his men have forgotten a brutal, double homicide in a town of fifty thousand people? Especially since the only murders around here were usually the result of a drunken bar fight or a crime of passion between two people who supposedly loved each other. He took a deep breath and prayed for patience. "Who was the second murder victim?"

Clayton shook his head, his smug look returning. "You got it all wrong," he said. "The second girl, Amanda Stockton, she got away."

AMANDA EASED HER tired body down onto her leather couch to take a much-needed break from her computer. Making a living by writing computer programs at home rather than having to go into an office was a blessing, but it was also a curse. She'd become the hermit her sister had once accused her of being, working inside on a beautiful weekend rather than going out. The sky—visible from her back windows—was so blue it hurt to look at it. And she knew if she went outside she'd smell the salt in the air, might even be able to hear the waves crashing on the shore a few miles away.

She'd enjoyed the ocean once, a lifetime ago. She'd loved hearing the sand crunch beneath her feet, feeling its cooling touch between her toes, listening to the cries of sea gulls overhead. But those days were gone, a part of her past. She could never be that carefree again, that ignorant of the people around her, that exposed, vulnerable.

Wary of the all-too-familiar path her tired mind was taking, she forced those thoughts aside and curled her legs beneath her. With one click of her remote, her brand-new, sixty-one- inch, high-def TV snapped to life. A decadent luxury, it had put a huge dent in her savings. But she'd only turn thirty once, so she'd splurged.

Instead of spending her birthday last week visiting her parents' graves like she usually did, she'd watched two action flicks on her new TV, and shoveled handfuls of fattening, buttery popcorn into her mouth.

She didn't regret buying the TV.

She did regret the popcorn.

An extra hour on the treadmill had been enough to keep her from indulging again anytime soon.

After clicking through the movie guide, she selected a crime scene drama. With her past, she knew most people would think her odd to like those kinds of shows, but it made perfect sense to her. It was all about control, facing and overcoming fears.

Not letting *him* win.

But instead of the show she'd expected, the screen filled with a live shot of the outside of the building that housed Shadow Falls' city hall and police station. A red banner underneath the picture declared "Breaking News."

When anchorwoman Tiffany Adams stepped in front of the camera, Amanda knew this was something far more important than another fluff piece on the upcoming mayoral race. Adams rarely left the anchor desk to report in the field, probably because her heavy makeup and hairspray didn't respond well to the Florida humidity.

In a tone far too upbeat for what she was saying, she

informed viewers that a jogger had discovered a woman's body in the city's main park early this morning, and that the mayor and police chief were about to give a news conference.

Amanda's stomach fluttered and she twisted the hem of her pink tank top between her fingers. Four solemn policemen filed up to stand shoulder to shoulder behind a podium at the top of the steps. She shook her head at the bitter irony. If she went to a store without a written shopping list, half the time she'd come home without the very items she most needed. And yet, even though she hadn't spoken to those policemen in years, she could still remember their names. Some things she could never forget.

Even though she wanted to.

Mayor Edward Montgomery heaved his bulk up the steps and stood red-faced in front of the officers lined up behind the podium's bank of microphones. His usual jovial personality and rotund appearance had given him the nickname of Santa. He wasn't jovial today. After giving one of his briefest speeches since the start of election season, he introduced Police Chief Logan Richards and motioned toward someone off-camera.

A man with short, dark hair strode into view and stood next to the mayor, towering over him. Impeccably dressed in a navy blue suit—in spite of the stifling heat—Richards radiated confidence and authority.

The previous police chief had retired about six months ago and moved to California. Amanda knew Richards was his replacement and that he was from New York, but she hadn't paid much attention to the news reports about him when he was hired. That part of her life was over and she wanted nothing to do with any more policemen.

He looked younger than she'd expected—maybe mid-thirties—although the tiny shots of silver in his blue-black hair might mean he was older. His skin was smooth and tanned, with a slightly darker shadow along his jaw. He was probably one of those men who always looked like he needed to shave. She bet it drove him crazy; it contrasted starkly with the rest of his crisp, polished appearance.

When he spoke, his rich, deep baritone cut across the chatter of the reporters and demanded everyone's attention. His speech was short and concise, confirming what Tiffany Adams had reported earlier but adding little else.

He nodded at a reporter from the *Shadow Falls Journal*, the same reporter who'd badgered Amanda with relentless, personal questions when she was released from the hospital four years ago. After suffering through his crass, intimate questions about her abduction, she'd never agreed to another interview—not with the press, anyway. The detectives had interviewed her so many times she'd sarcastically threatened to move into the police station to save them time.

"Chief, can you confirm the body in the park is missing college student Carolyn O'Donnell?" the reporter asked.

"Until the next of kin are notified, I can't speak to the identity of the—"

"Do you actually expect us to believe the dead woman isn't O'Donnell?" the same reporter shouted.

Richards pointed to another reporter, effectively dismissing the *Journal* reporter, leaving him red-faced and sputtering.

Amanda couldn't help but grin.

"Yes, the body was discovered just off the main jogging trail in a remote section of the park," Richards said in response to a question.

"No, the jogger who found the victim isn't a suspect in the slaying."

"I can't confirm or deny sexual assault until the autopsy is completed."

"No, I can't speak to the cause of death at this time."

For several minutes, the questions continued. When another reporter repeated the question about the victim's identity, Chief Richards thanked everyone for their time and walked away, abruptly ending the press conference. Amanda smiled at his audacity.

The angle of the camera shifted, focusing again on Tiffany Adams. Quoting unnamed sources, she callously confirmed that the nude body found in the park was the Florida State University sophomore who'd gone missing while home on summer break. She quoted an unnamed source and didn't express a twinge of remorse that O'Donnell's family might be watching the broadcast.

The anchorwoman seemed to delight in going into more detail, telling the audience about the multiple stab wounds and speculating that the victim was strangled. Then she mentioned something Richards hadn't: the victim was found clutching a long-stemmed, red rose.

Amanda shivered and clasped her arms around her

middle, barely feeling her fingernails biting into her skin through her thin, cotton tank.

*Was the stem smooth? Had the killer removed all of the thorns? All but one?*

The TV screen faded away and she was back in the cabin four years ago, lying on the hardwood floor in a puddle of her own blood, listening to the sound of Dana's terrified sobs behind her.

Amanda's attacker straddled her stomach and held a red rose above her, its sweet perfume wafting down and mingling with the metallic scent of blood. He plucked one thorn from the stem. "He kills me." He broke off another. "He kills me not."

His sickening version of the childhood chant continued as he snapped off each thorn to drop one by one onto her blood-smeared stomach. When only one thorn remained, his obsidian eyes shone through the holes of the hooded mask that covered his head and most of his face, but not the cruel slant of his lips as they curved up in a delighted smile.

He leaned down, pressing his lips next to her ear, his hot breath washing over her bare skin. She shuddered in revulsion and his hand tightened in her hair, painfully twisting her head back. "He kills me," he rasped.

Dropping the rose, he reached behind his back and pulled out a long, jagged knife. Its wickedly sharp teeth winked in the dim light as he raised it above his head.

With a muffled cry, Amanda tore herself away from the nightmare of her past, collapsing against the couch as she struggled to breathe and slow her racing heart. The TV gradually came back into focus. Channel Ten was still covering the gruesome discovery in the park. Adams speculated on a possible connection between this morning's murder and Dana Branson's murder years earlier. A picture of Dana at Florida State University filled the screen. Then the camera zoomed in on a closeup of her tombstone.

When they showed a file photo of Amanda leaving the hospital, she flipped the TV off and dropped the remote to the floor. She reached up and ran a shaking finger down the rough edges of the long, puckered scar that zigzagged down the right side of her face, a scar that four painful surgeries had failed to completely erase, a scar that reminded her every day of the horrors she wanted so desperately to forget.

But no matter how hard she tried, she could never forget the price of her cowardice: Dana's life.

Furiously wiping at the hot tears cascading down her cheeks, Amanda wondered who had really escaped all those years ago. Her? Or Dana?

LOGAN THOUGHT HE knew what hell was. He'd lived it for the past decade, trying to atone for a split-second decision that could never be undone.

But that wasn't hell.

Not even close.

Hell was telling the O'Donnells their daughter had

been murdered. Hell was watching the light of hope die in their eyes, watching Carolyn's mother crumple to the ground, her tear-streaked face ravaged with grief.

If they'd been angry or had cursed at him for failing to save their daughter, it might have been easier. Instead, Mr. O'Donnell shook Logan's hand, thanked him for trying, and patted him on the shoulder as if Logan was the one who needed to be comforted.

This wasn't the first time he'd told someone their loved one had been killed, but it never got any easier. Every time it was like a punch in his gut, reminding him of the tragic mistake he'd once made. Had the killer he'd let go hurt anyone else? How many lives had been lost, how many families destroyed because of his lapse in judgment all those years ago?

He blew out a shaky breath and blinked his tired eyes, trying to focus on the computer screen in front of him. The most important thing right now was finding Amanda Stockton. The similarities between O'Donnell's killing and what had happened to Amanda and her friend were too overwhelming not to have been committed by the same man. She was the only living witness to his crimes. If there was any chance the killer thought she might re-member something that would help the police find him, she could be in terrible danger.

None of the detectives understood Logan's obsession with finding her, but none of them could know the kind of guilt that ate at him every day. God willing, they never would.

He'd already browsed through dozens of law enforcement and government web sites searching for her, but he wasn't giving up. No one was going home tonight until he was certain Amanda Stockton was safe.

He glanced at his watch, cursing when he saw how many hours had passed since he'd begun his search. How could one woman be so hard to find? She wasn't on the tax rolls of any municipality within five hundred miles of Shadow Falls. The local utility companies didn't have her on their customer lists. Neither did the cable or satellite TV companies. If she'd gotten married or changed her name, she hadn't done it in Walton County.

Everything pointed to her not being a local anymore, which meant she wasn't in immediate danger, at least for now. But without knowing why the killer had shown up again after four years, Logan couldn't risk giving up on the search. Finding her, making sure she was safe, was his primary goal, but it wasn't his only goal.

He wanted to interview her about her abduction. Asking her to relive that horrific experience didn't sit well with him, but finding the killer before he could kill again was more important than sparing anyone's feelings. She'd been with her attacker for three days. Even though the killer had worn a disguise, Amanda had to have seen something that could help identify him. She could hold the key to the entire investigation without even realizing it.

A knock sounded on Logan's open office door, and one of the detectives helping him search for Amanda leaned in around the doorway, his eyes lit with excitement.

"Chief, I found her."

## About the Author

LENA DIAZ grew up a Navy Brat. But while two of her three siblings followed her father's footsteps and joined the Navy, Lena loosely followed her musically talented mother's footsteps by choosing a more creative path, writing. Her first novel-length manuscripts were paranormals, ranging from contemporary vampire stories to medieval druid tales. Since dead bodies kept creeping into everything she wrote, she eventually turned to romantic suspense. Today, Lena can be found in North Florida with her husband of twenty-plus years, her belly-dancing daughter, her mud-bogging son, a tri-colored Sheltie named Sparky, and a pair of Betta fish named Rocky Bal-Betta and Mr. T.